WOLF PIT

BOOK 2 OF THE PURPLE DOOR DISTRICT

ERIN CASEY

ISBN: 978-1-7329450-2-9

Dedicated to anyone who needs a community to call
their own.
You're not alone.
Welcome to the District.

Acknowledgments

As always, dozens of people were involved in the making of *The Purple Door District* series. Most notably is AE Kellar, my fellow author-in-crime, who couldn't stop laughing when I first wrote "the car crash" scene. I promise no more accidental Hollywood explosions. Much love goes out to my editor, Leona Bushman, and my proofreaders, Shakyra Dunn and AE Kellar. Artist Oni Algarra once again brought my characters to life through beautiful portraits. Sara Cunningham and Amanda Bouma helped develop marketing materials. "Les" made the incredible cover for both books. A huge thank you goes to Brian K. Morris who has helped me adopt the "rising tide" theory and has become an incredible mentor.

A very special thanks goes to my sensitivity readers. Leslie Kung and Jessica Larson-Wang helped me come up with Shen Yanlei's name and reviewed my cultural references. Shakyra Dunn also checked my character accuracy with Nick and several others. I'm thankful, and humbled, that they took the time to teach me and guide me so I could properly represent these diverse characters.

This book is about community, and that's what you see here. Thank you, everyone. I couldn't have done it without them, or you, the reader! To those who have taken the time to review my book and talk to me about how it touched them, I can't tell you how much I appreciate your words and encouragement.

Forward

The world of *The Purple Door District* started out as the stubborn brainchild of AE Kellar and myself. We have spent years writing together, researching, brainstorming, and developing characters and rules governing our parahumans and worlds. Our main series, *Fates and Furies*, is still in production but occurs in the same urban fantasy setting.

When we started to design the District, I latched onto it and suddenly had ideas blossoming in my head about creating one in Chicago. Plus, as a birdmom of seven feathered kids, it gave me the chance to professionally write about a werebird, even if I still get the side eye. With AE's blessing, I wrote *The Purple Door District* series to introduce you to our world and insanity.

We jokingly say that AE is the brain and I'm the heart, but I think it's very true. While AE fills our books with well-researched facts and logic, I add feeling, creativity, and literary flair. I couldn't have done it without my walking encyclopedia. All you see here exists because of our love for storytelling and our incessant need to get fewer than 8 hours of sleep a night.

Keep an eye out. *Fates and Furies* is on the horizon.

About AE Kellar

AE Kellar works as a professional wingman by day, while by night pretends to write by hiding behind a laptop and listening to a well-crafted, shuffled playlist. With a penchant for dark humor and plenty of snark, AE writes urban fantasy with a smattering of sci-fi and Paranormal thrown in for spice.

Serving as the creative consultant on Erin Casey's *The Purple Door District*, AE is also co-creator and co-author of *Fates and Furies,* an as-yet unpublished fantastical urban fantasy series upon which *The Purple Door District* is based.

In addition to the world of *Fates and Furies,* AE has written a sci-fi short story called *Remember Nevada,* with hopes to publish before Mars is colonized.

Chapter 1
Fae Way

Tess

Tess Montgomery lurched over the edge of the sticky bar top, waving at a gruff-looking satyr mixing the drinks. Her packsister, Carmen, bounced excitedly beside her as Tess finally got the bartender's attention. "Can we get two fizzy elixirs, one with extra spark? We got a birthday girl over here!"

"I hope that birthday girl is 21," the satyr grouched. The bar hid his furry, red legs, but the black, curved horns on his head were enough of a beacon to scream, "I'm not human." Not that Tess cared in the slightest. Her fire magic could send humans running, too.

Carmen pulled out her ID, almost dropping it in her haste. She thrust it forward. "See?"

Tess chuckled and rested her hand on Carmen's back. "She's got a designated driver, don't worry."

"Aren't you going to drink?" Carmen asked with a pout.

"Duh, I didn't mean me. Our designated driver's called Uber."

The satyr grumbled but pulled two shot glasses out and started to mix together a concoction that could only be found at a bar owned by creatures of the Veil, the magical realm of the fae folk. Tess didn't know all the mysterious ingredients, but it tasted amazing, so who cared? She grinned at Carmen and bumped her packsister's hip with her own. "My little Carmen's all grown up. Almost brings a tear to my eye."

"Oh, shut up," Carmen laughed. "You're only like, what, three years older than me? What is this thing anyway?"

Tess wiggled her fingers in Carmen's face, letting some fire magic dance on her nails. "*Magicccccc*. But it'll still give you a nasty hangover all the same if you have too many, so pace yourself."

"You do realize I've been drinking since I was like 18," Carmen whispered back to her.

"Don't you remember who bought you your first drink?" Tess winked.

The satyr placed two shots on the bar in front of them. The liquid swirled with myriad shades of blue and green. It mesmerized Tess and pulled her in as she picked it up in synchrony with Carmen. Suddenly, the green swirl shot up from the glass and fizzled like a living flame. Carmen squeaked in surprise, drawing a deep laugh from Tess.

"We didn't have a cake yet, so here's your birthday candle. Make a wish."

Carmen held the drink out at arm's length. "How am I supposed to drink it without burning my tongue off?"

Tess winked and blew on the sparks. They danced away into the air and coiled in on themselves, leaving tiny smoke rings behind.

Carmen's face lit up as she did the same.

They clinked glasses and tossed the shot back. Icy-cool liquid raced down Tess's throat, leaving behind the burn of alcohol and the sweet flavors of caramel and berries. She moaned in appreciation and slammed the shot on the bar with a gasp. "Hoo, forgot how good that tastes! What do you think?"

Carmen licked her bright red lips and slid the glass across to the satyr. "Another!"

Before the bartender had a chance to either serve her or make a scathing reply, a voice rang out above the dance music.

"Carmen!"

Tess looked over her shoulder and grinned as another Caucasian packsister walked in with her Latina girlfriend.

"Kat! Bianca!" Carmen shouted as she dashed through the crowd and threw herself into their arms. Kat caught her with a laugh, her golden hair sweeping around her soft white face. Bianca reached out to hug both Kat and Carmen, her green eyes crinkling with mirth.

"Happy Birthday," Bianca said. She pushed her red-tipped hair out of her way and gave Carmen a quick affectionate peck on the cheek. A pair of feathered earrings bounced against her face as she leaned back, reminiscent of her inner bird.

Kat tapped Carmen playfully on the tip of her nose. "You're drunk already, aren't you?" she teased.

"Ha! Just getting started! I…oh crap." Carmen scrambled backwards and bolted towards the bathroom.

Tess laughed and headed towards Kat and Bianca. "Broke the seal already. That girl's never been able to hold her alcohol." She rolled her eyes then reached for the pair. "I'm glad you could come."

"Wouldn't miss it," Kat replied and gave her a tight hug back before lacing her fingers between Bianca's. "Let's grab a booth and get some drinks while we wait."

Tess lifted an invisible shot glass in a "cheers" motion and headed towards the seating area around the bar. Emerald vines curled around the rafters, bearing glowing violet blossoms which lit up the dance floor. The flowers moved on their own accord and pulsed alternating colored beams of light, reminding her of lasers cutting through the dark. Both friends and strangers danced around each other, bodies thick with sweat and glitter. The dance club was a strange mesh of technology and foliage, as was to be expected in Fae Way.

The Purple Door District of Chicago housed two areas devoted to the fae; not every District could claim the same. And not every Fae Way generously allowed parahumans to come in and partake in their exotic drinks, magic, and eccentric customs.

She glanced around, looking for a good spot to sit, and caught sight of a group of men and women huddled near an intricately carved glass dragon, its mouth alight. They breathed in the hookah and flipped over tarot cards, reading each other's destinies. A woman picked up her wand and tapped two of the cards, making them float in the air and rotate in front of her companion. He scowled and swiped them away, causing the rest of the witches to laugh.

Near them, a small gathering of fae sipped drinks and chatted quietly amongst themselves. One, the size of a human, bore mottled blue and green skin and glittering gold wings. Another appeared to be little more than a child. Her hair flowed like molten lava, her wings quivering with fire that somehow didn't set any of the wall art aflame. Another wore no wings but rather fins which matched his blue skin along his back. A seashell headdress rested upon his brow.

Tess tried to hide that she was staring, but she couldn't help but admire them. She would never see them like this anywhere else due to their glamor spell. At least parahumans weren't the only ones who felt like they had to keep their true selves hidden.

She settled on a plush red booth with her friends, positioning herself so she could pay attention to them and still admire the fae.

Bianca picked up a drink menu while Kat looked around. "I've never been to this place before. I didn't even know it existed!"

"First time in Fae Way?" Tess asked. When Kat nodded, Tess cracked a smile. "You get used to it…eventually. I'm practically best friends with the bartender now." She waved at the satyr who gave her a dirty look and went back to his customers.

Kat rolled her eyes. "Making friends everywhere you go."

"You know it." Tess leaned over and pulled Bianca's menu back a little with the tip of her black nail. "You should try anything that has a little wing next to it. It's supposed to help strengthen flight."

Bianca moved closer as if to tell a secret. "Does it work on werebirds or only fae?"

"Won't know until you try."

While Bianca and Kat put in orders for drinks, Tess checked the crowd for her packbrother, Nick. She spotted the younger wolf grinding against a beautiful Black woman. He pulled her up against his broad chest, running his dark hands around her waist as she leaned back into his hold, mouth creasing in a sensual smile.

Finally, Tess thought, smiling. *At least he's gotten over his obsession with Kat.*

She glanced at Kat and Bianca, recalling how Nick's poor heart had shattered to pieces when he found out Kat had fallen for Bianca. Weeks of moping around the house finally forced their alpha to drag him to nearby social events so he could at least meet other people. It was a good experience for him, Tess thought. He was only 19; he had the whole world—and pack women—waiting for him.

Besides, Kat and Bianca were freaking adorable together, and

Tess wasn't interested in betting on any other ship. She watched the pair as Kat leaned against Bianca's shoulder, the werebird nuzzling her nose into the werewolf's golden tresses.

They were an odd group. Normally werewolves, magi, and werebirds didn't hang around each other, but that was the beauty of The Purple Door District. Everyone came together under a violet banner of peace. They had more things to worry about anyway, like humans, Hunters, and the occasional idiot dark-magic users called senkas.

Tess could go another few years without meeting one of those monsters again.

"Tess, come on. Let's dance!" Carmen cried as she returned to the group and grabbed Tess's wrist.

Tess laughed and let Carmen pull her up. "I've been summoned. Forgive me, ladies. Continue necking while I'm away."

"Tess!" Kat protested.

"Can't hear you. I'm dancing!" Tess followed Carmen out onto the dance floor and spun her packsister around. Carmen waved her arms not quite to the beat of the music. It was cute, so long as she avoided smacking people in the face. Tess caught a hand sailing towards the back of a guy's head and guided Carmen to a more open area, which was hard to find.

"Hey, birthday girl, let's not knock out the competition," she said. She grabbed Carmen's hands and danced her in a circle.

Carmen swung her head back, her hair flying through the air behind her in a golden and purple halo. "More shots!" she demanded. She spun Tess around so hard, it sent the magus stumbling back into someone seated at the bar.

"Hey! Watch it!" the patron snapped.

Tess quickly turned and held up her hands. "Sorry about that. We're just having a little fun…oh." Her good humor evaporated in an instant. "Trish."

The red-headed vampire glared back, her eyes a subdued crimson. She perched on a stool in a seductive black dress with lace that matched the choker at her throat. Leather boots hugged her calves, showing off her long legs. Anyone would do about anything to take someone so beautiful home. They'd regret it once they woke up to find Trish gnawing on their neck.

If they woke up. Not everyone survived around the vampire.

"What are you doing here?" Tess demanded, pushing Carmen

protectively behind her. "Joseph let you off the hook for good behavior, or did you sneak out?"

Trish snorted and picked up a chocolate martini with blue fae fruit coiled around it. "I'm trying to have a good night out. Back off, magus."

"Heh, yeah, you have a bad rep with magi, don't you?" Tess growled and leaned in closer. "You going to do me in like you did Gladus?"

Trish flew to her feet, forcing Tess back a couple of steps. Tess cursed inwardly. She hated how much faster vampires were than her. No matter how much magic she had, it wouldn't save her if a vampire sank fangs into her throat first. It didn't help that Trish's heeled boots put her a few inches above Tess.

"Tess…" Carmen whispered and gripped her shoulder.

Tess kept her arm out, blocking Trish from getting closer.

"I said back off," Trish hissed down at her, her eyes taking on a bright, threatening glow. Two vicious fangs slipped through her gums. "You don't know anything about what happened."

"I know Gladus is dead, and it's your fault."

Trish glanced away. Her hands fisted like she wanted to lash out. Instead, she took a deep breath, fangs retreating, and grabbed her martini. "I don't need this," she said and made to stalk off just as Bianca and Kat were coming to get drinks.

Bianca's laughter died when she saw the vampire. Her eyes shifted, taking on a birdlike appearance as her caracara started to break through. Tess couldn't blame her. Trish was the whole reason Bianca had been captured by the Hunters in the first place. "*You*," was all Bianca managed before Trish sashayed towards the group of witches around the glass dragon. They paid her little mind.

"You should worry less about me and more about your drunk friend," Trish called over her shoulder. "Not everyone here is going to treat her to a good time."

Tess made to follow, taking it as a threat, but Carmen enveloped her in a hug from behind.

"Tess, come on. I don't want there to be a fight. Not on my birthday!"

"Sorry, hon," Tess said. "She knows how to get under my nerves." She gave herself a shake and turned her attention back to Carmen. She pulled her packsister closer as the wolf danced to the music. In her excitement, Carmen nearly smashed her head into a young man. The guy turned, his mahogany hair slicked back with far too much gel, a sharp contrast to his overly tanned skin. He looked human, but Tess sensed the earth magic swirling around inside of him.

"Did I hear we have a birthday girl?" he asked with a coy smile. He gave his female companion a wink and held out his hand to Carmen. His fingers glowed green as he called on the Ether and created a long-stem rose in his palm. The ruby petals blossomed, releasing a sweet fragrance which made Tess's nose itch. "Let me get a shot for you. On me."

"That's beautiful," Carmen said. She took the rose and tucked it behind her ear with a shy smile then slipped her hand into his. "Thank you. But only one shot! Don't want to make *Mom* upset," she added, winking at Tess.

Tess narrowed her eyes at the man, but before she could say anything, he chortled and touched Carmen's hip, guiding her towards the bar and away from Tess. "I'll get you back to her in one piece. Promise."

Something about the guy rubbed Tess the wrong way. He seemed too smug, and the possessive hold he had on Carmen sent warning bells off in her head. Tess followed on their heels and caught Carmen's free arm. "Hon, come on. Let's get a drink and head back over to Kat and Bianca."

Carmen shook her off. "*My* birthday. If he wants to buy me a shot, let him."

"Let her have some fun. It's a special occasion." The earth magus pulled Carmen roughly out of Tess's hold and body-blocked her from getting back to her friend. A faint Ether shield built up between them, forcing Tess back a step.

Oh, hell no.

She reached for the guy's shoulder, fire magic starting to build around her hand, when someone else grabbed her arm and yanked her into a dance. The new man's breath reeked of stale beer and cigarette smoke. Mixed nut flecks peppered his unruly beard. He towered over her, his body a mix of muscle and beer belly. In his half-drunk state, his eyes flickered between human brown and wolf gold. Werewolf, but not from her pack. The Harvey Pack maybe. Great. "Show me what you got, sexy thing."

Tess glowered and tried to jerk her arms back, but he didn't let her go so easily. He spun her around and grasped hold of her so tightly, she felt her skin start to bruise. Tess squirmed and stole a glance at Carmen in time to see the earth magus slip something into her drink as he chatted amicably with her.

Screw this, Tess snarled to herself. No one was going to hurt her friend.

She suddenly leaned towards the werewolf and flashed him a coy smile. "You wanna see what I got?"

He looked down, his eyes roving over her cleavage poking out the top of her blue shirt. He licked his lips lasciviously. "Oh, yeahhh."

She kneed him in the groin.

Tess barely heard his squeak of pain as he dropped to his knees and released her to grab himself. She stormed towards the bar as the magus held out the glass to Carmen. Tess curled her fingers, calling flames into her hands. It was lost in the flashing lights as she sent it snarling towards the man's pants. Fire raced up his thighs to his crotch until he yelled in surprise and dropped the glass. It shattered on the ground around Carmen's feet. She jumped back with a shout and rounded on Tess.

"Tess! What the hell!"

Tess didn't bother to explain. She shoved Carmen behind her and faced the man, all 5 foot 4 against his 6 foot whatever.

"Bitch," he snarled and raised his glowing fist.

A hand caught his wrist before he could strike.

"Back. Down," Nick snarled. He pulled the guy's arm down, causing the man to wince in pain. Magi were strong, but they couldn't stand up against a werewolf's strength. Nick's eyes flashed gold, his body bristling and preparing for a fight. "Leave them alone."

The flames had dispersed by now, but a few nice holes showed off the drunk's raw, pink skin. "You better let me go, pup, if you know what's good for you."

Carmen tried to shove her way through. "Stop it! Stop it. He was just getting me a drink!"

"*No*, he was drugging your drink," Tess said, clinging to her packsister. "I saw him drop a roofie in it."

Nick's low, wolf snarl was the only warning he gave before he punched the man full in the face. The magus fell back against the bar, sending glasses clattering and shattering to the floor. Patrons yelled and scrambled out of the way. The satyr shouted in protest and threw a towel down over the glass as people ran to him for protection.

Nick pounded the guy's face twice more before the drunk managed to get in a half-hearted punch with both his fist and magic. Nick skidded but didn't let go of the magus despite the vines threatening to curl around his biceps.

"Nick, stop it!" Kat shouted and sprang forward. She grabbed him from behind and tried to drag him back, but Nick shook her off and went after the magus again.

In the guy's haste to escape Nick, he crashed into someone else, who threw a punch of his own. Kat got in the way of it and grabbed the man's fist inches from striking Nick in the side of his head. She threw the customer back, her eyes turning more wolfish, taking on a golden hue.

"Back off," she warned them.

Tess pulled Carmen out of the way and sighed as the wolves went at it. *Good job, Tess. Way to keep a low profile.*

By now, the whole dance club noticed something amiss. The witches rose from their cloudy table to watch, none stepping in to try to help. A few fae backed off, their gossamer or fiery wings glittering in the blossom lamps overhead. The fae stayed out of it, but more wolves came down on Nick and Kat, as did a handful of magi, their magic crackling like fireworks.

A drunk werewolf tried to get behind the bar to start up a fight with some of the hiding patrons. The satyr bartender wasn't having any of it. With a grunt, he bowed his head, and rushed the werewolf. He sent the wolf flying across the room into a table with his mighty horns. Wood and glasses splintered beneath the parahuman's body.

Tess grimaced and wrapped a shield around herself and Carmen to block some of the magical attacks. When a magus got too close, Kat wrapped her arms around him and bodily lifted him before tossing him against a soft leather seat. Tess hadn't meant for any of this to happen, but at least Carmen wasn't drugged. And she'd enjoyed Kat throwing her weight around.

A year ago she would have hid in a corner had a man raised a hand to her, not that Tess could have blamed her after her experiences. Being with Bianca had helped her grow in confidence and become an even stronger member of the pack. Funny how a little bird could instill more strength in her packsister than the other wolves could.

Kat blocked another blow and forced the new fighter away from Nick. As Bianca swooped in to help, Tess guided Carmen further away from the fight. To Carmen's credit, she'd gone quiet after finding out about the drugged drink. Tess glanced at the horrified expression on her friend's face and started to pull her towards the door. "I've got you, Carmen. Let's get some fresh air."

"He drugged it?" she asked in a whisper Tess barely heard above the fighting.

"Yeah, but you're okay now. I got ya." She wrapped her arm around Carmen as the sound of sirens screeched outside. Two swat cars pulled up, sending a few patrons outside scattering. A spell around the building made it impossible for humans to enter or even see inside. But if the cops were parahuman...

Tess winced and pushed the door open.

Don't let it be him. Don't let it be him.

As they got outside, an officer climbed out of one of the swat cars and stepped into the light. "Tess?"

"Dad..."

Shit.

***

"So, let me get this straight," her father, Officer Brighton, droned on in the front seat of his car. He sat dressed in full dark uniform, on duty for that night. Though his gaze remained on the road, Tess felt him giving her the side eye. "You saw him put a pill in her drink, and you thought setting his pants on fire was a good idea?"

"I had to think of something on the fly," Tess groused. She sat in the passenger seat, arms and legs crossed in frustration. Nick rested in the back behind her seat, holding Carmen against him, comforting her as she sniffed quietly. He sported a black eye and bloody nose, but otherwise, he'd made it out of the fight with barely a scratch. Kat had ended up with a bruise or two herself, but she and Bianca had taken another car home after getting questioned by both Tess's father and the other officer, a werecat.

"How about, 'Stop! Don't drink it!' or do something other than use your magic to start up a fight?"

"He was an earth magus. I wasn't going to give him the chance to do something else to her. Besides, he deserved it," Tess muttered.

"Catessa Montgomery," her father growled.

"Full name, uh oh," Nick snickered from the back.

Her father glowered at him in the rearview mirror. "Don't think I'm letting you off easy either, Nicholas. Paytah is going to hear about this. What were you *thinking* fighting members of the Harvey Pack? Do you want to start a war between their pack and ours? You're lucky you didn't punch an alpha or beta."

Nick shrank in his seat.

"And you," her father said, giving her a sharp look. "I'm sure Vic will have words for us after you attacked a magus."

Tess leaned her head back in frustration. "Why am I getting in trouble? I tried to keep my friend safe! He's the one who did something wrong."

"You didn't have to start up a fight. Either of you," her father retorted. "That makes things harder for all of us. Why couldn't you have stayed in a local District bar?"

Tess pointed her thumb over her shoulder. "Carmen wanted to try something new where we wouldn't be recognized so easily. It's not like we expected trouble."

"What did you think would happen when you shot off a fireball at someone's ass?"

Tess winced and tried to hide the hurt on her face. The scolding didn't bother her as much as the disappointment in his voice. She tucked her hair behind her ear and stared outside, letting the awkward silence build between them.

Her father sighed deeply and gripped the steering wheel in both hands. "Tess, I'm not upset that you defended your friend. That guy has a warrant on him; I'm glad we finally get to take him in. But you can't risk starting up fights between our different groups. The District is meant to be a place of peace, not—"

"I *know*," Tess replied defensively. "I screwed up. I get it. I'll be more careful next time."

Her father shook his head. "I'm telling Paytah on you, too, Tess. You need to stay in the District area and not visit Fae Way. There are too many rogues there, and the fae don't take kindly to us disrupting their peace."

Tess turned towards him, lifting a hand. "If I hadn't been there, some other poor girl might have gotten drugged tonight. And you know the sick thing? The guy would have gotten away with it too!"

"Tess…"

"No, people would have said crap like Carmen should have been more careful. Or it was because of how she dressed. Or she was asking for it. Why is it never the guy's fault?"

Her father eyed her. "You know I don't feel that way, Tess."

"It's not really your choice, is it? If he's some kind of star athlete, someone would let him off if he hurt her."

"Tess," Carmen whispered from behind. "Can you…please stop? I don't want to think about what he could have done."

The fight and anger whooshed out of Tess. She looked at her friend as Nick pulled her closer, nuzzling her shoulder. Tess's shoulders fell. "I'm sorry, Carmen," Tess said. "I really wanted this to be a special night for you." So much for an incredible twenty-first birthday. She shook her head and rubbed her neck. She wasn't making things any better, was she? "Dad, look, I'm sorry for causing a fight, but I couldn't let him get away with it."

"You're not above the law," her father replied. "One of these days, you're going to have to realize that magic or being the daughter of a cop doesn't make you immune to consequences. I know your heart was in the right place, but you need to learn to think things through more before acting and risking someone getting hurt. Do you understand?"

While Tess didn't appreciate the lecture, she could see where he was coming from. This wasn't the first time he'd had to pick her up or *save* her from jail time because she'd acted without thinking about the repercussions. That had to be hard on him being in the force and all. Being a magus had its perks, but she knew it also gave her father a bit of trouble.

"Look, Dad, I'm sorry," she said and turned back toward him.

Blazing lights poured into the car through the driver's seat.

Tess had a second to throw up a magical shield and scream, "Dad!" before a truck plowed into their cruiser.

Chapter 2
Missing

Tess

The metallic tang of blood bombarded Tess's senses, forcing her awake.

She coughed and gasped for breath, smoke and the starchy smell of deployed airbags filling her lungs. She opened her eyes and was met by the shattered windshield and crushed hood of her father's car. Shards of glass that should have impaled her throat and face rested against her weak magical shield. But her wounds meant little as she craned her protesting neck to search for her father in the driver's seat.

It was empty. Jagged metal glinted in a broken headlight where the door had been ripped off its hinges. The deflated airbag nestled in a cloud of powder against the steering wheel, the side slashed open. Blood splattered part of the bag and sections of the smashed car. Tess reached weakly towards the seat, her vision pulsing in and out with her heartbeat.

"Dad?" she croaked, her voice hoarse. She remembered seeing the lights and feeling the impact. Collison. A truck. Where was he? *Where was he*!

She grimaced and dropped her arm to the hood of the car. They were upside down; her seatbelt kept her from falling on her already pounding head. Her body ached, but at least she was alive.

"C-C-Carmen? Nick?" she asked. Her vision blurred and went out, though for how long, she didn't know. When she said their names again, it felt from afar, like she couldn't quite hear her voice. Her ears wouldn't stop ringing.

And the car was starting to get hot.

"Carmen?" she rasped again, more frantic. She looked at the review mirror, still in place save for a small spider-web crack in the corner. Carmen lay sprawled on top of the roof, blood dripping down her forehead and out of the corner of her mouth. Nick dangled next to her, also unconscious, but less bloody. He was lucky the truck hadn't hit his door.

Glass crunched near Tess's head. She tried to turn, but a stabbing pain stopped her and forced her to go still as she listened to something grind against Nick's door. A high-pitched squeal preluded a sudden tremble through the car.

Tess swallowed hard and croaked out, "10-1, 10-1!" If her father had been thrown from the car, they had to know an officer was down somewhere.

She heard no response. Nor did she notice any flashing lights from an ambulance.

How could an ambulance have gotten there that fast anyway?

Tess tensed.

The door fell with a loud clang and was dragged out of the way. Tess watched through the mirror as gloved hands reached in, snipped Nick's seatbelt, and dragged him out without much tenderness. No one bothered to grab Carmen.

"What do we do with the other one?" a woman asked.

"She's probably not going to survive. I told you not to hit them so hard. And the other one is a magus. We don't need her."

The smell of spilled fuel and the rising cloud of smoke started to clog Tess's senses. Her mind rifled through the information, moving as slow as molasses. But it was clear these people were not here to help.

She reached for her door and tried to open it. No way in hell would she let them get away with Nick or her father. But the door didn't budge. She glanced through her broken window and found a light pole pressed against it, trapping her inside.

"Light it on fire," a man said. "Get rid of the evidence."

The footsteps receded, but the smell of fuel and smoke intensified. Heat from the engine fought against her shield. She pushed more energy into it seconds before she saw a fiery line race across the pavement, guided by a spilled path of fuel. The heat from the engine burned and boiled hotter, the flames creeping past the hood and toward her window. Tess gasped for breath and fought a cry of pain as small fire spirts passed through her shield and started to blister her hands and arms. Her fingertips turned an angry red, flesh starting to darken and peel.

"Carmen?" she choked, hoping against hope her packsister would awaken and be able to escape. But Carmen remained still. Tess couldn't even tell if she was breathing.

Her hands started to quake with stress, her throat tightening with familiar panic.

Breathe. Close your eyes and concentrate. You're not going to be able to check on her if you're both dead.

In and out. In and out. She breathed slowly, deeply—or as deeply as she could with the smoke—and reached for the Ether which flowed through the Earth and her veins, the magic which gave her command over fire. She closed her fist, searching for the heat in the engine and started to draw it into herself. Cool the metal; stop it from burning them alive.

But the noxious fumes emanating from the broken gas chamber threatened to suffocate her. Her calm breathing turned into choked coughs, tears stinging her eyes. Her head started to spin. She had to free them before she passed out or the engine roasted them both alive.

Tess reached for her seatbelt and braced her blistering arm for impact. The strap came loose, and she fell, barely avoiding smacking her head on the metal roof. Her leg went out the window, sliced across glass, banged into the pole, and nearly fell into the fire. This time, she couldn't stop herself from yelling.

She pulled her shield inward, pressing it over her skin to act as a barrier against the heat, but it was almost too much to bear. She crawled across the hood to Carmen's side and shook her friend. "Carmen," she croaked.

Still, no response.

Tess didn't waste time trying to find a pulse. Either way, she wouldn't her packsister to burn alive. She grabbed Carmen by her arm and dragged her across the roof towards Nick's open door, leaving bloody fingerprints behind on the girl's arms. Glass and metal cut into them both, but better that than the fire steadily flowing into the car like some angry phoenix. Tears stung her eyes as she struggled to breathe and get Carmen free at the same time.

She crawled through the opening first then pulled Carmen out after her.

The heat and smoke belching from the ruined cruiser didn't let up. As much as Tess wanted to rest, they couldn't lay there.

"Come on," she moaned as she dragged Carmen further away from the car and toward a ditch on the side of the road. She propped them at the edge, but not well enough, and they both tumbled and rolled down into the blessedly cool grass.

Tess landed in a heap with Carmen beside her, hands still blistered and aching from the fire. She coughed and looked up towards the road to the smoldering heap, flames licking the sky. The truck that had smashed into them was nowhere to be found, nor were there any other vehicles. Her father and Nick were gone, and she didn't even know if Carmen was alive.

Tess struggled to rise, but she only made it halfway before crumbling back down to the dirt. The world spun and blurred, her ears pounding to the tempo of her heartbeat. As her vision darkened, she thought she heard a door slam and someone shout.

***

Tess woke to the rhythmic beats of a monitor and the sterile smell of a hospital room.

She grimaced and opened her eyes slowly. The lights of the room made her wince—they were far too bright. She turned her head away from them. Someone spoke quietly at the doorway.

"She'll need to be monitored for a couple of days. She suffered smoke inhalation, and we want to make certain her hands and leg don't get infected."

Tess glanced down at her hands. Bandages covered them from her fingertips up to the middle of her forearm. When she tried to move them, pain streaked through her nerves.

A fire magus burnt by fire. She didn't miss the irony in that.

Tess sighed and flopped her head on the pillow again.

A part of her wanted to panic and try to rush out of the room. But, despite being magical and not considered a pure human by Legion standards, she was still quite *human* in body. Yes, she could command the Ether and bring flames raining down from the sky if she wanted, but a car crash or infection could kill her like any other human. Her only advantage was her magical shield. That had likely kept her from dying when the truck plowed into the squad car.

"Thank you, doctor. Hopefully, she'll awaken soon," a familiar voice said.

Tess turned her head carefully to the left and saw a white-coated doctor step away, leaving her mother standing with slumped shoulders in the doorway. Her mother, Iris, a magus like herself, looked frail to the human eye: pale skin like a vampire's, jet-black hair that flowed down her back in waves like some cheesy Snow White character. But inside that short, lithe body resided a powerhouse of magic. Tess didn't know if her mother's magical abilities or good looks made Brighton fall in love with her.

Her mother walked back towards her bed, but paused upon seeing Tess's open eyes. "How long were you awake?"

"Long enough to hear that my magic couldn't fight the fire," Tess said with a half-hearted smile. "Pretty piss-poor fire magus, right?"

"You almost burned your hands off," her mother scolded. She sat down next to Tess and settled her hand on her daughter's arm. "You were a mess when they brought you in. Burns all over your hands, lacerations on your leg, and a concussion."

Tess squinted her eyes. "It would have been worse without my shield. I'm going to guess you had a hand in healing me?"

"I had to be careful. They took us to a human hospital." She sighed. "But yes. You idiot, what were you thinking trying to control the heat and flames like that?"

"I was thinking of saving my ass and Carmen," Tess aid. "Unless you wanted us to burn *in* the car."

"Why not smother the flames with your magic?"

"I was too busy trying to cool the engine." she scowled. "You know, it wasn't exactly easy to do two things at once. I acted to keep us alive."

Her mother frowned. "You never make things easy, do you?" She reached out and ran the back of her hand gently along Tess's warm cheek. "I thought I was going to lose you."

Tess leaned into her mother's soothing touch. "I'm all right, Mom. At least I didn't have a building fall on me this time." Now that had required a *lot* of healing including in a wheelchair.

But her mother didn't smile or chuckle. Her face remained perfectly still, her brow knitted together with concern, the tight lines of worry growing deeper on her lips.

Tess's smile faded as memories slowly returned to her. "Carmen? Is she…"

"She's alive. But she's in a coma. The car was hit on her side, and she had a piece of shrapnel go through her side and puncture her. They have her stable, but she hasn't woken up." She bowed her head. "They can't get much brain activity either. They're hoping once the swelling in her brain goes down, they'll see something."

"*No…*" Tess whispered. Damnit, not Carmen! Why had this happened? She shut her eyes and fought back tears of rage and guilt. She should have done more. What was the point of being a magus if she couldn't use her magic to help people? "Dad? Nick? Did you find them?"

"No. The car's too damaged to get any clues, and there's no sign of them. The wolves have been out searching, as has the CPD, but it's like they've vanished."

Tess set her jaw, fighting the rising panic. "They have to be alive. I heard two voices when I was still in the car. They wanted Dad and Nick, but they said they couldn't use Carmen because she was probably going to die, and they didn't need a magus."

"They knew *what* you were?"

Tess nodded and opened her eyes again. "It sounded like it." She shifted and tried to sit up. "I couldn't see them; I heard them."

"Stay down," her mother said. When Tess didn't listen, a soft push of magic pressed her against the bed. "I said *stay.*"

"I can't lay here while Dad and Nick are out there," Tess argued. "They need us. What about the rest of the pack? You said they're out searching. Where's Paytah?"

"He's calling a pack meeting."

"When?"

"Before you can get out of the hospital."

Tess glared. "Mom, come on, heal me. I need to be there. I'm the only one who heard anything! I have to help."

"And how do you think that'll look to the hospital staff?" her mother argued. She adopted a mock-innocent expression. "I don't know, doctor. It's a miracle! One moment, she was laid flat, and the next she was up and walking!" She sighed in frustration and glanced over her shoulder. "Look, I already put in a call to Legion Medical. An operator named Harding said he'd get the paperwork and make sure you get transferred to a parahuman hospital soon. You were too far outside of the borders to get help from a District hospital."

"Yeah, yeah, I know, we should have stayed near home," Tess muttered. "Dad already gave me the lecture."

Her mother arched an eyebrow at her. "Maybe next time you'll listen?"

Tess didn't respond. She couldn't help but think about the hands that had dragged Nick out of the car so carelessly, like he was a lump of meat and not a person. Were they hurting her dad? He was older than Nick, and he had scars from past pack battles and patrols. What if he was being tortured? How long would he survive?

"Tess," her mother said softly.

Tess didn't realize she was crying until her mother wiped the tears from her eyes. Tess rubbed them away stubbornly with the part of her arm that wasn't bandaged, but then her mother descended on her, pulling her into a gentle hug.

"We'll find him, Firebug."

"Oh my god, Mom, come on," Tess complained, but she mustered a choked laugh. She hated that nickname, and ever since her father had dropped it to Paytah, that was all she heard. She sniffed and rested her head on her mother's shoulder. "I know. But if he's hurt, I'll make those bastards pay."

"No, the *pack* will make them pay. You need to stay out of it. You're injured."

"But I'm pack!" Tess argued. "And my pack is in danger. Just because I'm not a wolf doesn't mean I can't help."

Her mother gave her a look. "As long as you're stuck in this bed, there's nothing you can do."

"Then heal me!"

"Tess—"

Someone knocked on the door.

Tess and her mother looked up as Vic stepped into the room. A pale-faced man with blonde hair, the magus walked with an air of purpose, his hands folded behind him. He wore simple jeans, a gray t-shirt, and an open red-plaid shirt which looked a bit too tattered and holey to keep in his daily wardrobe. A red stone embraced in golden wire bounced along his chest as he moved.

Her mother relaxed. "Vic."

"I came as soon as I heard," Vic said. "How's our patient doing? Being stubborn I presume?"

Tess stuck out her tongue at him.

Vic reigned as the priest of the local Oakland Ward, a group of magi who had once served under the former District's Violet Marshall, Gladus. Gladus's death still weighed heavily on everyone, but for Vic, part of his world had shattered and could never be mended. They'd been close friends, and he'd been forced into the priesthood much sooner than he'd expected or desired. Tess had noticed the bottles of alcohol growing at his house each time she visited him for a fire lesson. At least he never left the house drunk, not that she'd seen as of yet anyway.

"Stubborn, of course," her mother said. "I wasn't expecting to see you."

"I wanted to make sure you both were well and protected," Vic said as he approached them. He spun a seat around and sat next to her mother. Tess knew he fancied her mother, but he would never do anything to ruin her mother's happiness. Still, that didn't stop him from getting close to her and watching longingly from the sidelines. Maybe that was why he was so eager to work with Tess on her magical abilities.

He was a good guy, and he ruled kindly, albeit a bit sternly. When her mother had arrived in Chicago with Tess—little more than a toddler—he'd welcomed her warmly into the ward with Gladus's blessing. He'd given them a place to stay, food, and comfort. It'd been a nice change since her birth father had walked out on her and her mother after Tess had demonstrated proclivity to magic.

"I don't need two freaks in the family," he'd said, and that was that. No goodbyes. No kiss on the cheek. Vic, sadly, had been forced to endure Tess's "daddy issues" and her unwillingness to trust him. By the time he got her used to accepting another father figure, Brighton came into her mother's life, and Tess fell for him too. Then again, how could she not fall for a big, fluffy wolf who let her ride piggyback on him?

Tess always thought Vic got the shitty end of the stick, but he handled it with grace. And when it came down to it, Tess still saw him as a mentor, especially considering the amount of times they threw each other around while wielding magic.

Her mother touched her leg, pulling her out of her thoughts. "Well, she wants to get up and leave, of course. Paytah's having a pack meeting."

"Ah," Vic said with a nod. "Well, maybe I can put in another good word to Legion Medical to get you moved. Then a 'miraculous' healing doesn't have to go on file."

Tess smirked. "Trying to earn more brownie points?"

Vic nudged her shoulder playfully in return, but his smile seemed tight. "More like I want to make sure you're in the protection of the District." His eyes hardened, and he turned to her mother. "Word's going around that a wolf from the Harvey Pack went missing around the same time as Nick and Brighton."

"Really? Who?" her mother asked.

"Someone named Yanlei, Shen Yanlei. Her parents said she went out with friends, and someone grabbed her. The other wolves got away because Yanlei distracted whomever was after them."

Tess frowned deeply. "Any others missing?"

Vic shook his head. "That's all I know. I think Paytah will have more up-to-date news." He eyed Tess and leaned forward. "You need to rest. I'm sure your mother has told you that enough. Let me see what I can do about getting you out. But until then, you're not going to do anybody any good if you try to get up."

"I know, I know," Tess huffed. She settled back on the bed. "Stay put. Got it." She rubbed her face wearily and glanced at her mother. "Bianca and Kat? Are they okay?"

"You can ask them yourself," Vic said as he rose. "I saw them coming in with flowers."

"Wait, how long have I been out?"

"About a day and a half," her mother replied. "Speaking of which, I need to go talk to your doctor and have him check you over since you're awake."

"I'll go with you," Vic said and fairly leapt to her side. Tess hid a smirk as he walked at her mother's elbow out of the room. Tess would have loved to have seen her father's expression as Vic followed her mother around like some loyal puppy.

Her throat tightened at the thought of her father. *Where are you, Dad? And Nick? Are you even alive?*

In that quiet moment alone, Tess allowed her emotions to overcome her, and she wept into her pillow. She could put on a brave face so people didn't worry about her, but all she wanted to do was curl up in bed with Carmen and hold her packsister then run out and find her father and Nick. None of them deserved this, and she couldn't help but feel guilt gnawing through her stomach at being the only one to make it out free and conscious.

She was drying her tears when she heard a knock at her door. Tess rolled over and forced a cocky smile as Bianca and Kat walked in. "Hey, troublemakers. Looks like you got off easy this time."

"Tess, don't joke," Kat said. She brought a vase of lilacs over to her table and set them down before giving Tess a hug. "We were so worried when we got the call."

Tess smirked at Bianca. "You, too?"

"Duh," Bianca replied. The avian settled next to Kat and touched her girlfriend's leg as Kat joined her. They made a cute pair. She hadn't been overly fond of Bianca in the beginning, what with her showing off some kind of wicked seer power, but now that that was gone, she didn't think the caracara was so bad. Then again, she did manage to steal Kat away more often than Tess would like. But Tess had to learn to ignore her jealousy. "How are you feeling?"

"Like a truck smashed into me." Tess shifted and showed them her bandaged hands. "Apparently, I'm not immune to fire. Who would have thought?"

Kat shook her head. "We saw the car. Bianca said she had a bad feeling when she didn't hear from you, Carmen, or Nick after your dad drove you off, so we went to look for you and…" She gestured vaguely to Tess's body.

"Wait, were you the ones who found us?" Tess asked in surprise. She narrowed her eyes at Bianca. "And what do you mean bad feeling? You aren't getting those visions back again are you?"

Bianca quickly shook her head. "Oh geeze, no. I texted Carmen to make sure she was okay. I figured if she didn't respond, Nick at least might. And none of you did. So, we headed after you, and we saw the car. Kat found you two off the side of the road." She shuddered, not that Tess could blame her.

Bianca's parents had died in a car crash, though they'd gone off a bridge. Frankly Tess would have rather drowned than been burned alive. The latter death would have been a cruel irony.

"Well, thanks," Tess said. "Have either of you seen Carmen?"

Kat nodded, her hand squeezing Bianca's tightly. "She's still hooked up to the machines and in a coma. We're…well, we're hoping. Paytah is going to stop by and see if maybe having him close might do *something*."

Tess tried to lift a finger then winced when she remembered the pain. "Hey, remember, not a miracle hospital. I'm glad you two are okay. Especially you, Kat. If you'd been in the car too…" Either she'd be dead, or maybe they would have taken her, too.

Kat shut her eyes. "I wish it had been me instead of them."

"Kat," Bianca said sharply and squeezed her hand. "At least we can try to do something to help."

Tess felt inclined to agree. "And wishing you were in their shoes isn't gonna help them." She breathed out heavily and eyed the pair. "I don't know if I'm going to be able to get out of here before the meeting. Kat, you better tell me what Paytah says."

"I can do that," Kat said. She lifted Bianca's hand and kissed her knuckles lightly. "I don't get it. How did they peg your father's car, whoever did this?"

"Maybe he was being watched," Tess replied. "Pretty hard to miss a squad car like his."

"I know, it's just…it makes my fur stand on end," Kat replied. "Are any of us really safe?"

Bianca actually chuckled. "As someone who spent weeks running from Hunters, I might be able to at least provide some advice. So long as we stay in the District, we should be protected, right?"

Tess shook her head. "It doesn't sound like it kept one of the Harvey wolves safe." She swallowed hard. "I know there have been some unsolved parahuman murders here and there with no real pattern. At least according to my dad."

Kat and Bianca exchanged startled looks.

"How long has this been going on?" Kat asked.

"Since Bianca came to the District."

Bianca quickly held up her hands. "It's not my fault this time."

Kat chuckled and gave her a peck on the cheek. "We know, hon."

Tess couldn't bring herself to smile. "It makes me feel like this isn't random, like someone is hunting us down,"

Bianca tightened her hold on Kat's hand and tensed. "I think we can guess who."

Kat glanced at her. "But what if it's not Hunters?"

"If it's not," Tess said, "then who the hell is coming after us, and how are they strong enough to take down werewolves?"

None of them had an answer.

Chapter 3
Pack Meeting

Tess

With Vic's help, Tess and Carmen were transferred over to a Legion-certified hospital by the next morning. Between people poking her with needles and checking her vitals, combined with her own anxiety, Tess didn't sleep well that night. She sat up in her bed, eager to receive the "miracle healing" that would help her get out sooner rather than later. Paytah, fortunately, had pushed the time of the pack meeting so that Tess could be there to tell them all she'd seen.

Vic and her mother arrived after noon, and despite both wanting to heal Tess themselves, a Legion-certified magus handled the task. The rather quiet man healed the worst damage, leaving her with enough strength to get her to her feet. But the doctor still requested Tess stay under observation for twenty-four hours as even magic couldn't cure smoke inhalation. By the following day, Tess was released with her doctor's approval. Poor Carmen stayed behind, still on machines.

Magic could only heal so much.
Her mother drove her to her apartment from the hospital so she could change and get rest before the pack meeting. Tess didn't want to sleep; she wanted to find her father. Ether vibrated in her nerves, urging her to try and cast a location spell, even though she knew she was piss poor at it. It took a strong magus to locate someone, and Tess was nowhere near that caliber yet. Vic would

have a time of it, but he'd already tried with no luck.

She wouldn't consider the alternative.

While her mother fixed food in the kitchen, Tess headed into her bedroom and threw off the old pair of jeans and shirt she'd been given at the Legion hospital. Red paint covered the walls of her room which held black-framed pictures of her family, the pack, and a few signed records from her favorite bands. The vinyl looked more impressive than the CDs anyway, and it was a hobby she and her dad had gotten into when she was still a kid.

She stopped near the record of Sweeney Todd, the Demon Barber of Fleet Street, signed by the original cast. Her mom had had a fit when Brighton had taken her to it when she was only ten, but Tess had fallen in love with the songs. They still sang the lyrics to each other especially if there were any fresh-baked "pies" around.

Tess brushed her fingers over the frame and swallowed a lump in her throat. She glanced at a reflection in the glass and could see a family picture of herself, her mother, and her father across the room. Oh, she'd been a little hard ass when she first met Brighton. Vic had tempered her rage and won her trust, but she'd still had memories of her absent birth father. How was she supposed to know that Brighton would treat her any differently? Not only that, he was a wolf. What did a wolf know about magic?

Absolutely nothing, Tess thought to herself, fondly. But that hadn't been a problem. In fact, Brighton had been so eager to learn about her magic and encourage her to practice it, she forgot all about putting salt in his coffee or setting his newspaper on fire. He'd taken her under his paw, and when the pack had welcomed her, well, she'd found a place to call home.

She took a breath and glanced at her dresser where bundled sage sat filling the room with an herbal scent. A grimoire rested beside it, the old, crinkled pages bound in coarse red and brown leather. It had been made to look that way by the local apothecary just for fun, but Tess still used it to record spells. Though her magic could produce all sorts of fire power, she liked learning other spells, similar to what the witches used.

Tess headed into the shower and turned it as hot as she could stand. She looked at herself in the mirror, her face still somewhat battered from the car accident: stitches beneath the eye, bruises on her forehead. Minor compared to her other healed wounds. These would go away soon enough once she had enough sleep.

The glass started to fog with steam. She opened the medicine cabinet and pulled out a bottle of lorazepam for her anxiety. She wanted to pop about a handful of pills to quell her emotions, but she swallowed one instead. After tucking the bottle away, Tess climbed into the shower and dunked her head under the thundering water as the events of the collision played through her head. She still couldn't get Carmen's bruised face out of her mind.

Carmen. Her eyes stung at the thought of her packsister. She should have done more to save the wolf. If the people, whoever they were, had left Carmen behind, then they must have really thought she was better off dead.

"Get rid of the evidence." That's what they said. Clearly this wasn't their first rodeo. So whole else did they take, and why? What about the wolves caught their attention?

She'd been in better shape than Carmen, and they'd wanted nothing to do with her. How had they even known what Nick, Carmen, and her dad were? They'd been in human form. Unless they had someone who could scent what her dad and friends were.

Or we were being watched.

She shuddered at the thought. The District had already seen enough trouble with Hunters a year-and-a-half ago when Bianca had come to town. Granted, they'd only been after her, but others had died in their quest, and while Bianca now lived safely with a cloister, a group of werebirds, that didn't mean the threat was completely neutralized. *Those* Hunters were long since dead, but that didn't stop others from coming to town. Not all Hunters were bad, or so Vic and the others claimed.

She thought they were full of bullshit.

Tess squeezed shampoo into her hair and closed her eyes, letting the medicine work its magic. She hadn't felt anyone watching them at the bar except for the asshole who had drugged Carmen's drink and stupid Trish. Could he have been part of it? Probably not. She would have smelled the alcohol on him a mile away; no way was he coherent enough to be part of a bigger operation. And the same went for the crusty-bearded douche who had grabbed her.

So then who the hell had followed them and had the balls to take out her dad's squad car of all things?

Maybe Trish wasn't as innocent as she professed.

Tess dunked her head and washed the shampoo out before conditioning it.

Or maybe she was thinking too hard. It could have been a random attack. Her father was kind of a hotshot in town; they could have known who he was and been after him alone. Nick had been a bonus.

"Nick," she murmured. God, he was just getting his life on track, too. School was going well. He impressed everyone academically and on the college football team, not to mention all the ladies. Too bad he'd only had eyes for Kat for the longest time. He didn't need this shit in his life. At least he knew how to defend himself. Her father and Paytah had made certain of that.

"Tess?" her mother called. "Are you going to stay in there all day?"

Tess blinked and suddenly noticed the chill creeping through her skin from cold water. "Be out in a sec!" She washed the conditioner out quickly and scrubbed down her body with dial and lavender soap.

Tess climbed out of the shower and pushed her heated magic across her body, drying herself before she grabbed the towel. She went into her bedroom, searching through her drawers until she pulled out jeans, a black sleeveless shirt with lace at the throat, and fingerless gloves for her hands. She ran hot most of the time thanks to her power, and the gloves helped protect her palms when she went a bit too fire happy. She could have used them in the car.

She got dressed and braided her black hair behind her before heading out to the kitchen. Her mother stood over the stove, cooking up pancakes and sausage (her mother's go-to food when stressed). Though her mother stood with her head bowed, Tess spotted the tell-tale damp spots on her shirt.

"Mom," she murmured and went to her side.

"I'm fine," her mother lied.

Tess snorted and forced her to turn. "Yeah, your red eyes tell me otherwise."

Her mother swallowed hard, glancing away. "I'm worried about your dad."

"I know, me too." Tess pulled her close and hugged her tightly. She nuzzled her head under her mother's chin. "Look, we're going to find him. Paytah's too stubborn to let him and Nick stay missing."

Her mother didn't respond. Not a surprise. They both knew not every kidnapped person came back alive.

Brighton's birth-daughter hadn't. Neither had Carmen's mother.

They sat down and gorged themselves on pumpkin-spiced pancakes, sticky-sweet syrup, and thick sausage. Tess got a cup of chamomile tea for her mother and a shot of Jack Daniels for herself.

"Tess," her mother admonished when Tess threw it back.

Tess refilled the shot glass and pushed it across the table to her mom.

She refused for a moment, then downed it as well. "We should get going."

Tess nodded. "Let me get a few things." She grabbed a silver-studded belt which had a single pouch above her right hip. It looked like it could only fit her phone, but she'd spelled it to hold a lot more than that. She slid her wallet, keys, phone, and a few potions inside, then picked up a golden-chained necklace. A small jar which seemed to snarl with living fire dangled at the end of it.

Tess had steadily been storing her magic into the talisman so, if she ran out of energy to connect to the Ether, she could draw from her necklace instead. It seemed like something she might need in light of things. Unlike witches, she didn't necessarily *need* a talisman to help her use magic, but it still had its benefits.

She slid it beneath her shirt and headed for the door. "Let's go. I'll drive this time."

***

Tess pulled up to Paytah's house about 45 minutes later. Freaking rush-hour traffic. The driveway curved up the road, turning from asphalt to rocks briefly before becoming paved again. He'd bought the house a good distance outside of the heart of Chicago so wooded land was available for the wolves to run in. It was safe, private territory, and the witch occupying one of the other houses didn't seem half bad.

Cars lined the front yard. Most, she recognized. She spotted Kat's red Subaru and wondered if Bianca had tagged along. Paytah didn't seem to mind the bird, but pack meetings were different. The only reason Tess and her mother were allowed was because they'd been adopted into the family. Bianca was still considered an outsider since Kat had yet to put a ring on it to make it official.

Tess got out of the car and looked up at the large two-story house. It showed its age in the prairie style architecture. With strong horizontal lines, oversized eaves, and a massive chimney that separated rooms, the house had the spirit of Frank Lloyd Wright in its red and sandstone-colored walls, or so Paytah said. Tess usually dozed off about halfway through his speech.

The house had a homey air to it, and most importantly, it fit all of the wolves, even the ones who Paytah and his wife Rozene decided to adopt, like Nick and Kat. Kat might have moved on to another apartment, but Nick still lingered, though Tess wasn't sure if that was his own desire or Paytah's incessant need to keep an eye on at least one pup. He didn't do well with an empty den.

She tucked her hands in her pockets and headed up the stairs towards the more secluded entrance.

Before she reached the door, another wolf with bronze skin bounded up the stairs after them dressed in black slacks, white shirt, and a red tie. He looked ready for a business meeting except for the tattoos that poked up beneath his shirt-collar. Warm eyes crinkled as he smiled.

"Tess! Didn't think we'd see you out of the hospital," he said and scooped her up in a crushing embrace. "How are you, little sister?"

Tess gasped as his arms tightened around her. "Can't. Breathe!"

"Ray, they just fixed her ribs!" her mother protested.

Ray dropped then caught her and grimaced. "Sorry, Firebug, I keep forgetting how breakable you are."

Tess scowled at him. "You call me Firebug again, and I'll show you how easily I can break *you*."

Ray snorted with laughter and ruffled her hair. "You're so cute when you get angr—yow!" He yelped and pulled back a steaming hand. "Alright, alright, point made."

Tess straightened her hair and stuck her tongue out at him. Suddenly, despite her healing body and her mother's protests, Tess pounced on Ray's back and grabbed him around the neck, mock fighting with him.

He laughed and looked over his shoulder. "And what are you trying to do?"

"I'm not the only one getting pounced today," she said and nipped playfully at his ear. She flopped her chin on his shoulder.

"Augustine joining us tonight?"

Ray nodded. "I'm meeting her here." He wiggled until Tess had to drop from his back. "Come on, we're late and you know how Paytah is with punctuality." He grabbed the door and held it open for them. "After you, ladies."

"How chivalrous," her mother said with a smile.

Tess rolled her eyes and headed inside, poking Ray as she passed him for good measure.

Wolf packs had started out as a patriarchal society, with men leading and protecting the more submissive women. Over time, and in many packs, the view of gender had gone out the window, replaced by strength alone. It wasn't unusual for a woman to lead a pack, so long as she could put any challengers in their place. Tess might be able to defeat Ray at a battle of wits and words, but when it came to strength, a magus physically could not stand up to a werewolf. So she had to be careful with her attitude.

Augustine, however, a powerhouse of a wolf, could have probably taken their beta Jackson on had she really wanted the position. She towered over most of the wolves strength wise, while fellow she-wolves Becky, a local waitress and actress wannabe, and Tamara, a school teacher, were more than happy to let the "stronger" wolves take charge.

Pedro, a successful mechanic, and Quince, a nurse, had gotten married shortly after Illinois allowed same-gender marriage and adopted two Black twin girls named Eliza and Phoebe.

And what beautiful, smart little girls they were. Tess spotted the pair the moment she stepped into the house, Eliza lying on her stomach and reading a book while Phoebe sat on the edge of a couch, glasses resting on the tip of her nose as she talked with her Latino fathers. Quince leaned against Pedro, both listening with rapt attention.

Theirs was a melting pot pack of wolves.

The living room echoed with the chatter of those whom hadn't seen each other for quite some time. The pack had meetings once a month to check on everybody, but even then, sometimes wolves couldn't get off work, were out of town, or were sick. Tess heard the babble of Becky's three-year-old daughter, Heidi, and smiled sadly to herself. Her husband had been shot and killed in a house robbery about a year prior. The pack still mourned his death.

She pressed herself in amongst the wolves, slapping Ray

playfully on the right ass cheek when she passed. Augustine's snarl warned her she'd been spotted. She glanced back at the Hispanic woman and offered a playful smirk. Augustine glowered back, her broad shoulders stiffening, her hands resting on her thick, curvaceous body. She looked every ounce a murderous predator from her gold-tinted eyes, to the leather jacket, and the claws which formed on her hands, the tips covered in purple polish in the shape of a nail. Augustine seemed to notice the mistake she made and she groaned and glanced at her hand. "Damnit, Tess, you just had to go and piss me off."

"Sorry, Augustine, you know I can't resist dat ass." It was a joke between them. Augustine got overly protective of her mate, and Tess played off of that every time they were together. Otherwise, they hit it off pretty well.

Augustine snorted and drew her nails back in, checking over the polish. She wasn't vain per se; she just liked to look put together when she worked at the tattoo parlor. She wrapped her arms around Ray and pulled him into a tight, possessive hug. "*Mine*," she growled at Tess.

Ray nuzzled up against his mate and grasped her hand, kissing one knuckle at a time. "*Mine*," he said back with more force and adoration.

Tess broke away before they could start giving each other lovey-dovey eyes. She glanced around and spotted Mikayla rushing in, a satchel heavy with books dangling from her shoulder, her natural black afro in partial disarray. Probably running late after a class at Loyola University. Mikayla acted calm and collected like Tamara and Becky, but Tess knew the woman had a sharp tongue and could flatten most people when pushed. Taekwondo lessons helped.

"All right, settle!" a deep, rich voice barked above the noise.

As one, the wolves quieted down and shifted their positions to greet their alphas. Ray, Augustine, Pedro, and Jackson kept more to the front while Becky, Quince, Kat, and Tess's mother settled near the back. Tamara, as wife to beta Jackson, stuck close to him. And Mikayla? She plopped herself in the center.

Tess squeezed through the wolves until she came to the front where Paytah and his mate, Rozene, stood.

Both were of Native American descent, Sauk they said, and bore their culture proudly. Paytah crossed his arms, his black hair bound in two braids which rested over his chest. A sunburst piece held each braid in place. Dressed in jeans, red-plaid shirt, and a leather vest, he stood as a pillar of strength in front of the room.

Rozene softened him, a cool river to his fire. She wore her black hair in a single braid, held in place by another matching sunburst piece. A black and red rug dress with angled designs covered her body, cinched by a silver belt. She looked across the pack with grace and a quiet strength which seemed dwarfed by her husband's.

Paytah waited until he had every eye in the room. "By now some of you have heard about what happened to four of our packmates. But for those who have not, let me be blunt. Brighton, Carmen, Nick, and Tess were all attacked. A truck crashed into Brighton's car. Brighton and Nick were both extracted from the crash. Tess used her magic to save herself and Carmen, but Carmen remains in a coma."

A furious murmur started up amongst the wolves before Augustine snarled, "Who attacked them? What are we going to do next?"

Paytah's gaze quickly shifted to Tess, causing her to stiffen.

"Will you explain what you saw and heard?"

Tess felt angry and vengeful eyes zero in on her. Thank goodness she wasn't the source of their ire, otherwise they might have caused her to burst into flames. She headed to the front and turned to face her pack, a myriad of different faces, shapes, and genders. "I don't have much to report. I heard two voices, but I didn't see either person except for gloved hands." She explained what she remembered, how they'd taken their packbrothers but left her and Carmen to die in a roasting car.

Becky clutched her daughter close and huddled up against Kat for support. Jackson fairly gnashed his white teeth in rage, hungry for revenge.

Once Tess finished, she squeezed her arm and looked around until she caught Kat's eyes. Sure enough, Bianca didn't stand beside the golden-haired woman. "I don't want to say it was Hunters, but they seemed to know what we were, so…"

Kat's eyes lit with rage and fear at the same time Paytah's heavy hand fell onto Tess's shoulder.

"We can't jump to conclusions," Paytah said.

"But what if she's right?" Ray asked. He rested his hand on

Augustine's back and glanced around at the pack. "What if the Hunters have come back?"

Jackson folded his broad black arms. "There has to be a reason Brighton and Nick were chosen and not Tess and Carmen."

Augustine snorted. "Tess is a magus, and Carmen's a woman. They probably didn't think she was necessary for whatever they were doing." She sounded bitter about it, but Tess was more than happy they'd left Carmen behind. She'd have a better chance to survive under hospital care.

"Isn't that a good thing?" Pedro asked. The average-heighted Latino edged his way closer, little Eliza resting sleepily in his arms. Behind him, Phoebe clung to Quince's hand.

Paytah waited until the room settled. "It's not only our pack or our people who have been affected."

Tess grimaced as he told them about a young woman, Shen Yanlei, who had been snatched up off the street from the Harvey Pack. But there was more. Two other packs had lost wolves as well.

"Joseph," Paytah continued, naming the duke of the local coven, "also informed me that two of his vampires have gone missing. As of now, the cloisters, prides, wards, and groves have been untouched. But if vampires are disappearing, it's possible others may be attacked as well."

Tess wrinkled her nose. Missing vampires? She thought about the night at the bar then blinked. "Trish was there."

Paytah and Rozene looked at her.

"Trish?" Paytah asked.

Tess nodded. "Could she be involved? It wouldn't be the first time she helped Hunters."

Paytah shook his head. "Joseph assured me he's been keeping a close watch on her. As of now, she's not a suspect. I think it better we not expect one of our own to turn against us. Facing the Hunters is bad enough." He rubbed his firm jaw. "That being said, I'll have words with Joseph to make sure she is under heavy guard."

The murmuring resumed and turned into a low roar of worry and anger. Tess wormed her way through the group to Kat's side and squeezed the woman's hand. "I'm sure Bianca is fine," she said.

"Yeah…yeah, I'm worried about Nick," Kat replied, a half-truth. Bianca was, of course, at the back of her mind. When a wolf chose a mate, she did so for life. Granted, they weren't married or even engaged, but Kat and Bianca doted on each other like an old wedded couple.

Tess tightened her hold and looked over at Paytah as he brought peace back to the pack.

"I know you're all concerned," he said. "Until this threat is neutralized, I'm instituting a curfew and check in. The kidnapping seems to take place after nine p.m. I expect everyone to arrive at their homes before nine p.m. and to report in with me and Rozene that you made it safely so we can keep track of everyone."

"What?" Ray cried. "But some of us work late at night. We have evening shifts."

Jackson grunted. "We're on call for evening pickups if the kids we're watching try to run off," he said gesturing to himself and Mikayla. "We can't refuse to pick someone up because of a curfew."

"And I can get paged in the middle of the night," Quince added.

Tess felt the same. Eventually, these people would probably figure out the wolves were heading to their homes by nine p.m. Would they decide to strike then?

Paytah pressed his lips into a thin line of consternation. "Then you will take someone with you. Jackson, Mikayla goes with you on the ride." He looked at Ray. "And Ray, you have Coleen bring you back towards our territory after restaurant hours. But you are *all* to check in with me. If I don't receive a call by curfew, or you haven't cleared it with me that you can stay out later, I will come and find you. And you do not want that to happen, I assure you."

The wolves grumbled.

Augustine folded her arms. "So because of whatever psychopaths are out there, we have to completely disrupt our daily lives? How are we supposed to find our missing wolves if we can't even go and search for them at night?"

Paytah's eyes glinted with a silent warning for Augustine to watch herself. "Rozene and I are speaking to the other leaders about that. We'll find our lost wolves, but we need time to figure out who is attacking us and why. In the meantime, I need to know my pack is safe. Understood?"

"Understood," the other wolves replied begrudgingly.

Tess's stomach dropped. *He's not sending anyone out to look for Dad and Nick*, she realized in a mix of shock and anger. *What's he thinking? They could be out there getting tortured! And he has to talk to the other leaders? Since when does Paytah have to turn to anyone else for approval?*

And then she remembered he was the District's Violet Marshall, the leader of the Purple Door District of Chicago. When trouble was afoot, he was the first to know about it and the first to act on it. He'd chased rogue wolves away from their territory, helped pride and cloister parahumans alike to find homes, and settled disputes between a grove and a ward. Leading was his area of expertise. Yet, as the Violet Marshall, he was still meant to consult the other parahuman leaders before risking himself and the District. She understood, but that didn't mean she liked it as it meant another day without her father and friend.

Tamara moved closer to her husband, her eyes down. Jackson wrapped his dark arm protectively around her white shoulders as she whispered, "What about Legion? Can they help us?"

"I've already been in contact with them," Paytah explained, his voice softening for Tamara's sake. "They're dealing with some affairs at the moment, but they promised to send an agent over to help investigate."

"*An* agent? A single one?" Jackson scoffed. "They can't give us more time or protection than that?"

"One agent may be all it takes to find the perpetrators," Paytah said. "I only hope it's in time."

A cold silence settled over all of them at the implication. It was possible that neither her father nor Nick would make it out of captivity alive. Tess didn't want to think about it, but she had to face the truth, as did her mother.

She glanced at her mother, but she couldn't spot Iris amongst the crowd. Concerned, Tess wove between the wolves until she found her mother sitting on a couch with her head in her shaking hands. Tess settled next to her and rubbed her back. "It's going to be all right. You know how resourceful Dad is. And Nick's as stubborn as a mule. He's not going down without a fight."

"Fighting is what worries me," her mother choked out, tears dripping from her eyes. "What awful things are being done to them?"

Tess wrapped her arms around her mom, unable to answer. They sat together, comforting one another while wolves went to

Paytah to either thank him for his decision or to complain about his overprotectiveness. A curfew was unusual for the wolves, especially when they all had their lives to live, but Paytah didn't want anyone else to disappear.

At least, that was what Tess told herself.

She glanced around the room as her brethren huddled together, talking in low voices and making plans. It would be hard to stick with the new rule. Ray and Augustine both worked late often at the restaurant or tattoo parlor respectively. Becky only had herself, so another wolf would have to stay with her and her daughter so she could be watched. Jackson had already offered up his protest. No, the curfew wouldn't stick.

I wonder if I even count, Tess thought. *I'm not a wolf, and they're clearly not tracking magi at this point. If the other wolves can't help, maybe I can.*

Her mother shuddered, and Tess looked at her sadly. A deep love flowed between her mother and Brighton, tested by time and a grouchy, growing magus. They'd survived hardships together before; Tess wanted to believe her father would come back from this, too.

She glanced at Becky and whistled until she got the woman's attention. "*You mind sitting with my mom while I have a talk with Paytah?*" she said mentally.

Becky shook her head and hurried over, bouncing her daughter on her hip. Tess slipped away as Becky sat down and touched Iris's back. "Paytah knows what he's doing. He'll keep us all safe," she said.

Tess waited her turn until Paytah wasn't surrounded. He sighed in relief at the sight of her.

"I was hoping you'd be able to join us tonight. How are you feeling?"

"Well enough to do *something*," Tess said. "What can I do? I know my location spells aren't the best, but I have other magic which can help us out."

Paytah frowned at her. "As I said, I'm working with the Legion agent to find our wolves. I won't get home most nights until curfew, and you'll need to be inside too."

Tess wrinkled her nose. "Wait? The curfew applies to me too?"

"You're pack, aren't you?"

"But I'm not a wolf, and they're hunting werewolves, not

magi."

Paytah shook his head. "I don't care. You're still part of the pack, Tess, which means you may be in danger as well. You almost died in a car crash in their attempt to get your father and Nick. I'm not taking chances."

Tess took a step back and fisted her hands. "I can't sit back and *wait*. He's my father, Paytah!"

"You can and you will," Paytah said with a low, warning growl. "That's an order, pup."

Tess narrowed her eyes angrily. *Pup.* She did not like being called pup. That was meant for the troublemakers, not her. She leaned forward, pitching her voice low. "I helped stop the Hunters who were tracking Bianca. I can do more than sit still and look pretty."

"Need I remind you that you almost died during the fight as well when you were thrown into the ceiling?"

"But—"

"*No*," Paytah said firmly. "You're pack, so you follow pack rules. Curfew is at nine, and I'll be expecting you to check in as well."

Tess wanted to strangle him. It wasn't fair! She was the one who'd at least heard something. If the pair came around again, she might even be able to identify them based on their voices.

She turned away with a frustrated grunt. Paytah's hands were tied in this, but hers weren't. She couldn't bear the thought of another wolf going missing, and the longer they waited, the more likely it was they'd lose someone else.

If Paytah wasn't going to give her a way to help, then she'd take matters into her own hands.

Chapter 4
Housebound

Trish

I need to remember not to drink so much, Trish thought to herself as she upended a bottle of Excedrin into her hand. She grimaced at the faint rattle and popped a couple of the pills before settling back on her bed in the faint glow of her lamp. Nearly twenty-four hours had passed and her head throbbed like bricks were being tossed around in it. It seemed unfair that vampires got hangovers. Shouldn't her vampire *healing* have taken care of it already?

She gulped down water and propped her head on a pillow, bracing her neck to help offset the migraine. She sank into her bed and looked around her room, where she'd been housebound for over a year now. Joseph had *finally* loosened his hold on her enough that she could sneak out at night here and there. Otherwise, she stayed in her room of the coven mansion, a place many of the vampires shared together.

In the heart of Dearborn, Chicago, the mansion looked like a modified castle from the outside with stone walls and its turret-like red roof tops. Ten bedrooms were big enough to be converted into nearly 17 with siblings or married couples living together. Trish had one of the guest rooms assigned to vampires who had no other place to go or were deemed troublemakers. They might as well have given it to her for all the time she'd spent in there.

She looked around at the beige-colored walls and the elegant crystal chandelier hanging from a ceiling trimmed in dark wood which matched the flooring. Heavy pale gray curtains draped over the windows to protect her from sunlight. She had her own bathroom and a walk-in-closet a diva could die for. But it still felt sterile, cold. Saul had filled her shelves with books, and she even had movies and games she could play on her flat screen tv, but it wasn't the same as being *free*.

She'd gone from being a captive to her sire, to being forced under Joseph's watchful gaze by Gladus, to being kidnapped and used by Hunters, to once again being expected to serve her time in Joseph's care. Most of the household didn't really want her there. They tiptoed around her like they were waiting for the walls of their home to burn down because of the bad luck she brought.

Frankly, it surprised her something of the sort hadn't happened yet.

She sighed and grabbed the book on her nightstand and flipped it open. It was a YA novel about vampires who sparkled and a love triangle between a human, werewolf, and vampire. She didn't know why she read them; maybe she enjoyed the author's different perspective of parahumans.

Trish turned a page when she heard a commotion in the hall. She tried to ignore it, shoving part of her down pillow against her ear, but the tittering didn't stop. Rolling her eyes, she dog-eared the page and slipped off of the satin sheets. Voices stopped her at the door.

"Alpha Paytah is in an uproar," an older woman said. Jessabelle, most likely.

"Why shouldn't he be?" a young male replied, though Trish couldn't figure out which of the Harlem twins it might be. Darius usually had a softer voice than Miles, but when they were both nervous, they sounded exactly the same. "A car crash, and suddenly, two wolves go missing? And other packs are complaining about the same thing happening. Next, it'll be the prides or the cloisters."

"Or us," Jessabelle groused. "And here we thought the Hunter debacle with Trish and Gavin was over. At least we've had *some* peace over the past year or so."

Trish fisted her hand and pressed her head against the cool door.

Gavin.

Her throat tightened, and her heart ached worse than the pain of her migraine at the memory of him. The coven had moved on after his murder, but Trish hadn't. He'd been her best friend and one of her mentors, albeit more of the troublesome kind. But he'd made her feel at home, like she wasn't some sort of freak.

Like she belonged.

She leaned against the door and looked at her nightstand. A single picture sat atop it, tucked in a silver frame and decorated with three flying bats. Gavin and Trish stood in the center of the picture, Gavin's arm wrapped tightly around her, Trish rolling her eyes but unable to wipe the smile off of her face. He'd gifted the frame to her shortly after also *gifting* her the nickname "little bat." No one called her that anymore, not that she would have wanted them to. The honor had belonged to Gavin alone.

Trish slunk back to her bed and flopped face-first into the comforter. She rolled her head gingerly and stared at the picture, Gavin's half-cocked smile still making her flesh flush even after all this time. "Don't look at me like that," she muttered. "I tried to protect the coven with my actions." She swallowed a lump and ran a finger along his image. "I'm sorry I couldn't do the same for you."

She'd never get his dead eyes out of her mind. They haunted her in the depths of the night, and left her writhing and sobbing in bed. He wasn't the first dead person she'd seen, but she'd never been so connected to the dead before him.

Trish buried her face into her arms.

Someone knocked gently on her door.

"Trish? Are you awake?"

Trish lifted her eyes. She scrubbed a tear off of her cheek and slowly straightened. "Come in, Saul," she called, her voice as heavy as her heart.

The tall, dark-skinned vampire entered, shutting the door behind him. He dressed, as always, in one of his pressed suits. His dreadlocks wove around his head in an intricate pattern, braided in some places and left to hang in others. He walked towards her with purpose, his leather shoes leaving small imprints in her padded rug. "How are you feeling?"

"Ugh, migraine. I'll be fine once the pills kick in."

"Too much bad alcohol?"

Trish grimaced. He knew she'd snuck out, didn't he? Of course he did. Saul knew everything. "Yeah. I've been a little bit of a lightweight recently."

Saul stopped near the edge of her bed and tucked a hand into one of his pockets. He contemplated then sat down beside her with a deep sigh. "Trish, I know Joseph is slowly loosening the rules, but you can't sneak out like that. It puts you in danger, not to mention it makes it look like Joseph can't control his coven."

"It was just a drink, Saul."

"Yes, and now two wolves are missing."

Trish gave him the side eye. "What does that have to do with me?"

"They were at the same club as you, Trish. Don't you find that suspicious?"

An icy hand crawled up her spine and wrapped around her throat, silencing a retort. She stared Saul in the eye and knew deep down what his implication meant. Panic swept through her, images of Gavin's dead body flashing through her mind. "I had nothing to do with it, or with whoever took them," she insisted and shoved herself to her feet. "Saul, I learned my lesson. You know I only helped the Hunters to keep our coven safe! Why would I want to do anything to the wolves? It's been over a year. How could you think so lowly of me?"

"Trish, that's not what I'm saying," Saul said. "*I* believe you had nothing to do about the disappearances, but not everyone is so quick to forgive and forget." He squared his shoulders. "Joseph would like to have a word with you."

Trish slumped. If Joseph wanted to see her, then at least someone in the coven thought she was responsible. It wasn't fair! She'd done nothing but obey everything he, and the others, had to ask of her. She'd taken the abuse from fellow coven members who blamed her for Gavin's death and even Gladus's demise. Could she have done something differently? Yes, but in that moment, she'd thought she'd had a good plan, and it had gone awry. And now they despised her for it.

She closed her eyes. "Is he going to ask me to leave the coven?"

"No, no, of course not," Saul said, sounding surprised. "And even if he did, I wouldn't let him. He has a few questions, and that's all. Come along. You don't want to keep him waiting." Saul stood and held out his arm to her. "Don't worry, Trish. I'll protect you."

Trish reluctantly took his arm and followed him out of her room. The nearer they drew to the dining hall, the closer she huddled against Saul. She trusted him more than anyone else. He'd shown her nothing but love and respect since the first time she arrived at the coven, and especially since his mate, Fraula, was murdered by Alpha Paytah. He rarely spoke of her these days, but he carried a necklace with her ashes inside. The rest he'd scattered into the waters outside of the Shedd Aquarium. Fraula had been a bitch in life, at least to Trish, but she'd loved Saul and deep-sea life.

Probably because the bottom of the ocean was as cold, dark, and vicious as she'd been.

Trish glanced sideways at Saul. He wore more worry lines on his face, and his eyes bore dark bags of many sleepless nights. Fraula's death had shattered him, and being Joseph's second probably didn't help with the stress.

She wished she could do something, anything, to help him.

They stepped through the double doors to the dining room. Joseph sat doing paperwork at one end of the table while another vampire, their accountant, crunched numbers. The woman glanced over at Trish then exchanged a look with Joseph. The duke gave a single nod. In one graceful motion, the dark-haired beauty rose, swept her folders into her arms, and passed Saul and Trish.

Joseph settled back in his chair and gestured to the one across from him. "Please sit, Trish."

She did as he asked and perched at the edge of the velvet fabric, nerves sparking with tension. Joseph stared back at her, his skin paler than hers, and his hair slicked back. His eyes shone fiercely dark instead of red, demonstrating the control he had over his blood craving. Trish still had yet to learn complete control, a common case with most young bitten-born.

"So," Joseph began, steepling his fingers. "It's come to my attention that you went out last night against my wishes."

Trish shifted anxiously. "Only for a couple of hours. I needed to get out of the house. It's…it's become too much. Suffocating."

"Suffocating?" Joseph asked, his eyes roving around the expansive corners of the room. The table alone could seat twenty. Portraits of dukes long gone decorated the deep-red walls. Chandeliers, grander than the one in Trish's room, lit the room, their crystals sparkling. "I didn't think space would be such a problem for you. We have a bar here with alcohol if that's what you craved. And you're free to come and go around the house."

"Normalcy," Trish said. "I miss normalcy. I needed to be around other people. Our coven comes and goes, and not many people talk to me after what I did. I needed to get away." She rubbed her arm. "Saul told me what happened to the wolves. Yes, I ran into Tess, Bianca, Kat, Carmen, and Nick at the club, but I didn't do anything. We exchanged a few words. I backed off. And then they got into a fight with some magi and werewolves. I left before they did and came home. You can ask Jessabelle," she said with a roll of her eyes. "She caught me coming in at like one a.m. and gave me an earful."

Saul inclined his head. "She said as much to me."

Joseph grunted under his breath and looked down at a paper in front of him. "Alpha Paytah is calling a meeting of the leaders of the District. He's concerned this threat will grow bigger to encompass more parahumans."

Trish tensed. "Have any vampires gone missing?"

"No," Joseph said, quick to wave his hand. "Our coven is safe. Do you doubt my ability to protect us?"

"Of course not! I was…I wanted to be sure," Trish replied.

"The wolves seem to be the primary target. But with the threat of Hunters, or whatever beasts stalk in the night, lurking about, I want to make sure none of our vampires become victims. If I ask you to stay here, you will stay, Trish. Do you understand? I don't need you being blamed for the wolves' disappearances." He narrowed his eyes. "Nor do I need you to be targeted as a Hunter's helper again."

Trish's stomach twisted with both anger and disgust at herself. She'd never live this down, would she? "I understand."

"Do you?" Saul asked her from behind her shoulder.

She glanced back at him, surprised. She found it a little odd he stayed in there at all, since Joseph had dismissed his accountant. "I stay inside, otherwise, I might get taken. I get it."

Joseph cleared his throat. "It's more than that, Trish. If you cause a stir again, and make us enemies of the other leaders, I'll have no choice but to remove you from the coven."

Trish froze. She thought they were well past that threat! "But I've done nothing but obey you! I know I went out, but it was one time!"

"And it only took one time for you to turn to the Hunters. Mark me, Trish, I won't protect you again."

Trish fought back tears of anger and fear. She'd tried to protect her family. Did no one get that? She wasn't the villain. "I understand," she said again, her voice tight with emotion.

Joseph waved his hand, dismissing her. Trish flew to her feet and stormed out of the room. She expected Saul or Joseph to admonish her for her rudeness, but neither followed. She slammed the door behind her, causing it to bounce before the latch caught hold. Trish stood outside, hands pressed to her head and digging into her scalp. She should go back to her room, but her shallow breaths and tap-dancing heart stopped her. She meant it when she said the house suffocated her. Her room was the worst of it.

"I should have told her the truth," Joseph's whispered voice filtered through the crack between the doors.

Trish glanced at the slight opening as she counted in her head to slow her breathing. She shouldn't listen, but Joseph's words worried her. What was he not telling her? Did he really plan to kick her out? She moved closer to the door and listened with her sensitive vampire hearing.

"She doesn't need to know vampires are already missing," Saul said. "What would be the point of worrying her?"

"There are only two gone," Joseph agreed after a moment. "It could have been the Hunters, or it could have been humans who took them, we don't know."

"It could be the wolves, too," Saul remarked quietly. "They've shown little regard for our kind recently."

"Saul, I know you're still hurting over Fraula's death, but you can't keep blaming the wolves."

"I don't. I only blame the one who killed her." Saul shifted a chair and sat down. "Trish is fragile. If she thinks she can make amends for her actions, she'll do whatever she can, even if it means trying to find the missing vampires. The closer she stays to us, the safer she'll be."

"We can't know that," Joseph argued. "They could attack the coven house next. Who knows what they have planned or what they want? Perhaps this meeting with Paytah will bring some of our worries to light. I don't know what else to tell the coven, and my hands are tied in acting. Paytah, as Violet Marshall, *has* to take the lead."

Trish heard the bitterness in his voice. Many of the vampires suspected Joseph was sore over not being chosen as the next Violet Marshall after Gladus, but he usually encouraged them to support Paytah.

"It's what Gladus would want," he would say. "VM Paytah will keep us safe."

She wasn't sure if she believed him, nor was she certain if he believed his own words.

A long moment of silence passed between them, and Trish wondered if they were done talking. But then Saul spoke up again, his voice sounding sterner than usual. "It's a real pity you weren't named Violet Marshall. You've served this community for decades without ruling over everyone with a clenched fist. Paytah is even stricter than Gladus was."

Joseph grunted in frustration. "She had promised me at one time that she would choose me if I proved myself. She didn't even ask one of her own kind to lead the community. No, instead, she asked this wolf."

"The same one who killed our Fraula," Saul added. "She threw salt on the wound."

A chair squeaked across the wooden floor as someone rose sharply. Suddenly, Joseph's voice rumbled close to the door. "It doesn't matter now. Paytah is Marshall, and unless he's somehow removed, we're stuck with him. All we can do is make the best out of a bad situation and protect the coven."

"Of course, my lord. The coven's safety is of the upmost importance."

"And we'll keep it that way," Joseph said. "No matter the cost."

Trish backed away from the door and swallowed hard. She didn't like the tone in his voice, or the way they talked about Paytah. While Saul had grievances with the werewolf, he'd never acted upon them. He focused on keeping the peace. But Joseph? She didn't know if she could say the same thing about him. Would he bother to tell the rest of the coven that their members were missing?

Something isn't right.

She headed back to her room well before they left so they didn't know she'd been listening. That would be a sure-fire reason to get rid of her. Trish locked her door and paced the length of her room, thinking. The leaders were meeting. They would talk about what had transpired and who'd been taken. It wasn't her business.

And yet, did she have a right to keep it to herself? What if Joseph didn't tell Paytah about the missing vampires to try to demonstrate he had more strength than the alpha, or more control over his coven? Would that put the pair at a head? What did he mean he'd protect the coven no matter the cost?

She swallowed and glanced at the picture of Gavin and herself again. "What would you do?" she whispered to him.

"*Learn more and play the game. If we're going to be pawns, then we might as well be the best damn pawns we can be. Even a pawn can take down a King.*"

She swore she heard the soothing tenor of his voice echoing in her head. She closed her eyes and pressed her hands over her ears, shutting out the world, and imagined his playful tone. His advice. *You always said if something felt wrong in your very bones, then it was probably wrong. But what if listening to my worry gets me kicked out of the coven?*

She waited, but there came no reply. His voice and mannerism had started to fade over the year, no matter how she clung to them. "Please, Gavin."

"*Sometimes you gotta take the risk and hope to God everything turns out right.*"

Trish opened her eyes and stared at the picture. He probably would have made a joke about how he hadn't burst into flames using God's name. She missed him so much, she almost couldn't breathe.

Trish went to her closet and got dressed in comfortable clothing. She yanked on a pair of flat boots then pulled out a trench coat. It had belonged to Gavin and still had his scent faintly embedded in the fabric. She breathed it in to center herself then headed towards the window.

Trish slipped over the sill and leapt down, landing lightly on her feet a couple stories below her open window. She glanced around to make certain she hadn't been seen then glanced up at the mansion.

"Sorry, Saul," she murmured.

With a deep breath, she slipped away into the darkness.

Chapter 5
Captured

Nick

The cold gnawed at Nick's bones, causing them to creak and ache. He couldn't get warm, no matter what he did. He woke in a box with a few air holes which let in fluorescent light. Fighting, scratching, and punching the walls had only earned him bruised and battered knuckles. When he tried to shift, something around his neck shocked him and sent him back to sleep.

The next time he came to, he lay on a cold, dirty padded floor surrounded by silver bars. But the silver didn't bother him as much as the wolfsbane injected into his bloodstream. His body moved sluggishly, almost of its own accord. He'd been stripped from the waist up, leaving him in tattered jeans. Even his belt had been removed, along with his socks and shoes.

Nick reached up to his throat and ran his fingers delicately around a thick collar pressed against his jugular. It felt bulky and crude, but when he tried to pull on it, it didn't budge. He ground his teeth and pressed his other hand to it, intending to drive his wolf claws into the metal.

"I wouldn't do that, Nick," Brighton's tired voice called behind him.

Nick turned and looked over at the older werewolf. Brighton, likewise, had been stripped of most of his clothing except his torn uniform pants. His usually well-kept brown hair was askew, his hands as battered as Nick's. But that wasn't all.

"Man, what happened to you?" Nick asked, eyeing the bruises lining Brighton's face, neck, and chest. He thought he even saw bite marks on the man's right shoulder.

Brighton's expression turned grim as he glanced over his wounds. "They kept you unconscious for most of the ride here and after they threw you in the cell. Not sure why. But they dragged me out and tossed me into a pit." He clenched his jaw and narrowed his eyes. "We're part of a fighting ring, Nick. Wolves against wolves. Vampires against vampires. Wolf against vampire. They've made a sport of us."

"Who?" Nick snarled. "Who the hell has us?"

"Shh!" Brighton hissed. "Don't let them know you're awake."

"Who are they?"

Brighton's eyes flashed gold before he spoke in a low whisper. "Hunters."

Nick swore under his breath. Of course they were captives to Hunters. Who else would have the balls to ram a police cruiser and take them in? He glanced at his wrists, noting the silver-colored cuffs linking them together. His ankles remained free at least, but he'd only get so far without his hands. "Tess? Carmen?" he asked with concern, but Brighton shook his head.

"I haven't seen them. I don't think they were taken."

Nick wanted to feel relieved, but the tone in Brighton's voice worried him. "What? What is it?"

"The car was demolished, Nick. I saw it when they pulled us out. You were already unconscious." He shook his head, his expression grim. "I don't know if they're all right."

A chill raced down Nick's spine. Carmen would probably make it. She was a werewolf like him, and it took a lot to kill a were. But Tess? Magic could protect her while she was conscious, but he was pretty sure the crash would have knocked her frailer human body out. His packsister was lucky the truck had hit them on the driver's side. "They're fine," he said firmly. "They're stronger than they both look." But he had to wonder, if Carmen had survived, why wasn't she here with them?

Brighton looked less confident, and that honestly pissed Nick off. Wasn't the older wolf supposed to be comforting *him*, reminding Nick of the strength of their pack and how nothing could destroy them?

But they both knew Nick wasn't stupid. His own father had

gotten shot in the head and killed. Wrong place, wrong time. His dad had had nothing to do with the gangs, but he'd paid the price for their stupidity and violence, leaving Nick without a father or a home.

Brighton had been the one to come to the scene after the shooting happened. Paramedics had tried everything to revive Nick's father but to no avail. A bullet to the head left most people dead. Nick, consumed by both grief and hatred, had tried to rush off into the night to avenge his dad, but Brighton had stopped him. Brighton was likely the only reason Nick hadn't joined his dad in the morgue that night.

Still, a little reassurance would have been nice. "They're fine," he said again, this time with a growl.

Brighton glanced up and nodded. "Tess is too stubborn to go out like that."

"Yeah," Nick smirked. "She'd still want to get the last word in after your fight anyway." He glanced around slowly and touched his neck. The collar chafed and irritated his skin. He warred between anger and panic, not knowing which emotion to settle on. But then he thought of the lessons Paytah had taught him.

His alpha spent almost every night forcing him to sit down and meditate to calm his anger, because he had a lot to be angry about. Paytah was a ticking time bomb himself, but meditation helped them both. And Nick felt better about practicing it when his own alpha admitted that he needed it too.

He settled in the middle of the cage and crossed his legs. He gripped his ankles with both hands and bowed his head, focusing on his breathing. In. Out. In. Out. Air in, anger out. Air in, fear out. He silenced the world around him, the distant shouts from the fighting ring, Brighton's tired breathing, the drip of a broken pipe somewhere.

In. Out.

And he brought himself to a calmer place. To Paytah's house in front of the warm fire with his pack, Carmen and Kat on either side of him, Paytah kneeling in front of him and reciting some historical story about the house. Rozene and Iris making a soothing herbal drink. Jackson humming a spiritual in his deep tenor to little Heidi while Becky caught a nap on a nearby couch.

Tamara braiding Eliza's curly corkscrew hair while Mikayla periodically corrected her process between studying for biotech exams at Loyola University. Phoebe chatting her fathers' ears off about school and the newest boy she had a crush on. Ray cooking a delectable dish in the kitchen for everyone while Augustine sketched out designs and begged Iris to let her give the magus one *tiny* tattoo. Tess playing with small fireballs while chatting at Brighton's side. The warmth and strength of his pack flowed through him and broke past the rage and fear. He let his thoughts of them consume him and fill him with hope rather than despair. They were out there, searching for him and Brighton. They'd find Tess and Carmen and take care of them.

He had to have faith in the pack.

Nick blew out one final time then opened his eyes, feeling calmer than before. He caught Brighton's gaze and noticed the man smiling. "What?"

"Practicing Paytah's meditation? He used to do that with me too, you know."

"It helps," Nick said with a shrug. He looked around. "So, what do we know, what don't we know, and do you have any ideas how we can get out?"

Brighton settled down and rested near the bars. "They keep us injected with a steady stream of wolfsbane. Not enough to prevent us from changing, but enough to keep us weak. The collars shock us if we do something they don't like, or if they want to be dicks. I tried to get mine off, and it shocked me unconscious. There's enough room that it won't hinder us from changing; feels a little like a choker though. I think…oddly, it might be spelled to get bigger when we shift. I didn't see much when they dragged me through, but they have some of the cages set up around the ring. Others, like ours, are in more private sections. It looks like we're in some kind of underground cave network. Might have been part of an older subway system."

Nick snorted. "Lot of Hunters, then, to keep us guarded?"

"Yeah. At least 15 manning the fighting ring, excluding the crowd. Several up top keeping an eye on things. We got at least one Hunter posted outside our area at all times. Can't see him, but I can smell him lurking." He curled his lips over his teeth, showing off two vicious fangs. "Mix of men and women. Haven't seen this many Hunters together in an area for a long time. I'm wondering if there's trading going on, too."

"Trading?" Nick asked.

Brighton grunted. "Parahuman trafficking. Bring their captives here to force them to fight. The weak get killed. The strongest either keep fighting or get sold, probably to go to another fighting ring. Bad enough they invade our towns, but now they do this shit?" He leaned his head back. "We should have stopped this years ago."

Nick tilted his head, curious. He knew Brighton had worked as a cop for a long time, but he hadn't ever heard of a Hunter ring in Chicago before. "What do you mean?"

"You were a kid when parahumans went missing last time," Brighton said. "I worked with a special force of officers who had received some extra training from Legion. Well, we found out about the fighting and trafficking, and we set up a sting operation to bring them down. We would have gotten them too, but somehow, they got wind of it, and everything collapsed. They shot and killed one agent in her own backyard. Murdered a few more contacts we had put into place. It got personal."

"How'd you survive?"

Brighton's lips tightened into a thin line. "Tess," he murmured. "She somehow heard about the operation too. Followed me, wanted to make sure I was going to be okay. She saw the Hunter who had come to assassinate me, and she hit him with fire. Distracted him long enough for me to get him down and arrest him. If she hadn't been there, I would have been murdered."

Nick managed a half smile. "Sounds like she's your good luck charm."

"You might say that. We found the remains of a fighting ring, but by then, the victims had either been transported away or shot and killed, left behind for us to find and blame ourselves for. The disappearances stopped until about a year and a half ago." He shook his head and kicked the bar lightly. "If we'd put an end to it the first time…"

"Hey, it wasn't your fault someone blew your cover," Nick tried to console him. "You at least got it to stop for a while."

"Did we? Or did we just force them to continue it somewhere else?"

Nick didn't have an answer for that, but it scared him. How deep did the operation have its claws in the city? And how many other people were going to get dragged into it before—

Footsteps caught his attention. He sat up straight, Brighton doing the same, as someone walked down the hall towards them. A woman appeared first, dressed all in black, followed by a man standing about a foot taller than her. The woman smelled like lilacs; it made Nick want to sneeze. Her short black-cropped hair didn't do much to cover the scars on her face and neck. They seemed to glow white against her otherwise flushed skin, likely a memento left over from a pissed-off wolf. The man wore his long sandy hair in a man bun. He was taller and broader than the woman, but something about their faces made Nick suspect they were siblings.

"Ah, the pup's awake," the woman said without much feeling. She carried a steaming bowl in her hand which she dropped in front of Brighton's cage. "Eat, dog," she growled at him then looked at Nick. "Looks strong," she said, though Nick could tell she was talking to her companion, not him. "Think he can stand up against the newcomer?"

"Only one way to find out, Gale," the man replied. He pulled out a small control from his belt and—

Blinding pain knocked Nick onto his back with a yelp. Somewhere, he heard Brighton call his name, but the pounding of his blood in his ears drowned the other wolf out. When the pain subsided, he found himself on his side, panting, tears running down his cheek. His entire neck burned like it'd been wrapped in a flaming whip.

"Hendrickson!" Gale barked.

"Whoops, setting's too high. Well, at least it'll know what happens if it pisses us off."

Nick blinked through his tears as the door to his cage got yanked open. Rough hands dragged him out. He fought to get to his feet and regain his senses, but manacles were slapped onto his ankles and something latched onto his collar, forcing him to stay a few feet in front of Gale and Hendrickson. A cursory glance revealed a pole kept him at a safe distance so he couldn't try to launch himself at them or bite them.

Smart, but it ticked him off.

"Come on, pup," Gale said as Hendrickson started to drag him along. "Let's see what you're made of."

"Let him go!" Brighton shouted only to collapse in a pile of screaming pain.

Gale looked sharply back at Hendrickson. "*Enough.* Stop breaking them before they even get to the pit."

"Oh, lighten up. It gives them an incentive," Hendrickson scoffed. "They don't want to get shocked? Then they better win the fight. I got a lot of money riding on this one." He jerked the pole causing Nick to wince. "Hear that? You win, you get rewarded. You fail, you get the zap."

"Loud and clear," Nick snarled back.

Hendrickson barked out a laugh. "There, you see? They can be reasoned with."

Gale rolled her eyes and settled her hand near a ring of knives attached to her hips. "Come on. We're already late. Slater brought in his new one a few hours ago, and I hear it's a mean one."

"I love the mean ones," Hendrickson said. He jerked the pole one more time and forced Nick to look at him. He smiled, his teeth bright and filled with devious charm. "Make us proud, pup."

Chapter 6
Fighting Pit

Nick

Cheering and shouting assaulted Nick's ears as they made their way towards the fighting pit. They dragged him through dizzying tunnels, some he thought repeated as if they were trying to keep him confused, which likely wasn't far from the truth. The cave reeked of blood, sweat, tears, piss, and that damn lilac scent that kept wafting off the Huntress and clouding his senses. He didn't know if it was perfume or hair conditioner, but he hated it.

He stumbled through an entrance as Hendrickson jerked on the pole. Light poured down from fluorescent bulbs fixed into the walls and ceiling, nearly blinding him. He staggered and stopped, looking around.

A caged ring stood in the middle of the room surrounded by a few smaller prisons. Bleachers, old and rickety, lined the fighting pit, full of what he assumed were Hunters. Most of them smelled human, but again, the lilac scent distracted his nose. They cheered, passed around money, and made bids on the two people fighting in the ring.

Nick got a closer look at the two men battling. Vampires, fangs and claws drawn, flew at one another with speed werewolves envied. One was stockier in build, the other lithe and quick. His foot barely touched the ground before he was off running again. The only other parahuman who might be faster was a werebird. He had to wonder if any birds had been dragged down there as well. Or felines for that matter.

The vampires got in close, but the stockier man stepped wrong, misinterpreting a feigned attack. Suddenly, the smaller vampire grabbed him by the cheeks, twisted, and ripped his head clean off of his shoulders. The larger vampire collapsed in a pool of his own blood.

Half of the room groaned while the rest cheered.

Nick almost threw up at the sight of it. He'd seen people die before—he was no virgin to that—but it hadn't been as gruesome as the beheading. The winner dropped to his knees beside the body and *wept*, as if he had an iota of grief for the one he'd killed. Hunters swarmed in and got the winner shackled and back to his feet while more cleaned up the mess left behind. They shoveled sand over the blood until the pit looked clean again.

"Wow," Gale murmured. "Did *not* expect 42 to take down 43. Weren't they from the same coven?" she asked the man.

Hendrickson nodded. "Yep. Apparently loyalty only goes so far. Wonder what 42's master promised him."

"Heh, maybe no more shock collar," Gale said.

Nick struggled in his bonds and dug his heels into the dirt. "So is that what you're expecting? For us to kill one another?"

Gale looked back and shrugged. "Eventually. I mean, that's the only way we can figure out who really is the strongest. But for now, no, that'd be a huge disappointment if you went belly up right away. What a waste of time and effort to get you and the other dog." She looked Nick up and down, appraising him. "We picked you for a reason. You definitely showed some merit in that bar fight of yours. Too bad we broke the girl in the accident. We might have been able to use her too."

Nick's heart sank. "What did you do?" he said in a low, dangerous whisper.

"What do you think? Got rid of the evidence. A little fire, no one's the wiser. Though I guess we could have moved that magus into the driver's seat to add to the illusion. Oh well."

Suddenly, all of Paytah's calming lessons vanished. Nick threw himself forward with a snarl and tried to get his claws around the woman's neck. Carmen. Tess. They couldn't be dead. She had to be lying! But if she wasn't, he would rip off her stupid lilac-smelling face.

A sharp jerk of the pole yanked his head to the side and sent him crashing to the ground. He yelped in pain, cracking his shoulder and cheek against stone. Tears of anger and grief flowed down his cheeks followed by a whine. Tess…Carmen. No. Not them.

"Phew," Hendrickson spat on the floor next to him. "One fall, and he's already whimpering? Don't tell me we got a dud."

"Will you stop trying to break him!" Gale shouted. "You keep hurting them, we're not going to have anyone to bid on." She grabbed the pole and yanked, trying to force Nick back up to his feet. "Get up, get up! And stop sniveling. Save that anger and fight for the ring."

"Go to hell," Nick snarled. He wiped blood off of his cheek with one of his bound hands.

Gale didn't entertain him with a reply. Instead, she guided them down the slope to the main level of the ring. She pulled a ticket out of her pocket and rushed towards a broad white man at the entrance of the pit. "Here! We're next. Entrant 38."

The man eyed her and took her ticket. He looked it over then glanced at Nick as she dragged him forward. "Already battered? Are you two incapable of keeping control of your prey?"

Gale pointed her thumb back at Hendrickson. "Blame him. Is Slater here with his?"

The ticket master sighed and motioned to the other end of the pit. A tall Black man with stone-cold eyes and a chiseled frame towered over a figure huddled at his side. Nick couldn't see much of the other person, but he looked pretty small. Brown hair with reddish-orange undertones, his hands manacled in front of him like Nick. Collar, but no pole attached. The kid already looked defeated.

Gale waved a hand at the one named Slater, but the other Hunter rolled his eyes and growled something at his captive. Gale slowly lowered her hand and sighed. "Let me guess, he wants to do winner gets loser?" she asked the other man.

He nodded. "The usual."

Hendrickson chuckled dryly. "His fighter looks ready to fall over. I don't think it's going to be a problem. We might even be doing him a favor." He jerked the pole, causing Nick to wince. "All right. You go in. You both fight human. When we tell you, you go wolf. Got it?"

Nick didn't try to argue; what was the point? In all honesty, he was just trying not to panic. He wasn't afraid to lose. He knew how to fight, and he clearly had an advantage in size. He feared what they'd make him do to the loser. He wasn't a violent person! Yeah, he'd punched the shit out of the dick who'd tried to drug Carmen, but the guy had deserved it. He didn't want to hit some kid he didn't even know all for the sake of the Hunters.

"So what happens if I win or lose?" Nick asked.

Hendrickson lifted an eyebrow. "Wow, you're thick. You don't get it? You win, we get to keep Slater's fighter. You lose, you go to Slater. So if you don't want to be separated from your little friend back in the room, I'd suggest you take his bitch down fast."

Nick's head shot up. Wait, they wanted him to fight a *girl*? *Shit.* Every instinct told him to back down. He wasn't supposed to hurt a woman. It was ingrained in him to protect them, like Kat and Carmen, and even Tess, though she'd never thank him for it. He refused to throw his weight around and hurt another wolf, much less a woman!

But he didn't have much time to protest. The grate in front of the ring opened, and Hendrickson thrust him inside. The pole detached, sending Nick stumbling to his knees. The moment he hit the sand, the manacles on his wrists and ankles unlocked and dropped to the ground, freeing him. He looked over his wrists then glanced up as the other werewolf fell into the ring.

Now that he had a better look, he could see she was a woman. Her hair might have been cut in a boy's style, but her facial features, her hands, and even her scent told him otherwise. She shook her head and looked at him with rounded, prominent brown eyes. She glanced over her shoulder at Slater then slowly rose and rubbed her wrists.

Nick stood as well and kept as far from her as possible. He did not want to do this! Who the hell did they think they were forcing wolves to battle one another? He glanced at the sand and could faintly make out patches of red where the vampire had died.

"Fighters at the ready!" a voice boomed over a sound system. Nick ducked slightly, as did the woman. "1, 2, 3, fight!" A gong rang.

Nick didn't move. He stared at the other werewolf and set his jaw. No. He wasn't going to do this. They were wolves. Even if she served a different pack, he wasn't going to—

The woman threw herself forward before he could finish the thought. One moment he stood on his feet, the next he found himself on the ground, his face, throat, and chest smarting from three swift consecutive blows. He gasped and sat up, staring as the woman bounced from one foot to the next, her fists held up in front of her in a boxer's pose.

What the hell? he thought. He grunted and pushed himself up. "I don't want to fight you."

"We don't have much of a choice," she said and darted in again. He managed to dodge two blows before she nailed him in the spine, side, and right cheek.

Nick went down to one knee but managed to stay upright this time. His blood boiled with anger, and for a moment, he forgot all about wanting to protect the she-wolf. Her punches *hurt*. Her hands might have looked small, but she packed a wallop. "Stop it. We're not supposed to be fighting."

"We're in a fighting *ring*. What else do you think we're supposed to do, dance?" she asked. She moved around him, circling him, eyeing him like he was some kind of prey. The audience shouted, urging her on and booing and hissing at him for not standing his ground.

"Come on, 38!" Hendrickson shouted. "Are you going to let a little girl beat you?"

Nick glowered back at the man, then turned just as her fist connected with his nose. It crunched as he flew backwards to the ground. Damnit! He grabbed his face, blood sloshing over his lips and down his bare, broad chest. And all the while the woman kept bouncing around him. "Stop it!" he roared at her, his voice taking on a bestial sound.

"They're going to make us fight no matter if we want to resist it," she said calmly. "If we don't fight, they'll kill us. Now stop taking my blows and fight back!"

She came at him again, but this time, when she swung at his face, he caught her fist in his hand with a meaty slap. She looked surprised for a moment, and then her other fist nailed him right beneath the breastbone. The air whooshed out of him, and he stumbled backwards. But he didn't go down. He blocked another blow and swung out, barely grazing her shoulder. He thought of Paytah's lessons and the smooth techniques his mentor had taught him.

And then one of the woman's attacks sacked him in the crotch.

Nick went down to his knees with a gasp of pain, clutching

himself while he heard an audible wince from the male patrons. His vision pulsed with pain and anger.

Damn Paytah's lessons.

The woman was going down.

Nick launched himself forward and cracked his fist against the she-wolf's cheek, snapping her head around. He swiped his leg out and knocked her off balance before striking her between the shoulder blades. She pitched forward into a roll and let her momentum carry her back onto her feet.

Squirmy little thing, he groused. How the hell hadn't that put her down?

He followed her, but before he got close, she bolted out of the way and landed another strike to his hip and then a kick to the back of his knee. He staggered forward and felt her jump at his back, shoving him down until he landed with a loud belly flop in the sand. His lungs spewed air, winding him, leaving him floundering. The woman might have looked small, but muscle rippled through her body, and her weight had knocked him down *hard*.

"Get up!" Hendrickson shouted. "Shift! Shift you idiot!"

Nick blinked. Shift? Now? But—

"Shift, 85," Slater called to the woman.

She stood back and started to shift almost instantly, soft white and orange-red fur rushing over her body.

Nick looked down and panted. He had to do this. If he fought her in his human form, he'd likely lose in an instant. And he would not be separated from Brighton. He needed to be able to protect his packbrother, not be taken into some other crazed-man's custody.

He ground his teeth and started to change. He felt the dark fur break through his skin first and course along his body. His legs and arms tweaked and jerked, the bones restructuring and growing to give him a larger frame. His mouth itched as it elongated into a mighty muzzle filled with razor-sharp teeth. His ears moved up towards the top of his head, taking in even more sounds as they curled and created a tunnel for noise. His hands and feet doubled, then tripled in size, claws protruding and thick enough to rend flesh off of a man's arm. A tail sprouted from his tailbone, flicking back and forth as he crouched slowly in his biped form. He opened his eyes and stared across the ring at the she-wolf.

She looked different from the wolves in his pack, smaller, a little more elegant. She bore the resemblance of a fox with her reddish-orange fur and white underbelly, but with a wolf's larger frame and thicker face. He'd never seen a dhole wolf in person before, and he couldn't help but admire her beauty.

The clothes had vanished from their bodies. He rose and bared his teeth at her, eyes flashing and taking her in.

"Fight! Fight! Fight!" the crowd shouted.

Nick went down to all fours as he rushed her. She blinked in surprise and scrambled out of his way, but not fast enough. He smacked her legs out from beneath her and knocked her to the ground. His speed carried him past her, and by the time he turned, she rushed him, claws extended. He raised a furry arm to protect himself, but her claws sliced through the skin and flesh, causing him to roar in pain. He struck her along the belly and chest with his claws and bodied her across the ring.

The crowd cheered, sending a sick twisted feeling of hunger through Nick's stomach. The hunt, the need to take down his prey surged through his veins, urging him on. For a moment, it didn't matter that he was fighting a fellow wolf.

The woman crouched, panting. She glanced back at Slater then at Nick and opened her mind to him. "*Finally, we can talk like this.*"

Nick skidded, her voice shaking him out of his crazed state. "*What do you mean?*"

"*I came here alone. Did you come here with anyone?*" she asked him before he could fully gather his senses and realize that they could talk safely.

Nick backed off and crouched low. "*I came with a packmate. He and I were brought in together.*"

He thought he saw a look of disappointment on her face. "*Very well, I'll be the one to throw the fight.*"

"*Throw it? What are you talking about?*"

"*One of us is going to end up with the other, and it makes no sense to separate you from your packbrother. So I'll let you defeat me, and I'll go with you. It will make it easier for the three of us to figure out a plan of escape.*"

Nick stared at her. "*Wait, what do you mean you'll throw the fight?*"

A few people started to boo in the audience.

The she-wolf sighed in frustration and launched herself at him. "*Idiot, keep fighting! We have to make it look real.*"

A vicious slice across his chest felt all too real to him.

"Damn! Ow! Are you trying to flay my chest?" he protested.

"If it gets you to keep fighting, then yes! Hurry and end this." She struck out at him again, and Nick dodged, slapping her wrist away.

This was all a lot to take in. She wanted him to defeat her. He had no problem doing that, but he was a little offended that she'd *let* him win. As if he couldn't win by himself against a she-wolf. He scoffed and raced after her again, his claws digging through the dirt and propelling him along. They crashed into each other and traded blows, their claws catching each other on the face, chest, and back.

A sharp punch to his temple caused his ears to start ringing, and he backed off quickly.

"Finish it, 85," Slater said in a bored voice.

"Come on, 38!" Gale and Hendrickson shouted together.

Nick shook his head and rubbed his ear. The shouting and booing were like nails against a chalkboard. He wanted out of the ring, n*ow*.

"Finish it," the woman said. *"We need to give it a believable ending."*

Nick bared his teeth and howled, the sound vibrating through his entire body until each nerve pulsed with his challenge. Saliva dripped from his vicious fangs, pattering like rain on the sandy ground, mixing with blood both from his body and the vampire who'd died in the spot where Nick stood. He flexed his mighty paws and stared down his nose at the werewolf until she came at him again.

This time, Nick didn't hold back. He dropped to all fours and barreled his shoulder into her stomach. Her warm breath whooshed past his ear before he sent her flying across the ring. Her body crashed into the sand and rolled several feet, landing in a heap near the door she'd come through. Nick followed on the heels of his attack.

The woman tried to stand, but Nick dropped down over her and wrapped his thick mouth around her throat, pricking her skin. She froze and whined in submission, her ears laying back.

A bell rang through the arena followed by shouts and cheers. Nick panted, still holding the wolf down, and glanced over at Slater. The man scowled at them, especially the woman. Yet, he didn't approach them.

Gale and Hendrickson had less decorum. They cheered loudly, Gale throwing herself into Hendrickson's arms. He swung her around and then plopped her on her feet with a victorious cry. "That's how it's done!" he shouted and pointed at Slater, making the image of a gun with his pointer and thumb. "Told you she was no match for our dog."

"She threw the fight," Slater said calmly, but Nick's good hearing picked up on it. The woman tensed beneath him. "She held back. I want a rematch."

Hendrickson chuckled and spread out his arms. "A rematch? Sure, for twice the money. But we're keeping her until they've both recovered. Don't want to give yourself a disadvantage by having a wounded pup, right?"

Nick narrowed his eyes. "*What are they talking about, a rematch? I beat you.*"

"*If one of them suspects foul play, they can insist that we fight again. For now, I belong to them, though. Slater lost me.*"

Nick slowly removed his mouth from around her neck when it was clear he'd won the match. "*Did you really throw the fight?*"

"*Yes,*" she replied and started to change back into her human form. "*I could have laid you flat seconds after entering the ring if I'd wanted to.*"

Nick growled at her. Yeah, he'd believe it when he saw it. For the time being, he changed back to human. His chest burned as the fur sucked away, revealing the bloody gouges she'd left on him with her claws. His right leg looked a mess, too. He would have killed to have Tess there to heal them both up at that moment.

"What now?" he asked in a low voice.

The woman knelt and held her hands forward. "Kneel and wait for them to chain you back up."

Nick curled his lip. "Like hell! I'm not going to—"

"On your knees," Hendrickson said as he stepped into the ring. He grabbed the manacles from the ground and walked haughtily towards Nick, his hips swaying. Gale followed him, carrying another pair of manacles. "Do what she does."

Nick moved in front of the woman, blocking them from getting to her. "*No,*" he said in a low growl.

"Don't be an idiot," the she-wolf hissed at him.

Nick ignored her and started to grow his claws again.

Hendrickson sighed, disappointed. He pulled a silver device out of his belt and held it up. "Are you going to make me use this again?"

Nick eyed it then looked at the door they'd left open. He could try to run. He might get about five steps before Hendrickson shocked him and brought him down to the ground. Was it worth it to try to escape? Hunters surrounded the arena; who in their right mind would just let a werewolf run off?

"Well?" Hendrickson said.

Nick huffed out a breath and dropped to his knees beside the woman. He hated it, but he didn't want to get hurt, nor did he want the cocky wolf to get punished for his stubbornness.

Gale and Hendrickson descended, chaining them both and attaching poles to their collars. They were a little gentler about dragging them to their feet this time, though Nick still managed to growl. It was demeaning to be carted around like some animal, and he did realize the irony of that thought.

The two Hunters chatted annoyingly about their winnings as they brought Nick and the woman back to the cages. He kept glancing at her out of the corner of his eye, but she walked along with her head bowed, looking positively beaten down. It seemed so contrary to when she'd been talking to him and ordering him about.

When they reached the room where Nick was being held, Brighton rose to his knees and looked him over. Nick subtly held up a hand to say he was fine and let himself be pushed back into his cage. To his surprise, they shoved the woman in after him. He turned, catching her, and helped her down to her knees after Gale locked the door.

"Help her get acquainted to her new quarters," the Huntress said with a smirk. "You both will be fighting again soon enough." With a laugh, she and Hendrickson left the room.

Chapter 7
Shen Yanlei 申焰雷

Nick

Brighton broke the silence once the Hunters left. "Are you all right?" He shuffled closer to the edge of the cage so he could get a better look at them.

"Yeah, just a few wounds," Nick said and looked himself over. Blood leaked through a patch of his pants and covered part of his chest. It would have been nice to receive medical help, but he didn't expect that from Hunters. He eyed the woman. "Who are you?"

"Shen Yanlei, from the Harvey Pack. You may call me Yanlei."

Nick cocked his head in surprise while Brighton leaned forward. "You're from around our area then. How did you get caught?"

"Grabbed off of the street while helping my friends," Yanlei said. She settled down on the ground and started to massage her shoulder. "I've only been here maybe two days."

"Same," Brighton said. "I wonder if we were all nabbed at the same time."

Nick gave Yanlei an incredulous look. "Wait, if you've only been around for two days, why weren't you fighting that guy, the Hunter I mean? And why'd you give up so easy? How'd you know the rules?"

Yanlei rolled her shoulders and neck, brownish-red tips

brushing along her thin cheeks. Her skin glowed a beautiful shade of golden brown. "I'm not the first of my family to get dragged into a fighting ring. My grandfather landed in one, and he warned us what to expect from Hunters."

"He survived," Nick said in surprise. He didn't expect many people to escape these halls with their lives still intact. The Hunters would be stupid to let captives go who could lead the rest of the parahumans, and Legion, back to the base. "So, did he help get the others out?"

Yanlei shook her head. "He tried, but by the time he got anyone to listen and believe him, the Hunters were gone. They like to slip between our claws. But this was back in New Jersey, before we came here and joined the Harvey Pack. Apparently their customs are familiar amongst all Hunter groups. It's a shame the Hunters here aren't like the ones back home."

"Back home?"

"China," Yanlei replied. "American Hunters are so brutal. They're only interested in torturing parahumans and making the most money out of it. Hunters in China are more focused on the *bad* parahumans. They hunt to keep people safe, not to torture us. Granted, they'd probably wipe out anything that's not normal, but no torture. It was how my grandfather got caught. Hunters approached him in New Jersey, and he didn't know what they were or how cruel they could be. He learned quite quickly how to play the game."

Nick couldn't decide if he should find that comforting or not. Familiarity prepared them for what came next, but it also told them how bad things could get.

Better to be prepared, he decided.

Brighton settled down near the bars and looked Yanlei over. "What can you tell us of their operations? And how did your grandfather escape?"

"Simple. He died."

The hair stood up on the back of Nick's neck. "But you said he escaped and warned you."

"Oh he did, he just died first." Yanlei chuckled at their expressions. "My grandfather meditates and likes to challenge himself. He learned, long ago, how to slow his heartbeat until it stops. Or seemed to, anyway. My mother used to joke that he would do it to get out of chores. The Hunters checked him and tossed him in one of their dump spots for bodies when they thought him dead. But my grandfather, of course, awoke, and he returned to us. My mama thought he was a ghost when he walked through the door."

"Can you do that?" Nick asked.

Yanlei smiled a little. "I don't have his patience." She glanced around the room, her gaze sweeping between Brighton and Nick. "He tried to help the captives by telling a Violet Marshall. But, we did not see any of our people escape. You either came alive and left a corpse or as someone's slave."

Nick grunted defiantly. He wasn't so easy to kill, and they'd find that out very quickly. He flexed his hand, looking over the tight muscles beneath his dark skin. Paytah had trained him well in fighting and enduring pain. Whatever the Hunters had in store for him, he'd survive it. And he'd get himself and Brighton back home to his pack. No one else would fall victim to the Hunters under his watch.

Brighton caught his eye and nodded, as if reading his thoughts. "Well, then, Yanlei. My name is Brighton, and this is Nick. We're both part of the Chicago Pack led by Alpha Paytah."

"The Violet Marshall of the Chicago Purple Door District," Nick added.

"A big responsibility," Yanlei said. "Many PDD Marshalls decide to hand over their role as leader to another while they are in charge of the District. No conflict of interests, then."

Nick frowned. "What do you mean? Are you saying Paytah wouldn't be able to separate his feelings for his pack over the safety of the District?"

"That is exactly what I'm saying. I don't know your alpha, but I've heard it said before that some Districts ask their Violet Marshalls to step down from a place of leadership. Magi, for example, are vain and known for showing favoritism to their ward. If protecting *their* people means putting the District at risk, they don't care."

"That's not true!" Nick snapped, his face flushing with rage. Memories of Gladus flooded back to him. Though a priestess of the Oakfield Ward, Gladus had dedicated every moment of her life to the District and its people. She died saving Bianca; Gladus was the last person who would have put her ward before someone else. "Gladus gave everything, even her life, to the District."

"And I assume she was a magus?" When Nick nodded, Yanlei chuckled. "Well, obviously I don't mean all magi will show favoritism; it was an example. And I hardly could have known about Gladus. Paytah has been the Marshall since I arrived in Chicago."

"You're new," Brighton said. "What brought you here?"

Yanlei snorted. "We thought it would be safer than where we were. Apparently, we were mistaken." She started to rub the muscles in her legs slowly. "You want to know what to expect from the Hunters, yes?"

"Please."

"Nothing good," Yanlei said unhelpfully. "These Hunters like to hold fights in the pit against different parahumans. They usually don't bring in magic users. They might be human, but they're harder to control and boring in the ring." She glanced at Nick. "You could take off the head of a magus before she got a good shot in with as much as the Hunters keep magi drugged." She reached down to her ankles, stretching. "Daily pit fights. People come and go. Winner of fights usually get a new captive and money. More wins under your belt, the higher standing you have. They try to pick the strong ones who can do the most damage. Me? They'll think I'm weak and try to sell me off. They won't put me back in a ring unless they want to spare you two. The stronger parahumans stay in the pit for a long time. The others? Either die or get sent off to other places. Sometimes to get milked for our venom. Or have our bodies experimented on. There are humans who know about us and would love to explore how much mental and physical torture we can endure before death."

Nick shuddered. He'd thought that they'd grown past all that. The District was supposed to be safe! How had no one figured out this had been happening right under their noses, and why hadn't they been discovered? Well, no, that wasn't entirely true, not based on Brighton's story. "So what do we do then?" he asked. "Make ourselves look impressive or weak?"

"You have a better chance of survival if you're strong," Yanlei replied. She gave him a cursory look over and reached out for his arm. "You're in pain. I can help work out the cramps in your arms."

Nick shied away from her. "I'm fine; you didn't hurt me that badly."

"Don't be such a *male*," she grumbled. "I've studied physical therapy, and I'm training to be an athletic trainer. Let me see your injury."

Nick really hadn't noticed the pain until she mentioned it. Shifting towards her sent agony racing through his right shoulder and down his back. How the hell had she known? He turned his back to her and gasped when she pounced. Her hands dug into his flesh, pressing against muscles and nerves he didn't even know he had until knots popped and both brought and alleviated pain. He gasped out a breath and shifted to get comfortable, but she grabbed him and held him still while she worked. He gritted his teeth and tried to keep on a brave face. "So, physical therapy?"

"Yes. Initially, I think my father had hoped I would follow him in the neurological field. He works as a migraine specialist over at the Diamond Headache Clinic. But once he realized I was more interested in physical therapy, he supported my career. Helping people runs in the family." Yanlei pressed a nerve which sent a jolt through his body. "Though knowing which pressure points to hit during a fight is an added bonus of my profession."

Nick became putty in her hands. He slumped into her hold and closed his eyes, allowing himself to enjoy her touch, and her smell. Her brownish-red hair held a unique scent, spiced with something he didn't recognize, but he liked it. It almost reminded him of the Great Lakes, but in a good way. He focused on that and the pressure on his bare skin.

He didn't know how long he lingered under her spell, but her voice broke him out of it.

"I think if you were a werecat, you'd be purring right now."

Nick grunted and sat up quickly, his cheeks flushing red.

Brighton barked out a laugh. "I think you lucked out having her in your cage, Nick. You'll be ready for any battle after that."

Nick muttered and straightened himself out, brushing off flecks of dried blood on his chest, his wounds healing with his natural werewolf DNA. The wolfsbane slowed their abilities, but the dose they'd been given didn't completely stop it. Yanlei also looked better, her face a little less pale from losing blood. He rolled his shoulders and almost leaned against the bars until he remembered they were silver. That was going to get annoying quick. "Thanks."

"Don't need to be shy about it," Yanlei said, smiling. "It's going to be my job once I get out of here."

Brighton cleared his throat. "Well, if you two are done flirting, do you mind filling us in on what else we might expect, Yanlei?"

"*Job*, not *flirting*," she corrected him. She crossed her legs and rested her hands on her knees. "There will be pain. The longer you last, the more they'll work to condition you to last even longer. Not all fights are between other lycans, at least not with claws and teeth. Sometimes they will test pain threshold with this." She tapped the collar on her neck. "So, they may spend hours zapping you to see what you can endure."

Nick's stomach dropped. One shock had laid him flat. What would multiple do to him? He grimaced and touched his belly where phantom pain churned inside of him. He would have expected it more in his throat. "I wanted to throw up after one shock."

"Yes, they set it high, so you prepare yourself. They'll change the settings, make it weak once, then hard again. They like to get creative. And sometimes they'll do it if they get bored." She scratched her neck lightly, brushing hair off of her shoulder. "What else they might do, I don't know. That's all what my grandfather told me and what I've experienced so far."

Nick narrowed his eyes. "They've shocked you?"

"Slater? Several times. He wanted to test my strength." She wrinkled her nose. "I'm still not good at standing up to the pain, but I try."

"What about food?" Brighton asked. "Is it safe to eat and drink? Do they actually feed us?"

Yanlei went to respond when Nick heard a clang near the entrance of their prison. He looked up and growled under his breath as Gale walked in carrying three thick metal bowls. Each one held a raw cut of meat. Hendrickson followed behind her with water.

"Awake and healing already," Gale said with a note of pride. "Stronger than I thought. We have food and water for you. Now, make sure you eat it all up. Especially you." Her eyes darted to Brighton. "You have a fight tonight."

Nick scooted closer to the bars. "And what about us?"

"You get extra treats," Gale cooed. She put the bowls of food and water down outside of their cages and then another smaller bowl with red liquid. The sweet scent of fermented berries filled his nose. "Go on, eat."

Nick frowned. Exactly how was he supposed to eat with the food outside the cage?

Yanlei provided the solution. She shifted before his eyes into her biped form. Their cage was adequate in human form, but as bipeds, there wouldn't be much room. He moved away from her as her size grew, her tail brushing against him and tickling his skin. She padded forward and pressed her muzzle through the bars, her fur protecting her from the silver metal. With a growl, she chomped down on the meat and pulled it inside before tearing into it with gusto.

Nick reluctantly changed as well and watched Brighton follow their example. His muscles screamed in protest at being forced to take on his biped form so quickly after shifting earlier, but he didn't have much choice. He had to eat, and if Yanlei was devouring the food without protest, then it had to be safe.

He hoped.

He moved to her side and squirmed into the small space between Yanlei and the cage until he could get his muzzle through the bars as well. The metallic scent of meat made his mouth water with anticipation. He jerked it into his paws and devoured it, his newly-changed body craving the protein and calories. The thought of lapping at the water like dogs made him sick to his stomach, but he didn't want to die either. And if he was going to get thrown in fights, he needed the sustenance. He drank deeply from the water dish and eyed the wine. Something told him not to drink it.

Yanlei, however, gulped it up without a second thought.

"Well, maybe they can actually learn to obey," Gale remarked. She sat down on a ledge and rolled a knife around in her hands.

Nick eyed it while he ate. It looked like any normal knife except for the, what he assumed were, werewolf teeth decorating the hilt. That wasn't unsettling at all.

Gale caught him staring and waved the knife back and forth tauntingly. "A few keepsakes from werewolves who didn't follow orders. Do what you're told, and I won't add you to it."

Nick growled under his breath, but he didn't rise to the bait. Instead, he swallowed the last of his food and shifted back to human. The transformation started much slower this time. His bones twisted and creaked, sending minor streaks of pain through his limbs. Shifting drained him, and doing it multiple times in a day made it even worse.

Once human, he sat down and settled near the bars, eyeing Gale. She acted tough, but something about her made him believe it was all a façade. Hendrickson was the real tormentor of the two. Nick glanced at the other man and watched how his eyes roved over Yanlei as she changed back to human. Nick's ire rose, and he started to move to put himself in front of her, but Yanlei rested next to him too quickly and pulled her legs up. She wrapped her arms around them, holding her knees to her chest and looking hardly like a threat at all. Nick knew better.

Hendrickson spit on the floor and leaned back. "So what do we do with this one? She doesn't really look like a fighter."

"Did you *see* her in the ring? She was faster than the pup, and she marked him." Gale cleaned her nails with the tip of her knife. "I think she's holding back, but no matter. She'll learn soon enough to play the game."

"*She* is right here and can speak for herself," Yanlei said, surprising Nick. He glanced at her, but she had her eyes on Gale as well. "Slater asked me to fight. He didn't tell me to win."

Gale and Hendrickson both looked at her before the Huntress smiled and laughed. "Oh, you're going to grow on me. And so you know, when we ask you to fight, we want you to win, got it?"

Yanlei nodded and yawned deeply. Nick didn't know how she could act so blasé, but then he felt his eyes flutter. He blinked and struggled to stay awake, but sleep tugged at him, threatening to drag him under. It couldn't have been the wine. The food? The water? He didn't know, but he felt himself slump down. Yanlei fell against him and grimaced.

"Nick? Nick!" Brighton shouted and banged his fist against the bars before hissing in pain as the silver burnt him. "What did you do to them?" he roared.

"Not…part of the plan," Yanlei whispered to him.

He didn't know what she meant, but he didn't have much time to care. His vision blurred, and the last thing he saw was Hendrickson raising the silver controller to Brighton.

Chapter 8
Concocting the Plan

Tess

Curfew didn't sit well with anyone in the pack. Tess heard the complaints both first-hand and from her mother. Jackson and Mikayla grumbled about not being able to pick up kids who needed their help. Ray and Augustine struggled to keep both of their businesses running when they couldn't be there later at night. Becky lost much-needed tips at the restaurant by missing the late crowd, though Paytah compensated her for it. Quince broke curfew more than once to tend to a patient at the hospital and was treated to one of Paytah's vicious scoldings.

"He told me this isn't a game!" Quince growled as he paced through Tess's apartment. Her mother fixed all three of them a drink, but Quince waved off any alcohol, favoring a glass of iced tea instead. "As if I don't know that. He has to realize that Pedro and I are terrified our girls are going to get snatched. Or someone's going to attack Pedro while I'm at work. But I have a job and lives to save. I can't cower somewhere and wait to see what happens!"

"I know," Iris said soothingly. "He's worried about the pack, Quince. It's nothing against you, or Jackson, Mikayla, Ray, Becky, or Augustine. We all have lives, but I'd rather be safe than sorry."

Tess watched Quince deflate and sit down at the table beside Iris. Her mother had this way with the pack. Her calm nature could snuff the fire of the hottest wolf. Tess had tried to sense for magic, but her mother didn't use anything except her words to calm their brethren.

Tess folded her arms over the back of her chair and frowned. "There's still no sign of Dad or Nick or even their captors. Jackson and Tamara came back from scouting earlier, but there's nothing." And that worried her. It was like her father and Nick had vanished into thin air. She didn't want to think a magus had gotten involved in all of this, but how else could they disappear so thoroughly? "I'm really sorry Paytah scolded you. I know how important your job is to you."

"Yes, but your dad and Nick are just as important." Quince sighed and reached for Iris's hand. "I'm so sorry, Iris. I can't imagine what you're going through. If I ever lost Pedro—"

"I have hope he'll come home," her mother replied and patted his hand. "And we have to have faith in our alpha. Paytah knows what he's doing."

"Yeah…yeah, I think Pedro and I need to remember that."

Tess sighed and pressed her head against her folded arms. Paytah was a strong leader both as an alpha and a Violet Marshall, but his hands were tied. If he didn't want to anger Legion, he couldn't launch into a full scale investigation as he normally would have. Hell, when Bianca had gone missing, he, Tess, and Kat had gone together to get her back. He'd had no hesitation about jumping into danger for someone. Now? They had to play the waiting game, and Tess *hated* waiting, especially when it was affecting the lives of her other packmates. It was like they all had leashes coiled around their throats.

She found allies in Ray and Augustine at least. On the fifth day of her father's disappearance, she went to them near sunset. Ray arrived home early—he'd had his tail chewed out by Paytah when he didn't check in the night before. Augustine left her shop in the care of a protégé who, while talented, didn't have the same finesse and attitude as his mentor.

Augustine let Tess in when she arrived, and Tess followed her into the modest three-bedroom house that the werewolves shared together. "To what do we owe this pleasure? You sure you want to be here so late?" Augustine grumbled.

Tess took off her red coat and draped it over her arm. "That's what I wanted to talk with you and your mate about."

Ray and Augustine exchanged looks, but Ray waved his hand. "Let's discuss it over dinner. Are you hungry?"

"If you're cooking, definitely."

The two wolves went to work together in the kitchen. Ray might have been the chef, but Augustine could make a mean side dish. They moved side by side, curving around each other as if in an elegant dance. Ray pulled meat out and set about seasoning and cooking it. Augustine cleaned off asparagus and coated the stalks in a parmesan crust. She bumped hips with Ray playfully, and he leaned over to steal a kiss.

Tess watched them, fighting back a smile. For someone as gruff as Augustine, she could be a doting, head-over-heels-in-love mate at times. As Ray reached for the salt, Augustine snuggled up behind him and wrapped her arms around his waist. Ray sucked in a breath.

"Dear, we have a guest, and you're going to make me burn the food," he teased.

"You've never burnt it before. And last time, I was naked," she growled softly into his ear. "You're just afraid of putting on another sort of show for her," she added, glancing meaningfully down to his bulging pants.

The salt shaker clattered to the counter as Ray cleared his throat. "*Augustine*," he whined.

Tess chuckled and fingered her necklace. She couldn't help but long for a love like theirs. Independent as she was, the thought of someone holding her while she made—or burnt—dinner sent butterflies through her stomach. The warm, inviting presence of someone waiting for her when she got home at night. And the feeling that she was never quite alone. *I wonder if there's anyone out there who can handle my fire and won't try to tame me*, she thought.

Before long, and with Augustine keeping her clothes on, Ray set the table with a delectable dinner of steak mignon, parmesan asparagus, and red-skinned garlic potatoes that were to die for. Tess tried to enjoy the meal, but her intention of meeting them made the food taste more like ash.

"So," Tess began and set her fork down. "We all know Paytah is limited in the search."

Ray lowered his glass of red wine and frowned. "He's trying, Tess. But he's waiting for Legion and trying not to stir up fear in the District."

Augustine snorted and drained part of her beer. "People are

disappearing. Who the hell isn't going to be afraid of that?'

"Exactly," Tess said. "Vampires and werewolves have been the targets from what we've heard. We haven't seen anything since the accident, but that doesn't mean that they aren't still out there, lurking."

Augustine gave her the stink eye. "Your point?"

"I think we should get *them* before they get us."

While Augustine perked her head in interest, Ray grimaced. "Tess, what half-brained plan do you have this time?"

"They're not all terrible," Tess protested.

"Casting spells from a grimoire that's not your own?" Augustine said.

"Drinking an old potion to increase your strength to take on a werewolf," Ray added.

"Causing a ceiling to fall on you," Augustine and Ray said together.

"Hey! I was trying to save someone. I didn't think—"

"See? Right there," Augustine interrupted, pointing at her. "You didn't *think.* Sometimes, we gotta rely on our alpha even if we don't like it." She tapped her beer bottle lightly on the table. "Although, I am curious about what this plan is."

Tess brightened, but only a little. "Bait," she explained. "We set them up. Send our wolves out to draw the attention of the Hunters, but the rest of us are close by to help them. I don't want anyone else to get hurt or taken, so we take extra precautions. We wait for the Hunters to pounce, and then we catch them."

Ray smirked. "A double cross. My, so devious."

"I do have my moments," Tess said proudly.

Augustine *thunked* her beer down on the table. "And what's Paytah got to say about this?"

"Well, he doesn't know."

The Latina wolf snorted loudly and leaned back, propping her feet up on the empty fourth chair. "Oh, right, yeah, that's going to go well. You send us out there, and we don't come back. What do you think Paytah will do with you then?"

"I don't care!" Tess shouted, surprising herself. She half-rose out of her chair, her hands planted on either side of the table. Ray and Augustine stared back at her, mirroring her shock. Tess curled her fingers into fists and bowed her head. "Look, it's almost been a week, and there hasn't been a sign of any of them. I'm scared,

Augustine. For Nick, for my dad. My mom can't lose him. I know magi don't exactly share the same sort of bond that two wolves or two birds would, but she already lost one husband. I can't let her lose another. And I…I can't…I need my dad."

Silence permeated the room. Tess half-expected one of them to ask her to leave, but they didn't speak. They continued to stare even as Tess lowered herself down in her chair. *I didn't realize how much I was holding in*, she thought. *I was so busy worrying about Mom and making sure the pack was all right, I didn't check in with myself.*

Her therapist would have a field day with her the next time they met.

Augustine picking up her bottle broke the silence. "Well, at least you're dedicated to the cause," she muttered. "Who did you have in mind? Us"—she swayed the bottle to Ray and herself—"obviously, but who else?"

Tess bit her lip. "Bianca and Kat."

Ray almost spit out his wine. "Are you crazy? Kat just started warming up to the pack in the past year, and Bianca isn't a wolf."

"I know, which works to our advantage," Tess said. "They won't expect an avian to be around. If Bianca can scout from the sky, then Kat can be used as bait alongside Ray." She looked at Augustine. "You and I will follow. I'll keep us hidden with my magic so we can attack when we think Kat and Ray are going to get taken. And if something goes wrong, Bianca has wings; she can fly away and warn someone. Kat's also one of the fastest wolves. No one's going to catch her that easily."

"Why not just send Kat out there?" Augustine asked. "Not that I want her to be bait, but why two?"

"Because they left Carmen behind, so they might be less likely to take women. But if there are two unguarded wolves, we could have a better shot catching their attention. Besides, we're supposed to be traveling in pairs. It probably won't happen immediately, but after a couple of days, one of the kidnappers is bound to bite if they want werewolves."

Augustine grumbled and set her beer down again. Her thumb scraped at the label, growing until a claw slid through and nearly shattered the glass. "I'm a better fighter than Ray."

"No argument there," Ray said.

Tess knew where she was going. "Right, but we need to keep

our fighters in reserve. Ray is big and strong enough, he'll be pleasing to the eye. They won't expect you to come out of the shadows and trounce them."

Ray reached for the Cabernet Sauvignon. He poured himself another half-a-glass and touched the wine to his lips. "Why do I feel like I'm on display at some date auction?"

"Kinda making a date with death," Augustine said bitterly. "Tess, I don't know about this. It could all go wrong, and we don't need any dead wolves. What do Bianca and Kat even think about this?" When Tess didn't answer, Augustine dropped her feet to the floor and leaned forward. "You didn't even ask them yet? Girl, what the hell are you thinking?"

"I'm *thinking* I want to get my packmates back. And if we have to take matters into our own hands because Paytah *can't*, then fine. If I was a wolf, I'd—"

"But you're not." Augustine rested her arm on the table and moved closer to Tess. Her size, strength, and the intensity of her stare made Tess shrink back. "Like it or not, Tess, you're a human with magic. You can't stand up to shit like the rest of us can, and if it comes to blows, Ray, Kat, and I are going to take them because you won't be able to."

"Augustine," Ray murmured. "Don't be so harsh."

"It's true! I'm not trying to sound like an ass, but we have to look at both our strengths and our weaknesses. And you, Tess, are a weakness when it comes to the pack."

Tess's breath caught in her throat. Didn't they think she considered that when she watched the wolves spar, knowing she could never join in? She could burn down a house with the flick of her wrist, but a sharp blow to her torso could easily break bones, something a werewolf didn't necessarily have to worry about. Their fast-healing enabled them to stay on their feet whereas a human, like herself, would be laid flat.

But a weakness?

She gripped the table for stability. "Is that all I am to you? A liability?"

Augustine sighed. "Tess, that's not—"

Tess pushed herself up before she could finish responding, heart thumping painfully with the threat of a panic attack. "Thanks for dinner. Sorry to have bothered you."

"Tess," Ray said gently.

Augustine took a different approach. She slammed the beer down and shot to her feet, blocking Tess's path so she couldn't leave. Tess jumped back in surprise before steeling herself and trying to brush past the wolf even while anxiety tightened her throat. When Augustine reached for her, Tess's stress got the best of her, and she swung up two fingers. A bar of fire raced between them, blocking Augustine from touching her without burning her hand. The werewolf paused and slowly lowered her arm. "Grow up," she grouched. "You can't solve everything by taking matters into your own hands. That's how you get people killed."

Tess fought tears as she stormed past her and grabbed her coat from a peg. "Yeah, 'cause wolves *never* let their emotions take over, and they *never* run headlong into a battle without thinking things through. You go ahead and sit there and sulk over the curfew. I'm actually going to do something." She reached the door and yanked it open. As her foot hit the first step, Augustine called after her.

"I didn't say we wouldn't do it."

Tess paused, hand on the door. "No, but you think it's a bad idea."

"Clearly, but you're right about one thing. We're running out of time. Yeah, it'd be better if Legion got involved or Paytah had a plan, but since there's nothing, we have to do what we can to save our pack. Besides, at least you're taking precautions to keep us safe. You tell us where and when, and we'll be there."

Tess turned and looked back at the two wolves. Augustine stood next to her chair, arms crossed over her generous bosom. Ray remained seated with wine in hand, but when their eyes met, he lifted his glass to her in kinship. The tension in her shoulders eased, and she nodded. "I'll let you know. I'm not trying to be rash or stupid. I just can't sit still any longer.

"Neither can we," Augustine said in parting.

Tess shut the door quietly behind her and leaned against it with a sigh. Her panic attack ebbed with each slow breath. *I know the risks*, she thought. *But that's why we go in with a plan. I hope Bianca and Kat are more reasonable.*

***

"No," Bianca said, shaking her head. The avian paced back and forth in the apartment she shared with Kat. The whole building actually belonged to Bianca's cloister Father, Carlos. He'd bought it about six months ago to house all of his avian members, including his family. The elevator had been the selling point to help support Carlos's wife who used a wheelchair. Kat and Bianca likely appreciated it, too, since they were up on the third floor.

The apartment appeared modest, the walls painted a soothing shade of blue with navy accents. Pictures of Bianca's adopted family decorated several spaces. Tess admired two portraits which hung side by side. One showed the family in their human forms with Bianca sitting in between her younger siblings, a young boy with curly red hair named Henry, and his older sister Maddie.

Their mother sat in her wheelchair, a tired but contemplative expression on her face. Old eyes peered out from behind thin-rimmed glasses, contrary to her younger complexion. She held her husband Carlos's hand in her white one while he leaned over his family, smiling, his bushy mustache revealing more white than the year prior.

The second picture showed them all in their bird forms. A red-tailed hawk and a ringed-neck dove sat on either side of a large caracara. A beautiful barn owl nestled on a bed of blankets in the chair while a massive golden eagle perched behind her.

Pictures filled with Bianca's and Kat's smiling faces took up more empty space. The most adorable picture though showed a golden wolf looking back to the caracara sitting on her back. Mixed-parahuman relationships weren't unheard of—hell, Tess's mom and dad were a prime example—but it did come as a bit unusual to have so many in the same pack. They were fortunate Paytah was such a lenient alpha when it came to the matter of the heart.

Now if he could get a move on with everything else.

Tess leaned back in an old leather chair and crossed her arms. "You're not exactly the one I'm asking permission from." Her gaze swept to Kat.

The wolf sat on the couch, holding a mug of tea between her hands. She'd gained weight since arriving at the pack a half-starved beaten shell of a woman. Bianca had helped her find her strength again and heal some of the damage Kat's abusive boyfriend had left behind. Tess knew she still struggled with PTSD nightmares; Tess had created a spelled bracelet Kat could wear at night to help, but it didn't stop all the nightmares. Nor did it wash away the memories of what had been done to her.

Kat brushed golden hair behind her ear and glanced sideways at Tess. "I don't know if I'm the best one for the job. I agree with you that we need to do *something*, but I might blow our cover."

"You're stronger than you think," Tess said. "You helped fight the guy who tried to drug Carmen."

"True," Kat admitted and allowed herself a proud smile. "I wasn't even afraid of him. I wanted to help Carmen."

"See?" Tess said. "You have one of the best noses, *and* you can change into a four-footed wolf form. That means you'll be able to escape and blend in better than, say, Becky could." Werewolves had two forms, a biped one which looked like a typical tv werewolf, and a four-footed one. Granted, the wolf forms were a bit larger than what one would find in the wild, but they could pass off as a husky if they really tried.

Bianca stopped at Kat's side and laid a comforting hand on the wolf's shoulder. "And what if she doesn't escape? What if none of us do? We could all be taken into captivity by Hunters or whoever is tracking us. You don't mess with them, Tess."

Tess sighed under her breath. Bianca had every right to be afraid. The whole reason she'd come to the Chicago PDD in the first place was to escape Hunters chasing her. They'd murdered Bianca's sister, and her parents, too, and had turned their sights on her. Though they'd been driven by the orders of a power-hungry senka, they'd still been Hunters and had used their skills to make Bianca's life a living hell.

But this was different. Bianca wasn't alone. None of them were.

"Bianca, I get it," Tess said. "I'm not trying to hurt any of us. I know what you went through. But we have to do *something*. Ray and Augustine are willing."

"Then why not let both of them be bait and leave Kat out of it?" Bianca asked.

"It's because I look weak," Kat said simply, catching on. "If they see two powerful wolves walking side-by-side, they might be more cautious about attacking. If they think I'm easy to take down, they could make a mistake. Besides, Augustine is a powerhouse. We need to have her as backup." She gripped Bianca's hand and kissed it softly. "Hon, I love you, and I know you're worried, but maybe Tess is right. If I can help my pack, I should do it. If not me, then it'll end up being someone else."

Bianca huffed and squeezed her hand back. "You can't help them if you're dead or in captivity."

Kat didn't say anything in reply. She leaned against Bianca's hip and wrapped an arm around the shorter woman's waist. They were adorable, and Tess felt a little envy at not having someone to fret over her as much as Kat and Bianca did over each other. At the same time, it had to be hard to watch a loved one walk off into the jaws of the enemy.

Tess sat down on the edge of a chair and dropped her arms between her knees. "You know I wouldn't do anything to intentionally put my pack in danger if I didn't think I could get us all out again. I was caught off guard when the squad car got hit. I won't be this time."

Kat glanced up at Bianca. The avian looked away and tightened her hold on her girlfriend's shoulders. Finally, she leaned down and kissed her head. "It's your decision, Kat. I'm sorry, I shouldn't speak for you. If you decide to go, I'll be there at your side, and if you refuse, I'll support you."

"Thanks." Kat kissed her back and nodded. "I'm in. What do I need to do?"

Tess laid out the plan, indicating times, locations, and contingency plans in case anything went wrong. The pair listened, though Bianca squeezed Kat's hand harder the longer Tess spoke. Kat's face remained contemplative, her eyes shut as she took in the information.

"It's bold," Kat said. "But it could work. You're strong enough to keep the spells up?"

Tess nodded and pulled her necklace out from beneath her shirt. Inside, fire Ether burned brightly. "I've been storing magic for a situation like this. I can do it."

The wolf nodded. "Then, I'll do it. I—"

Tess's phone went off suddenly. She picked it up and frowned when she saw her mother's name. *Now what*? She thought. She held up a finger and answered. "Mom? Is everything okay?"

"It's Carmen," her mother said. A jolt of icy dread passed through Bianca's spine as she looked at her friends. But the next words shocked her more. "She's awake."

Chapter 9
The Witness

Tess

Tess offered to drive and brought them all to the hospital. The clock rolled over to 8:45 pm by the time they arrived. In the back of her mind, she ticked down the minutes to nine, wondering if Paytah would have words with them for visiting Carmen so late at night. At least they were together and not going separate. Sometimes, she could follow Paytah's rules.

She fidgeted in the elevator on the way up, practically bursting with excitement. She was awake. Carmen was awake! After days without much change in her tests, Carmen had defied the odds and come to. Tess could have cried in joy to have her little packsister back in her life, and she probably would have if other questions weren't bubbling inside her. She remembered what she'd seen that night, but what about Carmen? Maybe she had the clues they so desperately needed to find her father and Nick.

"This way," Kat said as she guided them off of the elevator, going the direction the receptionist at the front desk had given them. The large hospital had two floors dedicated specifically to parahumans and their doctors. The owner of the hospital knew of the mixed population, and he made certain that humans stayed on human floors and parahumans stayed with parahumans. At least, employee wise.

They rounded the corner, and Tess spotted her mother sitting next to Carmen through the glass window. Carmen rested in her bed, smiling wearily.

Oh thank God. She really is okay. Tess thought. She followed the girls in and froze mid-step.

Paytah sat in a chair near the foot of Carmen's bed, his hand resting on her blanket-covered leg. He glanced up at the three women as they entered and arched an eyebrow.

"I called them," Iris said. "I thought they'd want to see her."

Tess met Paytah's eyes then dropped them quickly. "We thought it was better for the three of us to come together."

Paytah's gaze swept over them before he nodded. "Quince and the doctor will be back soon," he said and then rose, offering them a seat.

Tess didn't bother with the chair. She hurried to Carmen's side and scooped her friend in a warm, gentle hug. "Hey, birthday girl," she whispered, fighting tears of relief.

Carmen hugged her back weakly and offered a lopsided smile, her blonde and purple hair laying in disarray around her shoulders. The superficial wounds on her body were gone, but apparently some internal damage remained. Only one side of Carmen's face seemed to work; the other remained limp.

"Not my birthday anymore from what I heard," Carmen said, her voice hoarse from having been on the ventilator for so long. She lifted a shaky arm and touched Tess's hand. "I'm glad you're okay. Thank you."

"For what?"

"Paytah said if it wasn't for you, I would have roasted in the car." Tears filled her eyes and she sucked in a breath. "I thought I was gonna die."

Bianca and Kat swooped in and touched Carmen on her arm and leg, offering her physical comfort as only a pack could. "We're here for you," Kat said.

Tess gave Carmen another loving hug. "I'm sorry I couldn't get us out faster." She held onto Carmen for a few moments then leaned back, her eyes searching Carmen's. "Do you remember anything?"

"Tess," Paytah said. "She just woke up."

"I know, I know, it's…we only have so much information." She hated to push Carmen like this, but they had to know. She settled on the side of the bed and took Carmen's hand in hers. "What do you remember?"

Carmen scrunched the right side of her face. "Lights. The sound of the crash. Pain. I heard Nick yell and felt him wrap himself around me and then everything went dark." She looked up at the ceiling. "I was awake when we landed. And I saw people walking towards us."

"Yes?" Tess pressed, her hope rising.

Carmen blinked then shook her head. "And…and that's it. There were three people, and—"

"Wait, three?" Tess asked. She could have sworn she'd only heard two voices. This could definitely be a breakthrough!

"I didn't see anything else. They walked towards us, but the lights shining behind them made it hard to see their faces." Carmen deflated a little. "I'm sorry."

Tess's shoulders slumped but she continued rubbing Carmen's hand affectionately, trying to soothe them both. "You can't remember anything? No features? Hair color? What they were wearing?"

"Tess," Paytah warned.

Carmen grimaced and touched her forehead. "I'm trying. It's all mixed up."

"You can do it, Carmen," Tess urged. "Dad and Nick need us. If you can—"

"That's enough!" Paytah barked and marched forward.

Tess almost argued, but she paused when she noticed Carmen's vitals rising. Her heart beat faster, and she started to tremble from the stress. Tess leaned back and caught a glare from Bianca. Guilt washed over her. She squeezed Carmen's hand and set it gently back on the bed. "I'm sorry, Carmen. That wasn't right of me. You need to get some rest. I'm so glad to see you're awake."

"I'm sorry I can't remember anything else," Carmen said in a small voice. "I'll try, Tess."

"No, no, honey, rest," Tess said and hugged her again. "You worry about getting better. That's all that matters." Carmen could have died, and here Tess was grilling her for answers. What was she thinking? Yes, she wanted to save her pack, but not at the cost of hurting her already injured friend.

She released Carmen and slunk near the wall, letting Kat and Bianca replace her.

Stupid, she scolded herself. *You should know better than that!* Her throat tightened with anxiety, her chest growing heavier with guilt. Everyone had their attention back on Carmen, but Tess could feel the frustration radiating off of them.

She should have brought her pills with her.

While she took a few moments to breathe and calm her panic, Quince and the doctor stepped into the room, helping to distract her packmates from their frustration with her. The doctor gave pause at the sight of everyone but said nothing. The one other nice thing about having a parahuman-friendly hospital was the doctors understood if more people needed to be in the room than usual; that was how packs, cloisters, prides, covens, wards, and groves worked.

"Hello, Carmen. I'm Dr. Jenkins. I was in here when you woke up. Do you remember me?"

Carmen squinted at him then nodded. "Vaguely."

The doctor smiled kindly and motioned for Quince to take her vitals again. "We've been running tests while you've been asleep. You had swelling and damage at the base of your skull, which is why you seem to be suffering from facial paralysis." He took a metal tool out of his pocket and lightly touched the left side of her face with it. Carmen didn't even flinch.

Paytah frowned. "Will feeling come back?"

"Only time will tell. I will say this. If she wasn't a werewolf, she wouldn't have survived the crash. You're very lucky." He glanced at the machines as Quince took her blood pressure. "We're going to keep a close eye on your vitals and have someone with you to make sure you stay awake with us. We'll take good care of you."

Carmen relaxed into her pillows and offered a half smile. "Thank you."

Dr. Jenkins nodded and glanced around. "Who is her caretaker?"

"I am," Paytah replied. "When she's released, she'll be staying with me and my mate."

"Good, good. It may be some time before she's discharged. She'll need physical therapy for her legs."

Tess looked up in surprise. "Her legs?"

"We were struggling to get feeling in her legs when she came in." He reached for the blanket and gently flipped it over to reveal Carmen's feet. When he poked the flesh, her toes moved a little, but not as much as Tess expected.

Carmen shook as she watched. "I'll…I'll be able to walk again, right?"

"With time and therapy, I think we can get you back on your feet. Be patient with yourself. Brain injuries are no easy things to mend." He put the blanket back over her then reached gently for her shoulder. "We'll do everything possible to help you."

Carmen fought back tears. "Thank you."

"BP is 95 over 55. Heart rate is 73," Quince said. He entered the numbers into a tablet and smiled at Carmen. "I already drew blood. We're going to try to get some food in you while you're up. You still like cinnamon apple sauce?"

Carmen brightened. "Yeah. Warmed up."

Quince winked. "I can do that. Maybe I can even convince them to give me two servings."

He and the doctor departed, and Carmen sank into her bed. She snuggled closer to Bianca and Kat and grasped the werewolf's hand. "I'm so tired."

"Rest," Paytah told her. "I'll be here when you wake up." He gave Kat, Tess, and Bianca a look. "You three should get home. I'll let you know if anything changes or if she remembers anything. She doesn't need to get excited." The last part he said pointedly at Tess.

She glanced away sheepishly. They took turns giving Carmen a hug. As Tess leaned down, Carmen swallowed a lump and buried her head against Tess's shoulder. "I'm sorry I don't remember."

"It's not your fault. I'm sorry for getting you worked up. We're gonna help you through this. Promise." She kissed Carmen's forehead and then went to her mother's side and gave her a hug, too. With that, Tess, Kat, and Bianca left the room.

Tess stuck her hands in her pockets and took a shaky breath. Carmen was lucky to be alive, but her legs were still damaged. Tess couldn't help but think that if she'd acted faster, done something different, her packsister might still be mobile.

She reached for the button on the elevator when Paytah's voice caught her ear.

"Tess, a word."

Tess winced. She saw the pitying looks from Kat and Bianca as they stepped away from the elevator.

"We'll wait for you over here," Kat said, and she and Bianca took a seat in the waiting area.

Tess headed back towards Paytah, his eyes burrowing into hers as she reached his side. She dropped her gaze. "I'm sorry. I wasn't trying to get her worked up."

"I know. But I also know how you are when you get certain thoughts in your head. Plans."

Tess lifted her eyes enough to see him staring at her. "I get distracted by what's on my mind," she agreed hesitantly.

"Waiting is hard for us all, but I promise you I'm doing everything I can to get help to find your father and Nick. I'm going to be meeting with the other group leaders shortly, and we're going to devise a plan to keep our people safe."

Tess tried not to comment how that would take up even more precious time. Time their packmates didn't have. "And Legion?"

Paytah shook his head. "Still can't get involved except for the one agent."

"Why not?" Tess snapped. "People are missing."

"People go missing every day. They have to pick and choose their battles."

Tess looked at him furiously and raised her arms. "How can you be so calm about this? These are *our* people who are missing. Why can't you—"

"Tess, I'm doing *everything* I can as Alpha and as Violet Marshall." Suddenly, his stern face changed. The years fell upon him in worry lines and age marks. "Please, trust me."

Tess wanted to argue that she'd trusted him this long, and yet, nothing had happened. But she kept her mouth shut. It wouldn't help, and he already looked so tired. Instead, she nodded briefly and glanced up at the clock. "I should get them home and then go home myself. I have work in the morning."

"Get some sleep. And be safe. Call me when you're settled."

"Yes, Paytah," Tess said. She didn't give him a hug or offer him any more than a fleeting smile. She turned her back on him and headed towards Kat and Bianca. They were silent as they rode the elevator down and then went to her car.

As Tess sat in the front seat and gripped the steering wheel, her stomach twisted, and her nerves broke. Paytah had said it plainly enough; he couldn't do anything yet. He was stuck. So someone had to act. "You still with me on the plan?" she asked the women.

This time, neither one hesitated. "Yes."

Chapter 10
Bait

Waiting was not Tess's forte.

The pack had a plan, at least a small fraction did, but it still took time to enact. They had to figure out a place Ray and Kat could meet up that would make sense. Tess, Augustine, and Bianca had to scope out the terrain to find the best vantage points. All of it had to be perfectly plotted out. But each day that passed without word about her father pushed Tess that much closer to the edge.

Her therapist started to wonder why she kept running out of lorazepam so quickly.

Her mother could barely hold back her tears and often hid behind alcohol to ease her worry. Paytah prowled about, fretting over both Brighton and Nick. Tess knew the bond and responsibility Paytah felt to his pack, especially to Nick. She couldn't understand why he didn't do *more*.

At least *some* of her packmembers were willing to put their necks on the line. Practicing and planning took her mind off of her father's plight. Sometimes, though, she swore she felt eyes on them while they worked together. If it was the Hunters, well, at least they knew the group lingered nearby. If it was someone else, she hoped it was friend and not foe. She mentioned it to Augustine at one point, and the she-wolf admitted she'd felt it too.

They started watching their backs more after that.

Tess stood in her apartment, dressing in a comfortable, nonrestrictive outfit. Dark jeans, black shirt over an undershirt, and sneakers, none of the heel bullshit that she saw in so many comics. Who the hell wore heels on a mission? Tess wasn't clumsy, but even she knew she could break an ankle in one of those things. She pulled her hair back in a braid and tucked her necklace into the shirt. The glass jar throbbed with stored Ether magic. Whoever came after them would regret messing with a fire magus.

Tess grabbed her wallet and reached for her phone.

It rang with her fingers hovering over it. Tess pulled back her hand to check the caller.

Paytah.

She hesitated. Why in the world would he be calling her *now* of all times? She checked the clock, the arms pointing almost to nine. She winced. Shit, she'd forgotten her nightly check in.

"Hey, Paytah," she answered and headed for her living room. "Sorry, I was about to call you and let you know I'm home."

"Good, but that's not why I'm calling," his deep voice said on the other end.

A chill raced up Tess's spine. Did he know? Had Ray or someone else ratted them out? "Oh? What's up?" Sudden panic swept through her. "Is it Carmen? Is she okay?"

"Carmen's fine." The line grew quiet for a moment. "I wanted to see how you were. We haven't spoken much since Carmen woke up and we heard her prognosis. You know it's not your fault, right?"

Tess jerked her head away from the phone. How…her mother. Of course. She rolled her eyes. "Mom told you I was beating myself up?"

"She alluded to it."

"I wish I had done more for Carmen. If I'd acted faster, I might have saved her legs."

"You don't know that they can't be saved. The doctors were optimistic. Tess, we could have lost you both in that fire, and you got yourself and her out of there. You should be proud."

Tess snorted. "She's still in the hospital. My dad and Nick are still gone. I don't know what there is to be proud of."

Paytah sighed on the other end. "I know you're cross with me, but your father and Nick's safety is of utmost importance to me."

Tess paused and sat down on the edge of her couch arm. "Paytah, I know. I was upset, and I kept blaming myself for not doing more." She swallowed. "Has there been any change with Carmen? Is therapy starting soon?"

"Yes. Her face is still paralyzed, but they're trying to get her up on her feet. It's going to be a long journey for her. She'll need all of us to support her."

Tess shut her eyes. 21. Her friend was 21. All she'd wanted was to celebrate her birthday, and now she was relearning how to walk. Carmen's fate made Tess even more determined to catch the bastards.

Paytah went on, oblivious to her rage. "Your mother also said you've been distant, and you haven't been sleeping. She's worried about you, and so am I. I want you to know that I'm still talking with Legion and the District. Legion's doing what they can on their end, but they're having trouble finding information, too."

Tess snorted bitterly. "What's the use of having them if they can't even track down Hunters?"

"You have to look at the bigger picture, Tess. It's not just Chicago they have to protect. And we're still losing people."

Tess sat up sharply. "What do you mean? Who else is gone?" she asked in a panic. Everyone had been checking in!

"Not from our pack," Paytah assured her. "I spoke with Joseph this morning. Trish has gone missing."

"*Again*?" Tess spat. "She was supposed to stay under Joseph's watchful eye. You sure she's not helping the Hunters again? I mean, considering her track record."

"She's demonstrated good behavior for the past year and a half. If she decided to sneak out to the bar again, like she did on the night of the accident, she could have been easily snatched up. "

Tess sighed. "All right, so she's gone. Anyone else?"

"At this time, no. The pride is safe. The wards and groves have all their members accounted for. I spoke with Carlos, and his cloister is safe. I think only the wolves and the vampires are being targeted."

"I'm surprised the cats aren't," Tess said. "They're good in a fight. Well, no, take that back. They're better at a verbal fight unless you really piss one of them off."

"Let's hope it stays that way." Paytah fell quiet again. "You trust me, right, Tess?"

That's a weird question, she thought. *And out of the blue.* "You're my alpha. Of course I trust you."

"And you know that I'll do everything in my power to bring your dad and Nick home."

"I wouldn't expect any less."

She heard him grunt. "Then let me remind you not to do anything rash. I know how you are, Tess. You like to take things into your own hands when you don't think someone else can get the job done. A Hunter problem is nothing to mess around with."

"I know, Paytah," Tess said. She glanced at a long mirror in her living room. Her dark, sleep-deprived eyes stared back at her. When had she last gotten a full night of sleep? If she wasn't busy working on the plan, she was up fretting over her father, imagining all the horrible things that were being done to him. Her mother struggled with the same issue, and it killed Tess that she couldn't tell her that they were trying to do something about it. She'd run to Paytah and blow their cover. "You got a hard job, and you're trying to keep us all safe. I get it, and I respect it."

I just might not follow it, she added silently.

"Good. I'll let you know if I hear anything in the morning."

"Thank you. Sleep well, Paytah," Tess said. She sat still on the couch for a few long moments after he hung up and stared at herself.

Second thoughts flooded her mind. It almost felt like he knew what she had planned but wasn't telling her. Was he giving her the chance to back out and save face? If she told the others Paytah was on to them, they'd back out for sure. If she didn't tell them…

Tess looked at one of the records she and her father had gotten together. A signed version of, "Live and Let Die."

She clenched her fist and pushed herself off of the couch. She was done waiting.

***

Tess crouched on the top level of a fire escape with Augustine and Bianca. Bianca perched on the railing in her caracara form, her black feathers catching the moonlight and drinking it in. Her white breast feathers stood out against the darkness, and her red cere did so even more. She preened a wing anxiously and stalked back and forth on the metal bar.

Augustine leaned against the building, her arms crossed over her chest. Like Tess, she'd dressed in comfortable, casual attire that let her both move and shift with ease. She played around on her phone while Tess kept an eye on the alley where Ray and Kat were supposed to meet up.

Tess had tossed a protective ward around the stairwell to keep them out of sight. They chose different fire escapes each time, just in case they were, indeed, being watched. No sense in giving up their position. She glanced over at Bianca who shuffled her wings again for the fifteenth time that hour. "*I know you're restless,*" she said mentally, "*but all we can do is wait.*"

"*Tell me that when you have your lover out there,*" Bianca bit back. The caracara gave her the stink eye and shifted around again.

Tess sighed and turned on her phone. 10:30 p.m., and there was no sign of anyone. No messages from Kat or Ray either. They'd promised to text if they noticed any problems. She leaned back next to Augustine and glanced at the woman's phone.

Colorful figures exploded on a grid. "Candy Crush? Really?" Tess asked.

"It helps me unwind. Lay off," Augustine growled. She pulled her phone away then lowered it and peered into the darkness. "I don't like it. It's too quiet."

Despite the sounds of cars zooming down the road, police chasing after them, and the random shout or laugh from passersby, Tess had to agree. The air buzzed with tension, like the calm before the storm. She checked her phone again, only to grunt when Augustine nudged her with her elbow.

"Down there," she whispered.

Tess followed her gaze and spotted Ray first, carrying a bag of food. Kat appeared next to him a moment later, chatting amiably. They'd decided to have the two meet at Ray's restaurant where he gave her extra food and then walked her home. The apartment wasn't far from the restaurant. She doubted the Hunters would know about the werewolf curfew, so it wouldn't look overly strange.

Ray touched the small of Kat's back as they walked together, keeping protectively close as he always did. They stopped in the alley and continued talking to one another, seemingly oblivious to the world around them.

The minutes ticked by and still no sign of any attackers.

Tess sighed and tucked her phone back into her pocket. "They gotta come at some point, don't they?"

"Unless they've caught onto us," Augustine replied. She watched her mate with sharp, worry-filled eyes. "This is the fourth time we've done this, and still nothing. Maybe we need another plan."

Tess had to concede. At least they'd tried this area. It was better to move on to another if they weren't getting any bites. She grabbed the railing and pulled herself up.

Ray pitched forward with a gasp of surprise and pain, Kat scrambling to grab hold of him as he went down to one knee.

Tess froze, startled, but Augustine lurched towards the railing.

"*Kat?*" Tess called mentally. "*What's going on?*"

Kat kept her attention on Ray, but she responded using the Ether necklace Tess had provided to both her and Ray. "*He said he feels like a bus hit him. Wolfsbane. I'm checking him over. He—a dart! I have a dart! Someone—*" Her voice cut off as she fell forward next and dropped to her knees. Ray struggled to shift beside her while Kat yanked something out of her arm. "*I'm hit, too.*"

"*Keep playing the part,*" Tess said. "*We're here. We're not going to let anything happen—*"

Something clinked behind her then exploded. Smoke wrapped her, Augustine, and Bianca in a thick, suffocating cloud. Tess clapped her hands over her mouth, coughing, and heard the clinks hit two other fire escapes.

They don't really know where we are, she realized in relief. She lifted her hand, pressed two fingers together, and swirled them in a circle. "Silence," she rasped and put a silencing spell on them as well, just in time.

Augustine doubled over coughing and pulled the hem of her shirt over her mouth and nose. "*I can't see them!*" she shouted mentally, causing Tess to wince.

She covered her face with the top of her shirt and waved her hand. Though not a wind magus, she still had enough magic to create a small whirlwind and push the smoke outward. It whooshed past them, leaving an open pocket of clean air. Tess and Augustine gasped for breath, but Tess didn't see Bianca. "*Bianca? Bianca!*"

"*Down here!*" the caracara shouted.

Tess coughed and looked down towards the alley. Somehow, Bianca had gotten clear of most of the smoke and gone down to help protect Ray and Kat. The caracara zoomed around the two werewolves, lashing out at a man trying to get close to their packmates. Kat was down, but Ray was still conscious and standing over her now in his biped form. Deep gray fur covered his entire body, saliva dripping from his fangs. Apparently, he hadn't been hit with enough wolfsbane to stop him from shifting.

The man attacking them snorted and pulled a gun from his holster. Bianca dove in and clawed at his face, but he lifted a leather-gloved arm to protect himself. He swiped out with the other, punching the caracara in the side with brass knuckles and sending her flying to the right. Bianca flapped frantically to keep herself up. Her wingtips grazed the ground, but she caught air and soared upward.

Ray leapt at the man as he recovered, directly into the path of the gun. The Hunter fired, but it didn't sound like a normal gun, and Ray didn't pitch back like he would have if hit by a bullet. He swung twice at the man, but the Hunter dodged both attacks. He fired again, and this time Tess saw the tranquillizer darts protruding from Ray's leg.

"Gotcha!" the man crowed.

Ray took another step forward, wavered, and collapsed next to Kat's body with a grunt. He fisted his paws and struggled to get up, but to no avail.

Augustine snarled, already shifting into wolf form.

"*Augustine, wait!*" Tess cried, reaching for the wolf, but Augustine shoved her hand back and bolted down the fire escape. Tess swore and wrapped a shield around the woman to help protect her from attack, but it got harder the further away Augustine ran. She had no idea how the woman could transform while on the run, but she managed. A gigantic, black wolf in biped form emerged where a woman had stood. She roared and threw herself at the Hunter.

"*Bianca! Get out of here!*" Tess shouted mentally. She ran towards the stairs to help protect Augustine. At the very least, she could make sure Bianca got to safety.

"Gale!" the man shouted.

Shimmering light burst in front of Tess's eyes. She gasped and fell backwards, covering her face, but she felt something hard strike her shield followed by Augustine's howl of protest. Tess shook her head to clear her vision and scrambled forward again.

A glowing net snarling with electricity hovered in midair

around Augustine. Tess's shield had managed to hold, protecting the werewolf from getting tangled up in the net, but it also prevented her from getting closer to the Hunter. Augustine glowered at him through the holes, lifted her arms, and jerked them forward. Tess waved her hands, following her motion. Her magic caught hold of the net and hurled it at the male Hunter.

"Whoa!" he shouted, scrambling out of its way.

Augustine leapt over it and chased him, teeth snapping, claws slicing the air. Bianca came down from the sky to block him from escaping. Tess waved her hand, sending fire racing across the ground to create a protective wall of flames around Kat and Ray so they'd be safe.

And then everything went to hell.

Tess heard another clink before a second smoke bomb exploded next to her. She'd had enough sense to put a new shield up to protect herself from being suffocated by the smell, but it still blinded her from the battle below. She fought to clear her vision.

Suddenly, Augustine roared in agony both mentally and physically. Tess cried out in reply, her head pounding with the wolf's tortured voice. She collapsed to her knees and held her skull. Augustine yowled again and again in between what sounded like electric blows.

By the time Tess managed to gather her senses and clear the air, Augustine was hunched over with severe burns all over her body. A female Hunter stood next to her, wielding poles which sizzled and popped with electricity. Daggers glinted on her waist. Tess searched for Bianca and almost cried out when she saw the caracara lying in a heap on the ground, one wing bent awkwardly. The male Hunter stood over her, panting, scratches lining his face. He grabbed the unconscious bird by her legs and pulled her up.

"*Bianca!*" Tess shouted mentally, but the bird was out.

The female Hunter struck Augustine again in the spine this time. The she-wolf screamed and fell, coils of smoke rising from her fur. Tess called a fireball to her hand at the same time the Huntress pointed a gun at the back of Augustine's head, and this one wasn't a tranquilizer. "Put the fire away, magus, and come down those stairs. Don't make me kill her."

Tess swore, realizing her concealing shield had broken. In between trying to protect Augustine, Ray, Kat, and herself, she'd lost hold of it. Still, she wasn't going to give up. "You touch her again, and I'll burst you both into flames."

"Would have done it already if you could," the man taunted and shook Bianca's limp body. "I could smash this one's head instead. We don't need her."

Tess panted, her eyes flickering with fire magic. Kat and Bianca were unconscious, and both Ray and Augustine were barely holding on. She couldn't risk losing any of them because of her own stupid mistakes.

She waved the fireball out with her hand. "Let them go."

The man laughed. "'Let them go,' she says. I don't think you're in any position to be making demands, darling." He glanced at the fire wall still around Ray and Kat then looked at Bianca and reached for her neck. "Giving you to the count of three to come down and drop the rest of the fire, otherwise we're putting bird on the menu tonight."

Bile rose in Tess's throat. Were they so perverse they'd actually *eat* a werebird? She didn't want to tempt fate. She made her way slowly down the steps, her head buzzing a bit. She assumed it was from breathing in all of the smoke. But as she got closer to them, she felt a headache build up in her temples, a familiar one. The fire wall wavered and sputtered until it vanished completely against her will. She paused on the last step and stared at her hand, but she barely felt the connection with her magic.

"You're feeling it, aren't you?" the woman asked. An odd scent of lilac wafted off of her, the smell far more pleasant than the smoke. "I thought that elderberry smoke bomb might work."

Tess's heart skipped a beat. Elderberry…oh no. No, no, no! She tried to call fire to her hand, but her magic flickered and died.

She heard a click and looked up as the man leveled another gun at her. "Knees. Now."

Tess had no choice. She knelt down close by. She made sure to stay in Augustine's eyesight. The wolf remained bent over, barely moving, her breath labored and weak. Still, when she met Tess's eye, hers were full of fire and rage. She wasn't out yet.

"What do we do about the spares?" he asked his partner.

The woman frowned. "We don't need a magus, and the bird looks half dead. The wolf is strong. She'd do well in a ring, but I think she might be too hard to control." She cocked the gun and sighed. "We need to stop leaving bodies."

Tess sprang to her feet. "No!" she shouted.

Augustine snarled and whirled as the woman pulled the trigger.

Ray shoved himself up at the same time, throwing his body over his mate. The bullet slammed into his back with a sickening squelch. He collapsed against Augustine, dragging her down with him even as she howled in rage and grief.

At the same time, something zoomed past the male Hunter and yanked Bianca out of his hands. He staggered with a shout of surprise and ran after the figure.

The Huntress shook herself out of her dazed shock. She fired her gun at Ray again and then grabbed the tranquilizer, pumping Augustine full of darts.

Tess threw herself at the woman. She made it two steps before something crashed into her spine and sent an electric shock through her entire body. Her eyes rolled back, and she collapsed into darkness.

Chapter 11
Death Knell

Paytah

Paytah poured steaming coffee into a ceramic mug and passed it to vampire duke, Joseph, who waved it off. They'd gathered at a round table with all the leaders of their immediate Purple Door District community. Carlos, a Hispanic cloister father rested across from him, arms crossed, bushy mustache drooping over his frowning lips. On either side of him sat Vic, the Oakfield Ward Priest, and Akeno, the grove's High Witch.

Akeno looked about five years Vic's junior, but Vic was actually much older than he appeared. Ether kept him young, and while Akeno, as a witch, could also access the Ether, it wasn't in the same capacity. Akeno sat with his back straight, his hand resting beside a tablet for note taking set to Chinese characters. His black hair was slicked back, revealing a firm, serious jaw.

Mia, the pride queen, lounged in all her regal glory to Paytah's left. He and Mia rarely saw eye to eye. Mia often accused him of being too "emotional," and "eager for violence" to lead. It wasn't easy, but he and Mia could get along well enough when discussing things outside of pack and pride. But he'd never challenge her to a battle of words and wit; felines were naturals at verbal sparring. She drummed her golden-tipped nails on the table, her natural afro embracing a beautiful but severe ebony face. The only person missing was one of the fae elders who already had other business to attend to.

Joseph sipped from a mug of tea that Rozene poured for him. Mia eyed Rozene as the werewolf offered the feline queen tea as well. "Still needing your women to do the easy things for you, hm?" Mia asked with her usual bite.

"No more than your males do for you," Paytah replied.

Mia snorted and sat up straighter. "Let's get to it then, eh?"

Paytah grunted. Always the type A personality, wasn't she? "I've spoken with Legion again. They've informed me that the amount of people missing is too small scale for them to reassign resources."

"Too small scale?" Joseph scoffed. "When his *bird* vanished," he motioned to Carlos, "they had a group of people go in to help find her!"

Carlos bristled. "That likely had to do with the fact that a Violet Marshall had just been murdered, and a certain vampire had been coerced into joining Hunters to kidnap a magic-filled avian."

"Don't bring Trish into this," Joseph said with a growl.

Vic leaned forward with a scathing glare. "And how is dear ol' Trish? Still *missing* as well? Are you sure the Hunters took her, or is she back to doing their bidding?"

Joseph started to rise at the bait, but Paytah quickly put out his hand. "Vic, Carlos, enough. I brought you here so we could discuss the situation, not to get into a quarrel ourselves. It does nothing for our people."

Vampire, avian, and magus glared at one another before settling back down in their seats. Paytah sighed and rubbed his eyes. He hadn't expected the meeting to go well, but really, they'd only been talking for five minutes, and already, they were getting at each other's throats.

"*Well,*" Mia said in a long tone of suffering. "This is starting off so delightfully well. Maybe we should have poured something stronger." She lifted her tea and sipped from the mug.

Paytah tried not to roll his eyes. "Legion doesn't want to step in, yet. They've heard about parahumans going missing, but compared to some of the other towns, we're not on their radar."

Akeno shifted and slowly folded his hands on the table. "What, then, do they expect us to do? Werewolves and vampires are already being threatened. When will the werecats or werebirds be next? Or the magi and witches?"

"That's the question," Paytah said, "and why we're all here.

I've put my wolves on curfew and ordered them to call me in the evening when they get home so I can keep track of everyone. So far, no one else has gone missing."

Joseph grunted. "That won't stop whoever is after us from attacking them in the middle of the night. Or even during the day. They knew Brighton's route and took his car out mid-drive. They're not stupid; they're watching us. They're going to figure out that your wolves are heading home at the same time. All they have to do is wait for your wolves to check in and then take them out. You won't know until the next morning, or next evening at the latest, and by then, it'll be too late."

Paytah set his jaw. He didn't want to admit it, but Joseph had a point. Had he painted a larger target on his wolves' heads? He glanced at Mia. "They haven't taken any of your werecats. Do you do anything different?"

"My cats work close together and tend to travel in pairs, too. Since the attacks started up, I've asked them to scatter. Change up their routine. Make it so no one can really track them." She stretched out her hand and eyed her nails. "I also asked Vic for a favor and have a few wards around the houses. Keeps humans out at least."

"And if the attackers aren't human?" Joseph asked.

"Well, that'll give us more information, now won't it?" Mia replied with a Cheshire smile. "I do think things through, my dear. Paytah, I'd suggest doing the same with your people, and have them call in at different hours. For all we know, your phone is tapped."

Paytah glanced at Rozene, but he had no reply. She could be right. Any one of their phones could be unsafe. "Mix it up. I'll talk with my pack about it. Joseph, you might consider doing the same for your coven."

"I know how to lead it, thank you," Joseph snipped. "I'll address it with them as I see fit."

"So haughty," Mia drawled. "You're losing people, too. And, I'm sorry, but I have to agree with Carlos about Trish. After what she did last time, is it really so safe to have her out there?"

Joseph clenched his mug in his hands. "She could just as easily be a victim as the rest of the people who were taken. And need I remind you that she did the Hunters' bidding to protect our coven? She wasn't trying to be malicious."

Vic scowled at the vampire, magic burning in his eyes. "She still helped murder Gladus. And you did nothing to punish her."

"I punished her enough!" Joseph shouted. "I don't charge in and tell you how you should lead your magi, so let me mind my own people."

"*Boys*," Mia sighed. She curled her perfectly manicured fingers beneath her chin and glanced between the two men. "Can we not make this a dick measuring contest? Trish being out there is a concern; we can agree to that. But until she's found, we can't assume that she's working against us. Joseph, who else has disappeared?"

"Christina and Marco have both gone missing. We haven't heard word from them for at least two months now. I fear they're already dead."

Akeno shook his head. "We can't think like that. As soon as we give up on anyone, the rest of our people will notice it. We must not do anything to make them believe we don't care or we're not going to do everything in our power to bring them home."

"Two *months*," Joseph repeated. "That's a long time to be away from the coven. At least Paytah's wolves were just taken. They may still be alive."

Rozene reached out and took Paytah's hand. "That's our hope."

He squeezed it back affectionately. "I spoke to the Harvey Pack. So far, Shen Yanlei is the only one to have gone missing. Have any of you spoken to the smaller groups?"

Mia nodded. "Two felines were kidnapped from a pride in Olympia Fields."

"Five avians were taken from the same Homewood Cloister," Carlos said. "All strong adults."

Paytah wrote the notes down. He glanced at his fellow leaders and frowned to himself. No matter the bravado Mia and Joseph showed, they were just as afraid for their people as he was. And to have Legion refuse to come in except for one measly agent hit like a slap in the face. He'd done what he'd been asked as a Violet Marshall. The attacks were beyond what he could handle. Legion was supposed to help with that. What could be so important that it kept them from helping out the Chicago District?

"I'll talk with my ward and see if we can create talismans people can hang around their houses to add in another layer of protection," Vic said, pulling Paytah from his thoughts. "I can't promise it'll stop the threat, but it might slow it at the very least."

Paytah nodded and made to agree when a sudden commotion at his front door halted him. He jerked to his feet, claws slicing through the tips of his fingers. The others bolted upright, and he felt the snarl of magic as Vic called a ball of fire to his palm.

A familiar shout eased Paytah's aggression, but only slightly. "Paytah!" Jackson cried.

Paytah launched himself through the hall with Rozene hot on his heels. Jackson held the door open for Tamara and a hysterical Quince. The nurse, still in his scrubs, scrambled into the house, his face twisted with worry and grief.

Paytah's stomach dropped. The only reason Quince would leave duty was if something had happened to either the pack or his family. He didn't look bloody, but Paytah thought he scented the faint metallic smell on him. "Quince, what happened?" he asked in a growl brought on by stress.

Quince opened and shut his mouth, his eyes filling with tears. Tamara gripped his arm tenderly and touched his back. "Tell him," she whispered, her own voice laced with sadness.

Quince looked at Jackson then back at Paytah and shook his head. "Ray is dead."

The room spun for a moment in a blur of red as his heart lurched then skipped a beat. Dead. Ray was dead. How was it possible? Who could have done it? He tried to ask the questions, but he couldn't get a single word out.

Rozene came to his rescue. "*How*? What happened?"

Jackson held Quince's shoulder gently. "Quince got called into an emergency. Paramedics brought Ray in with gunshot wounds all over his body. They tried to resuscitate him."

"We did everything we could," Quince said. His voice broke. "But he just…he died. Blood spilled everywhere. He wasn't healing. I could smell wolfsbane in his blood. He was drugged with it. If he hadn't been, he might have survived it. But he….he…oh, God." He dropped his head into his hands, trembling.

Rozene faltered. Paytah turned and caught her so she didn't fall. He held her close and stared at his three wolves. Ray was dead. "Does Augustine know? Where did they find him?"

"That's the thing," Jackson said. "We think Augustine was there."

Before Paytah could ask what they meant, Mia stepped up

behind him and grasped his elbow.

"Paytah, I'm sorry for your loss, but I think the rest of us need to hear this."

He bristled at her touch, but he didn't snap at her. She was right, of course, but all he wanted to do was shake the information out of his wolves. Still, he motioned for them to follow him to the dining room where the others waited at rapt attention. Carlos and Vic watched the werewolves anxiously while Akeno and Joseph kept stony expressions on their faces.

Quince sank into a chair and wrapped his hands around the back of his neck. Tamara sat beside him but Jackson stayed behind him, hands on both of Quince's drooped shoulders. The beta sighed. "I went where they found Ray," he said and held up his hand at Paytah's reproachful look. "I went with a few of Brighton's officers. There was a fight there, Paytah. I could smell wolfsbane and elderberry in several places and found a couple of dropped darts. I scented smoke, too, from canisters. It was hard to breathe, but I caught whiffs of Augustine, Tess, Ray, Kat, and I think maybe a bird. I'm guessing Bianca."

"What!" Carlos cried.

"Carlos, please," Rozene said. "Go on, Jackson. What else?"

"There's not much to tell," Jackson said. "There was a struggle and blood. A lot of it. Ray was the only one brought in. His rescuers didn't see any of the others. They did see what looked like burn marks on the ground, though."

Paytah gripped the back of his chair and bowed his head. *Tess.* Of course Tess would be involved. She must have agreed to bring Augustine, Ray, Kat, and Bianca into some crazy plan to help save her father. Why else would they have been out that late and together? And with no sign of any of them, he could only assume they'd all been kidnapped.

Tess hadn't been lucky and spared this time.

Joseph clicked his tongue. "So that now makes five of yours taken, plus an avian. I'm sincerely sorry for Ray."

Paytah's arms trembled with emotion, his fingers itching as his claws begged to tear into something. He obliged and heard wood splinter beneath his grip. Normally Rozene would have scolded him for losing his temper, but she held her tongue this time.

This couldn't be happening again. They'd already lost Gladus, and even if she hadn't been pack, she'd been family. And now Ray?

Augustine would be inconsolable if she was even still alive. *But why leave only one body behind if they killed several*, he reasoned? How could he have let this happen? He was supposed to protect his wolves!

Mia broke through his self-deprecation with a quiet, tentative question. "In light of this new development, do you think this is enough to bring Legion in? A werewolf was killed, and now four others are missing, including Bianca. That has to be enough to gain their attention."

"I don't know," Paytah said. "I don't know!" His calm tone turned into a stormy shout as he grabbed his chair and hurled it across the room. The wooden boards splintered against a stone wall, clattering to the floor in a broken mess. He heaved for breath, fur pushing through the pores on his skin. He needed to run or rip into something. He couldn't be here, not with everyone. Not knowing Ray, one of his own… Not another person he'd failed.

"My love," Rozene said, coming to his side. She grasped his cheeks, despite the sharp fangs forming in his mouth. "*Breathe. Stay with me. I know you're hurting, but we still have a job to do. Your pack needs you.*"

Paytah struggled to catch his breath. His blood pounded in his ears, drowning out the other sounds. He clenched and unclenched his fists, the claws digging into his tender flesh.

Suddenly a body pressed up against him. Tamara leaned into his side. And then there came Jackson, and finally Quince. They closed in around him, creating a cocoon of his pack's scent. He leaned more into Rozene's hands and breathed slowly, steadily, until the anger ebbed.

"Are you in control?" Rozene whispered.

Paytah nodded slowly and cupped her chin. He kissed her deeply then turned to each one of his wolves and touched them. "I'm here," he said.

Tamara took his hand and placed it on her cheek for comfort. Quince dropped his head and settled it against Paytah's chest. Quince had a good heart; Paytah didn't know what he himself would have done if he'd seen Ray die in front of him. He patted the wolf soundly on his back and tilted his head.

Joseph cleared his throat. "As touching as this is, it's not going to help us find your wolves or stop the attackers."

Jackson growled at Joseph for disturbing the peace, but Paytah touched his arm. "Hush, he's right. Jackson, were there any leads? Anything that could help us find where they were taken?"

Jackson shook his head. "I don't know, Paytah. I wasn't allowed to stay long enough. The area is wrapped up with police tape now."

Paytah grunted under his breath and glanced at the other leaders. "I'm going there to see what we can find."

"Are you mad?" Vic asked. "You just lost four more members of your pack! Do you think it's really safe for you to go out there alone?"

"I'm not going alone," Paytah said and looked at Jackson. "Pack stays together. So, we go together."

Mia snorted. "Don't be an idiot. Your wolves have already proven they can't stand up to the Hunters." She stretched her claws. "I think it would be in your best interest if I came along, too. They haven't been hunting cats as often. They may not want to mess with us while I'm there."

Vic threw his hands up in the air. "You're all fools."

"I want to go, too," Carlos said, rising. "I have to know for sure if Bianca was there."

Akeno scooped his tablet into his arm. "I can use my magic to provide some protection."

Paytah nodded in thanks. "Then let's go before we lose anything from the crime scene. Maybe there's something that one of you can find to help you with a locator spell," he said, eyes darting between Vic and Akeno.

Vic glared. He pushed back his chair, the legs scraping against the wooden floor. "I never said I'd go, Paytah. I learned from Gladus's death. If there's been another murder, I'm going home to protect my ward and warn them. If Tess was involved, and she's not there, then it means she's been kidnapped, too. They're prepared for magi."

Paytah frowned at the magus. "Then I'll collect items and bring them to *you* if you won't brave the streets."

"Don't," Vic hissed, raising a hand. "You know what I lost when Gladus died."

"You aren't the only one who lost a friend, Vic."

"I lost my priestess!" Vic shouted and brought his fist down on the table. "The ward lost its priestess, and I had to take her place. It's my responsibility to make sure that none of my own join

Gladus or Ray in the grave."

"I have to agree with Vic," Joseph said, clapping the magus on the shoulder. "We need to protect our own."

Paytah glared at them. "What's the point of the Purple Door District if we're going to run at the first sign of danger to tend to our own groups?"

Joseph laughed. "That's rich coming from you, Paytah. You're an alpha and Violet Marshall, but now that your wolves are being attacked, you're putting yourself and our District at risk to save them. And weren't you the one to run into danger the last time Hunters attacked?"

"Yes, to help save Bianca," Paytah retorted. "Who is part of our District and *not* part of my pack."

Joseph shook his head. "And in doing so, you managed to get one of my vampires killed."

"Joseph!" Carlos snapped. The avian's eyes shifted, becoming more birdlike for a moment. Feathery patterns raced across his face but didn't emerge. "Not now."

Paytah straightened his back and met the vampire's eyes boldly, regardless of the charm that Joseph had the ability to throw on him. Joseph wouldn't dare, not while the other wolves were around. "You've been wanting to say something about this since it happened, haven't you? Out with it, then!"

"You killed Fraula!" Joseph shouted back. "You might have been under a senka's magical hold, but answer me this, Paytah. How were you able to stop yourself from murdering one of your wolves and Carlos, but you couldn't spare one of my people?" He moved towards Paytah despite Jackson's snarl. "My coven wanted war for the blood you spilt, but I calmed them, assured them that you would have stopped yourself if you could have. Maybe killing one person brought you back to your senses. Maybe you don't have a vendetta against vampires."

"Enough!" Mia growled and got in between them. "As much as I love to see you boys trying to one-up each other, we do *not* have time for this. Joseph, Fraula died over a year ago. If you had grievances with Paytah, you should have brought them up before now. Her blood was spilled, and now, one of his is dead. You're even. Get over it and move on." She turned to Paytah. "Can we stop this squabbling and go?"

Paytah wanted nothing more than to tear into Joseph for his

accusations. In truth, Paytah still suffered the pangs of guilt for what he'd done to Fraula. He'd tried. He'd resisted the senka's hold as long as he could, but Fraula had become the unfortunate victim. He still didn't know how he'd managed not to kill Kat or Carlos.

But Mia was right. Now was not the time. "Jackson, did you bring the van?" When he nodded, Paytah looked around. "Everyone who is going, let's ride together. Stay close and make sure we don't get separated."

"Fine by me," Mia said and motioned to Jackson. "Lead the way, hon."

Jackson filed out with the others, leaving Vic, Paytah, and Joseph momentarily behind. Paytah stared at the pair and set his jaw. "I understand what you've both lost," he said. "And I'm sorry that I caused one of the deaths. But letting other wolves, a magus"—he gave Vic a look—"and an avian die because of our disputes isn't going to help anything. Please, come with me."

Joseph looked away. "I have my coven to look after."

"And my ward," Vic replied. He grabbed his jacket and stepped past Paytah. After a moment, he paused and glanced back at the wolf. "I'm sorry about Ray, Paytah. I can't let the same happen to my people. Please understand. We've already lost too much."

Paytah heard the genuineness in his voice. He nodded and let Vic go. Before he could say another word to Joseph, the vampire turned and followed Vic out. Paytah took a steadying breath and prowled after. He reached out, catching the man's arm gently. "Joseph, what happened is between us. Don't take it out on my wolves."

"I'm not the one killing or capturing them, Paytah," Joseph said. "*You're* the Violet Marshall. You're the one who is supposed to be fixing all these problems, not me. My hands are clean in this."

"For how long?" Paytah asked. "If more of your vampires go missing, you'll be involved like the rest of us. You should already be trying to do something!"

Joseph glared and tugged on his arm, freeing himself from the werewolf's hold. He turned to leave at the same time another figure entered the house.

Saul approached them, dressed in one of his typical suits, his dreadlocks pulled back behind his head. Though his suit was pristine, his tired eyes and the worry lines rippling across his forehead betrayed a more haggard appearance.

Paytah dropped his eyes. Joseph and his vampires still blamed him for Fraula's death. They didn't seem to realize Paytah blamed himself too. There were nights when she visited him, her dead eyes capturing his, her bloody mouth open in a soundless scream. She only came to him as a head, never a full person.

Therapy helped only so much.

Saul stopped in front of Joseph. The pair exchanged a look before the duke stiffened and turned on Paytah again. "That's not the first time you've questioned my ability to lead my coven, *Alpha.* Do you doubt my role as Duke? I'm not one of your pups, Paytah. I lead a portion of the District, just as you do, even if I don't wear the mantle of Violet Marshall."

Paytah took a small step back, startled by the anger in Joseph's voice. The vampire's eyes flickered with faint embers, as if his control over his rage was slipping. "I'm not questioning your ability as a leader, Joseph. I'm trying to get us to all work together. Our unity saved Bianca and eliminated two Hunters and a senka."

"And cost us Fraula," Saul said in a quiet voice.

Paytah sighed. "Saul, I have tried to make amends with you. There is nothing I can say or do that can bring her back, but—"

"No, there's not," Saul agreed. He touched Joseph's arm and squeezed it. "We should go. I still haven't found Trish, and no one has seen her. I'm concerned for her safety."

Joseph grasped the man's shoulder and nodded. "Wait for me in the car. I'll be there shortly." As Saul obeyed, Joseph straightened out his shirt and looked at Paytah. "Gladus was a great many things, and everyone felt like they could trust her. But she didn't have the blood of our people on her hands. You haven't gained my trust or my coven's trust, *Marshall.* You can't lord over everyone like you do your wolves. The District won't stand for it." He squared his shoulders. "*I* won't stand for it."

With that, the vampire swept through the hall, leaving Paytah standing alone with a dangerous silence surrounding him.

****

The crime scene appeared as Jackson had described it; littered with police tape. Investigators had already come and gone, obscuring the scents more, but Paytah could pick out his packmates' individual smells. He walked slowly through the alleyway and glanced around at the different stairwells where Jackson had said someone had seen smoke. He could imagine Tess hiding up there with someone, waiting to draw out the Hunters. Foolish girl…he'd wring her neck after he smothered her with a hug.

He stepped over two colored tags on the ground and blood that had yet to be cleaned up. He crouched and took a deep breath.

Ray.

This was where Ray had died.

He touched the asphalt with two fingers and bowed his head. Why hadn't Paytah been there? Why hadn't Ray *listened* to him and not gotten involved in a stupid rescue attempt that ended up in his death? He didn't want to face Augustine when she found out. This would break her. And Colleen, how would his restaurant partner react?

"Bianca was here," Carlos said quietly, breaking the silence. He stood up from beside a building and held out a feather. "Caracara. She was in her feathers."

Rozene held a shawl tightly around her shoulders as she looked over the feather. "If Bianca was here, so was Kat." She rubbed a hand along her face and sighed. "It looks like most of whatever was left behind was cleaned up. I don't know if this is going to help us."

Akeno inspected the feather as well. "It may. If you'll allow me to have that. And if one of you can sniff out Augustine's or Kat's blood, I might be able to create a spell to help us find them. But it will take some time."

"Any help would be appreciated," Paytah said. He went around to the areas he smelled Kat and Augustine the most.

Quince waved his hands. "Wait, wait, don't wipe it up without being sanitary. We don't need to spread germs." He reached into his scrubs and pulled out a couple of swabs and baggies. "I thought these might help." He went to the spots Paytah indicated and swept blood up with the cotton swabs and put them in the baggies. He passed them along to Akeno in yet another clean baggie. "How long do you think it'll take?"

"A few days. If I had Vic's help, less. Locator spells aren't easy for witches. But that doesn't mean we can't do them." Akeno tucked the items in his pants pocket and looked around. "I sense some Ether, but that could have been from Tess. There's only one Ether signature I can make out."

Paytah glanced at the witch. "If it feels like fire, it was definitely her."

Akeno nodded. "I feel the heat of it. Fire for certain."

Paytah almost wished Akeno was wrong. He'd rather it have been some other magus and not his Tess. But he knew deep down it was. *What were you thinking? I told you to wait. I told you not to run into danger!* But when did Tess ever listen to him? As much as she adored the pack, she was still a fire magus at heart.

Rozene laced her fingers between his. She hadn't cried yet, but the tears would come later that night, he was sure of it. "I want to see Ray," she whispered.

Paytah did, too. He simply hadn't been able to voice it. He looked over at Quince who stood awkwardly to the side, hands shoved in his pockets. The sight of Ray must have been agonizing; blood didn't normally twist Quince's stomach. "Quince. Can Rozene and I see him?"

Quince blinked, taking a moment to understand. His face paled. "I'm not…I don't know if you want to see him like this."

"He's family," Rozene said.

Quince glanced at Jackson who gave a nod. Not that they needed Jackson's permission, but his beta also knew what Paytah could handle. Quince pressed his lips together. "Let's drop the others off. Then I'll take you. But only you and Rozene. Getting myself down there is hard enough. The fewer people who go, the better. Since the death happened so late at night, they're holding him at the hospital until tomorrow to transport him to the Cook County Medical Examiner. I'll do my best to get you in."

"Thank you." He patted Rozene's hand then went over to Carlos. The avian stood at the spot where Bianca had been. "We'll find her, Carlos."

"I promised to keep her safe," he said softly. "I promised the Hunters would never get ahold of her again."

"I know. Now you just have to keep that promise and go save her. We won't leave her in their clutches."

Carlos looked up and gave a shaky nod. "Thank you, Paytah."

When they had finished searching the area, they clambered into Jackson's van and headed back to the house where everyone's cars awaited them.

Paytah bid his goodbyes to the other leaders, promising that he would be in touch and they would figure out what to do next. But his words were lackluster. The more he thought about Ray's final moments, the more he couldn't focus. He needed to see his packmate. He needed to know it was true, because at that moment, he still couldn't believe that Ray was gone.

They headed to the hospital in Paytah's car.

"I don't have clearance to go in the morgue," Quince explained on the way there. "But I know a fae in Environmental who owes me a favor. She'll get us there."

"You're sure?" Paytah asked.

"Mostly," came the hesitant reply. "It's still against protocol, but I think we can manage it."

When they arrived, Quince took them through the hospital and into an empty room. No one stopped them; why would they if Paytah and Rozene were with a nurse? Quince touched the Vocera on his chest. "Page Matilda Lawrence."

"Paging Matilda Lawrence," a mechanical woman's voice replied. A moment later, another feminine voice answered.

"This is Matilda."

"Matty, it's Quince. Are you free?"

"That depends on what you need."

"A favor."

She heaved a long sigh. "Where are you?"

Quince gave her the directions, and they waited.

Paytah paced the room, counting the minutes that passed while Rozene tried to coax him to sit down. But the thought of Ray lying dead somewhere in the hospital kept him moving and on edge. He shouldn't be alone.

The door opened and a tall, thin Black woman with red-rimmed glasses stepped in. Nothing about her looked unordinary, but Paytah sensed a faint magical vibe around her. She glanced briefly at him and Rozene then back to Quince. "Well?"

"I need you to get us into the morgue undetected."

Matilda grunted and turned on her foot. "Not part of the favors, Quince."

"Wait!" he called and slid in front of her, blocking her from leaving. "Matty, please. One of our wolves…" He bowed his head and glanced sideways at her. "My packbrother died today. These are my alphas, and they want to see him for themselves."

Matilda glanced at Paytah again, and the hardness in her brown eyes softened. "I'm sorry," she told them. She nudged Quince.

"This makes us even, Quince," she remarked and rolled her shoulders. Paytah thought he caught a purple glint of magic in her eyes as she pulled out her badge. "Stay close to me. I'm going to wrap my magic around you so no one sees us go in or out of the morgue. We get caught by security, you're on your own."

"Understood," Paytah said. He took Rozene's hand and moved close to Matilda and Quince. The fae didn't wave her hand or speak a spell. One moment everything seemed normal, and the next, Paytah noticed an odd purple shield around them.

"Not a word," Matilda said. "And Quince, get that badge in your pocket before you set a scanner off."

"Oh, right," Quince whispered and shoved his badge out of sight.

Matilda opened the door and guided them out of the room. She walked with purpose, her head up, her white sneakers sweeping across the floor. Paytah wrapped his arm around Rozene to keep her close and followed the fae into an elevator. They went down a few floors before traveling through a wide hallway. She swiped her badge at a door and continued through. It didn't look different from any other hallway, but Paytah swore he caught whiff of something that reminded him of death. He doubted any human would have noticed it.

Matilda stopped in front of another door and pressed her badge over it. Before it opened, Quince glanced at Rozene and Paytah and whispered, "I should warn you…it wasn't an easy death. Ray… doesn't look like himself."

"Let us see him," Paytah said.

Quince nodded, and the door swung open.

It was like entering another world. Silver doors lined one wall, an icy breeze wafting off of the surface and making the room frigid. The smell of death hung heavily in the air, along with decaying flesh. Every fiber of Paytah's being told him to turn around and leave, but he pushed himself onward, clutching Rozene's hand for support. .

Matilda shut the door behind them and turned her back to them to give them privacy while Quince brought them over to the silver wall. He searched the clipboards hanging over the doors. Paytah glanced at one near him. Female. 20. Slit throat. Another read, Female. 50. Gunshot wound, stomach. He shivered, reminded for a moment of Gladus.

"Here," Quince said and set a clipboard quietly onto a metal tray.

Paytah held Rozene as Quince took a shaky breath and opened one of the doors. He pulled a body draped in a white shroud out. Paytah knew it was Ray before he even saw the wolf; his smell betrayed him.

Quince hesitated then slowly pulled back the cloth.

Rozene broke. She fell to her knees beside Ray's body and sobbed against the cold metal pan.

Ray had not died in peace. His face was contorted in pain and seemed to have frozen that way upon death. Bullets had ripped through the side of his head and punctured several spots on his body. The silver residue was still strong; bullets meant for a werewolf.

Paytah clenched his teeth and went to Rozene's side. He pulled her to her feet and held her to him as she sobbed into his chest.

"I told you it was bad," Quince whispered. He turned away and tried to hide himself, but Paytah caught his arm. He pulled the younger man close to Rozene and held them both lovingly and protectively.

And inside, Paytah died a little. He should have been there. He should have tried harder to protect his pack, but he'd failed. And now, five were missing with a sixth slowly hardening on a table in front of him. He forced himself to look down at Ray's face and swallowed a lump in his throat.

You'll be avenged, he swore silently. *You will be avenged, my brother.*

Chapter 12
Match

Nick

Nick flew backwards as his opponent landed a blow to his chest. He hit the ground and rolled until he ended up on his stomach in the sand. His body ached and screamed with protest as he struggled to get back to his feet. His human form bore ugly, thick purple bruises and claw marks across his skin. He glared at the vampire he faced off against and crouched, hands curling into fists.

The vampire was older and not one he recognized from Joseph's coven. He stood about a head taller than Nick, and despite his frail appearance, he delivered a vicious punch. And he was fast, which Nick really began to detest. Nick was muscular and a force to be reckoned with, but extra bulk slowed him down and made it a hell of a lot easier for his enemy to get in quick jabs. He'd be even more screwed against an avian.

He panted and wiped blood off of a split lip. The vampire circled around him, dressed only in pants. His shirt had been ripped off him before he entered the ring, exposing years of abuse on his white flesh. Most of the scars looked like claw marks from werewolves or cats. Nick had to wonder if the man was forced to fight against his own kind, too.

He'd lost track of the number of times he'd been in the pit. He found it easy to immerse himself in the fight, because if he didn't, he'd end up on the losing side. So far, he'd fought against werewolves and vampires, but that was it. He didn't blame his opponents for being forced into the ring, but he also knew he couldn't take it easy on them. Gale and Hendrickson had already showed him more than once what would happen if he tried to throw a fight. His neck burned with ghostly memories of punishment.

But Gale and Hendrickson weren't there at the moment. They'd been gone for some time now, but someone had left orders to keep Nick and Brighton both limber. They were still training Yanlei to "fight better." They were idiots. Yanlei could wipe the floor with them if she wanted. She kept them in the dark, biding her time when she could actually use her skills to—

Whack!

Nick fell again, chest smarting. He swore and leapt forward, raking thin air with his claws as the vampire dodged away twice before roundhouse kicking Nick in the face. The blow dropped him to his knees. He bowed his head quickly, avoiding another kick that had been aimed for the back of his skull. He turned and grabbed the vampire's leg out of midair and pulled as hard as he could.

The vampire yelped and fell to the ground. Nick threw himself on top of him and grappled with him, getting the man's arms pinned behind his back before he pressed wolfish teeth dripping with venom against the back of the vampire's neck.

"Yield," he hissed.

"You wouldn't really bite me," the vampire said, but Nick heard the fear in his voice. Nick pressed his teeth against the vampire's flesh until the man cried, "I yield!"

Nick pulled back with a relieved grunt and listened to the roar of the crowd. They'd all started bidding on him now, and he had yet to disappoint them. It helped to know that if he lost, he might be taken away from his friends. So he fought to his full ability, no matter who he hurt.

It was getting easier not to feel anything at all. Thinking too much created mistakes, and he couldn't risk losing. Brighton and Yanlei needed him.

He spit into the dirt then held out his hand to help the vampire up. "Good fight."

The vampire smacked his hand away with a growl. "Savage. Keep those fangs to yourself." He rose without Nick's help and stormed to the other side of the ring.

Nick sighed. Maybe using the venom and fangs had gone a bit

too far, but it had ended the fight. A bite from a werewolf could kill a vampire, just as a vampire's bite could kill a werewolf. It, at the very least, made them ill as their body warred between which creature to turn into.

Nick went to his side of the ring and grabbed a towel, mopping up sweat and blood. The Hunter who had taken charge, Abel, Nick thought, nodded. "Good. You're not done yet, though."

Nick paused. "Gale and Hendrickson only have me fight once."

"Yep, but they just texted and said they want you to battle one of their new catches to see if the wolf is worth keeping. All they said is not to kill her, unless they ask you to."

Nick snorted. Like he'd listen to them if they told him to kill someone. He tossed the towel back at Abel and turned around, wondering what poor sap would get thrown in with him next.

The ring fell quiet for a bit save for the Hunters chattering with each other. Nick leaned against the cage wall to rest, grateful it wasn't silver, and inspected his body. Scars lined his chest from days of fighting. His wounds healed at a relatively good speed despite the wolfsbane in his system. Either he'd adjusted to the dosage, or they had diluted it so he could put up a bigger fight.

The noise grew suddenly, and Nick glanced up as Gale came in first. Hendrickson followed her, dragging someone behind him, though he couldn't see who with the bag shoved over her head. What a way to get introduced to being in captivity. At least he'd woken up in a cage, not in the middle of a fight.

Gale opened the cage, and Hendrickson undid the cuffs. He grabbed the bag and shoved the woman inside before slamming the door behind her. "Not too rough, now," Gale called. "Just show us what she can do!"

Nick glared at her then looked down at the poor soul huddled in the dirt. Golden hair poured over her face, blocking it from view. He started towards her, figuring he could be kind and knock her out quick, but then she swung her hair back.

A familiar scent washed over him as warm but frightened eyes met his. He staggered with a gasp of surprise.

"Kaitlyn?" he whispered.

Kat knelt in front of him, staring around the room with wide eyes. She held her freed wrist to her chest and huddled, trembling as people shouted and urged them to fight.

"Kat?" he said again.

Her eyes snapped to him, and she blinked a few times, suddenly recognizing him. "Nick!" she cried in relief. She jumped to her feet and ran to him.

Nick didn't hesitate. He swept her into his arms and held her tightly to his chest. "Jesus, Kat, what are you doing here? Are you all right?"

"We were trying to find you and Brighton, but we got ambushed," Kat said into his ear. She buried her head into his neck and clung to him, her entire body shaking. "They drugged us. I was unconscious until only about a half hour ago. I woke up with a bag on my head." She shuddered and hugged him tighter. "Thank God you're alive."

"What is this?" Gale shouted. "Come on! Fight!"

Nick ignored her and lifted Kat's chin. "Did they hurt you?" He didn't see any bruises on her, but it didn't mean there weren't any under her clothing.

She shook her head. "I don't think so. Nick, they were too strong. Augustine, Tess, Ray, Bianca, and I, we all tried to save you, but—"

Blinding pain shot through Nick's neck and spine. He cried out and fell away from her, even as she shouted his name. He hit the dirt and writhed, struggling to fight through the agony. They'd been working on Yanlei to get her used to the shocks, but he still couldn't bear them.

"Nick!" Kat shrieked and shook him, which only added to the pain. She looked around. "Stop it! Stop hurting him! He—ahh!" Kat collapsed next to him, thrashing as shocks ran through her collar next.

"Noooo," Nick moaned low and reached for her hand. She convulsed, her body trembling. He endured as much as he could and roared, "I'll fight! Stop!"

Mercifully, the shocks stopped. Nick gasped for breath and stared at Kat as she shook and sobbed beside him. Her torment had ceased as well, but he knew the aftereffects. She wasn't going to be able to get up very quickly. Which meant they'd probably be shocked again until they were on their feet.

He crawled on his knees to Kat's side and grasped her chin. "You have to get up," he said in a strained whisper. "If we don't fight, they'll keep hurting us."

"Fight?" Kat rasped. "I-I can't. I can't fight you, Nick."

He bowed his head. Why did it have to be Kat? It wasn't that she couldn't fight. She was damn good at it when she tried. But she'd come from an abusive pack, and he knew fighting was the last thing on her mind unless absolutely necessary. He'd have to take some hits on purpose so they didn't find her useless. "Yes, you can. Fight me like I'm one of the guys at the bar. Like I'm the one who tried to drug Carmen."

God, Carmen. Was she even still alive? Would Kat know?

He tugged on her arm then pushed himself to his feet. She sat up slowly and looked around the arena, taking it all in. He saw her eyes widen in alarm as it dawned on her what the cage and the bleachers filled with Hunters all meant.

"Hurry it up!" Hendrickson shouted.

"Kat," Nick said more firmly. "Do what Paytah taught you. I can take it. Thank about our backyard spars. It's just us. Focus on me and kicking my ass."

Kat met his eyes, and much to his relief, he saw her nod in understanding. She struggled to get up, still wobbly on her feet from the shocks and the wolfsbane. She walked in a circle to clear her head and then faced off against him. They'd sparred before to help them both get stronger. They could do it again now.

Nick attacked first, sweeping out his arm and aiming for her chest. She blocked it with her forearm and ducked beneath it, landing a quick, sharp blow to his torso. Nick grunted and backed off before blocking her strikes against him. It wasn't the savage fight the Hunters were used to, but he and Kat were still obeying orders.

They danced together in the sand, delivering sharp jabs, kicks, all part of the routine Paytah had taught them. He kept his eyes on hers, pulling her in, trying to distract her from the people watching them. Each time she made to look away, he shifted and got into her line of sight. "Stay with me," he whispered to her then swung at her chest. She blocked it again and nailed him in the gut, which genuinely surprised him.

He stumbled back with a huff and caught her eyes again. She'd gotten better! He couldn't deny being a little impressed.

Unfortunately, the rest of the Hunters didn't sound amused. They grumbled and complained about how slow and forced the fight seemed to be. Gale and Hendrickson kept shooting looks at him, but when he continued to ignore them, Gale sighed loudly.

She looked out into the crowd. "Slater, you want to bring one of yours in just for the fun of it? No keeps?"

Slater rose to his feet. "I have been wanting to break one in. Give me a moment to retrieve him."

Nick hesitated and looked back at Gale. Kat paused at his side. "What's happening?" he asked. "Who is he bringing in?"

"Someone to motivate you," Gale said. "You two are going too soft on one another. Let's see how you do now."

Nick heard the snarl before he saw their opponent. It was enough to make the hairs on the back of his neck rise.

Slater returned, holding a chain connected to the collar of a great, hulking beast. A wolf with fur, which must have at one time been white, towered over him, fangs dripping saliva. A half-mad look gleamed in the werewolf's one good eye, the other a milky white. A deep scar traced a jagged line over his bad eye. He peered at them through his good one and growled darkly, his muscles rippling beneath his powerful frame.

Nick backed up and held out his hand. "Kat, shift. Whichever form is stronger, shift into that one."

"They aren't seriously going to make us fight him, are they?" she asked in a terrified whisper.

Nick could only nod. He started to shift and glanced sideways at his friend. "If you don't fight, you'll feel all those shocks again, and so will the rest of us." He heard her whine as his body grew in height and size. Dark gray fur raced over his skin, swallowing up his clothing. He arched his back and growled in pain as his bones shifted into the right direction. The dose of wolfsbane made his transformation slower and more painful, but not impossible. He shook himself and crouched low, front paws down in the dirt, hackles raised.

Kat shifted beside him, golden fur flowing over her body. She could take on two different forms, but he wasn't entirely sure which one was stronger. Her four-footed wolf had more speed, but he felt her biped form had more strength.

Kat went with speed. She landed on her four paws and crouched low, ears laid back and her lips quivering over her snarling teeth. But the snarl would hardly intimidate anyone. Her tail tucked between her hind legs betrayed her absolute terror.

Slater opened the gate and pushed the wolf inside. He unhooked the chain and shut the door. "Don't kill," he told the wolf. "Challenge, yes. Kill, no." And then he raised a silver device and pressed it. The wolf howled in pain as streaks of electricity ran through his body.

Nick swore and moved in front of Kat protectively seconds before the other wolf barreled towards them. *"Stay behind me!"* he ordered her.

He pushed himself to his hind legs and lashed out at the white wolf's face. He struck, but the beast kept coming and slammed into him like a bus. The wolf's strength and size threw Nick backwards violently into the caged wall. He smacked into it and fell to the ground, gasping. Kat had thankfully moved out of the way in time and missed his body crashing into hers.

He struggled to get up and looked at his friend as she bolted away from the white wolf, leading the male on a mouse and cat chase. Any time the beast turned back towards Nick, she snapped at his leg or tail and dodged away before he could strike her. Smart. She was so smart, but Nick dreaded that one blow would take her down for good.

"Get up!" Gale snapped at him and raised the controller threateningly.

Nick didn't need a second urging. He pushed himself up and ran after the wolf. The white monster managed to corner Kat, but before he could strike, Nick leapt at his back and wrapped his arms around the wolf's throat. He jerked as hard as he could and snapped at his ears.

His opponent yowled in anger more than pain. He reached back sharply and caught Nick across the cheek with vicious claws. Nick bit again until another set of claws scraped against his side. He fell off with a cry of pain and scrambled backwards, but the white wolf came after him and rammed him again. This time Nick didn't try to fight it. He went limp and let himself get tossed like a ragdoll, but the blow was less severe.

He rose as Kat leapt onto the white wolf's back and caught the nape of his neck in her teeth. Their opponent reached back for her, but she jumped away before he could catch her. He snarled furiously and turned his full attention on Kat.

Nick dashed forward and scraped the wolf's legs. The male staggered with a growl, but he kicked back, barely missing Nick, and kept on after Kat. Nick scratched, bit, punched and kicked, but still the wolf shoved him off like a pesky mosquito and kept his sights on Kat.

"*Kat*!" Nick shouted. "*Stop antagonizing him and get behind me! He wants* you."

"*I can't get around him! He's too fast!*" She ducked a blow and tried to go left, but the wolf blocked her with another sweep of his paw.

Nick ground his teeth and took a breath. "*When I move, go right.*"

"*O-okay.*"

He waited after the male swung again then threw himself into the white wolf's side to block him from getting to Kat.

Somehow, the male guessed his attack. He turned at the same time Nick moved and thrust his fist into Nick's gut. The air whooshed out of his lungs. He dropped to the ground, gasping like a fish out of water.

The wolf leapt over him and scooped Kat up with his huge paws. She howled, bit, and scratched, but it was no good. Nick could only watch in horror as the big wolf hurled Kat into the side of the cage and held her up by her throat. Kat kicked and shook her head frantically, trying to get in a single breath. But the wolf's hold tightened and kept her pinned.

"*Stop it*!" Nick shouted at the other wolf. "*Stop it! You'll kill her*!"

The wolf flinched as if Nick's voice in his head hurt him. He gave his entire body a shake and tightened his hold on Kat until Nick thought her neck would snap. She stared back at him with frightened eyes, her tongue lolling out of the side of her mouth.

Nick couldn't let it happen. Despite the pain, despite his near inability to breathe, he pushed himself to all fours and ran. He didn't care what damage he did; he had to get Kat free. He hit the back of the white wolf's legs, causing him to lose his footing. He fell to the ground, letting Kat drop in his surprise. Nick rounded on him and jumped on his chest. He scraped his claws across the white wolf's face over and over again. He even tore them down the other wolf's chest until his flesh wept crimson.

For a moment, the world fell away, and only he and his opponent existed. No Hunters. No Kat. No chains, or collars, or cage. Just this male who had tried to hurt his friend. His vision blurred with rage as he let his anger pour into his strikes.

And then there was nothing but pain.

Nick fell backwards to the ground, grasping at his collar, but still the electricity didn't ease. Suddenly he realized his vision hadn't been blurred by rage, but by tears. He fought to stay conscious, but the shocks continued until merciful darkness took him.

***

"Why won't he wake up?" a soft voice asked, rousing him.

Nick felt the cool, padded floor beneath his body, and he almost sobbed in relief. A pad meant he was no longer in the pit. Something soft and warm braced his head, a hand running through his hair. He opened his eyes, expecting to see Kat.

Yanlei smiled sadly down at him. "You survived," she said.

Kat sighed in relief from across the room. "Oh, God, Nick. Nick, are you all right?"

Nick blinked and took a few slow breaths. The air wheezed out of his bruised lungs and made his ribs vibrate with pain, likely left over from being thrown into the wall. He lifted his hand to his face and paused, noticing the bandages wrapped around his knuckles. The pain hit him next like a sledgehammer, and he groaned. "What happened?"

"You beat the other wolf," Kat said in a raspy voice. Nick looked over and saw a thick bruise around her throat where the wolf had held her; her collar likely covered the rest of it. She was lucky he hadn't crushed her jugular. "And I mean, literally beat him. They had to shock you off of him because you weren't listening."

"I didn't even hear them yell," Nick admitted. He tried to sit up, hissed in pain, and fell against Yanlei again. "Ow."

"Ow is right," Yanlei remarked. She touched his chest lightly. "Fractured ribs, and likely one poking into your lung. You need to rest. No more fighting for you for now."

He went to argue that the Hunters wouldn't care about his condition, but paused when he noticed there was another cage in the room. Brighton was gone, again, but someone sat in the new cage, back to them. "Augustine?"

His packmate glanced over at him. "Hey, kid…glad to see you're mostly in one piece."

He stared at her long and hard. Her usual fire had been reduced to a flickering flame. She wore a collar like the rest of them, and he could see the wounds on her body. But no, something else seemed different.

Instinctively, he reached and grasped Yanlei's hand for support. "What happened?" He remembered Kat telling him a few things while they were fighting, but his mind buzzed with pain, fogging his memories.

Kat wrapped her arms tightly around her legs. "Tess devised a plan to help get you all back. We were going to capture one of the Hunters and make him or her tell us where you all were. But…they knew. They came in force and took us down. It was me, Tess, Augustine, Ray, and Bianca."

Nick frowned. "Are Ray, Tess, and Bianca here?"

Augustine shook her head. "I don't know what happened to Tess and Bianca. Ray…Ray's dead."

Nick stared at her like she had grown another head. "What?"

"They shot him. They were trying to shoot me because I didn't stop fighting, but he jumped in the way." Augustine looked down at her hands. "He died because of me. It was my fault."

"Augustine…" Kat whispered. "You were trying to protect us. You couldn't have known."

"I let my mate die!" Augustine snarled, her eyes taking on a crazed golden hue. Her teeth started to elongate into vicious fangs. But just as quickly, the transformation faded, and she dropped her gaze.

Nick wanted to reach out to her, but he could do nothing. He could barely sit up on his own. Still, that didn't stop his heart from aching for Augustine. He shut his eyes to hide his own grief. Ray, why Ray? He was the puppy dog of the pack who could get along with anyone. How could someone snuff out his light?

His eyes burned with unshed tears as he fought to control his emotions. He had to be strong for Augustine and Kat. Listening to Kat weep for their lost brother didn't help. Yanlei squeezed his hand, as if sensing his struggle. He looked up at her and brought it to his chest. "Augustine, I'm so, so sorry. I know it doesn't fix anything."

"I told Tess it was a stupid idea," Augustine said.

Of course it had been Tess's idea. The girl couldn't sit still and let things be. She always had to act. Paytah was going to murder her, once they found her.

"I shouldn't have gone along with it. I should have told Paytah."

Nick shook his head. "It's too late for that now. We need to focus on healing and getting out of here before any more of our pack is brought in."

Augustine opened her mouth as if to give him a piece of her mind, but she looked away instead. Nick didn't mean to sound heartless, but they would have time to mourn later, once they were away from this God-awful place.

Everyone sat in silence for a time as if too afraid to speak and disturb the peace. Yanlei was the one to break it.

"Augustine, is it?" she asked. When Augustine glanced at her and nodded, Yanlei offered a tender smile. "My name is Shen Yanlei. I'm sorry for your loss. Truly, I am. If we can escape, we can avenge your mate and ensure no one else falls victim to their murderous ways."

Augustine cocked her head. "Yanlei. You're part of the Harvey Pack, aren't you?"

Yanlei looked surprised but nodded. "Yes, they took me around the same time as Nick."

"Our alpha knows about you. The other packs are keeping in touch to warn us if any of their people have gone missing."

Yanlei relaxed a little against Nick. "Thank you for telling me. Again, I'm sorry for your loss."

"You and Nick are right," Augustine said. She sat up taller, tears welling in her eyes, but the dam didn't break. "We need to get out of here, and I'm going to kill that witch who took my Ray. What do we know so far?"

Nick and Yanlei took turns filling Kat and Augustine in on the routine. "We're forced into one to two fights every day, either against another wolf, or sometimes a vampire," Nick started. "Vampires are few and far between. It's usually just wolves. I haven't recognized any of the vamps who have been forced to fight us. It's a 'winner gets all' type of scenario unless otherwise specified, like what happened with the white wolf," Nick added, looking at Kat. "If that had been a regular battle, and we'd lost, we would be under Slater's rule now."

"Slater?" Kat asked.

"He's one of the other Hunters," Yanlei continued. "He's the one who kidnapped me. He's brutal. Calm on the outside, but he's not afraid to shock you until you're convulsing on the floor in a pile of your own feces." She gave Nick the side eye. "Yes, I've had experience with it. He, Gale, and Hendrickson are the main trio that works around the Chicago area from what I've heard, but they're enlisting more Hunters."

"Are we still in Chicago?" Augustine asked.

Yanlei shook her head. "I don't know. None of us have seen outside, and we were unconscious when we were brought in. I've heard people talking in difference languages. Chinese, Japanese, French, German. Wherever we are, it's a central location for a lot of Hunters. I fought against a French werewolf the other day. Our Hunters agreed to a spar, neither of us would be taken, but the Hunters could still make bets on us. He'd been collared for five years."

Kat's head shot up, her eyes growing wide. "Five *years*?"

"Yes. Another wolf, she said she came from Florida, has been stuck in captivity for closer to nine. This is the fifth ring she's been brought to. Some of the Hunters focus on longevity and put their attention towards building up their wolf for the battle. Both of those wolves beat me; there was nothing I could do to stand up to them. They were too strong and experienced. I know how to fight," she added. "But they've learned how to play dirty to come out on top."

Augustine gestured to Yanlei. "Is that where the bruises on your face came from?"

Yanlei nodded.

Nick rubbed her back soothingly and leaned against her at the same time for support. "I fought against someone from Iowa. She could barely stand on her paws. She said that her Hunter prefers to torment his wolves, and it's likely they won't last more than six months before the body is dumped. He throws his wolves in death matches."

Kat and Augustine exchanged disconcerted looks before the latter spoke. "Do I really want to know?"

"It's like it sounds," Yanlei said. "The winner walks away from the field. The loser doesn't."

"I saw one when I was brought here," Nick explained. "Two vampires battled one another. One lost his head. The crowd went nuts over it." He shuddered. "I managed to fight against one of Gale's old captives, and he said Gale and Hendrickson don't make a habit of putting us in death fights, so we can take comfort in that."

"Slater, however, does like those rules," Yanlei said. "But I think they prefer to build up bigger crowds for those events. They're special. That's not to say a wolf doesn't accidentally die in the ring. I've heard there have been mercy killings, too."

Augustine shook her head. "How have you learned all this?"

"We talk," Nick said. "When we're in our wolf forms, even when we're fighting, we exchange information the Hunters can't hear. It's the only thing they can't take away from us, and the only way we can resist." He squeezed Yanlei's hand and took a shaky breath. "We're trying to work a coup amongst the wolves. If we can get everyone to rise up against the Hunters, at least some of us might make it out and bring help."

Augustine made a face which caused his heart to drop. "If they know one of you escapes, they'll either track you down or try to move the pit, I'm sure. They—"

A loud bang from outside interrupted her. Nick quickly settled back into Yanlei's lap, looking more hurt than he was. Kat huddled in a corner of her cage, but Augustine faced the noise head on.

Gale and Hendrickson came in dragging Brighton between them. Blood flowed from the werewolf's forehead, leaving a trail behind him. For a moment, Nick thought the top of his head was missing entirely from all the blood and gore. They dropped Brighton unceremoniously into his cage and slammed the door shut.

"That was disappointing," Hendrickson said with a grumble. "I would have expected him to last longer than that. Oh well, at least we didn't bid too much on him."

Gale wiped blood off on a piece of cloth dangling from her belt. "If he survives the night, we'll try again tomorrow. I want that red wolf." She glanced at the other cages. "Maybe this one will be able to beat him. She put up quite a fight in the streets." She crouched down to get a better look at Augustine. "What do you say, dog? Think you can take down a former alpha?"

Augustine glowered and jerked forward in the cage. She thrust her hand out, trying to claw Gale, but her fingers barely grazed the tip of Gale's nose. To the Hunter's credit, she didn't jump back or scream. She just smirked and nodded.

"You have fight in you. I'm impressed. Keep your energy until tomorrow." She pushed herself up and looked over at Nick and Kat, her expression souring. "You two were a great disappointment today. I expect better from you the next time you go up against Slater's wolf."

Kat whimpered while Nick glared. "It's not even for keeps? What's the point of fighting that thing?"

"Bragging rights," Hendrickson replied in a bored tone. "Slater is a cocky bastard. We like to keep him on his toes. Besides, we get a lot of money if you win. Which means better food for all of you. And medical supplies and new clothing." He gestured to Brighton. "Your failure means he doesn't get the medical treatment he needs, and neither do you," he said, looking at Nick.

Kat shook her head. "You-you can't leave him like that. He'll bleed to death!"

Hendrickson pulled out one of the controllers, his thumb hovering over the button. "We can do what we want, sweetheart. If we want him to bleed out, then he'll bleed out. You battle and win, you'll be treated well. Otherwise…"

"Don't!" Nick cried, but too late. Hendrickson pressed the button.

Kat fell backwards against the bars with a scream of pain. When Hendrickson released her, she flopped to the floor, trembling.

Nick saw red. No one hurt his packmates and got away with it, especially not Kat. He tried to lunge at the bars, but between his wounds, the silver, and Yanlei's hold, he was forced to stay still.

Hendrickson pocketed the controller and folded his arms. "Get some sleep," he ordered and turned to leave. "You'll all have a big day tomorrow. We're training."

Nick tried to argue that half of them weren't even in shape to train, but Gale and Hendrickson left before he had a chance, leaving a trail of Gale's lilac scent behind. He swore and banged his fist on the floor. They were going to get the werewolves killed at this rate. Maybe they were more sadistic than he thought and enjoyed fights to the death. If that was the case, he didn't know if any of them were getting out of there alive.

Chapter 13
The Hunter's Dwelling

Tess

Tess awoke to searing pain in her spine and hammering inside her skull. She groaned and shook her head, but that made the raging migraine worse. What the hell had happened? And where was she?She opened her eyes and stared at a head of dark, curly hair.

Tess jerked, finding a man lying in the bed right next to her. Wait, a bed? Why was she in a bed? How had she ended up here? Who was he? She tried to sit up, only to feel something tug on her wrists and ankles.

She looked up to the thick metal cuffs wrapped around her wrists, chaining her arms above her head to the bed railing. A tug on her ankles told her she was similarly tethered to the foot railing as well. Tess grunted and tugged hard, muttering against something thick and rubbery in her mouth. It pressed back against her tongue, silencing any spells she thought to cast. A thick piece of leather wrapped over her lips, keeping the thing inside. She tried to reach back behind her head and undo it, but her fingers couldn't reach.

Tess flopped back into the soft folds of the mattress and tried to calm her pounding heart. The last thing she remembered was fighting against the Hunters and then a shock of pain in her spine. And now she was in a bed with a strange man. What *happened*?

She stared at him, a thick white comforter wrapped around his waist and legs. His torso was barren, leaving his muscular back exposed. Scars lined the flesh in several places, but otherwise, his back looked like something an artisan had chiseled out of stone. His skin was darker than hers, bordering on warm brown. Was he even wearing pants?

Tess glanced down at herself and found her lower-half covered by a blanket too. She could feel her shoes and socks had been removed, but her pants were on. Her bra was still in place, and her undershirt on. She didn't feel sore. But still, why was she here?

And where were her packmates?

Flashes of memory returned to her in sharp bursts. Bianca getting grabbed. Kat and Ray lying on the ground. Augustine howling and racing after a Hunter. The gunshot.

Ray!

Tess yanked against the bonds, growling into the gag. Ray, was he okay? What had happened to the others? She tried to call fire to her hands to free herself, but it was no use. The sting of elderberry flowed through her veins, cutting her off from her connection with the Ether. Whoever this was, he knew *what* she was.

She continued her struggles for about five minutes before the man suddenly sighed loudly.

"Can you sit still for five more minutes?" he asked, his voice laced with something akin to a British accent. "And maybe don't snore in my ear this time."

Tess snarled into her gag. She did *not* snore. And what right did he have telling her what to do? He'd chained her to the bed in the first place! She hadn't asked for this. If he wasn't going to let her go, then she wasn't going to let him get his five damn extra minutes of sleep.

She thrashed more, trying to hit him with a knee, or *something* to get him up so he could give her answers. After a few tries, the man sighed again and rolled over.

Tess's breath caught in her throat.

Black hair fell in a light wave on either side of his cheeks, matching the thin mustache beneath his nose that ran down his face and around his strong chin. His eyes were as deep as an abyss, swallowing up her gaze and leaving her breathless. He looked like some hot Bollywood star, though his accent suggested otherwise.

"Please settle down, love," he said. "It was a long night, and we both need our rest. Sleep for a few more minutes then I'll get up and fix us breakfast." He rolled over again as if that was it.

Tess stared at him incredulously. He acted like she wasn't tied up next to him. Who did he think he was? If she had access to her magic, she'd show him a thing or two. But no matter how hard she reached for it, it remained elusive. She only managed to make her head hurt worse.

Begrudgingly, she gave him his five minutes.

And five minutes was all he took. One moment he was still, and the next he rolled onto his back and stretched his arms above his head, revealing dark hair beneath his pits. "See, wasn't that better?" He tilted his head towards her but she continued to glare back. "If you're trying to cast some spell to burst me into flames with your eyes, it's not going to work, though I do enjoy your pretty eyes. By now, you should know there's elderberry in your system. In fact." He leaned away for a moment, opened a drawer, and came back with a syringe in his hand.

Tess tensed and then struggled to get away from him, but to no avail. He pushed the needle into her arm and dosed her again. Her head swam and her vision blurred as the elderberry took over. She barely noticed him get out of bed, as well as the mix of relief and disappointment he was clothed.

"I'll be back shortly," he said, his voice seeming to echo.

She shut her eyes until she felt something warm settle over her chest. She blinked and looked down at the blanket he'd draped over her before disappearing from the room. *I need to get out of here,* she thought dizzily. *I need to fight it. I need to…*

But her thoughts flickered and faded, leaving her in a half-asleep state. She didn't know how long she rested, but it was long enough to listen to him take a shower in the other room. The soothing scent of soap and body wash wafted out of the bathroom and comforted her with its normalcy.

The man came out several minutes later, his waist wrapped in a towel. Water dripped from his dark hair and shined as it rolled down his bare skin. Tess stared at him, appreciating it in her dazed state. He grabbed clothing and went back into the bathroom. When he stepped out again, he was dressed in black pants and belt, and he was pulling on a navy blue tank. He rubbed his arm, drawing Tess's attention to a thick tattoo on his bicep.

A black arrow with a heart-shaped point traced down his skin with two arched markings on either side of the shaft. A drop of black blood dripped off of the tip. Tess squinted at it then gasped into the gag. Hunter. That was a Hunter mark.

Damnit! Where are the others? Were they caught, too? They'd gone out to capture a Hunter, and she'd been taken instead. She looked around, half-expecting to find her friends in cages or chained up, but the innards of a loft met her eyes instead.

It was a simple abode with a small kitchen, dining room, and bedroom all in one room. The colorful tapestries lining the white walls hardly screamed evil villain. It didn't make any sense. If she was a captive, why keep her *here* and not with her friends?

"I see you're confused. We can discuss things over breakfast," he said. "Let me get you some coffee and Excedrin. That'll help your head."

Tess stared at him. *He chains me and gags me, and then he wants to make breakfast and coffee for me?* All she could do was watch in silence as he ground up fresh coffee and started a brew. He pulled pans out from a cabinet and gathered the fixings for an omelet.

"I hope you don't mind a vegetable omelet," he said and cracked a couple of eggs. "I've been trying to give up meat. Three years so far. I think being able to have eggs saved me." He chuckled, a pleasant sound which still made Tess want to punch him in the jugular.

The coffee machine hissed as it poured fresh, ebony perfection into a pot. Tess sniffed appreciatively. It smelled spiced, even though he hadn't added anything into it that she could see.

He left the eggs in a bowl next to the stove and poured two mugs of coffee. "Sugar? Creamer?" He looked back at her then rolled his eyes. "Where are my manners?" He brought one of the mugs and a water bottle over and set them on the end table near her. She shied away from him, but he reached out and grasped the buckle behind her head. He gently worked it free then started to pull the gag out, only to stop. "Now, I'd like to have a conversation together, so I ask that you don't scream, otherwise this is going to go right back in. There's no one around to hear you anyway. I just don't like loud noises first thing in the morning. Can we make that agreement?"

Tess glared but nodded.

He removed the gag, taking some of her saliva with it. She coughed and licked her dry lips, her jaw protesting the sudden freedom. He picked up the water bottle and held it near her face. "Drink."

She took a small sip, then swallowed several large gulps before he pulled it back.

"Easy, you're going to make yourself sick," he said and capped it off.

Tess glowered at him. "Okay, what the hell? Who are you? Wh—"

"I'll answer your questions once we have breakfast," he interrupted. He pulled a key out of his pants and reached up to her wrists. "Please don't try to do anything stupid. I don't want to tase you again."

"You tased me?" Tess snapped. So that explained the searing pain in her back. Good to know.

"I had to get you out before anyone noticed me." He unlocked her chains and took hold of her wrists. She expected him to flip her over and bind them behind her back, but instead, he massaged her skin gently, working life back into her limbs. He let her go after a moment and pushed the coffee closer to her.

"Go on and drink. Oh." He picked up the mug and took a sip. "See? Nothing in there. I'll finish breakfast and bring you to the table." He put the coffee down then walked away before she even had the chance to think about throwing the hot mug at him.

She grabbed the water instead and drained the bottle, then picked up the coffee. It warmed her cold hands; how long had they been chained above her head? Her aching shoulders suggested at least several hours.

She sipped the coffee and glanced around the loft. The windows were covered up, so no natural light came through. Lightbulbs and a UV ray provided the only source of light. She glanced at the UV light and the tiny herb garden nestled beneath it. The man grabbed a few pieces of oregano and crushed them into the omelet.

Tess took another drink. "So, am I at least allowed to ask you your name?"

"If I can ask you yours."

Tess snorted. "My guess is you already know." She ran her thumbs along the chipped red mug. "Tess."

"Arjun," he replied.

Arjun, well, it sounds Indian. "Okay," she said. "I'll bite. Where are you from?"

"Heh, isn't that a bit racist?" Arjun teased.

"Your accent is throwing me."

"It usually does." He sprinkled herbs onto the dish. "My mother was born and raised in India. My father went there on a business trip and fell in love with her. He grew up in Wales. So, he moved her to England with him and had me about six years later. I grew up listening to people speaking more with a British accent, though my mother used to tease me and say I needed to learn to keep my homeland tongue." He flipped the omelets and slid them onto a plate. "She died when I turned sixteen. My father was nearly inconsolable. Tried to take his life but remembered he had a son to care for, so he did whatever he could to make my life worthwhile."

"So you became a Hunter," Tess said bitterly.

"Yes," Arjun replied with pride in his voice. "By your tone, you aren't fond of us."

"Why should I be? You and your fellow assholes keep taking my friends and almost killed my father. You left my packsister in a coma, and now you've gone and kidnapped me. Where are the others? What did you do with them?"

Arjun sighed and brought the plates of omelets to the table. "You really don't beat around the bush, do you, love?"

Tess slammed her mug down, accidentally causing hot coffee to jump onto her hand. She shook it out with a hiss. "Tell me what you want and where my friends are!"

"I don't have them."

His response startled her into silence. *What does he mean he doesn't have them? He was there!* But all she could do was stare dumbly at him as he walked over to the bed. He rolled the blanket off of her legs, exposing the chain linking her cuffed ankles to the bed.

"Hey," Tess said softly, suddenly nervous.

"I'm not going to hurt you." He pulled out the key again and undid the link to the bed, but he left the cuffs on her ankles. "It's for both of our safety," he said. "I can help you to the table." He put the key away and held out his hand. "Come on. You must be hungry."

Tess stared at his offered hand suspiciously. She didn't want his help. She didn't even know this guy. But her rumbling stomach, and her desire for answers, finally made her reach out. His hand felt rough, but his grip remained soft as he pulled her up to her feet. He grabbed her coffee mug and clicked his tongue. "You chipped another piece," he admonished and helped her towards the kitchen.

Tess considered putting him in a headlock, but she realized pretty quickly why he wanted to help her, and it wasn't just because of the chains. Her head spun from the elderberry, and her legs wobbled like jelly. She gratefully sank down into a chair and looked at the omelet.

Five pieces of avocado placed purposefully smiled back at her. "Seriously?" Tess said. "What are we, five?"

"What?" Arjun looked back at the omelet and laughed. "Oh, sorry. My friend's daughter insists on smiley faces with all her food when I cook for her. Bad habit when I make for two. I'll take them if you don't want them." He reached for the plate, but Tess yanked it back.

"My avocado," she grouched.

Arjun looked taken aback, but he smiled and laughed all the same.

His laugh was annoyingly adorable.

She dug into the food and started to eat, trying to ignore the chains on her ankles. They weren't that heavy, but they were uncomfortable and unnecessary. What'd he think she could do without her magic? Well, the fork gave her some ideas, but she put it to work on her omelet instead. "Ugh," she said after the first bite.

Arjun paused, his fork in the air. "Is it bad? I can make you another."

"No, it's *good*, and that pisses me off." She ate another bite and then set the fork down. "Okay, this is too weird. Will you tell me what happened and why you brought me here?"

Arjun ate a couple bites and took a maddeningly slow sip of his coffee before he spoke. "You and your friends were tracking two Hunters. I was tracking them, too, and I had things all put into place to catch them, but your friends came at the wrong time and interfered."

"Excuse me? *We* came at the wrong time?"

"Let me rephrase that. You did what I'd hoped. You provided yourself as bait, but then you got sloppy, and Gale and Hendrickson got the drop on you."

"Who?"

"The two Hunters. The ones you were tracking?" At Tess's look, he barked out a shocked laugh. "You didn't even know the names of your targets?"

"We were trying to get ahold of one of them so we could figure out where my friend and Dad got dragged off to."

Arjun paused, mid-slice on his omelet. "Your father?"

Tess sighed and rubbed her face. "Yeah, they took my dad and my friend Nick. Put my other friend in a coma."

Arjun set his fork down and reached out, placing a warm hand on her shoulder. "I'm so sorry. I assumed you'd been affected, but I didn't realize family was involved."

She slapped his hand away, more surprised than angry. "Pack *is* family. So Nick and my dad are both important to me." She gave him the stink eye. "So you were tracking us and waiting for us to be bait so you could get the Hunters. Why?"

"Because, they're an embarrassment to Hunters."

Tess stared at him. Had she heard him right? "What do you mean?"

Arjun folded his arms and leaned forward. "How much do you know about Hunters?"

"Asides from the fact that they want to capture and kill the people I love, what else is there to know?"

Arjun shook his head. "Know your enemy, first rule of battle. That's one kind of Hunter. There are several. I'm, what I'd like to call, a true Hunter, who follows the original oath of my people. We protect humans from parahumans who would do damage to *anyone*. So the vampires who kill for sport and risk exposing your people to the rest of the humans? We take care of them. The dark magic users like senkas who sacrifice people for their rituals, or magi who cut up beastlies for their scales, claws, or other pieces of their body? We take care of them, too. We have no interest in kidnapping fathers or kids or people who have done nothing wrong."

Tess stared and cleared out an ear. "I'm sorry, did you call us people?"

"Well, yeah, that's what you are." He poked his omelet. "Hunters who took your friends, they're abominations. They hate all parahumans and will kill without asking questions. They believe humans are superior, and they rarely work with parahumans unless it benefits them."

"Why would they work with parahumans at all if they hate us so much?"

Arjun cracked a smile. "Considering you could incinerate me with a wave of your hand, let's just say, sometimes those Hunters feel like they need to fight fire with fire. Our fragile human bodies can't always stand up to magic or bites from lycans." He sipped his coffee. "Then there's Legion. They have licensed Hunters who go out and kind of do what I do. They take out the threats."

"So why aren't you with them?"

"Frankly, I think licensed Hunters enjoy being able to kill without repercussions. Too many of them are trigger happy. Plus, Legion has all their rules, and I'd rather work to my own oath. Legion has their hands tied most of the time anyway. They can't take care of *every* crazy Hunter or parahuman who wants to ruin the lives of the innocent. So we walk that grey line and do it for them. Believe it or not, Hunters like me are good friends to a lot of parahumans. You tend to see the bad ones more often and think we're all the same." He bit off another piece of egg. "I can assure you we're not."

"Huh," was all Tess could bring herself to say. She poked at the food and furrowed her brow. "All right, so say I believe you. Why did you kidnap me? What about my friends?"

"I grabbed you because they would have killed you. They don't want magi around. Too unpredictable and hard to control. That, and you're no good in a ring fight if you can't use your magic. If I'd tried to grab you while you were conscious, can you honestly say you wouldn't have blasted me with your magic?" When she didn't answer, he chuckled. "Thought so. Fastest way to get you out of there without anyone noticing was to incapacitate you. I dragged you into a nearby abandoned apartment and stayed there while your friends were taken."

"Why didn't you try to stop them?" Tess protested. "You're supposed to protect parahumans, right?"

Arjun sighed. "In the time it took me to get you secured, they already had your friends. If I'd tried to attack, they would have become collateral. I didn't want to risk it. One death's enough."

Tess dropped her fork with a clatter. "*What?*" she whispered, a cold wave of dread washing through her.

Arjun bowed his head. "The male wolf. He died trying to protect the big female. I'm sorry, Tess."

Tess fell back into her chair, her hands clasped over her mouth. *Ray! No, not Ray!* Oh God, what had she done? She'd urged both him and Augustine to come on this crazy mission with her, and now, Ray was dead. Tears ran down her cheeks and into her hair.

She shook her head. "He can't be dead. He was fine! He was just fine. You're lying!"

"I checked him before I took you away. And I made a call to the local hospital to get someone over, but, Tess, he's gone. I checked his pulse."

"Why didn't you stop it?" she cried. She shoved him hard, her vision blurring. "If you were so close, why didn't you stop them from killing him? What about the others? Are they dead, too?"

Arjun shook his head as he straightened himself. "I don't think so. I saw them take the two female wolves and leave the male behind."

"And the avian? Did they kill her?"

"That's the strange thing," Arjun said. "Someone else was there. They grabbed the bird and bolted. Gale and Hendrickson didn't have her when they left."

Tess covered her face. Both Augustine and Kat were captured. Bianca was, who knew where. And Ray, dear sweet Ray…

Tess wasn't the type of person to cry easily, but she sobbed for his death, for the pack's loss, and especially for Augustine. Did she even know that her husband was dead? Paytah would never forgive Tess for this, and she doubted she'd ever forgive herself either. First Carmen and now Ray. Who would be next? How many more people would she fail?

Arjun touched her arm, but she jerked away from him. "Don't," she said in a broken sob. "Why should I trust you? You could be like the rest of them and messing with my head."

"I thought you might say that." He got up and went over to a bag on the counter. He opened it and pulled out a small device. It took her a moment to realize it was a miniature camera. How was that supposed to get any shots, especially when everything had happened in the dark?

He sat down and tapped three tiny buttons on it. Suddenly, the camera grew to three-times the size. Tess blinked in surprise and wiped her tears away. "What did you do?"

"A gift from a magus," he said. "She spelled it so I could use it on missions. Take pictures to get information without actually having it very visible." He turned it toward Tess as he flicked through pictures. "This is what I saw."

She grabbed the camera and stared at the picture of the woman Hunter, Gale, standing over Ray's fallen body. Kat and Augustine were both unconscious on the ground and chained, Hendrickson looming above them. She swiped back and forth between the pictures, pulling up ones of the fight and where they'd gone wrong. He'd taken a blurred picture of something grabbing Bianca, but the camera speed couldn't catch whoever had stolen her.

As she swiped through more, she started to notice a trend. A lot of them were of *her*. Side angles, front views, shots from the back. And it wasn't of that night alone. It showed other evenings of practice. Sure, she saw her friends in there too, but she remained the primary focus.

She swallowed hard and glanced at Arjun before returning to the first one he showed her.

"You don't want to go past that one. I took a closer picture of him."

Tess stared at him, took a breath, then swiped.

Ray's lifeless eyes stared back at her, blood dripping from a bullet wound in his head.

She dropped the camera into Arjun's waiting hand and turned away from him. Her stomach lurched, her breakfast rising up. She panted, trying to breathe as panic clawed its way through her chest.

"I'm sorry," Arjun said.

"Why?" she whispered. "Why take the pictures? Why take so many of *me*?" When he didn't answer, she looked back at him and saw the blush blossoming on his cheeks. "Well?"

"I wasn't quite sure if you were a wolf or not. You didn't use your magic in the beginning, but then I caught some clips of your glowing eyes, and I knew. I thought, maybe, of your whole pack, I'd be able to convince you to let me help."

"Help?" Tess said. "How can you help us?"

"Because, while they were busy trying to capture your friends, I snuck something on one of the female wolves." He pulled something else out of the bag and showed her a cellphone with a crimson dot moving slowly around in one area. "I stuck a tracer on her. It's a very small, pin-point device you can shoot out of something like a dart gun. I hit your friend with it at the same time the Hunters took her down with the tranquilizers. It got lodged in her hair. It'll probably get washed out eventually, but it doesn't matter. The tracer already showed me the general location where she was brought." He put the device back in his pocket. "I wanted to show your alpha and see if my friend and I can help you get your friends back *and* take down the Hunters."

Tess stared at him in disbelief. *This seems too good to be true. Why bother helping us? He doesn't even know us, and he's a Hunter for crying out loud! But how else are we going to find them?* "Why didn't you bring me to Paytah to convince him?"

Arjun snorted. "Oh yeah, I'm sure that would have gone over real well. I walk into pack territory carrying your unconscious body. 'Excuse me, Alpha Paytah, I watched your packmates get kidnapped and shot and rescued your magus. One died, but I think I know how to find them. Oh, by the way, I'm a Hunter too!'" He spread his hands.

"Point taken," Tess mumbled. Still, keeping her here had wasted time. "Where are they?"

"Looks like near the Washington State subway station."

Tess frowned. "But isn't that abandoned?"

"Ideal spot, right? And so close to the heart of Chicago, it'd be easier to snag and sneak parahumans away without anyone noticing." He went back to his meal and tapped his plate. "My guess is they enlisted a magus to help out and dig a deeper area near the Washington station and below it. While businesses are happening above ground, no one realizes that a fighting ring is hosted below."

Tess wrinkled her nose. "Why would a magus help Hunters if they wanted to hurt other parahumans?"

"Well, here's the thing. Some Hunters still view magi and witches as humans. They have magical powers, but they don't shift into lycans, animals, you know? Some Hunters will work with them. Maybe they'll lie and say why they want the area built. Maybe they offer the magus a lot of money and then later kill them. Or threaten their family."

Tess balked at the thought while Arjun nibbled lightly on his meal, as if the thought of a family being threatened didn't faze him.

"In the end," he went on, "they find a way to get what they want from the magus and have their area built. If it's spelled, even better. It means people can't come in so easily. That makes it harder for us to find them though. I had a feeling that's what was going on under Chicago, but I couldn't be sure without getting a tracking device on someone. I still need to investigate, but I have enough information I'm willing to talk with the Violet Marshall and see if we can get Legion involved."

Tess settled back in her chair and stared long and hard at the man. Her stomach twisted, conflicted. On the one hand, he'd saved her, had proof of where her friends might be, and was willing to bring her back to her pack. On the other, he was a Hunter, he hadn't tried to help anyone else, and it seemed too damn perfect.

He watched her, waiting, but when she didn't respond, he offered a sad smile. "I understand not wanting to trust me. I'm supposed to be the bad guy, right? What if I gave you the chance to talk to your Alpha? You can call him, tell him what happened, and then we go to him. Your whole pack will be there. What am *I* going to do?"

Tess narrowed her eyes. "You'd be walking into the lion's den. You know what they could do to you."

"If I'm lying, then I deserve it, but I'm not. They need to know that not all of us Hunters are awful people." He motioned to his tattoo. "This used to mean something good back in the day. Hunters wore this as a sign of pride. We eliminated the ones who tried to harm the innocent. Over time, our duty got perverted, and this symbol? Parahumans started intentionally marking us to show us as a threat. As a danger." He shook his head. "I still wear it with pride. I know my purpose."

Tess stared at the tattoo for a long time then pinched her eyes shut. What did she have to lose? "Fine. I'm going to guess you won't let me use my phone."

"You can. I have a blocker on it so they can't trace it back to us anyway." He went to a bag hanging on the door and brought it over. She found her over shirt in it, her belt, her Ether necklace (not that it would do her much good right now), shoes and socks, and her phone. He pulled the phone out and put something on the back of it before handing it to her. "Please put it on speaker."

Tess took a breath and dialed Paytah. She set the phone down and pressed her hands to the back of her neck anxiously.

The phone picked up on the third ring. "Tess?"

Tess's mouth went dry. Ray was dead and the others were gone because of her. Would he even want to speak to her?

"Tess? Please, is that you?"

Arjun nudged her leg under the table; her chain rattled.

"Yeah, it's me."

"Are you all right? Where are you?"

The concern in his voice almost broke her heart. Tears pricked her eyes, but she fought them back. "With a…friend."

Arjun lifted an eyebrow at her.

"Tess, where are you? Let me come get you. You need to be home with the pack."

She shut her eyes. "Paytah, do you know where Ray, Augustine, Kat, and Bianca are?"

Paytah was quiet a moment. "Augustine, Kat, and Bianca were kidnapped. We thought you were too. Ray…he's dead. We can talk about this in person. Where. Are. You?"

Tess's eyes flooded again. So it was true. Ray really was dead. The fact Paytah knew about it and wasn't screaming at her shocked her. But maybe he was desperate to have her home so he could scold her in person…or he honestly, truly missed her. She couldn't imagine what her mother was going through.

"Tess!" he barked.

Tess jumped and swallowed. "I'm coming to you. Paytah, a man rescued me before the Hunters could take me. He said that he has information he can share with you that can help us find the others. Can we set up a meeting?"

Paytah drew in a breath. "Is he listening?"

"Yes."

She could hear the growl over the phone. "Who are you?"

"My name is Arjun, sir," Arjun replied in a respectful tone. "What your packmate neglects to tell you is that I'm a Hunter, but I'm not like the ones who took your friends and family. I assume, as a Violet Marshall, you're aware of the Hunter's code. At least, the original one?"

Paytah grunted. "Go on."

"I'm from the old order. Help the good, get rid of the wicked, whether they're parahuman or Hunter. I brought your packmate to my home to help her recover; I didn't immediately return her to you because, well, to be blunt, sir, I wasn't sure if I'd have my head ripped off."

"A wise presumption," Paytah agreed.

"I'll bring Tess to you, as well as my information with the promise you won't kill me."

"And how do we know we can trust you?" Paytah asked.

"I could ask you the same thing," Arjun said. "At some point, someone has to break bread first. So, Alpha Paytah, will you accept my offer?"

Tess glanced anxiously between the phone and Arjun. Trifling with Paytah was the last thing anyone should do. Arjun had already dug his grave by kidnapping her. He didn't need to nail down his coffin, too.

"Very well. Tess, have him bring you to your apartment, and your mother and I will meet you there."

Tess nodded. Probably a good idea. It was likely the Hunter already knew where she lived, but not necessarily where Paytah resided, which was a good thing. She had to keep him and the rest of the pack safe. "I will, Paytah."

"When?"

Arjun glanced up at the clock. "This evening. I have to get a few things taken care of, and then we'll head your way. Say around five."

"*Fine*," Paytah growled. "Five, and no later."

"Of course. We'll be in touch." Arjun took her phone and hung up before Tess had the chance to say goodbye. He pocketed it and gave her a look. "I'm trying to earn your trust, but I need to keep myself safe too."

Tess shook her ankle. "Is that why the chain is still on?"

"Well, that, and there's somewhere I have to be, and I can't have you running off. I'll leave you with the tv remote and books and things to read while I'm out. Your ankle will be chained back to the bed."

"And if I have to go to the bathroom?"

He winked. "I'll make it long enough that you can reach the toilet. This isn't my first rodeo or the first person I've tied up in my bed." His face went scarlet suddenly, and he cleared his throat. "That sounded worse than I meant it to."

Tess stifled a chuckle. The hope that she would see Paytah soon stopped her from trying to rip his head off then and there or stabbing him with a fork. She went back to eating her breakfast, glancing periodically at his pocket where he kept her phone.

After food, he helped her first to the bathroom then back onto the bed. He pulled out a longer chain from a trunk and attached it to the middle link on her ankle cuffs then tethered it to the bed. His bed wasn't some flimsy metal. It could withstand a lot of pressure. Which also made her wonder more about his "tying people up in his bed" comment.

He passed over the remote and some books then reached into

his end table for something else. "Sorry about this."

"Sorry for—"

The syringe pierced her arm before she had the chance to finish speaking. Tess hissed in pain and swung at him. "Oh, come on! What the hell? You already…dosed….me," she slurred, her eyes rolling. That didn't just feel like elderberry. What had he put in there, some kind of sedative?

She fell backwards against the bed, shaking her head, dazed. He propped a pillow up behind her head and pulled the blanket over her. "Rest," he told her in a soft, soothing tone. "You'll be back with your pack before you know it."

Tess weakly swatted at his face. "Asshole," she growled and slumped down. She drifted, her hearing fading in and out. Before she went completely under, she heard him speak into his phone.

"Skye? It's Arjun. Yeah, I have information for you."

With a sigh, she fell unconscious.

Chapter 14
History

Nick

The night dragged on as they waited to see if Brighton would pull through. Nick stayed awake, his head in Yanlei's lap, and watched the male's chest rise and fall. The blood eventually stopped flowing not long after they brought him in, but the line of it covering the floor made Nick dread that he'd lost too much to wake up again.

Consoling Kat was another problem in and of itself. After recovering from Gale's shock, she huddled in a corner and sobbed quietly for nearly an hour before Nick got her to calm down. It wasn't so much the shock that had impacted her. It was the memories that came with being helpless. Trapped.

Augustine said little except to ask questions about their situation. Nick had some answers, but not all of them as he and Yanlei were still trying to figure out how to escape. So far, no one had any good ideas.

They were brought food sometime in the evening, he thought. Fortunately, the cheap cut of meat was cooked so they didn't have to shift into their wolf forms to eat. Nick doubted he could make the full shift with the condition of his ribs. They ate, drank, and eventually, Yanlei, Augustine, and Kat fell asleep.

Nick watched over Brighton. His eyes grew heavy more than once, and he pinched himself to stay awake, too afraid Brighton would slip away from them when they weren't watching. But the older wolf kept fighting despite his wounds, pale face, and weak breaths.

Nick started to drift again when he heard movement at the entrance of their cave. A low light caught his eye, and he squinted as Gale stepped inside. She brought a lantern over to Brighton's cage and knelt down next to him. She shifted the light back and forth, inspecting Brighton as Nick had been doing. After a moment, she pulled a syringe out of her pocket and stuck it into the wolf's shoulder. An odd, glowing liquid flowed into Brighton's body. A few moments later, he took a deep breath (the first Nick had really heard in the past hour), and began to breathe more easily. The color returned to his cheeks, and the head wound began to slowly heal over.

Nick sat up carefully, trying not to disturb Yanlei. "What did you do?" he asked in a whisper.

Gale jumped then shined the light on him, causing him to wince against its harsh glow in the dim cave. "What are you doing awake? You have a match tomorrow."

"What did you do?" Nick repeated.

Gale glanced at Brighton and pocketed the syringe. "I had a spare shot of an Ether healing tonic. He's a good fighter; didn't want to lose him too soon." She checked the lock on the cage then made her rounds to look over the others.

Nick followed her with his gaze. Her response made sense, and yet, he felt like there was more to it than that. He gently helped Yanlei settle on the ground behind him and sleep. "So, be real with me. Why are you doing this to us? What made you hate parahumans so much?"

"You're joking, right?" Gale asked with a low chuckle. She checked the collar on Kat. "Look at you. You lot are an abomination. You're not like us. The only thing you're good for is fighting."

"Even though there are some parahuman Hunters," Nick countered.

"Pft, those aren't real Hunters. They're wannabes and disguising themselves as Hunters in order to save their own skin. A real parahuman Hunter doesn't exist."

"Then where'd you get the syringe?" Nick asked. "If you hate and don't trust us so much, why use a parahuman's magic?"

Gale glanced over her shoulder at him, annoyed. She brushed

her hair back, showing off her scars, and pressed her hand to her cocked hip. "Is there a point to all these questions?"

"Just trying to figure out what happened that made you despise us."

Gale bristled, her hand tightening over the lantern. "Maybe it's because you always take what you want with little regard for the rest of humanity. Maybe it's because you use your disgusting disease to change people against their will so they can be monsters like you. Maybe it's because you freaks of nature don't belong in *my* world."

Nick mulled over her words and leaned back. Forced change… that sounded rather specific. "Look, we're going to be stuck together for a long time unless you trade me in a fight or find a way to take me out. Level with me. Who did we hurt?"

Gale actually paused at his question and stared at him. Her eyes wavered with emotion. Outside, she kept her composure, but inside, Nick could imagine a scared, hurt girl screaming and beating her fists, wanting to break free and spill the truth.

He scratched his neck. "How about you tell me who we hurt, and I'll tell you what humans did to make me loathe you. Who am I going to blow your secret to anyway? Not like anyone of us are going anywhere soon."

Gale shifted on her feet, her fight or flight instincts kicking in. And yet, just when Nick thought she might bolt, she sighed heavily and sat down on the floor, lamp at her side. She faced him, well out of arm's reach, not that he could have moved quickly enough to hurt her anyway. A faint scent of lilac wafted towards him. "My parents were Hunters, and they taught me, Hendrickson, and our sister Daniella how to track and capture parahumans. Daniella was several years older than us, so she went out into the field and bagged a few wolves. And then she fell in love with one." She snorted. "Perverted version of beauty and the beast. She kept him a secret from our parents, and us. The more she talked to him and fell in love with him, the more she wanted to be like him. She started to tell us that hunting was wrong and that werewolves, vampires, all parahumans were the same as us. Only special.

"Dad hated her going on about it. Took a switch to her whenever she fought him on the subject and made me and my brother watch. 'Parahumans did this,' he'd say. 'They've corrupted your sister's mind.'" Gale chuckled dryly. "You know, for a time, I started talking and listening to my sister, and I briefly believed that maybe this wolf she'd fallen in love with wasn't so bad." She fell quiet and reached into her belt. She drew one of her knives and started to clean it with a whetstone. In the glow of the lamp, Nick saw etches of wolves running across the pristine silver blade.

"What happened?" he pressed.

"The wolf promised to change my sister and bring her to his pack where they could live together happily. So he bit her. And she went through the transformation." She narrowed her eyes. "But we've learned that some bodies don't do well with the transformation, or they mentally don't stay the same person. Daniella lost her mind. The pain fried her affections for the werewolf. She went to our parents, begging them to help her, but there's no cure. Once you're changed, it can't be undone. She lost her temper, screamed at my parents, lashed out at them."

She inspected the dagger and stared long and hard at her reflection.

"One moment I had two parents and two siblings. Then I had two dead parents at the claws of my sister. We woke up to the commotion and didn't realize what was happening. So Hendrickson and I rushed downstairs and attacked the beast hurting our parents, as we'd been trained to do. We captured her and forced the information out of her.

"You see, we'd hoped her werewolf lover had done the deed, not her. But the blood under her claws and in her teeth were irrefutable evidence." She wiped the knife off. "We couldn't bring ourselves to kill her, so we sold her into a fighting ring, buried our parents, and never looked back. The thing that kills me is, my father died on the stairs headed up to our bedroom. I think she had intended to go after us, and he got in her way. If it hadn't been for them, I'm sure my brother and I would be dead. All because a werewolf took what didn't belong to him."

"She had a choice, too," Nick reminded her. "She didn't have to ask to be changed."

"He offered it!" Gale hissed.

"And what happened to him?"

Gale narrowed her eyes and looked down at her blade. "My brother tracked him down and cut his throat out. He deserved it. That monster offered to change my sister, and she took it because she was a coward, and now our family is broken because of what parahumans did.”

“And you know what you did?” Nick argued. He pointed at Augustine’s sleeping form. “You killed her mate.” He pointed at Brighton. “You tore a loving father away from his daughter, a husband from his wife. We’re people, just like you. Sure, we might change forms, but we’re still people! We don’t deserve to be treated like—”

“*Animals*?” Gale sneered. “But isn’t that what you are? You might look in the mirror and see human now, but deep down you know you’re a beast that can kill and tear apart families.”

Nick curled his lip. “I bet you see the same thing when you look in the mirror.”

Gale glowered and pulled out the controller, but Nick didn’t stop.

“Tell me something, are you down here just to get back at parahumans, or are you really here because you feel guilty for selling your sister into bondage?”

He waited for the pain. It was a harsh, cruel thing to say, but he couldn’t help it. He could sympathize because she’d lost her parents—he knew what that felt like—but to sell your own flesh and blood? That could never be forgiven.

Gale’s hand shook as she held the controller, thumb brushing the button, but she didn’t push it. With a defeated look, she lowered her hand and glared at the floor, her teeth clenched so hard her cheekbones stood out. “You don’t get it.”

“No, I do. You told me your story. Here’s mine. I lied to you.” When she looked up, he caught her eyes with his. “I don’t hate humans.”

“What?”

“My dad and I were out shopping. Doing daily errands, nothing big. We stopped at a gas station to pick up some stuff. He left me in the car to listen to music. When he came out, these gangbangers came flying through shooting at one another. Guess one of the other gang’s members worked at the store. My dad got hit in the crossfire. He was a werewolf, but, as I’m pretty sure you already know, a straight shot through the skull isn’t something we generally survive. He died. Not because he was a werewolf. Not because those humans hated us. But because we were in the wrong place at the wrong time. I hate them for what they did, but not ‘cause they’re human.”

He snorted. "Your sister fell in love with someone who was different from her. And instead of embracing it, your family shunned her. And when she changed? You didn't try to get her help. You lost her because of your hatred and bigotry." He laughed. "Damn, people like to say prejudice and shit doesn't exist in the United States any more. If people ain't hating on you because of your color or where you're from, they're hating on you because you can change forms. Real progressive, aren't we?"

"If that werewolf had stayed away from my sister, this never would have happened!"

"And if she'd never hunted him, they wouldn't have met. Did he know she was a Hunter?" Nick lifted an eyebrow and waited, but Gale didn't answer. "I bet he did. And yet, he didn't try to kill her or call her a demon or something. He loved her. I want you to remember that. That *beast* loved your sister more than you and your brother did."

This time the shock did come. Nick tried not to scream so he wouldn't wake the others. He fell against the floor, gasping for breath, his hands grabbing his skull. He banged his head twice to try to distract himself from the pain in his neck, but it did little to help. The shock didn't last as long as usual though. When she stopped, he slumped down and held his aching ribs. "Shit…," he rasped.

Gale got to her feet and snatched her lantern. "You don't know shit about me or what we went through," she growled defensively. "I don't even know why I'm talking to you, you mutt."

"Heh, I was wondering that, too. But hey, if you want to talk *without* shocking me, I'll give you an ear."

Gale spat and stormed out of the room. Nick watched her and started to turn away when she reached the entrance, but movement caught his eye. Gale had already turned out the lantern, leaving the hallway mostly in darkness, but he saw a dark figure standing outside the cave, partially covered by the shadows. Gale shied away from the person at first, then sighed. "I wish you'd stop creeping in the dark like that."

"My apologies," a low, deep voice said. It sounded familiar, but Nick couldn't place it. "I have the information you were seeking. There's to be another pack meeting with Paytah and a few others this evening. It would be the perfect time."

Gale took the paper he handed her and looked it over. "Good, thank you. You're sure this information is accurate?"

"Have I steered you wrong before?"

"No. Thank you."

The figure bowed then retreated into the shadows. Gale stared at the paper for a long moment then looked into the cave. She met Nick's eyes, smirked, and departed.

Nick felt a rock sink into his stomach. The only reason they'd want to know Paytah's location was likely to either capture him or go after other wolves while he wasn't present. Damn. He doubted he'd get the truth out of her now, not with that smirk.

"That was ballsy," Yanlei whispered at his side.

Nick jumped only to hiss and wince as his ribs protested again. "Ow, damn, how long have you been awake?"

"Since she got in here. I wanted to listen and see if I could piece any information together." She sat up slowly and brushed her hair out of her eyes. Her poor face was blotched with bruises, but he could see some of the flesh beginning to turn a normal color. "Where did you learn to analyze her like that?"

Nick chuckled. "Paytah and Rozene. Mostly Rozene. She always told me she could learn the most when she listened or pushed people's buttons. Paytah prefers pushing." He rubbed his throat. "I don't know how much of what she told me will help us, but it's a start. I wish she'd stop with the shocking."

"Come here." Yanlei held out her hands. When he leaned over, she started to massage his shoulders and his throat tenderly. "Who was that at the door?"

"I don't know. I recognized the voice. Probably one of the other Hunters around the ring." He swallowed hard. "They're going after Paytah."

"I heard. It's stupid to try to capture an alpha."

"You heard what they said, though," he argued and glanced at Yanlei. "The red wolf who took Brighton down was a red-furred alpha. They're bold enough to do it once, they could do it again."

"Legion won't stand for that," Yanlei said. "It's one thing for us to go missing, but for Alphas to vanish, especially a Violet Marshall? They won't let it happen."

"They have before," came Brighton's exhausted, weak voice.

Nick looked sharply at the man. "Brighton! You're okay."

"Alive…not really okay," Brighton replied. He grimaced and touched his scalp which was mostly healed by now. "I feel like my head got split open."

Yanlei scooted closer to Nick's side. "It looked like it when you were brought in. How are you feeling?"

"Like I took an axe to my skull." Brighton rubbed his face tenderly and rolled onto his stomach. "Heard you talking. Alphas have gone missing before, and Legion didn't step in. Over ten years ago, we knew where the Hunters were hiding in Chicago and keeping wolf pits. We planned to go in without Legion because they were too busy. Someone found out, and our forces got demolished. Legion only came in for the cleanup."

Nick grimaced at the thought. "Why wouldn't they do anything?"

"Legion has to be careful who and what they tangle with," Brighton explained. "They like to say there are both good Hunters and bad Hunters out there. From what I heard, they tried to say they couldn't be sure if the Hunters we were going after were the good ones keeping the bad parahumans in check, or if it was the other way around." He scoffed.

"By the time they decided, most of my forces were dead, I guess Legion had their answer, but it was too late. We'd lost almost everyone. A lot of distrust grew between us and Legion after that. Gladus built it back up, but with them refusing to come in and help? Yeah, I wouldn't put your money on them, or good Hunters. I've never met one."

Well, that's comforting, Nick though despairingly. He sighed and gave Yanlei a look. They were no closer to getting out than before, but at least they had a little more history to mull over.

Brighton shifted again and curled up on the floor. "With that, I'm going to try to sleep off this splitting migraine. Try to keep it down if you can."

He sighed and drifted off within moments. He must have been tired to not have noticed Kat and Augustine. Or maybe he'd seen them when they'd been brought in earlier. Who knew?

Nick sank against Yanlei as she returned to massaging him. He rested his head on her shoulder. "I can't believe you were awake during all that. You sounded like you were asleep."

"I've had practice. I used to do that when I wanted to eavesdrop on my parents. I'd 'fall asleep' on the couch and listen to their conversations. My grandfather taught me. I could never trick him, though."

Nick grinned. "I think I'd like to meet your grandfather one day. He sounds like an interesting guy."

"He is, and I think he'd like that." She placed a hand gently on his chest. "I'm sorry to hear about your father. How old were you?"

Nick closed his eyes. He didn't really want to talk about it, but when did he ever? It was a memory he'd rather leave buried in the grave with his dad. "Almost 15. Paytah and Rozene took me in after that. Kat came at the same time."

"You show such protection and affection towards her," Yanlei said. "Are you two, I mean…"

"Together?" he guessed and chuckled. "No. I had a huge crush on her when I was taken in by the pack, but then Bianca came into the picture, and, surprise, Kat realized she was bisexual. It hurt, but I'm happy for them. They seriously do well together." He frowned at Kat. She lay huddled on her side, arms wrapped around herself. "Bianca has to be worried sick about her. I wish we knew where she was. Tess, too."

Yanlei leaned her head on his. "I admire your protectiveness of your pack. That shows signs of an alpha in the making."

"Paytah said that to me before. I wish I could save everyone. I'm trying, but, I'm not strong enough."

"You're plenty strong," Yanlei replied and draped her other arm around him in a hug. He nestled into it, his shoulders and body relaxing in her embrace. "You don't have to just be strong in body, you have to have strength of mind. And compassion. So many alphas are rigid and don't show their emotions. You do. You show tears. I saw how you wept over your lost packmate."

Nick grimaced, the pain of Ray's death striking him in the gut all over again. "He was a good guy. Cared about the pack a lot. He was funny, too. Especially when he and Tess got into a mock fight." The tears started up again, but he did his best to push them back.

"No, no," Yanlei said and hugged him tighter, mindful not to put too much pressure near his ribs. "We're the only ones awake. If you want to mourn, then mourn. I won't judge you for it."

Nick wanted to argue. He wanted to say that he could mourn after they were safe—just as he'd told Augustine. He wanted to shove away his feelings and work through their next plans. But all he could think about was Ray's smiling face, and then imagine the bullet in his head.

The tears fell, and he curled into her as he wept for his

packbrother. All the while Yanlei held him and comforted him in the dim light of the room. The stress of the day, his grief, and his wounds finally wore on him, and he drifted asleep, still nestled in her embrace.

***

A loud bang jerked Nick awake. He sat up sharply, breaking free of Yanlei's hold, and looked around. The cave lit up with bright lights. Hendrickson stood over Kat's open cage with a bar in his hands. She scrambled to get away from him, but he poked and prodded until he managed to get the bar attached to her collar.

"Come on now, pretty. We need to get you trained to fight in the ring."

Kat struggled to get free, but a yank of the pole dragged her out of her barred prison.

Gale stood by as Hendrickson pulled Kat around by the collar, causing her to trip and whimper.

Nick snarled and slapped the floor of the cage. "Stop it! That's enough!"

Gale walked towards him with a piece of paper. "Save your energy. You'll need it for when we start the sparring bracket. New contest just went up. Winner gets $10,000 and pick of three parahumans to fight in another ring." She grinned at him maliciously. "Don't worry. You'll have time to recover before I throw you in. Did you notice your ribs aren't hurting as much today?"

Nick touched his torso. The swelling had gone down, and he didn't feel anything poking his lungs. He thought to thank her then laughed inwardly. Why should he thank her? She was the reason he was in the situation to begin with! "And what do we get out of this?"

"You get to stay alive," Gale replied. "And like I said, the more you win for us, the better we treat you. We're going to start sparring and training today. Oh, and look who's on the list first? Your new friend and—" She pressed the controller in her pocket and sent Nick back to the ground. He heard the cage open, but he could do nothing as Gale thrust in a bar and attached it to Yanlei's collar. He watched in horror as Yanlei was dragged out and the door slammed shut behind her. "This little one. We'll let the females go easy on each other first. Don't worry, you'll get the chance to fight both of them, and if any of you refuse, the other gets shocked."

She gave him a mock salute and dragged Yanlei out the door. Kat struggled and looked back at Nick with wide, terrified eyes.

"Nick! Nick, help me!" she shouted and reached out towards him.

"Kat, be strong! You can do this!" Nick cried and watched as the two were dragged away. Augustine and Brighton both looked at him after the women were gone. Nick swore and crashed his fist into the side of the cage before shrinking back near the bars.

He couldn't lose anyone else.

Chapter 15
Friend or Foe?

Bianca

Bianca woke with a start. She pushed herself up on a warm bed, surrounded by familiar sights and smells. The screams from her friends echoed briefly in her ears then started to fade into throbbing silence. She looked around slowly and furrowed her brow in confusion. What was she doing in her bedroom? She could make out Kat's scent and her own. A purple down comforter covered her lower half. A lamp in the corner spilled light through the room, chasing away shadows, and helping her see.

This isn't right, she thought to herself. *I'm not supposed to be here. Or was it a dream? Was I dreaming?* She rubbed her sore head and glanced at the partially open door. "Kat? Babe?" she called.

There came no reply from the living room or the kitchen. Everything was perfectly, eerily, silent.

Bianca started to throw back her blanket when the door moved. She relaxed a little. It had to be Kat. Maybe it *was* all a nightmare.

"Kat, I had this awful dream."

"It wasn't a dream," an oddly familiar voice said.

The door swung open, and Bianca jerked back in alarm.

Trish stepped into the room, her red hair hanging in waves around her face. The vampire looked at her with fierce crimson eyes, her body swathed in a black-laced shirt, jeans, and leather jacket.

"Trish?" Bianca gasped and scrambled to get to her feet. Only, when she tried to move her legs, she realized they were bound to the foot of her bed. She lurched forward to free them and started to shout. "Help! He—mph!"

Trish threw herself on Bianca and shoved her into the mattress. Her knees pressed down on Bianca's arms as the vampire clapped a hand over her mouth. "Shut up!" Trish hissed and stared hard into Bianca's eyes. Trish's grew redder until Bianca felt compelled not to scream. She closed her mouth, and Trish moved her hand slowly, her palm hovering over Bianca's face. "Be quiet. I'm not going to hurt you."

"What do you want?" Bianca growled quietly, unable to hide her hatred for the vampire in her tone. The last time they saw each other for an extended period of time was at Legion headquarters as Trish explained how she'd been coerced into joining the Hunters who'd helped kill Gladus. Bianca hadn't believed her. After being attacked by Trish and then watching her rough up Henry, a *child*, Bianca wasn't willing to believe anything she said.

Trish leaned back and got off of Bianca carefully. "I need your help."

Bianca barked out a laugh. She braced herself up on her elbows. "You want *me* to help *you*? In what world would I do that? You helped kill Gladus. You hurt Henry! You turned me over to those monsters!"

"I did it to save my coven," Trish snapped. She sighed loudly and held up her hands. "But that's neither here or there. Listen, the vampires and werewolves are *both* in trouble, and I need your help to make sure no one else gets taken."

Bianca narrowed her eyes. Suddenly, memories of Tess's plan rushed back to her, along with the screams. "Kat!" she gasped. "Kat? My friends? Where are they, Trish? What did you do to them?"

"*I* did nothing to them," Trish said. "I got your sorry ass out of there while you were being held upside down by one of the Hunters. If it hadn't been for me, you either would have ended up as roadkill, in a cage, or on some Hunter's plate. But you didn't." She lowered her arms and bowed her head. "I'm sorry for what I did. I know that doesn't make up for anything, so let what I'm doing now make it right."

"What you're doing now? You think kidnapping me is going to

make things right? Or forcing me to abandon my friends?"

"They lost anyway," Trish argued. She brushed her red hair back, exposing a few white scars on her face, tokens left behind by her precious Hunters. She'd survived being in captivity to them, but the scars remained. For everyone in fact. "Your friends were taken. I got you out so that I could save your life and also give you some information. I doubt anyone will listen to me, but they'll listen to you."

"And why should I trust you?" Bianca asked and tugged on the leg restraints. She'd tied the rope tight enough!

"Because I don't know who else to go to," Trish admitted. She gripped her hair and tugged on it. "More vampires are gone than what's been reported," she said.

Bianca paused. "Wait, what?"

"You heard me. Some of my coven members have vanished, but no one has said a word about it. Joseph told me no one was missing, but when I stood outside the room and listened to him and Saul, he said he lied. That he said it to protect me. Why would he do that?" She pinched the bridge of her nose in frustration. "I don't want to say my brethren have something to do with the disappearances, because I honestly think some have fallen victims themselves. But Joseph won't listen to me, and neither will any of the other vampires."

"Why?"

"Because of what I did. I've had a handful of them tell me that they would have died rather than work for a Hunter."

"Well…"

Trish shot her a glare. "You don't get it, do you? Or wait, maybe you do since you gave yourself up to save that boy. What's so different between you turning yourself in to save a kid and me giving myself up to save my coven?"

"Because I didn't try to kill anyone!" Bianca snapped. "You kidnapped people. Hurt and killed people. How can you justify that?"

"You killed, too," Trish argued. "What about Lanzel? You murdered him with a single shot to the head. Pretty cold thing to do for a self-righteous avian."

Bianca shuddered as the memory crashed over her in an icy wave. She tried not to think about that night. Lanzel had been her first kill, and she was terrified it wasn't her last. He'd been a monster, forcing other people to take serums that made them sensitive to the Ether. He'd just never counted on Bianca having visions of the future that had led to his ultimate demise. "I was trying to stop him from killing everyone."

"And I did the same with the Hunters," Trish said.

Bianca eyed her sideways and huffed out a breath. Part of her wanted to believe the woman, but the other begged her to throw the vampire out the window. No one would have to know she was the culprit. She could say it was self-defense. But Bianca couldn't imagine spilling more blood. "Okay, fine, so some of your people have gone missing. Why do you think Joseph hasn't reported it?"

"I don't know, but I thought if anyone would listen to me, it would be Paytah. He's the Violet Marshall, after all."

Bianca frowned at her. "And you didn't go to him why?"

Trish gave her a deadpan expression. "Didn't you just scream at me that I'm a murderer?"

"Can you blame me?"

Trish grunted under her breath. She pulled a knife from her pocket and leaned forward. Bianca struggled, but only for a second before Trish snipped the bindings free from her ankles. Bianca pulled her feet in and scooted away from the vampire until her back hit the headboard. Trish didn't come after her, like Bianca expected. Instead, the vampire slid the knife back into her trench coat and leaned back on the bed.

"I brought you back home," Trish said slowly. "To your own bed. To your cloister. If I wanted to do anything to you, don't you think I would have dragged you somewhere hidden? You're not tied to a chair. There aren't any Hunters or a senka. It's just you and me."

Bianca glanced around at the familiar comforts of home. If she wanted help, she could send her bird out to Carlos. He, or one of the other avians, would likely be home. Trish really was taking a chance coming to her like this. And what other lead did Bianca have to go on? Kat and the others were gone.

She lowered her legs and leaned forward, hands resting on her folded ankles. "Fine, let's talk."

Trish's shoulders relaxed a little, and the hardness in her features softened. For a moment, she looked like a tired, beaten down woman, not the villain that Bianca had painted in her own head. "When I followed the Hunters the first time, it was because they murdered one of my coven members in front of me. He…was my best friend." Her tone and the way she hugged her leather jacket to her chest suggested they'd been more than that. "I couldn't watch that happen to any of my other coven members. I'm not saying what I did to Gladus, or to you, or to Henry, was right. But I didn't do it out of malicious intent." She looked up. "I'm sorry. I'm trying to do the right thing now."

Bianca ran her fingers through her dark hair, tugging lightly at the red tips. *I still don't trust her, but, I would have done anything to keep my cloister safe, too.* "I can't say that I forgive you, but I understand better what you did." She squeezed her ankle to ground her. "Why were you at the bar that night? When Nick and Brighton were taken?"

"It's one that Gavin and I used to go to when we wanted to get out from under prying eyes." Trish touched the trench coat fondly. "That night would have been his birthday. I was getting a drink in his honor, and…I needed a break from the coven. It just happened to be the same place you and the others were. I wasn't spying on you. I wasn't feeding information to Hunters. I went there to drink and forget."

She sounded sincere and honest at least.

"Okay, so then what happened?"

"I left around the time the bar fight broke out. I didn't want to get involved in it and have Joseph ground me for another year. So, I went home and didn't hear about the attack until later. Saul came to me and had me speak with Joseph who warned me what would happen if I helped the Hunters again." She rubbed her neck. "Guess my coven still thinks I'll turn against them."

This time Bianca didn't make a snide remark. "You said Joseph kept secrets from you?"

"Both he and Saul have," Trish said. "They both lied to my face. I started doing some digging and calling coven members who don't live in the area. There are several who have gone missing. And Joseph, he's been acting strange."

"How so?"

"He's usually calm and collected, but he's more furious about Paytah being named Violet Marshall than I think any of us thought." She shook her head. "I don't think it has to even do with Fraula's death."

"The coven still blames Paytah?"

"What, have you been living under a rock?" Trish scoffed. "Obviously. Big bad wolf bit off a vampire's head. Wouldn't you be nervous if he'd eaten Carlos?"

Bianca blanched at the thought. "Point taken. But then why is it so strange for Joseph to act that way?"

"Because he normally doesn't. He's been trying to comfort Saul and bring him more into the fold to distract him from what happened to Fraula. They were mates for decades. You don't forget a love like that. Ever since Joseph and Saul have been together, Joseph's temper has gotten worse." She glanced at the window and held her coat closer. "And Saul, he's acting like his old self again, and that scares me."

"Why?"

"Because I can tell it's fake. He's being nice and open to the other vampires. He spent months secluding himself from us. He even vanished for a while. And I don't know if that was under Joseph's orders or not. I just…" She pinched her eyes. "Look, what I did put a black mark on my coven. I'm not trying to blame my people, but if they're behind *any* of this, then I'd rather it be a vampire who solves the mystery and helps save the District."

Bianca nodded and glanced at the spot of the bed where Kat should be. Grief rippled through her heart. "I understand. I also get what it feels like to be thought of as the bad guy. Kind of went through that with my cloister before they accepted me."

"At least you didn't try to kill any of them," Trish mumbled.

"To be fair, you didn't try to kill any vampires either," Bianca said.

Trish lifted her eyes and let a tiny smile touch her red lips. "Hm, maybe Saul is right. Maybe you aren't so bad."

Bianca couldn't help but chuckle. "Glad I have someone else's approval." She sighed. "So, you want to tell Paytah, and you think the only way to do it is through me."

"Exactly." She reached into her coat and pulled out a folded letter. "Bring this to him. It's in my writing and signed in my blood. He'll know my scent, and if you tell him you saw me, then he'll really know it's from me."

Bianca blinked. "Wait, you don't want to come with me?"

"No," Trish said, shaking her head. "I don't think Paytah would try to do anything to me, but I don't want to risk it. And if Joseph or Saul happens to be around, let's just say I don't want them to know where I am or realize I'm behind any of this. As far as they're concerned, I've gone missing too."

Bianca didn't like it. This wasn't her information to tell, and it would be better coming from a vampire. Otherwise, it would sound like she was pointing fingers. Would a blood-signed letter be enough? She glanced at Trish and pressed her lips together, thinking. "I'll take it to him, but on one condition."

Trish narrowed her eyes. "What?"

"You need to come with me to see Carlos."

Trish jumped to her feet, snatching the letter away. "Are you crazy? He has even more reason to hate me after threatening his kid."

"*Exactly*," Bianca said. "You want us to trust you, right? Then you need to make amends. Talk with him. Let him see you mean what you say. I'll take the letter to Paytah, but then you can stay with Carlos or the cloister and be safe. You're in danger, too, if vampires are being hunted."

Trish opened and closed her mouth, looking like a fish out of water. She paced, shaking her head in a dumbfounded way. "This is the stupidest idea."

"So kidnapping me during a Hunter raid and then tying me to my bed to try to convince me to bring intel to an alpha is a completely sound one?"

Trish glared. "Don't make me hate you again."

"I don't think I'd be alive if you did." Bianca pushed herself off of the bed and approached the vampire. Trish rolled to the balls of her feet, ready to bolt like some sort of scared gazelle. "That's my offer," Bianca said. "You talk to Carlos with me, or I don't take the letter." She held out her hand.

Trish eyed it and looked at the paper. Her eyes smoldered, her lips pressing together so hard, they started to lose color. Finally, she slapped the letter into Bianca's hand in a partial handshake. "Fine. But he meets you here so I at least know I can escape, and so I don't have to face a very angry avian mother."

Bianca couldn't blame her. "Probably a good idea. If you should be afraid of anyone, it's Haley." She tucked the letter under her arm and went to her nightstand. She'd left her phone behind, not wanting it to go off at the worst possible moment. When she dialed Carlos, the phone only rang twice before his worried voice sounded over the other end.

"Bianca! Where are you? Are you hurt? What happened?"

Bianca blushed as warmth filled her. She was sorry for worrying him, but it heartened her to be reminded how much he cared. He and Haley had become second parents to her, and she couldn't have asked for anyone better. "I'm all right, Carlos. A…" She glanced at Trish. "Friend saved me. I'm back in my apartment."

He sighed deeply. "Thank the Mother. Haley and I thought we'd lost you."

"Bianca! Is it Bianca?" Henry's young voice chimed in on the other end.

Carlos grunted as if fending off the boy. "Yes, it's Bianca. She's okay. Now sit there before you make me drop—"

The phone clattered to the ground, causing Bianca to wince from the impact. Something scrambled on the other end before Henry shouted into her ear.

"Bianca! You're really okay? Are you coming home? Are the bad guys after you again? I'll fight them!"

Bianca fought back a smile. "Yes, Henry, I'm fine, and I'll come see you soon. The bad guys aren't here, but I know you'd protect me if they were."

"Yep! I'm not going to let anyone hurt you."

She closed her eyes. "Thank you. But I need to talk to your dad. Can you put him back on?

"Oh, okay," the boy whined. "Dad!"

Bianca waited until she heard Carlos's exasperated sigh. "I have to talk to you. And only you. Can you come to my apartment?"

The thick air of suspicion could have been cut with a knife. "Bianca…are you safe?"

"Yes, but I have news that I only want to relay to you. You can tell Haley later, but right now, I need your clear head."

Carlos grunted into the phone. "Fine, I'll be there in a moment." There was a pause. "Should Haley be prepared?"

Bianca knew what he was asking. She glanced at Trish again, took a breath, and spoke quietly. "No. I think everything is fine."

He hung up after that, and Bianca gestured to Trish. "Let's head to the living room. It'll be a little less claustrophobic that way."

The vampire fiddled with a necklace at her throat anxiously

before she nodded and followed Bianca into the other room. They barely made it to the couch when Carlos knocked. Bianca motioned for Trish to stay back and opened the door. Carlos enveloped her in a tight hug and swept her out into the hall, much to her surprise. He spun her around, pushing her behind him and stood at the entrance of the door with his great wings out and at the ready. Avians had the ability to shift into two forms; a bird and a seraph, the latter of which gave the avian wings and fierce talons on their hands.

"Carlos, what are you doing?"

Carlos didn't answer and peered into the room, his body in attack mode. It didn't take him long to spot Trish. His wings flared. "*You.*"

Bianca grabbed his arm before he could launch himself at her. "Carlos, stop, you don't understand! She's not trying to hurt us."

Carlos looked sharply at her and met her eyes. "How do you know she hasn't charmed you?"

Trish sighed loudly in the other room. "You could just ask me," she muttered. "I didn't charm her. Well, other than to shut her up. If I wanted her to do my bidding without anyone knowing, do you really think you'd be able to see me right now?"

Bianca shot her a look. "Not helping."

Carlos glared at the vampire and took a step towards her. "Why should I believe a damn thing you say after what you've done?"

Trish's shoulders slumped. She glanced over Carlos's shoulder at Bianca. "I told you he wouldn't listen. No one is going to believe me after what went down."

Bianca set her jaw firmly and brushed past Carlos's golden wings. He made a startled noise as she bodied her way back into her apartment and stepped towards the vampire. "We don't have time for this," she snapped at them both. She crossed her arms, standing at Trish's side, and pushed her caracara out of her mind and into Carlos's. The black and white bird flew to him and broke through the haze until she found his golden eagle also at the ready.

"*She's not controlling me,*" Bianca said to him mentally through her caracara. "*She has information about the vampires that she wants to share with Paytah, but she's afraid he won't listen because of her reputation. I thought if you talked to her, you could see for yourself that she actually wants to help. I hate what she did, too, but right now, we can use all the help we can get.*"

The tension eased in Carlos's shoulders, and he folded his

wings down his back. Still, his raptor-like eyes darted towards Trish. Mentally, his golden eagle preened the caracara, tugging lightly at the black feathers around her red cere. *"I don't want to lose anyone else."*

"I don't either, which is why we need to listen to her. There may be more behind this than we thought." She withdrew the letter from beneath her arm and held it out to him. "Here."

Carlos finally dared to step into her apartment. He shut the door and approached them, still in his seraph form. Trish backed off a step, but she didn't bolt away into the night, like Bianca kept expecting. Carlos took the letter and started to read it. After a few moments, his bushy eyebrows rose, and his gaze swept to Trish. "Is this true? Joseph isn't reporting all the vampires that are missing? He said you had vanished and mentioned two others."

"I did that by myself," Trish said. "After the meeting I had with him and Saul, I had a bad feeling that something was going on behind the scenes, so I took a chance and left before I became the next target." She shoved her hands into her pockets and shrugged. "I'm not the same person I was when the Hunters used me. If it's any consolation, I have nightmares about Gladus's death more times than I care to count. I'm living with what I did to her, and I regret it." She bowed her head and shifted on her feet. "I'm sorry for what I took away from you and the District."

Carlos held the letter tightly in his hand, his eyes misting. Not a single tear fell, though. Instead, he cleared his throat and glanced at Bianca. "You vouch for her?"

That's a loaded question, she thought. She looked at the vampire and the letter. It could all be an elaborate scheme meant to throw them off the scent. But deep down, Bianca didn't think that was the case. Trish could have exacted revenge any time over the past year and a half, and she'd chosen not to. Maybe it was time to give her the benefit of the doubt.

"Yes," Bianca said. "I do."

Carlos looked at the letter again and folded it, his fingers running over the creases slowly, deliberately. "I'll bring this to Paytah. For now, Trish, it would be better if you stay put for your safety."

"And so you can keep an eye on me," Trish added. "Where exactly do you want me to stay?"

Bianca glanced sideways at Carlos. Trish being around Carlos's kids would be unacceptable, and with Kat gone—the reminder hit Bianca like a blow to the stomach—there was room in her apartment. "Stay here with me," Bianca told the vampire. "At least until we get things settled."

Trish looked less than pleased with the idea, but she nodded all the same. "Thank you." She spread her arms at Carlos. "See? All safe and no trickery."

"We'll see," Carlos muttered. He touched Bianca's cheek and rubbed it tenderly with his thumb. She leaned into his palm. "I'm glad you're safe, little bird."

"Me too. But we need to bring the others home. Kat…she…" She fought back the tears, but they flooded her eyes this time.

Carlos pulled her into a hug and stroked her hair tenderly. "I know, Bianca. We'll do everything we can to get her back." He kissed her hair and tightened his hold. "We'll find her. I promise."

Bianca shook her head. "Don't make promises you can't keep." She'd already lost her birth parents and her sister. She couldn't stand the idea of losing Kat as well. She sniffed and tightened her hold on Carlos. "Be careful," she whispered to him. "I don't want anything to happen to you either."

He patted her back before releasing her. "If you need something, go find Haley. She's taking care of Henry and Madison."

"I will." Bianca stepped back and dried the tears from her eyes with her sleeves. "Go."

With a final nod, Carlos slipped out of the apartment, shutting the door quietly behind him. Bianca leaned against it and faced Trish, the vampire who had caused her so much trouble when she'd first reached the District. And yet, for the moment, she was grateful not to be alone.

Chapter 16
Marked

Tess rubbed her sore arm, loathing the syringe Arjun kept using on her. The elderberry burned, and she wasn't shy when it came to complaining about it. Arjun left her for a few hours while he ran his errands. She woke up without him in the loft and spent a good hour trying to get the cuff off her ankle, but to no avail. Calling on her blocked magic was just as useless. So, she settled back to watch tv and fret over her packmates.

Ray crept like a ghost into her mind. Each time his smiling face arose, quickly followed by his death gaze, she dissolved into tears. It didn't help that she'd missed her anxiety medication and now felt everything far more intensely. She didn't know how she would face Paytah after she'd let one of her brothers die. And what about Augustine? The wolf would never forgive her, if they ever saw each other again. How could Tess have been so stupid?

After Arjun returned, they shared a quick dinner of Mexican fast food together before Arjun finally released her ankle bond. A tentative push at her magic revealed that the elderberry still hadn't cleared out of her system yet. She craved the familiar heat which came with her magic and chased away the chill in her veins.

They sat in a jeep together, all the windows fully tinted despite it being illegal in Chicago. Tess nestled in the passenger seat up front and looked outside, watching the streetlights pass as she guided him towards her apartment. Her stomach twisted and reeled at the thought of facing Paytah. He'd told her not to do anything stupid. She hadn't listened, and now Ray was dead because of it. Because of her. The others were missing. And she was the only one who had been lucky enough to escape.

Sort of.

She glanced at Arjun. He hadn't said much since they started the drive. In fact, ever since returning to his loft, he'd become a man of few words. A foreboding grimness surrounded him that made Tess shift anxiously. He sat dressed in solid black, his guns hidden away in holsters on his hips. She'd spotted him sheathing a mean looking blade sideways on his spine. He was a walking arsenal, which made her worry for Paytah's safety even more. She'd tried to insist they should meet with Paytah without weapons. Arjun had laughed.

"You're staring," he said suddenly, making her jump. His dark eyes darted to her then back to the road. "I already promised you I wasn't going to hurt your alpha. What else do you need me to say?"

"Can you blame me for being nervous?" she asked. "I don't know you, and you're armed to the teeth."

"This is light compared to my usual arsenal."

Tess wrinkled her nose. "That's not exactly comforting." She motioned to another street for him to turn down. "You don't need me to guide you, do you?"

"No, but I enjoy your voice, so you can keep doing it."

I can't decide if I should be amused or want to smack him, she thought to herself. He was charming, she'd give him that, but that didn't make up for what he was. And no matter what code he talked about, she'd only ever known bad Hunters. Could she trust him to be any different? *Why save you if he's like the rest of them? Unless he's trying to use that to get close to Paytah. I don't know.*

"You're brooding," Arjun commented. "If you have questions, you can ask them, you know."

Tess glanced out the window again. "Who were you talking to on the phone after you dosed me?"

Arjun tightened his hands on the steering wheel. "A friend of mine. A Hunter who also follows the same code I do."

"How many are there of you?"

Arjun shrugged. "There's no telling. Some of us stay in touch with each another, but mostly, we keep to ourselves. Take care of problems in our, heh, districts, and reach out if we need help, which isn't often. I wish there were more of us than the other breed of Hunters."

"Yeah, me too," Tess admitted. She fidgeted uncomfortably. The elderberry made her body twitchy when it started to work its way out, almost like little needles poking at her skin, not enough to leave marks, but enough to agitate her. "Are you done dosing me?"

"I have no intention to do it again. Like I said, the only reason I dosed you was for my protection. I had to make sure you believed me."

"You think I do?"

He grinned. "If you really wanted to blast me out of the jeep, you could. The last dose I gave you was strong, but it should be almost out of you by now."

Tess decided not to let him know that he was right. She might yet need her magic. "How long have you been in Chicago, doing your thing?"

"Couple of years. Basically, once I got whiff that a fighting pit had formed, I came over. I've stopped a few people from getting taken, but I can never catch the perpetrators. They're fast. Strong. It's a wonder more people aren't missing, though if I had to guess, homeless parahumans probably have been taken more than anyone."

Tess frowned. "Why don't they come to the District if they don't have a place to go? Our community protects our own."

"Some folks are too prideful. They don't want to admit they need help, so they go about their own lives. And, no offense to your District, but sometimes, people don't want to be in covens or packs or cloisters. They want to be seen as normal."

Tess glared. "Are you saying that being a parahuman isn't normal?"

"It's not the norm," Arjun said. "You're targeted because you're different, the minority. People fear you because they don't understand you. If you're in a big group, that can breed even more fear."

"And what about you Hunters? You're not exactly normal yourselves."

"No," Arjun agreed and looked at her. "But if I take off my guns and go out on the town, no one's going to suspect I'm any different than what I am. A human." He pulled up to a light. "It must be hard, watching over your shoulder everywhere you go."

"I don't feel that way," Tess argued. "Because my pack is there to protect me, and I can protect them."

"Like you did against the Hunters who killed your friend?"

Tess's breath caught in her throat. The words stabbed her in the abdomen like a knife, driving deep and bringing tears of guilt and frustration to her eyes. She turned away from him furiously and tried not to let him see her get upset.

Arjun sighed. "I'm sorry for being harsh, but you can't always rely on others to save you."

"Then why are you helping me, huh? Why do you give a damn about my pack if we're all just a bunch of animals to you?"

"I never said that," Arjun replied, his voice softening. "I lamented how hard it has to be for you all to feel so different, but I never called you animals, or monsters, or any other term people like to use."

Tess thought about it, but he was right. He hadn't made any derogatory remarks. Still, she wasn't sure he didn't feel that way. Most humans who knew about them thought they were monsters. Granted, Tess could pass as human unless she used her magic, but she was still *different*. She felt no shame about it either. She proudly proclaimed to be a magus and part of a pack.

And yet Arjun made her question how much she unintentionally watched her back for people who would want to see her dead.

She grew quiet as they traveled to their destination. When they pulled into her apartment complex, she spotted both Paytah's truck and her mother's car outside. Waves of joy and fear crashed through her, joy to see her family, and fear of how they would react to what she'd done.

They parked, and Tess started to open the door.
Arjun caught her wrist, holding her back. "I'm sorry," he said. "I didn't mean to offend you. I have seen countless parahumans get tortured or die at the hands of idiots who think anyone who is different should be shot dead. I'm tired of it, which is why I walk the life I do. I don't want to see something like that happen to you."

Tess glanced at his hand then into his eyes, his gaze soft and repentant. She wanted to believe him, but he was right about one thing. "Like you said, you don't know who you can trust." She twisted her wrist free and got out of the jeep.

Arjun followed her and walked at her side to the downstairs door. They went up the stairs together, Tess's heart weighing heavier with each step she took. When she reached the door, she barely had a chance to stick her key in when it lurched open to reveal her mother.

"Tess!" Her mother wrapped her up in a tight hug, which Tess quickly returned. "Oh God, I was so worried about you. When we heard about Ray—are you all right? Are you hurt?" She pulled back and looked Tess over, touching her cheek, hair, and arm. She seemed oblivious to Arjun standing behind her.

"Mom, Mom! I'm fine." Tess caught her hands and smiled tenderly. "Let's go inside. I want to introduce you to someone."

Her mother looked over at Arjun for the first time, and the worry vanished, quickly replaced with cold, calculated rage. Tess couldn't hide her surprise. She'd never seen her mother give anyone that look before (save maybe Ray after he'd eaten a whole supply of bake sale cookies her mother had spent all night making). "Paytah's waiting," she said and stepped into the apartment.

Tess blew out a breath and followed her mother inside, motioning for Arjun to do the same. She locked the door behind him and looked slowly over to the hulking figure standing near the patio doors.

In a few quick strides, Paytah came to her side. He grasped her arm and pulled her way from Arjun, planting himself between the Hunter and Tess protectively. While her mother held Arjun at bay, Paytah turned to look down at Tess.

His gaze burned into her, making her feel like a child. He'd sounded worried on the phone, but she could only imagine his anger blazing over her disobedience.

She swallowed and bowed her head low to him. "I'm sorry, Paytah. I should have listened to you."

"Yes, you should have," he said in a low, deep voice with the echo of a growl behind it. But then the anger ebbed, and Paytah's softer features came through. He sighed and pulled her into a tight hug, almost smothering her. "You had us worried sick, Tess."

Tess buried her face against his chest and hugged him back, breathing in his warm, comforting scent. Tears stung her eyes. "I'm sorry. I know this is my fault, but I was just trying to help." She felt him stroke her hair, and she relaxed into his embrace. Maybe he didn't hate her after all. "Has there been any word from the others?"

Paytah grunted and reluctantly released her. "I'd rather we not go into details and instead see what your *rescuer* has to say."

He advanced on Arjun, towering over the Hunter in both height and attitude. No one in their right mind would want to tangle with the werewolf alpha right then.

Her mother joined her and grasped her arm, pulling her close. "We still haven't found the others," she whispered. "Did you see your father?"

Tess shook her head. "No. Arjun only took me to his loft. I didn't see anything."

"Quiet," Paytah ordered them into silence. He rounded on Arjun. "You said you wanted to talk. So talk."

Arjun bowed his head politely. "It's an honor to meet you, Alpha Paytah. I've been tracking the people following Tess and your wolves for some time. Like you, I'm interested in finding them and liberating the captives."

"*Why?*"

"It's what I do," Arjun said and rolled up his sleeve to show off the Hunter mark. "My family once helped protect parahumans from threats be they from humans or other parahumans. Some of us still follow that code."

"That mark doesn't exactly evoke a sense of comfort any longer," Paytah said.

Arjun pulled down his sleeve. "That's why I hoped my bringing Tess back to you would at least help me earn your trust. These kidnappings have been happening for years. It's reminiscent of a Hunter ring which formed ten years ago."

"I remember," Paytah said bitterly. "They were never caught."

"I think some of them returned and were spurred on by something. Most Hunters aren't stupid enough to go after Purple Door Districts." He reached into his pocket, but hesitated when Paytah stiffened. Tess met Arjun's eyes, and he slowly pulled out the tracking device he'd shown her. "I followed your members while they practiced to take down the Hunters. I got a tracer in one wolf's hair, and I've been tracking her ever since to see if it'll take me to the secret base. I want to help you find and free them. I have another Hunter who's interested in lending her services as well, if you'll have us."

Paytah held out his hand for the device.

Arjun kept it close, fingers curling around it. "Forgive me, but it's the only one I have."

"And you expect me to trust you? How do I know you're not leading us into a trap?" Paytah asked.

"I can't convince you of that. I thought bringing her back would help."

Tess set her jaw. She didn't like how he kept referring to her like she was some kind of prize token. But he had been kind to her, fed her, treated her with respect—despite chaining her to the bed. She swallowed. "Paytah, I think he's telling the truth."

"Do you?" Paytah grunted and kept staring harshly at Arjun. "And do you think I should jump headlong into danger like you?"

Tess grimaced while her mother shot Paytah a look and touched Tess's arm. "Paytah, that wasn't—"

"No," Tess said, shaking her head, "I deserved that. Paytah trusted me to obey him, and I didn't. And Ray paid the price." Paytah tensed again at the wolf's name. "I should have listened to you. I know that now, and I'm sorry. But if we have a chance to get the others back, then we should take it, shouldn't we?" She motioned to Arjun. "He could have killed me. Tortured me. Raped me if he wanted. But he didn't. He took care of me, fed me, and brought me back home. I owe my life to him, because those Hunters seemed pretty damn determined to kill me this time around."

Arjun nodded. "They don't usually keep magi alive. They're too hard to control, even with elderberry."

Paytah stiffened. "You know this from personal experience? I assume you used it on Tess as well?"

Arjun rolled his shoulders. "I had to keep myself safe, you understand."

Paytah glared and held out his hand again. "The device. If you want to help, then I may be able to accept that if you give me control of the tracker. I don't need you leading us down the wrong path."

Arjun gripped the device harder and shook his head. "I'm sorry, but I can't do that."

"Why not?"

"This is my job. I—"

Whatever he had been about to say was lost in the crash of

glass. The patio doors exploded, sending shards slicing through the room. Tess cried out in surprise and pain as pieces cut into her seconds before Paytah threw himself into her and her mother and sent them both tumbling into the kitchen, out of the way of danger. Tess hit the ground and shouted as her mother's head smacked against the linoleum.

"Mom!" She scrambled to her mother's side and quickly touched her neck. Thankfully, her pulse beat strongly.

Paytah's roar of anger and pain drew her attention to him. She looked up as he turned on Arjun, his body already starting to change into his biped werewolf form. Blood flowed from the cuts on his chest, arms, and legs. His lips pulled back in a vicious snarl as he yelled at the Hunter. "Liar!"

"I didn't do this!" Arjun tried to argue and sprang out of the way when Paytah swiped at him.

The werewolf grew in height, muscles bulging under his skin as black fur burst forth. His face elongated into the muzzle of a great wolf, his eyes shifting to golden orbs that burned with rage, a rage which fueled him through the pain.

He was halfway shifted when metal canisters rolled into the apartment. They exploded in blinding flashes of light and spewed noxious smoke through the room. Tess threw her arm over her eyes. She couldn't see! But she could hear people clambering over her balcony and rushing Paytah. The werewolf howled in pain as something squelched in his body.

No...no, no no! Paytah! Tess shoved her mother under the kitchen table to provide some kind of protection for her then struggled to her feet. She reached for her magic and felt her body scream in protest before the fire ignited in her palm. She raised it in the air in time to see a woman shove a blade into Paytah's thigh. The werewolf yowled and went down to one knee, blood coursing down his body where he'd been stabbed in his side and shoulder.

A man, wearing a mask, approached Paytah with a long blade in hand.

There was no sign of Arjun.

Tess called the flames into her other hand and threw both balls forward. The fire snarled through the air, cutting through the smoke, and crashed into the masked male Hunter. The force of her fire blazed so strongly, it sent him flying outside and off of her balcony.

The woman and another man rounded on her. "Take care of the bitch," the woman snarled, her voice familiar. Was this the same pair that had taken down her packmates? "I'll finish the alpha."

A gun went off, and Tess whipped up a magical shield, blocking herself form getting hit by a bullet. The male Hunter scowled at her and advanced while the female kicked Paytah hard in the side.

"Why won't you die?" the man snapped at Tess. "This is the last time you're going to interfere with us." He pulled out a second gun, brass knuckles gleaming on his hand, and started firing at her.

Tess ducked behind the table and shoved it onto its side, using it and her magic to block herself and her mother from the rain of bullets.

Her mother groaned and shook her head weakly. "Tess?" she asked and started to cough.

"Stay down, Mom." Tess touched her back and hurled a fire ball over the table at the man. She heard him swear and one of the guns clatter to the ground, but he fired with the other. Only the wooden table and Tess's shield kept them safe. She knelt beside her mother. "I'm sorry. I'm sorry."

Her mother blinked a few times as she listened to Paytah's roar and the gunfire. Magic blazed in her eyes, and she touched Tess's arm. "Help Paytah. I'll take care of this."

"But—"

"*Go*. Keep your shield up."

Tess nodded and clenched her fists. She waited until the firing ceased momentarily before she burst out from behind the table. Her shield hugged her close as she passed the Hunter. He moved towards her, but he never got the chance to fire. Her mother's flames lashed out in a fiery whip and coiled around the Hunter's arm, drawing a cry.

Tess moved through the smoke-covered room. Her one advantage was she knew the placement of all the furniture in the apartment, unlike the Hunters. She wove around an end table and the couch, making her way towards Paytah and the Huntress. The woman drew her gun and pointed it at the werewolf. Paytah managed to smack her arm away fast enough that the bullet fired off in another direction, leaving yet another hole in the apartment wall.

Her landlord was going to murder her if these assholes didn't first.

As the Huntress stepped back to shoot again, Tess hurled a fireball at her. The woman lifted her other arm, blocking the flames somehow. Had they come prepared, knowing a fire magus was going to be here? She looked around again for Arjun, but still, there was no sign of him.

Tess swore under her breath and wove around Paytah. She could smell the blood on him more than she could see it; he needed help. His raspy breathing worried her even more than the wounds.

When she passed a heavy picture frame sitting on her tv, she picked it up and hurled it at the Huntress. The corner caught her on the shoulder and knocked her back with a shout of surprise. Tess launched herself at the woman and kicked her legs out from beneath her. As the Hunter fell, Tess pressed her hand against the woman's cheek and called on her fire.

Flames crawled along her fingers and the Huntress's mask, burning it and leaving her sensitive skin exposed. She felt the woman's skin blister beneath her grip before she heard the Hunter's screams of pain. She didn't want to kill the woman. A mark like this would be hard to hide and would help them recognize her.

Something banged loudly in the kitchen, and Tess heard her mother shriek then start to cough. Tess peered through the smoke, trying to see what had happened, only to find her mother on her knees, grasping a bloody arm. A pale, violet smoke swarmed around her, making it hard for her to breathe. The male Hunter stood above her, gun drawn.

"Mom!" Tess shouted.

The distraction allowed the female Hunter to punch her in the gut. The air whooshed out of her, and Tess staggered. Another blow to her head knocked her off of the woman. She rolled away and watched the man point the gun at her mother's head.

"Mom," Tess rasped.

Suddenly, another person broke through the smoke and grabbed her mother by the shirt. He jerked her backwards and slammed a kitchen knife into the Hunter's shoulder. The man yelled, dropping his gun to the floor.

"Come on! We've done enough!" the Huntress shouted and slipped out onto the patio.

The man didn't hesitate. He ripped the knife out and hurled it back at his attacker before fleeing the scene. As he made it near the patio, Paytah, still wounded, lumbered after him, roaring so loudly, Tess thought her ears were going to bleed. She huddled and held her head while searching for her mother.

Her mother's savior knelt down beside her, and it took Tess a moment to realize it was Arjun. His face and head were covered with black cloth, obscuring his features. The only thing she recognized about him was his eyes. He helped her mother to her feet and over to a couch.

Tess struggled to sit up. "What happened?"

"Elderberry," her mother said and coughed again. "He had some kind of condensed vial of elderberry. The moment it exploded, I breathed it in and couldn't use my magic." She glanced at her arm and slowly pulled a shaky hand away from the bloody wound. "He shot me in the arm."

Tess touched her mother's knee and slowly got to her feet. Her stomach and head hurt, but the injuries were minor compared to the ones both her mother and Paytah had sustained.

"Paytah," Tess said and looked over at the werewolf.

He stood framed in the shattered remnants of her glass patio doors, his body heaving with each labored breath. Blood pattered on the floor around him, knives sticking out of his legs, side, and arm. The wounds would have killed him as a human, but his biped form was much bigger, stronger, and more resilient. Still, as Tess approached him, she saw a madness in his golden eyes.

"Paytah?"

He snapped his head towards her and glowered. She held up her hands. "It's Tess. It's okay, I'm not going to hurt you."

But she realized, after a moment, his gaze wasn't on her but rather on Arjun. He'd pulled the mask down from his face, which happened to be one of the black cardigans from her room.

Tess swallowed and opened her mind to Paytah so she could speak to him and he could respond. *"Paytah, easy. He helped us."*

"You're a naive child to think that," he said to her, his voice sounding more animal than human. Pain laced every word. *"He hid during all this until it was convenient. That tracking device, who was it really for?"* He looked at her with a mixture of pain and rage in his eyes. *"You brought a traitor to the pack. To me!"*

"No!" Tess cried out loud. "It wasn't him! He saved my mother."

"To try to gain your trust! When are you going to learn to do

what's best for the pack and not for you?"

Tess's breath caught in her throat. "Paytah…I…I didn't mean for any of this to happen."

"You never do, but it still happened." He clutched his side and staggered, eyes shut. *"Ray is still dead. And those monsters tried to murder us all, and you're defending one of them!"*

"He's not a monster!" Tess shouted.

"Hey," Arjun said gently and approached them, both of his hands up. One glistened with blood from trying to staunch her mother's wound. "I had nothing to do with this. I was trying to help you. *They're* the real enemy."

"Liar!" Paytah shouted, his eyes snapping open to reveal a monster rather than the man she knew and loved.

Tess moved at the same time as the werewolf. He raised a mighty paw to strike Arjun down. Tess got between them, knocking Arjun back with her shoulders, and threw out her hand instinctively. When she realized what she was about to do, she tried to stop herself, but it was too late. A fireball flew towards Paytah's stomach at the same time his paw met her face.

The world exploded in fragments of light and pain. She was barely aware of falling to the ground before her head smacked against the wooden floor. Tess gasped, her ears ringing with sudden pain. Her face burned and wept crimson tears. She touched it with a trembling hand; her fingers came back sticky with blood.

Suddenly, she smelled burnt fur and flesh. She rolled partially onto her back and stared at Paytah in horror.

He stood hunched over, his chest burnt from her magic. The look in his eyes showed nothing but a single emotion; betrayal.

"Get out," he said in a low, dangerous voice. *"You're no longer pack. Get out*!" He roared, bloody teeth gnashing in a threatening snarl.

The world slowed and shifted. The ground opened up beneath her and she plummeted with no lifeline to reach out to.

She choked back a sob, unable to beg him to reconsider. Her vision started to blur as the pain in her face won out.

And then there were arms around her, picking her up off of the floor, cradling her against a broad chest. She heard Paytah roar again, but it wasn't at her this time. She blinked and looked up as Arjun carried her through the smoky room.

"I have you," he said, though her foggy ears barely heard him.

He ran towards the patio even as Paytah struggled to follow him. In the distance, Tess heard her mother shout her name as Arjun leapt off of her balcony and into the night.

Chapter 17
Walking With Ghosts

Paytah

Pain.

Nothing but pain raged through his body and heart.

In all his long years, Paytah had faced many insubordinate wolves, but never once had he been forced to throw someone out of the pack. There was always a way to help them, to save them. But when Tess had stood in front of the Hunter who had brought nothing but sorrow and bloodshed to his pack, his resolution to repair any relationships between himself and his packdaughter had gone up in flames. *Her* flames.

He wobbled near the patio, staring off into the dark where the Hunter had fled with Tess. Without Tess using her magic in his head, he heard nothing but blood drumming in his ears. He was losing too much. The wounds numbed more with each passing moment which meant death was lurking around the corner, waiting to welcome him like an old friend.

And for a moment, death sounded peaceful. He'd find Ray and Gladus there. He'd meet the packmates he'd lost over the years. His duty as Violet Marshall would end.

But the desire was fleeting as images of his beloved mate, his pack, and the community he'd sworn to protect flooded his mind.

He staggered and fell to the floor, his body slowly shifting from wolf back to human. He pulled the blades free before he transformed so as not to worsen the wounds. His natural healing struggled to take over, but he could feel the burning sensation of wolfsbane gnawing at his torn flesh.

They'd come for him, there was no doubt about that.

"Paytah!" Iris shouted and shook his shoulder, jarring his poor wounded body. "Paytah, stay with me. Stay conscious. Help is on its way." Her warm hands ran over his skin, searching for his wounds. He felt a faint spark of magic, but it vanished as quickly as it had come. "Damnit, my magic is still blocked. I'm sorry, just stay with me."

And then his head was on something soft; Iris's lap. He blinked a few times and gasped as the final bone snapped back into place, leaving him a bloody human mess in her arms. He heard sirens in the distance, but he drifted, too dazed to wonder if they were for him.

His heartbeat drummed slower, his vision pulsing to the same tempo until it went out completely.

"Iris," he said, voice slurred.

"Paytah, hold on!" she shouted.

He swallowed hard, closed his eyes, and slipped away.

***

Paytah found himself in the middle of a smoky purple room. Pale light filtered around him from the sky, playing tricks on his eyes as it wove through the fog. He walked slowly, glancing around for signs of trouble, but only silence greeted him. Was he still trapped in Tess's apartment and fighting the Hunters? Was this some sort of dream? Lack of pain should have been his first indication he was no longer conscious, but he couldn't get his mind to focus long enough to be reasonable.

"I left a huge mess in your paws, didn't I?" a familiar voice echoed around him.

Paytah blinked and turned, searching for the speaker. As he moved, the smoke began to clear until a room appeared before him. A cheery fireplace popped and crackled behind a round table covered in lace, a violet teapot, and cups. A thick, red couch sat to one end of the room, resting atop a beige rug with intricate black markings. The rest of the room was shadowed, like an artist had forgotten to complete his painting. Still, Paytah knew this place.

When he blinked again, one of the two chairs at the table was occupied by a beautiful Black woman. Colorful cloths bound her hair on top of her head. Purple silk robes flowed off of her body, the hems lined in gold. She looked as she had the last time he saw her alive; healthy, alert, hopeful.

"Gladus," he said deeply, his throat tightening with emotion.

"Hello, Paytah. Come take a seat. I made your favorite tea." She poured it into the cup for him, the scent of earl grey and lavender making his nose twitch. "You look like you have a lot on your mind. I thought I could help."

"Is this a dream? Or am I dead?"

Gladus shrugged and picked up her tea cup. "Maybe you conjured me. Maybe I'm here. Does it really matter so long as you have someone to talk to?"

Paytah took a seat and grasped his cup. "No. It's good to see you. I've missed you so much."

She reached across the table and grasped his free hand. Her warm touch brought a wave of comfort that loosened his tense muscles and made him sink down in his chair. She felt, smelled, and looked real. Maybe he'd just imagine she was. "I've missed you, too."

Paytah wasn't exactly certain how much to explain. If this was all in his head, then she knew it already, and if not, it seemed weird confessing his life's story to a ghost. "My packmates are going missing, and one is dead. Ray. A few other parahumans are vanishing, but my pack seems to be the primary target. And Legion won't do a damn thing about it."

"Legion is not at your beck and call," Gladus said. She held her cup between her hands and peered into the dark liquid. "Do you think Chicago is the only place that loses people? Legion covers the entire world and has to put their focus on the most important issues. For a place like Chicago, people vanishing is a dime a dozen. Drugs. Murder. Trafficking. Plenty of things can make a person disappear."

"But these are parahumans. It's Legion's job to help us."

"It's Legion's job to help stop the most dangerous threats. It's our job as Violet Marshall to take care of the smaller ones. Finding missing wolves is under our jurisdiction, not theirs." She chuckled. "Or should I say yours.*"*

Paytah grunted under his breath and drank some of the tea to calm his nerves. The fact he could both taste and smell the earthy, floral mix made him wonder if he hadn't quite survived the Hunter attack. "It feels like ten years ago all over again. We knew what the Hunters were doing. People were going to move in on them, and it all fell apart." He shook his head. "I don't want that to happen again, Gladus. I knew being a Violet Marshall would be hard, but each step I take forward, I feel like I take two back. I don't know who to trust."

"You mean like Tess?" Gladus asked.

Paytah stiffened. He barely remembered shouting at her. In a moment of rage, pain, and betrayal, he'd told her to leave the pack. He was starting to regret that now, and yet, Ray was dead because of her. And those Hunters had almost killed him. Who was to say her friend hadn't helped in the attack? How else would they have known where Paytah was meeting Tess? She was too hot headed, and it made her a threat to the pack. "I guess I have my own Trish."

"Ah, Trish," Gladus said and shook her head. "They were both trying to protect their people, even if they did it in a foolish manner. They had good intentions."

"How can you say that?" Paytah gasped. "Trish killed you."

"As I recall it, she wasn't the one who held the gun to my head." Gladus lifted an eyebrow at him and took another sip of tea. "Paytah, the world isn't black and white. There isn't only good and evil. We walk a very gray line, and sometimes we have to take chances or potentially trust the wrong people to make headway in this world. I brought in many parahumans, some who turned into upstanding citizens, and some who didn't make it. I mourn the ones I lost and celebrate those who survived and prospered. I can't help but think that I could have done something more to help the ones who struggled. Trish is one of them, but I don't think she's lost.

"If she'd wanted to kill me, she could have easily ripped my throat out with her fangs. I wouldn't have had a chance to stop her. And Tess,...if this Hunter did betray you, then he betrayed her as well. Trying to amass a rescue attempt may have been stupid, but she felt like she needed to do something." She smiled. "Not unlike a werewolf I know who thought it wise to rush into an abandoned warehouse to rescue a kidnapped avian."

Paytah fought a small smile. He'd been pretty bullheaded, hadn't he? He'd put Tess and Kat at risk when he'd allowed them to help him save Bianca. In fact, it had been Tess who had called upon Legion and gotten them the help they so desperately needed. In times of trouble, she did think with her heart over her head, but she meant well. Gladus was right about that.

He wasn't so sure about Trish.

"You think I made a mistake banishing Tess from the pack."

"I think you should look at what you stand to lose by doing so," Gladus replied. "You remove Tess, you're likely going to lose Iris and Brighton as well, if he makes it out of this alive. And then what of your other packmembers? I'm sure many will side with you as their alpha, but some might feel put off that you banished her without a vote, especially when she helped save your life."

Paytah frowned, the worry lines on his brow deepening until they made his head hurt. She had saved him from the female Hunter, hadn't she. She'd put herself between him and the woman and used her magic to stop her. And when he'd spoken of Ray, she'd reacted as any of their wolves would have; with heartbreak. "I know you're right, but I don't even know where she is now. That Hunter took her and fled." He leaned back with a frustrated sigh. "Iris is going to kill me. If I'm not already dead."

"Oh, they tried to take you out. You're lucky you had two packmates to help defend you." She patted his hand fondly. "You're not a weak alpha, Paytah. But you do have trust issues. And you try to take the world on your shoulders when you should be sharing it with the others. That's especially important as a Violet Marshall. You can't fix everything."

He tilted his head in her direction. "Meaning I should be talking with my wife about this and having more pack meetings."

Gladus lifted her teacup to him and chuckled. "That would be a start. There's no shame in asking for help. I did it enough during my time."

Paytah nodded and clutched the cup in his hands. His large palms dwarfed the fragile porcelain; one move, and he could crush it into a thousand pieces if he wanted. But he couldn't tighten a chokehold around his pack like that. They needed the chance to breathe and grow, including Tess. They would stand stronger together.

He rubbed his eyes and looked at her between his fingers. "I miss you."

"I miss you, too, you stubborn pup," Gladus said. She lifted her arms and motioned to him with a flick of her fingers. "Come

here. Give me a hug before you wake up."

Paytah went to her and wrapped her in a tight hug. He breathed in her herbal scent and sank against her motherly hold. He'd never had the chance to say goodbye. Only ashes had remained. "I'm sorry I couldn't save you."

"Stop," Gladus said and tugged on one of his braids. "It was my time. Now, you go back there and do what you must to save your wolves. Pack stands together. And the pack is strongest when it works side by side." She kissed his cheek. "Give Rozene my love."

"I will." Paytah lifted his head to say something else, but Gladus had vanished, leaving him once more in the smoky violet world. He looked around for any sign of escape, but he was as lost as when he had arrived.

And then, out of nowhere, a burst of light blinded him and yanked him back to life.

***

Paytah jerked awake, sweat rolling down his skin, his chest heaving with frantic breaths. The sterile smell of a hospital made him sneeze and wince in pain. Everything hurt. Even his nose.

"Paytah! Is he okay?" a man asked.

"Be careful! He's going to hurt himself," a softer female tone insisted.

"Pups, give him some space. Paytah, lay back." Rozene's gentle yet stern voice pulled his attention to her like a lifeline. His mate took his hand and touched his brow. Her palm felt mercifully cool. "You're burning up. Vic did what he could, but you need to rest."

"Vic?" Paytah said in a weak slur.

The magus bent over in a chair in the corner of the room, his own body drenched with sweat, likely from the effort of healing him. Vic wasn't as powerful of a healer as Gladus. "Iris called on me after she dialed emergency. The doctors have seen to you, and I've offered what magic I have. Though I will say, it would have been easier to work in less cramped quarters."

Paytah then realized that most of his wolves had squeezed into the room. Quince checked his vitals, frowning grimly as he jotted Paytah's numbers down. There was no sign of Pedro or their children, so Paytah could only assume the other father wolf had stayed at home with them. Jackson and Tamara crowded close to his left side while Rozene and Quince hovered over his right.

Carmen sat in a wheelchair a short distance away, looking at him anxiously. Her cheeks blossomed a rosy color, much better than the last time he'd visited her.

Becky and Mikayla hovered at the foot of his bed, the waitress frowning, and Mikayla shaking her head admonishingly. "You don't do anything easy, do you?" she asked.

"When have I ever?" he replied in a gruff voice. He looked at their laps, noticing Heidi sprawled across their legs, passed out. "You should get her home."

Mikayla snorted stubbornly. "Uh, with all due respect, Alpha, hell no. We're not leaving until we know you're safe."

Rozene rubbed his arm. "They've been keeping watch since you were brought in last night."

Paytah blinked. "I've been out that long?"

Quince made a strangled noise in his throat. "You're lucky you woke up at all! Stab wounds in your abdomen, one in your back above your kidney, burns across your chest, bullet wounds in your right arm and leg, another stab wound in your shoulder, and one a hair shy of your femoral artery in your other leg. If it had been half an inch closer, you wouldn't be sitting here. You'd have bled out before you even made it to the hospital!" The man shuddered and tapped into his tablet. "You should be dead, Paytah."

"I think that's what had been planned," Paytah said. He looked around the room at all of the worried eyes staring at him. He missed Ray and Augustine cracking jokes to lighten the mood. They would have known what to say to shake off the stress and anxiety clouding his packmates' minds. It took him a moment to notice another missing pair of eyes. "Iris? Where's Iris?"

Rozene smiled sadly. "Resting in another room. She was shot and doused with elderberry. She stayed awake long enough to tell us what happened, but she's been asleep for the past few hours."

Paytah tensed. "How much did she tell you?"

The room fell eerily silent. Jackson finally sighed. "You met up with Tess and a Hunter, then Hunters attacked you. You banished Tess, and the guy ran off with her. And now you're here. Does that about cover it?"

Paytah heard the disapproving tone in his beta's voice, but he didn't correct him for it. Gladus—or his manifested guilt—had done enough to make him think over his rash decision. "Tess also saved me. If it wasn't for her, I would have been killed."

Tamara paled. "But why? Why attack *you*?"

Paytah shook his head. "Maybe to make it easier for them to steal you away? I don't know, Tamara. But if they're bold enough to try to take down an alpha, none of us are safe apart." He cleared his throat. "We work better together." He rolled his face towards Carmen. She looked so small wrapped up in the blankets in her wheelchair. "How are you feeling, little one?"

"Me? You should be worried about you," Carmen said. She sounded better without the breathing tube inserted in her throat. "I'm working on getting stronger." She moved her blanket and shifted her leg slightly. "See? Got some movement."

Paytah smiled, though he didn't miss the frustration in her voice. She wanted to be up and out of that chair as fast as possible. Stubborn, like the rest of them. "I'm glad." He glanced at his beta. "Thank you for watching over them while I slept."

Jackson nodded. He wrapped his arms around Tamara and pulled her close until her cheeks turned rosy again. "Someone else stopped by to see you. He said it was urgent."

"Who?"

"Carlos."

Paytah blinked in surprise. Why would Carlos be looking for him? Had he received word about Bianca? Or were the Hunters on the prowl for avians now? "Is he still here?" When Jackson nodded, Paytah blew out a breath. "Bring him in."

"Are you sure?" Rozene asked. She laid her hand along his arm soothingly. "Paytah, you barely survived an assassination attempt."

"He wouldn't be waiting around unless it was important." He tried to lift his left arm, but between the bandages and the IV sticking out of it, he only made it about a quarter of the way before being forced to drop it on his stomach again. He saw Quince's look of disapproval, but he didn't buy into it. "Make some room for him, will you? Mikayla, why don't you and Becky take Heidi out into the hall and let her rest?"

Mikayla started to protest, but Becky silenced her as she rose and scooped her sleeping daughter into her arms. "You stay," she whispered and slipped out of the room. Mikayla snorted and gave Paytah a look that dared him to remove her.

Had he been in better condition, he might have tried just for the fun of it.

Jackson followed Becky out and returned a few moments later with Carlos on his heels. The avian took one look at Paytah and grimaced.

"You look like hell."

"I feel worse," Paytah said with a dry chuckle. The sound quickly dissolved into a wheezing cough. "Damn, ow…hmm." He shook his head. "Jackson said you had something for me."

"I'd hoped to discuss it more…privately," he said, glancing at the six other wolves surrounding him.

Paytah shook his head. "Whatever needs to be said, my beta and mate at the very least have the right to hear it."

Carlos sighed. He pulled a piece of paper out of his jacket and passed it over to Rozene so she could open it and hold it out for Paytah to read. "We received a tip that not all of our District leaders are being honest with us."

Paytah looked over the note, his brow creasing once more. A familiar scent lingered on it that he couldn't quite identify. "Joseph lied? But why?" he asked.

Carlos shook his head. "I don't know, but I find it very suspicious. Especially since Saul, too, seems to be in on the lies. If anyone had a vendetta against you, it would be Saul."

Paytah gave Carlos a look. "You think Saul is behind the assassination attempt? If he wanted to kill me, he could have done it himself."

"I'm not saying he is, but the letter suggests we're not getting the full truth, and there's no reason why Saul and Joseph would be lying unless they're somehow in cahoots with the Hunters."

Paytah growled under his breath. Could he trust no one? "Where did you get this information from?"

Carlos hesitated. "You're not going to like it."

Paytah stiffened, as did just about every other person in the room, including Vic. "Well?"

Carlos sighed and bowed his head. "Trish."

"What!" Vic exploded. "You saw her? *Trish* brought this information to you, and you let her go?"

Rozene held up a hand to try to bring some semblance of peace. "I thought she was missing."

Carlos nodded. "That's what Joseph and Saul want us to

believe. And no, Vic, I didn't *let her go*." He tucked his hands in his pockets. "She rescued Bianca from the Hunters, and they're both currently at Bianca's apartment."

Vic's face turned the same shade of red as one of the "are you in pain" emojis on the scale chart. "You left Bianca *alone* with that bitch? After what she did?"

Carlos rolled his eyes to the ceiling for patience. "She had no reason to lie to me."

"Unless *she's* working with the Hunters, too!"

"We don't know that," Carlos said.

But that didn't stop the argument. Paytah listened to the two men squabble back and forth. Jackson tried to get them to stop, but avian and magus got into each other's faces and continued bickering while Paytah stared between them.

Suddenly, he started to chuckle. The chuckle turned into a low laugh, then a loud one which shook his poor, tender belly.

It brought the men's argument to a grinding halt.

"What's so funny?" Vic snapped.

"Nothing, it's just…Gladus was right. This world really isn't black and white." At the confused expressions on the men's faces, Paytah shook his head. "Never mind. As much as you hate to hear it, Vic, I'm going to have to side with Carlos on this one. She hasn't tried to harm any of us for over a year and a half, and she's provided valuable information."

"She killed Gladus!" Vic shouted.

Paytah sighed. "Vic—"

"I'm not going to stand by this. You can believe what she says, but I'm not letting my ward get used." He rose, shaking his head furiously. "I wish you well, Paytah, but I have to protect my own." And before Paytah could say another word, the magus turned on his heel and left.

Everyone fell silent for a moment before Jackson broke it with a snort. "Well, that could have gone worse."

Paytah turned his attention back to Carlos. "This is the closest lead we have to go on. I want you to reach out to Joseph and Saul and tell them to visit me here."

This time Rozene bristled and raised her voice. "Have you lost your mind? If one of them is involved in your attempted murder—"

"I'm in the safest place possible," Paytah said. "And surrounded by my packmates. They won't do anything stupid in plain sight."

"No," Rozene agreed. "They'll wait until you're left unguarded."

Paytah took her hand in his and squeezed it. "You have to trust me, my love. If this brings us any closer to the truth of what happened to our wolves, I'm willing to risk it." He glanced over at Carmen. "There's something else I'm wondering about. You said you saw three people during the attack, while Tess saw two, right?"

Carmen nodded and bit her lip. "I still can't remember anything more than that, though."

"I know, that's okay, Carmen. You haven't seen either Joseph or Saul since the accident?"

"No."

"Good. I want you to be in the room when they come. Just observe."

Carmen frowned in confusion, but she didn't argue. She settled back in her wheelchair, fighting to keep a brave face.

"I don't like this," Rozene said and clutched his hand between hers. After a long, suffered moment, she sighed. "Call him, Carlos." She looked at the avian, her hands tightening around Paytah's. "Call on them both."

Chapter 18
Charmed

Paytah

It took a lot of convincing, orders, and some snarls to get his pack to clear out of his hospital room. Having a doctor practically explode over the amount of people around his sick patient helped —not all parahuman doctors believed in having an entire pack present. They were sent into the waiting room under Jackson's guidance. Only Rozene, Carmen, and Carlos remained behind well after Carlos had made the call to Joseph.

"He wasn't very inclined to make a trip to the hospital," the avian remarked. "Something about having other affairs to address, but I insisted it was important. And that he and Saul would want to hear what you had to say."

"Good," Paytah said. "If what Trish indicated is true, we may be closer to finding our people than we expected. Though, I hate to think that either Joseph or Saul is behind this."

Rozene sat on the edge of his bed and wove her fingers through his, lending him strength while his body struggled to stay awake. "They both have reason to hate us. Saul because of Fraula's death, and Joseph because of not being named the next Violet Marshall."

"He never wanted it, though," Paytah insisted. "Every time we talked about it, he said that was the last thing he'd want bestowed on him. He didn't like the idea of putting everyone else above his coven."

Rozene shrugged. "When a power struggle comes into play,

people change. Their ambitions can become less...desirable. Perhaps he saw the power you received and felt jealous."

"Or Saul decided he wanted to avenge his mate," Paytah added with a quiet sigh. "I still have nightmares about it. I never wanted to do that to her, and I *did* try to stop. My bond with the vampires isn't as strong as with the pack."

"I know, love," Rozene said. She lifted his hand to her cheek and kissed his palm affectionately. "You don't have to explain it to me. I've heard you cry out in the night. If Saul would *listen*, maybe he'd understand the hold the senka had on you."

Paytah shuddered. He'd been a puppet, the spell tying a string to every nerve in his body, forcing him to obey, no matter how Paytah tried to fight it. He hadn't been in control of himself, which was one of his greatest fears. Werewolves had to be careful not to lose their tempers because of the damage they could inflict (though the same could be said of all parahumans). Wolves, generally, could do more harm, as Paytah well knew. Could vampire charm take control as well? Could other magi manipulate his mind and body? He thought of Vic's rage over Gladus's death, but he knew it was due to passion and grief. He wouldn't do anything to upset the balance between his ward and the rest of the District.

Joseph and Saul...Paytah wasn't so sure. And not knowing made his fur stand on end. He wanted to be able to, at the very least, trust the duke. The rest of the District leaders would need to be informed if his suspicions were right. Mia, frustrating cat that she was, would have a field day with this.

He glanced over at Carlos. The avian sat near the closed window and Carmen. He kept checking his phone, texting Bianca every few minutes to make sure she stayed safe. Apparently Paytah wasn't the only one unsure about trusting Trish.

He needed to call Tess, if she actually answered. What if her Hunter kept her cellphone? What if he wouldn't let her speak to the pack? What if she didn't want to hear a damn word Paytah had to say?

Gladus's gentle advice suddenly echoed in his mind, reminding him not to take on the world alone.

He squeezed Rozene's hand and kissed it. "Once we talk with Joseph and Saul, I need to call Tess. I have to fix this between us." He shook his head, his grip tightening. "I'm worried about her. If the Hunter is working with the others, she's in grave danger, and

Iris won't forgive me for losing her daughter."

"No, she won't," Rozene agreed. She leaned towards him and brushed dark hair out of his eyes. "One challenge at a time. We can't solve every problem at once. Joseph and Saul are our priority now."

Paytah offered a small smile. "Thank you. You always know how to ground me."

"You do the same for me." She grinned back at him, little laugh lines forming at her lips and eyes. They made her look even more beautiful to him.

But her expression faded when they both caught scent of vampires approaching. Paytah sank down in the bed, looking more wounded than he felt. Jackson brought Saul and Joseph into the room and shut the door a little loudly behind them as he left.

Joseph stood tall, clothed in dress pants, a red button-up shirt, and a long black coat. Saul, as always, wore one of his dark suits. Paytah took note that his tie was missing, an unusual absence for the vampire. Both vampires surveyed the room, Saul's gaze resting briefly on Carmen before rushing back to Paytah. They seemed calm and like themselves. Paytah breathed in deeply, catching an odd, faint scent, but he couldn't quite recognize it.

Joseph bobbed his head. "I'm glad to see you alive. When we heard of the attack, I feared the worst."

Paytah grunted and grimaced, shifting to get more comfortable. "They certainly did their best to kill me. They had wolfsbane with them, so I can only assume I was the main target."

Joseph clicked his tongue. "This is getting out of hand. First wolves have gone missing and now their alpha is being hunted? What are they hoping to accomplish?"

Paytah cocked his head. "I've wondered the same. I'm also wondering why you and Saul haven't been telling me the truth."

Joseph stiffened slightly and shot a glance at Saul then back to Paytah. "What do you mean?"

"One of your vampires came to me and informed me your coven has lost more members than you've revealed. The last you told me, only Trish and two others were missing."

Joseph shifted anxiously on his feet until Saul touched his arm lightly. The suited vampire muttered something quietly to him, his voice so soft, Paytah couldn't hear it. The duke nodded and seemed to regain his composure. "They were members who haven't been at the coven house for some time. When we didn't hear back from them, we weren't certain it was because they were taken, or if they were busy living their own lives. I never meant to deceive you. Besides, your wolves have been targeted more than anyone else. I would assume that would be your main concern."

There was a bite to his tone that Paytah didn't like. "Everyone in the District is my concern, whether they're werewolf, vampire, cat, avian, magus, or fae. It's my duty to make sure you're all safe."

"*Safe?*" Joseph said with a laugh. "Since the first day you took on the mantle of Violet Marshall, you've focused on your wolves over anyone else. Would you have even cared if I told you vampires were missing if your precious wolves weren't disappearing as well?"

"Mind yourself," Rozene said with a low growl. "You assume too much."

"Do I?"

Paytah narrowed his eyes. He looked between the two vampires. Joseph kept his hard gaze on him, his eyes flecked with red as if hunger yearned to take over. Saul didn't move a muscle or speak a word, other than in a whispered tone to Joseph. He stared at his duke and listened, hands behind his back, eyes fixed on his duke's, hardly blinking.

Joseph folded his arms over his thin chest. "Paytah, if we're going to talk about honesty, then you need to come clean, too. You took on this role so you could protect your wolves, no one else."

"You know that's not true, Joseph," Paytah argued fiercely. "I've done all I can to stand by the District and watch over everyone. I've called on Legion. I've—"

"You've asked others to clean up your mess," Joseph snapped. "But you won't get your hands dirty, not until you have reason to."

Paytah shut his mouth with a loud click. *This doesn't sound like him at all. Joseph can be confrontational, but usually not to this extent. He has no grounds to blame me for playing favorites. I brought them all in when people went missing.* Yet, when he thought about his conversation with Joseph days ago, the duke had been more aggressive then, too. "What would you have me do then?"

"Step down," Joseph said without hesitation.

Paytah couldn't stop himself from snorting. This smelled wrong in so many ways. Joseph could be outspoken, but he was mindful about announcing his feelings. He didn't want them to be used against him. "And who would you have it go to? Carlos?" He nodded towards the avian. "Mia, perhaps? *You*?"

"Any one of us would be a better fit for the position. Gladus might have groomed you to take her place, but the only reason you did was because she named you in her will and the others didn't fight it." Joseph glared. "Maybe someone else should be in charge. Someone who hasn't blatantly killed another District leader's member."

The red in his irises burned brighter with each uttered word. Paytah looked at Saul. He watched the man's eyes carefully and noticed a slight glint which hadn't been there before. The vampire glanced at him then back to his duke.

Charm? Is that what Saul's doing?

"You don't believe that," Paytah said calmly, causing Joseph to frown. "You and I spoke about the incident. You were angry, but you understood the severity of senka magic. We came to an accord, Joseph. This isn't you." He swept his gaze to Saul. "What have you done to him?"

The vampire's eyebrows shot up in alarm. "What do you mean? I've done nothing but stand by my duke this entir—"

"Cut the act," Paytah snarled, his teeth starting to sharpen with his anger. Movement out of the corner of his eye caught his attention as Carmen stiffened. He let her be for now. "I saw your eyes. Those aren't his words. They're *yours*. You've blamed me long enough for Fraula's death, and I have tried to make things right. But you won't have it."

Saul straightened out his jacket calmly. "And why should I? You murdered my mate."

"Is that why all of this is happening?" Paytah asked in a low voice. "Are you filled with so much hatred that you would violate your duke's mind so he'd lie? That you'd take out your revenge on me by kidnapping or killing my wolves?"

Joseph blinked and looked over at Saul. "What does he mean?"

Saul lifted his chin boldly. "I don't know what you're talking about. Our vampires are missing, it's true. But we've been trying to find them under covert operation while you wasted time talking to Legion. Isn't that right?" He peered at Joseph.

"Joseph!" Paytah shouted, startling the vampire and forcing him to break his gaze with Saul. "Stop letting him control you!" He pushed himself up despite the pain screaming through his chest and body. Stitches pulled. Wounds sent fire streaking through his limbs. He felt Rozene move closer to him for support, but he ignored her as he put his full attention on Saul. "If you have a vendetta against me, then take it out on me, not on my wolves. Not on your own vampires." Something clicked inside, and he touched one of the wounds on his arm. "The assassination attempt, that was you, wasn't it?"

Saul didn't visibly change, but Paytah sensed a silent rage that suffocated the room. "You don't know what you're talking about. You're tossing accusations at me with nothing to go on except—"

"*You…*" Carmen whispered.

All eyes turned towards the young werewolf as she stared at Saul. Her shoulders stiffened so much, they almost swallowed her neck. "That voice…you were there that night. You opened Nick's door and pulled him out. You kicked me in the face."

Saul glared at Paytah. "More false accusations. I expected more from you, Paytah. You have no evidence."

"I can *smell* them on you," Paytah hissed, his nose finally piecing together the familiar scents. "The Hunters might have hid their faces, but they couldn't hide their scents. I smell them. On. You." He jerked his head, and Carlos went to the door, blocking Saul and Joseph from leaving. "What I can't figure out is if it's only you or if Joseph is behind this too."

Joseph shook his head and turned towards Saul with confusion written across his face. "What is he talking about, Saul? What smells does he…" his voice faded as he breathed in. Suddenly, his eyes lit up, and he took a small step back. "Why do you have wolfsbane on you?"

Saul's red eyes were Paytah's only warning.

The vampire glared at Joseph, and in a flourish, the duke suddenly flew at Carlos with fangs and claws bared. Carlos ducked, barely avoiding nails gouging his face. Still, Joseph's impressive claws left deep marks in the hospital door.

Saul threw himself at Paytah, a syringe in his right hand. Paytah braced himself for impact.

Rozene got there first. She swung her fist into Saul's chin, snapping his head and causing him to spin from the force of the blow. He recovered quickly and backhanded her, but Rozene was stronger than she looked.

She ducked and knocked Saul's legs out from beneath him. As he toppled, she tried to pin him, but the vampire punched her twice in the throat then the stomach. Rozene choked, only to give a strangled yelp as he shoved the syringe into her belly.

"Rozene!" Paytah shouted.

Saul glared at her and grabbed her head as she fought for breath. He spun her around, one arm across her throat, his free hand twisting her wrist behind her. The vampire glowered up at Paytah. "You took mine. It's only fair."

"No!" Paytah screamed and threw himself off the bed.

Saul lunged for Rozene's throat.

Joseph's body crashed into him before he had the chance to bite. The blow sent Saul and Joseph rolling across the floor. Rozene broke free and scrambled backwards until she bumped into Carlos's legs. The avian bled from several wounds, but his golden-brown wings were out and his talons held blood of their own.

Paytah groaned where he landed on the floor. Rozene reached for him and managed a strangled snarl of warning at the vampires.

Saul shoved Joseph off of him and sprang to his feet. He took one step towards them when the door flew open and the pack started swarming the room, led by Quince. With a glower, Saul ran for the window.

"Don't let him escape!" Paytah shouted.

Carmen remained the only person between Saul and the window. She shoved herself out of her wheelchair and managed to grab Saul around the legs, but it wasn't enough. With a streak of vicious claws, he scraped Carmen across the face and kicked her hard. She cried out in pain and doubled over on the ground in a crumpled heap.

Saul threw himself out the window, shattering the glass with the force of his body. Black smoke curled around him, and just as he started to fall, he transformed into a huge, vicious-looking flying fox with dark fur and an orange throat. The great bat slipped out into the night, faint coils of smoke trailing off of him.

Before Paytah could say anything, Carlos darted after the bat in his seraph form. He leapt through the window, spread his mighty eagle wings, and vanished from sight.

Jackson went to Paytah and Rozene. "I'm sorry we didn't come in sooner. We wanted to give you the time you needed."

Quince looked him over fervently. "Are you hurt?"

Paytah didn't answer. Instead, he reached up to his mate's cheek. She touched his hand. "I'm fine," she said then coughed. Bruises were already forming at her throat.

"I thought I was going to lose you," Paytah whispered.

"I'm not that easy to kill." Rozene chuckled and kissed his temple. "Jackson, help him in bed."

As Jackson hefted Paytah up, Tamara went to Carmen and helped the young woman back into her wheelchair. Mikayla and Quince both grabbed Joseph and twisted his arms behind his back. Paytah settled back in bed and looked down at the dazed vampire. He didn't resist. If anything, he looked lost and a bit scared.

"Gentle," Paytah said to them. He watched the vampire closely, but all the aggression had gone out of him without Saul there to, presumably, guide his actions. Joseph wasn't the type to jump into fights or flash his fangs at other parahumans. He could manipulate a person much easier with his charm and not even break a sweat. "Jackson, did you bring that mistletoe concoction I asked for?"

Jackson nodded and pulled out a small bottle made from a local apothecary witch. Paytah sighed and glanced at Joseph. It would hurt the vampire, but it was worth it to free him of Saul's control.

"Give it to him."

Jackson hesitated. "Are you sure? What if he's working with Saul, and this is all an act?"

Paytah set his jaw. He wouldn't consider himself and Joseph friends, but they'd been acquaintances for a very long time. And during their disputes, Gladus was usually there to knock their heads together so they'd get along (sometimes literally). In all that time, Joseph had never raised fang or fist against Paytah, nor had Paytah ever threatened Joseph with bodily harm.

The vampire before him was not the duke he knew.

And he wanted the duke back.

"Do it," Paytah ordered.

Jackson nodded and walked towards the restrained vampire. "Get his mouth open."

Quince made a face. "And what if he bites us?"

Jackson wrinkled his nose and then sighed. "Fine," he muttered and reached forward. He grabbed Joseph by the nose and pinched it tightly. The vampire opened his mouth for a breath, and to protest. It gave Jackson enough time to upend the bottle and pour the liquid down his throat. As Joseph gurgled and tried to spit it out, Jackson grabbed a cloth and shoved it over his mouth, keeping his own hand away from Joseph's fangs.

The vampire thrashed and tossed his head, the potion tearing at his insides like wolfsbane did to Paytah. Paytah regretted doing it, but sometimes there was no other way to break the charm on another vampire. At least it wouldn't kill him.

Joseph struggled in Quince's and Mikayla's arms, yelling into the gag, but to no avail. Between the shouting and convulsing, fear shined in his red eyes, a fear Paytah wasn't used to seeing. It made the guilt of hurting him sting that much more.

Rozene squeezed Paytah's hand suddenly. "He shouldn't go through this alone."

"Rozene," Paytah said and tried to stop her, but his wounds stilled him.

She rose carefully from his side and braced her hand against the bed, the wolfsbane from Saul's syringe still in her system. Sweat dotted her brow, and yet, she moved to Jackson's side and bumped him with her hip, gently nudging him out of the way. She pulled the cloth from Joseph's mouth (he would have swallowed the potion by now), and knelt in front of him, trusting her wolves to keep him at bay. "I know it hurts," she said and touched his chest. "We're not doing this to be cruel. We want to clear your mind and help you come back to yourself. Don't fight it; it'll hurt worse. We want to help you, Joseph. We're your friends."

"Friends?" Joseph spat, his voice hoarse from shouting. His crimson eyes darted madly, the charm and mistletoe fighting each other. "Friends wouldn't poison me."

"Friends also wouldn't charm you," Rozene said. She scooted closer and settled her hand against his cheek. Paytah stiffened in alarm, but Rozene showed no sign of fear. "What Saul did to you was wrong…criminal. I know what it means for a vampire to charm another, how it violates the mind. But, we want to help you. We wouldn't have used the mistletoe to free you otherwise."

Joseph's fangs slid through the top of his gums, but he made no move to bite her. He stared at Rozene, his breaths coming in ragged huffs. The red faded more, and as the mistletoe broke through the charm, his fangs slid back into his mouth, and his features softened then turned to cold, horror. He leaned his pale head against her hand and closed his eyes, his shoulders shuddering.

Rozene glanced at Quince and Mikayla. "Let him go."

Paytah bristled. "Rozene."

"Trust me," she said. She nodded at the pair. Quince exchanged glances with Mikayla and slowly released Joseph. She kept a firm hold on him until Rozene sent her a sharp look. With a sigh, the woman let go and stepped back.

Joseph slumped against Rozene and rested his head in her hand. She held him steady, whispering quietly to him. Rozene could be as sharp as nails, but she had a tenderness to her that brought the pack to her.

Joseph's breathing slowed before turning ragged again, not in rage, but grief. He didn't cry or wail. Instead, he curled his hand around Rozene's wrist so tightly his fingers trembled. Paytah stopped Jackson from doing anything as the vampire clung to Rozene for support.

Eventually, Joseph's grip loosened on Rozene, and he lifted his head off of her hand. "I'm here," he said. He sounded more like himself and less like the arrogant asshole of the past few days. The vampire sat back on his heels and looked around the room slowly. The wild glint lingered in his eyes, but not from charm. Paytah could only imagine what was going through his head. "Where are we?"

Paytah sat up a little more in bed, fighting against the pain. "What all do you remember, Joseph? What's the last thing that's clear to you?"

Joseph rubbed his head with sharp nails. "I-I don't know. Everything's been such a fog lately. Making phone calls to my vampires who are out of the state? Yes, I remember doing that. I wasn't getting answers from some of them. Then everything became a dream. I could see myself doing things and hear myself saying things, but it wasn't *me*." He looked over at Paytah and his eyes widened. "What happened to you?"

Paytah glanced down at his bandaged body. He must look a sight. "Assassination attempt."

"What? By who?"

"Hunters," Paytah said honestly. "And I think Saul."

Joseph balked. "Saul?"

Paytah opened his mouth to speak when he heard the whoosh of powerful wings outside the hospital window. He twisted slightly as Carlos landed on the windowsill, still in his seraph form. The avian carefully slid into the room, mindful of the glass shards sprayed across the floor and sticking out of sections of the window. He dusted dirt off of his arms and eyed Joseph warily. "He's back," Paytah said to soothe him. "Saul?"

"Escaped," Carlos replied with a growl. "He was too fast, and I couldn't see him in the dark."

Paytah grunted. Golden eagles weren't exactly built for night flight. "Are you sure no one spotted you in *that* form? What happened to being inconspicuous?"

Carlos flexed his wings. "No, but I had a better chance of taking Saul down like this." He glared at Joseph. "What's he doing free?"

"Excuse me!" Joseph barked then winced at the sound of his own voice. "Will someone explain what's going on here?"

Paytah held up his hand. "Carlos, back down. Jackson, I want you to get everyone in here and settled down." He glanced at the vampire. "It's a long story, so I'll try to be as concise as possible."

Once the pack had gathered, Paytah laid everything out for Joseph, from the change in the duke's attitude, to Carlos telling him about Trish, to their suspicions of Saul. Carmen added in her memory of Saul at the accident while Quince gently treated the bloody claw marks on her face.

Through it all, Joseph sat silent as the dead, his dark eyes never leaving Paytah's. The wolves shifted anxiously, not liking how the vampire had such a firm gaze on their alpha, but Rozene knew he wasn't being charmed. There was no red hue to Joseph's irises, and the duke looked more shocked than on a quest for vengeance.

As Paytah finished, Joseph ran his hands roughly over his face and stood. "I should have noticed something amiss," he growled and paced the small room like a trapped animal. He kept his hands on his head as if that would stop it from getting controlled again. "I barely remember Trish going missing. She should have told me about her suspicions about…Saul. Saul." He shuddered deeply and shot a look at Carlos, still pacing. "She's safe?"

The avian nodded brusquely. "She chose an interesting person to seek sanctuary with, but yes, she's safe. No harm is going to come to her under my protection."

"Good…good." Joseph stopped, realizing the amount of wolves around him and eyes on him. He crept back towards Rozene and knelt beside her. She tried to touch him, but he flinched away, one hand still on his head. "I'm sorry for what I did, but I don't remember it. I don't remember!" He gripped his face with both hands and snarled under his breath. "I can't believe he did this. He was my right hand. The one I could trust above all else."

Paytah swallowed and glanced at Jackson before his gaze darted to Joseph. "I'm sorry, Joseph, but is there anything you can tell us? Anything you remember about where Saul might have gone or where the Hunters might be hiding?"

"I don't even remember half of the things I've done, so how do you expect me to answer that question and trust my memory? What are my thoughts? What are his *orders*?" Joseph said with a growl mixed with rage and grief. "I never thought he'd go this far. He betrayed me. He betrayed me and his own coven!" The shout ripped from his throat. He dragged his hands down his face and stared at his palms, his nails growing sharper. "Fraula's death is no excuse for what he did. What he stole from *me*. That conniving son of a bitch," he hissed.

"His goal has been to hurt me," Paytah said, struggling to keep the rage out of his voice. He wanted to be angry that Joseph hadn't kept a leash on his vampire, but Joseph was a victim in this, too. "My wolf was killed. Others were taken. And an attempt was first made on my life and then on Rozene's."

Joseph shook his head. "If he had truly wanted revenge, he would have killed your wife in front of you. I think this goes deeper. There's something more to this than we know, but I can't fathom what." He looked away sharply and pressed his clawed hands onto the linoleum floor. "I'm compromised. He should not have been able to charm me so easily. I'm better than this. I'm… I'm stronger." His voice became a whisper. "I'm stronger."

Jackson shifted closer to Paytah and exchanged looks with him. Paytah nodded, giving him permission to speak. "Do you think he wants to take over as duke of the coven? Could he have been wearing down your mind for longer than this?"

"I don't know!" Joseph snapped again. "By the Night Mother, I don't know. He's never expressed interest in being duke. He likes diplomatic missions. He prefers to travel, but since Fraula died, he's barely left the coven. He's taken more interest in Trish, so the fact that I barely remember her disappearance makes me wonder if there was something else behind her vanishing."

Rozene frowned. "What do you mean?"

Joseph gave a bitter, dark laugh. "They've both betrayed me

once already. What's to say they aren't working together?"

Paytah snorted and glanced at his mate. "Why betray you both, then, if they're working together?"

"I don't know. Maybe she didn't feel like she was getting as much out of it. Maybe it was meant to be a distraction. Maybe Trish has her own target like Saul has his."

The color drained from Carlos's face. He scrambled for his phone and bolted for the hallway, nearly crashing into Tamara in his hurry. The woman frowned then went out the door after him, much to Paytah's relief. If something had happened to Bianca or the rest of his family, Carlos would need someone to center him. Tamara was good at that.

Paytah sighed. "So who can we trust?"

Joseph gave a half-crazed laugh. "Clearly, I know my vampires so well. Why, I'll let one invade my head. I can't even trust my own mind! How am I supposed to know who to trust?"

"Are there vampires you think who would stand beside you? Ones who won't try to corrupt you?"

Joseph bowed his head wearily. He started to shake his head then paused. "My mate," Joseph said. "She'll be returning from a trip soon."

Rozene arched an eyebrow. "She hasn't noticed a change in you?"

"She's barely been home," Joseph said then blinked. "I must have sent her away on more missions than I realized. Saul wanted her out of the way."

Paytah bristled. He didn't like the sound of that. "What sort of missions?"

"Talks with other covens. Trying to keep good relationships open with them. We've also taken in some vampires who have had trouble adjusting to other locations. She was supposed to come home with a young man who has far too much of a thirst for blood."

"Great," Quince moaned. "As if we need more vampires like that in this District."

Paytah shot him a look until the wolf flinched and went back to cleaning Carmen's face.

Joseph didn't take offense to the comment, but when he looked up at Paytah, a furious fire smoldered in his eyes, the shock and hysteria slipping away. "If Saul realizes he's caught, and he feels cornered, he's going to do something drastic."

"Such as?" Paytah pressed.

"Kill your wolves. Have them moved. Send the Hunters back in for one more attack on you. On *me*." He looked around and met every eye in the room. "No one is safe. No one can be *trusted*. Who knows now what Saul's capable of doing? He might even deliver the killing blows himself."

Which included Tess, Paytah realized. If the Hunters got the order to attack, then she might be the first to die if her friend wasn't being honest with her. His stomach twisted again and he shut his eyes. He needed to have a pack meeting.

Before he could suggest it, Carlos and Tamara walked back into the room. The avian looked exhausted, but he was composed otherwise.

"They're safe," Carlos said. "I spoke with Bianca, my wife, and Trish. I informed them of Saul's betrayal. Trish sounded disappointed, but not surprised. Haley said Trish hasn't tried anything. The vampire actually went to sleep soon after I took the letter."

Paytah nodded, relieved. Finally, one good piece of news. He glanced at Joseph as the vampire's claws dug so hard into the linoleum it cracked beneath his hold. He was a ticking time bomb, boiling with rage and hurt. And he was right; he didn't know who he could trust, including his own coven. Well, except for one vampire. "Carlos, I hate to ask more of you, but do you think you could bring Joseph to your cloister, and to Trish? I think he should be with someone he can trust, and I need to have a pack meeting. In fact, if Becky is still out there with Heidi, can you send her in?"

Carlos nodded and reached out to squeeze Joseph's shoulder. When the vampire looked up at him, the avian offered a smile. "Come on, hermano. Let's go."

"Why would you even think to trust me after what I tried to do?" Joseph asked.

Carlos shrugged. "You're not the first person to be forced to do something against your will." His gaze swept to Paytah meaningfully. "And we District leaders have to be there for each other, isn't that right?"

Paytah nodded.

Joseph stared at Carlos's offered hand and shut his eyes. He grasped the avian by the wrist, his claws slipping back into his fingers, and shook it in camaraderie, nodding in thanks. As the pair made to depart, Joseph looked back over his shoulder at Paytah.

"I hope you get your family back. And if you find Saul, bring the bastard to me *alive*. He's mine to deal with."

"We will," Paytah said with more confidence than he felt.

Rozene went out after them and returned a short while later with Becky and Heidi in tow. Becky held her daughter to her chest and sat down near Mikayla as Rozene shut the door. "Iris should be here," she reminded him.

"Iris also needs to rest. And I know where she'd stand on this." He looked around at his packmates. His heart ached to see so few. "You all know what transpired tonight, including between me and Tess."

"Yeah," Mikayla said shortly. "Again, with all due respect, why would you kick her out, especially after she saved your life?"

Quince glanced at her. "She did also bring a Hunter to Paytah and then a bunch of Hunters tried to kill him. Coincidence?"

"Even if it wasn't, that doesn't mean Tess was behind the assassination attempt too!"

Becky held her daughter a little tighter and frowned. "But she did disobey Paytah and led an ambush on the Hunters and ended up getting Ray killed and Augustine and Kat kidnapped."

Jackson bristled. "You can't blame that on Tess."

"Yes, we can," Quince argued. "There's a reason we have an alpha in charge. A reason why we have *him* make the decisions, and she didn't listen."

"Ray and Augustine knew what they were getting themselves into when they agreed to help," Jackson countered. "Just as Bianca did. Tess would have been killed herself if that Hunter hadn't saved her, and we all know that she's probably guilt tripping herself better than any of us could guilt her." He looked at Paytah. "*Why*? She's one of us."

Paytah looked down. Rozene's hand slipped into view as she took hold of his. "I did it out of anger. And I did it out of fear. I didn't want to lose anyone else. Trish turned against her coven. For a moment, I thought maybe Tess could have turned against us."

Mikayla made a strangled noise, a mix of a laugh and a scoff. "Yeah, 'cause helping the very people who have her packmates and her *father* held captive seems like something Tess would do."

"Point taken," Paytah said. He breathed out a short breath and then winced as pain raced through his body. He touched his abdomen and gave Quince a pleading look until the man pushed another dose of morphine into him. It would put him to sleep soon, but for now, it would at least keep the pain at bay. "We need to talk to her. Get what information we can from her. And then make a move to help our wolves. Now that Saul realizes we know he's behind this, he'll act soon, and I don't want to risk more people dying." He squeezed his mate's hand. "You should call her."

"Why me?"

"Because I don't think she's going to want to say a word to me after what I did."

Jackson slowly lowered his arms. "Did something else happen?"

Paytah set his jaw and ran his hand along his face. "I clawed her. Marked her. I was trying to chase off the Hunter, but she stepped in the way and took the blow. I don't know how badly she's injured."

Jackson grunted under his breath, and Mikayla growled quietly, her eyes glinting gold. She looked sharply away and pushed herself to her feet.

"She's pack," Mikayla said firmly. "Pack doesn't abandon pack. Nor do we mark each other."

"What about the marks she left on Paytah?" Quince asked. "Those burns were from magic, not Hunters."

Becky and Tamara shuddered while Mikayla shook her head. "Pack doesn't abandon pack," she repeated.

Before Paytah could explain further, Mikayla left the room and slammed the door loudly behind her, causing Heidi to jump and start to cry into her mother's shoulder. Becky shushed her gently and rubbed her back.

Jackson glanced at Paytah. "You should be the one to talk to her, Paytah."

"You can use my phone so she'll pick up," Rozene said.

Paytah nodded and patted her hand. His eyes fluttered a little, and he grimaced. "I'll call her once the medicine isn't about to send me to sleep. Quince, check on your mate and kids the moment you get a chance. I think everyone should stay here tonight, or gather at my house. We need to be together."

Quince nodded and glanced at his watch. "I'll be off shortly. Rest for now, Paytah. You'll need it for the coming fight."

Paytah settled back into the pillows and turned to look up at his mate. "I'm getting too old for this."

She chuckled and leaned down to kiss his forehead. "I think we all are. Sleep, my love."

"Stay with me? You need time for the wolfsbane to wear off anyway."

"I don't need an excuse to sleep with you," Rozene said. She smiled before sliding onto the mattress, mindful of his wounds. She shifted the covers around them, and Paytah rolled to his side, pulling her lightly against his chest. He breathed in her scent, reminding himself she was alive and safe in his arms.

"Sleep," Rozene whispered.

Paytah didn't need much more encouragement than that.

Chapter 19
Plots

Trish

Tess hugged a down pillow to her chest, welcoming the painful, scratchy pricks that helped distract her. She stared forlornly at one of the few pictures on Arjun's studio wall. An albatross flew over the ocean, its mighty wings carrying him through a fierce storm that tore at his plumage, threatening to send him tumbling into the hungry waves below. Still he flew on, heading towards the faint outline of a lighthouse in the distance.

She wished she had the same fortitude as that stupid bird. Arjun had ferried her away from her demolished apartment. The blow to her face had rendered her nearly senseless and more than a little heartbroken. She'd huddled against Arjun while he carried her to his waiting vehicle and brought her back to his home.

She didn't fight him when he stitched up her cheek, closing the wound tenderly but unable to do anything to prevent scarring. The fire had been snuffed out of her, and she sat hunched while he tended to her. After the bandages were applied and she changed out of her bloody, dirty attire into soft sweatpants and a black t-shirt, she crumbled into his bed and sobbed for what she'd lost. It wasn't just that she'd upset Paytah and lost his favor. Her family was gone, too. Being banished meant no one from the pack was supposed to interact with her. That included her mother. All the friendships and connections she'd built over the years, her stability, were ripped out beneath her, sending her tumbling into a dark, lonely hole.

She held herself and wept bitter tears, barely aware of Arjun as he crawled into the bed behind her. He tried to ask her what he could do to help, but when she couldn't answer him through the sobs, he wrapped his arms around her and held her close.

Tess didn't resist.

She rested against him and cried until the tears dried up and sleep helped her escape the depression.

Neither sunlight nor moonlight greeted her in the covered studio. She woke up sometime in the afternoon (according to his clock), but Tess couldn't bring herself to get out of bed. So she stared at the dumb bird and tried to ignore the pain gnawing through her heart and face. She hadn't even had the chance to say goodbye to anyone or apologize for the part she'd played in Ray's death. Would Paytah tell them what had transpired? Why he'd banished her? Would any of them even care?

Tess touched her bandaged cheek and swallowed as she felt the heat radiating beneath the cloth. It burned like she'd been stretched out in the sun for days. Even opening her mouth hurt. Whether Paytah had meant it or not, some of the venom in his claws had gotten into her skin. It wasn't enough to change her, but it still burned hotter than her fire; unfortunately aloe couldn't soothe this pain.

Pans rattled quietly in the kitchen. Tess glanced over her shoulder and watched Arjun move around the dining table, filling plates with food and pouring juice and coffee into cups. He was still dressed in black pants, but he'd pulled on a deep red shalwar kameez which went down to his knees. He'd rolled up the sleeves, revealing several scars lining his arms that she hadn't noticed before.

He glanced over at her, a few curls from his hair falling into his eyes. "You're awake. I made some food for us." He glanced down at the filled table and frowned. "Let me check your cheek first."

Tess nodded and slowly sat up in the warm pillows and blanket. Some part of her felt like she shouldn't be there. It was true, he very well could have betrayed her and brought Hunters to kill Paytah, but at that moment, she needed *someone* in her corner. Someone she could trust and believe in. She'd grown up in a wolfpack, and she followed that old ideology that wolves didn't do well alone.

Arjun brought a medical kit to the bed and sat down beside her.

His hands were wrapped in white bandages, hiding his own wounds. He reached for the wrap over her face and started to pull it away.

Tess hissed in pain but didn't fight him.

"Sorry," he said.

"Not your fault." She glanced sideways as he set the bandage in a disposable bag. Red lines streaked across it, outlining Paytah's vicious claw marks. "How bad is it?"

"It looks better than when I first treated it." He dabbed at her cheek with a warm cloth, cleaning up some of the blood. "The stitches are holding."

"Something to be happy about," she murmured. Tess shut her eyes and started to tug at her fingers. "I meant to ask, he didn't get you too, did he? I saw your hands."

"Hm? No, that wasn't from your alpha. I got it in the fight." He rubbed a salve across her cheek that smelled a bit like minty earth. It chilled her skin and sent pleasant waves of numbness through the wounds. "I have some pain killers if you need them, but you should eat first so you don't take them on an empty stomach."

Tess opened her eyes. He spoke so calmly and pleasantly, like they'd known each other for years and she hadn't woken up tied to his bed a day ago. "Let me ask you one question, and then I won't ask again."

"All right."

Tess turned her head to meet his eyes, searching his warm gaze for a lie. "Did you have *anything* to do with the attack on Paytah?"

Arjun didn't flinch or look at her with anger. He stared back resolutely and shook his head. "No."

Tess nodded and dropped her eyes to the bloodied bandage. "Good."

"That's it? No other questions?"

"No. Maybe I'm being stupid by trusting you, but apparently, I can't trust my own pack right now." She pulled her legs close and tilted her head away once he'd finished with her cheek. "I don't know what I'm going to do. I've never been alone like this before."

"Well," Arjun said and closed the bag. "You're not exactly alone. You have me."

Tess snorted. "I barely even know you."

"Didn't stop you from trusting me." Arjun ran his hands along his thighs and nodded towards the table. "Sit with me and eat, and ask me whatever you want. I think we could both use a friend right now."

"Both?"

"Well, it's kind of disheartening to have Hunters try to kill you when you're a Hunter as well."

Tess frowned. "Fair." She slid her feet over the bed and pushed herself up. The room spun a little, but Arjun grasped her elbow and steadied her. She nodded her thanks and followed him into the kitchen. Whatever he'd cooked made her mouth water. Her bowl was filled with bright yellow rice, cuts of chicken, and a splattering of nuts. She recognized the scent of ginger and guessed the yellow was from turmeric. The spices made her stomach growl with anticipation. "What is this?"

"Chicken biryani. A slightly faster version than what I usually cook, but I wasn't sure how long you would sleep."

Tess gave him a look. "I thought you didn't eat meat."

He tilted his bowl towards her, showing off cubes. "I used tofu in mine. I thought you could use the meat." He started to munch on his meal and gestured to a glass of milk he'd poured for her. "I wasn't sure how sensitive you were to spice."

"Yeah, me and my weak American tongue," Tess said with a weak chuckle. She took a bite and rolled her eyes back as spices, liquid, and flavor exploded in her mouth. "Oh my God," she moaned. "The chicken is so juicy."

Arjun chuckled and mixed his food around a little more. "At least I can still cook it even if I don't eat it."

Tess offered a faint smile and focused on her meal. She hadn't realized how hungry she was until that first bite. The spice warmed her mouth, throat, and belly pleasantly, though she stole a few sips of milk now and again to help dilute it. She liked spice, which prompted her to frequent Carlos's restaurant, but she still didn't quite have the tongue for it yet.

She drank another gulp of milk and stared at her half-eaten bowl. "When you left me in your bed to run errands, you said you called a Hunter friend of yours. Who?"

Arjun scratched the tip of his nose and set his bowl on the table. "Her name is Skye. She's been a partner of mine for years, and I wanted to let her know I was going to speak with your alpha in case something happened to me."

Tess arched an eyebrow. "So, didn't trust us either?"

"Well, I knew your people had issues with 'bad' Hunters, so I wanted to keep myself safe and also let her know I hadn't skipped town. At least someone would come looking for my shallow grave if I went missing."

"Skye, huh?" Tess poked at a chunk of chicken. "So, is she just a friend or something more?"

"Contrary to what people might believe, a man and a woman can work together and stay friends. Besides, I'm not exactly her type."

"Oh?" Tess replied trying to fight back an odd sense of relief. "And you're sure she's not with the other morons?"

"Very certain. They would be more interested in killing someone like her."

"Why?"

"She's a witch. And generally, unless they have full control over a parahuman, the other Hunters won't even entertain having one help them. Or they'll plan on backstabbing them later." He picked up another piece of tofu. "She's tried to settle down a bit from the Hunter life with her partner and her kid. But she can't seem to stay still. She likes to know what I'm up to and to help out here and there." He grinned. "She and her daughter are the reason I make the smiley face omelets."

Tess chuckled. "They sound like good people."

"I thought you magi weren't fond of witches."

Tess shrugged and ran her fingers lightly through her hair. "Usually not, but I can respect someone who tries to learn how to use the Ether."

She'd have to remember this Skye person in case she ever showed up in the pack—Tess caught herself mid-thought and grimaced. She supposed it didn't matter. The pack wouldn't want anything to do with her after this. They'd be expected to turn their backs on her like Paytah. It was just the way of things.

Suddenly, her appetite vanished, and any lingering flavors tasted like dirt. She set her fork down and glanced at her drinks, wishing they were something stronger.

As if reading her mind, Arjun stood up and reached into a low cabinet. He pulled out a bottle of vodka and poured some into a shot glass. Tess downed it and held it out for another. "Thanks."

"Did he really mean it? That you're banished?" Arjun asked as he offered her a second.

Tess ran her fingers along the cool glass and nodded. Her face stung as she thought about the claw marks. "Paytah doesn't make threats lightly. If he wants me out, then I'm out."

"I imagine it's like losing your family."

Tess fought back tears of grief. "Yeah, something like that." She tossed back the second shot and gave a bitter laugh. "The twisted thing is I still haven't gotten my dad back. Screwed up so much trying to rescue my friends and family, and now I can't even help my pack find them."

Arjun cocked his head towards her. "Then don't help them," he said. He reached into his pocket and pulled out the tracking device. He set her phone next to it. "Help me instead. We still have this. We can go in, scope things out, and locate where your friends are. Skye and I can enlist the help of some other people to give us a hand. And, you can also send the info to your pack, even if they don't want you there. You can still help, Tess."

Tess picked up the tracking device and stared at it. The dot hovered relatively in the same location it had been before. She traced her hand along her swollen cheek and down her jaw, warring between what was right and what was smart.

Hell, when did she ever do the smart thing?

She smiled and looked up at him, her heart thumping with a little bit of hope rather than despair. "You think we can save them?"

"It wouldn't be the first time I went into a fighting pit to help parahumans," Arjun said confidently. "Won't be the last either."

"How do we get in?"

Arjun leaned back and crossed his muscular arms over his chest. "That's where you come in. Hunters are more easily accepted if they bring an *offering* to the table. You come with me as my *captive*, and I can get us in. Getting us out will be a little harder, but if I convince them that the pit isn't the right place for me and my parahuman, there usually aren't too many questions, especially since you're a magus. We might at least be able to see if your friends are alive. You'll be the one to identify them. I can't."

Tess nodded and swallowed a lump in her throat. It would be dangerous, and she knew her powers would have to be subdued somehow so no one suspected that she wasn't fully restrained. But she could do that.

Especially if it meant she'd get to see her father again.

"Let's do it," she said and rose.

Arjun reached for her hand and squeezed it gently. He leaned forward, his gaze intent. "Are you sure, Tess? I'll do everything to keep you out of danger, but you need to be aware of the ramifications if things go wrong."

"I know," Tess said as she squeezed his hand back. "But my family and friends need me. It's especially my fault Augustine and Kat got into this mess." She grimaced. "I need to apologize to Bianca."

Arjun nodded. He pushed the bowl of food towards her and tapped the rim with a spoon. "Eat first. You're going to need your strength. I'll get things together, and we'll go in tonight. I'll have to dose you with a little elderberry, but not enough to completely suppress your powers. I have something like a perfume of it I can put on your skin so the Hunters will smell it too and think you're under control. We'll test your powers out before we go to make sure you can still use them."

"Yeah, okay," Tess said. She picked up the bowl and started to eat it while he finished off his meal. She watched him rise and rinse the bowl out before putting it in the dishwasher then heading into his "bedroom" to get some things. She ate slowly, letting her stomach settle as she thought about going into the Hunter's den. Mostly she was terrified that she would find her friends and father dead. And it would be her fault.

She pulled at her fingers again, her anxiety threatening to cascade over her and drown her. It wouldn't be the first time. It was a shame she hadn't been able to grab her pills while they were at her apartment. What was left of it, anyway.

She really was without a home, wasn't she?

As Arjun returned to the table with a pair of guns, she touched his arm. "Thank you, for everything you're doing."

He looked down at her hand then at her and let a warm smile fill his lips. "You're welcome. It's nice to actually help people again."

"I hope it works."

"We'll make it work," Arjun promised her. "Come hell or high water, we'll at least get answers."

Tess went to say something else when she saw her phone go off. Mikayla's name scrawled over the screen. Her heart jumped in her throat. Did Mikayla not know what had happened? Why was she calling? She looked at Arjun and he nodded, gesturing for her to take it. She picked up the phone and stood. "Mikayla?"

"Tess? Are you all right?"

Tess grimaced and ran her hand along her cheek. "What…do you know?"

"I know Paytah kicked you out of the pack, and Jackson and I are pissed about it."

Tess almost smiled. Ah Mikayla, she didn't hold back her opinions. But the smile didn't quite reach her cheeks. "Then why are you calling? You know Paytah won't like it."

"Yeah, well, Paytah's currently having morphine dreams, so what he doesn't know won't hurt him."

Tess glanced at Arjun. "Is he going to be okay?"

"It was close, but Quince says the doctor told him Paytah will survive. He's a tough old wolf." She quieted for a moment. "A few of us don't agree with Paytah, and we're going to fight him on your banishment. But until then, if you're with your Hunter boy, you might want to put yourself on speaker, because I got some news you're going to want to hear. Especially if you decide to be, well, *you*, and do something dumb."

"Thanks for the vote of confidence," Tess snorted. She turned the speaker on and set her phone on the table. "Okay, go ahead."

"No, no, we're not going into it that quickly. You, Hunter boy, what's your name?"

Arjun gave Tess a look. "Arjun."

"Why'd you save Tess?"

"Um, because it was the right thing to do. I didn't want her to end up with the other Hunters."

"Uh huh. What are your intentions for her?"

Tess's cheeks turned scarlet. "Mikayla."

"Shush! Come on, Arjun, what do you want?"

Arjun cleared his throat. "Nothing sinister. Just want to help. She seemed like she could use a friend."

Mikayla grumbled to herself. "Fine. So here's the deal. We found out who's behind the kidnapping and Paytah's assassination attempt."

Tess blinked in surprise and grabbed the phone without thinking. "What? Who?"

"Saul."

Tess felt the color drain from her face. She stared at the phone for a long moment until she noticed Arjun mouthing, "Who's

Saul?" to her. "Saul? Like, Joseph's Saul?"

"Yep. Apparently, he held a grudge against Paytah for what happened to Fraula, and he's been taking it out on our pack. Not only that, he's been charming Joseph. More vampires have gone missing, too, and Saul made Joseph lie about it. No one really knows why, though my guess is Saul's probably grooming the coven for his own takeover."

Tess shook her head in disbelief. Saul. After all this time. And here they'd made Trish the easy target. "You're sure about this? He confessed? Where is he now? How did you find out?"

"One question at a time, Girl. Yes I'm sure. Carmen said she recognized his voice from the night of the accident. And his confession came in the form of him trying to send Joseph to kill Carlos, him almost killing Rozene, and then Saul breaking out of the hospital window and escaping. We don't know where he is now. We found out because of Trish."

"*Trish?*"

"Heh, yeah, believe it or not, she rescued Bianca and then told her all her suspicions. I don't think Saul or Joseph had any idea."

Tess leaned against the table, dumbfounded, and looked over at Arjun as he listened intently. Well, that was quite a bit of news. The most surprising part of it was probably Trish. But that also meant they could get more help. Maybe. "Anything else, Mikayla? Is everyone else safe and alive? My mom?"

"Yeah, we're all good here. Carmen got a face full of claws, but Quince took care of it, and your mom is resting. Paytah wants us to stick together until we can get things under control. What about you, firebug? You holding up?"

"Firebug?" Arjun whispered.

Tess pressed her hand over his mouth and groaned loudly. "Mikayla, really? I'm…I'll be fine. I need some time to heal and figure things out."

Mikayla grunted over the phone. "You have a plan, don't you?"

"I got to go. Let me know if you find out anything else. I miss you."

"Miss you, too. Don't you worry, we'll get you back in the family. I promise."

"Thanks. Love you, wolfsis."

"Love you, too, firebug."

Tess hung up and pressed the phone to her chin. Saul. That

would complicate things. No wonder they'd known where Paytah was! They'd had a mole within their District this entire time. Oh, she could kill him for it.

Trish created another interesting element. She had insight no one else did. And Tess did need to apologize to Bianca.

She turned towards Arjun. "How would you feel about making a detour on our way to track the Hunters?"

"Does this have anything to do with this Trish person your friend was talking about?"

Tess nodded. "Yeah. I think she can help us. Which I never thought I'd say."

"Because she helped kill your former Violet Marshall?"

Tess almost dropped the phone. "Wait, how do you know that?"

Arjun sighed. "Word travels fast in a District, and I have my own connections. When a Violet Marshall goes down because of Hunters, you tend to hear about all of the details. Why do you think she'll help?"

"She's trying to make up for her part in the murder." Tess brought her bowl to the sink and rinsed it out before grabbing her phone again. She hesitated a moment then dialed a number. It rang twice before Bianca picked up. "Bianca, it's Tess. Are you all right?"

"Alive and worried about Kat, but I'm fine. You?"

"Fine. Look, is Trish with you?"

Bianca fell silent. "Yes."

"I'm coming over to your place with a friend. Can it just be you two? I need to talk with you both."

"I'm at my apartment. But, Tess, you want to be careful. Carlos is going to be home soon, and based on what I heard, I don't know if he's going to want you around, especially if your friend is with you."

"Then don't tell him. We won't be long."

Bianca sighed. "We'll be here."

Tess hung up and stuck the phone into her back pocket. "Okay, we should get over there. I can guide us."

Arjun looked her up and down. "You're not exactly dressed like you're ready for the occasion. Let's get you prepared, and we'll head out. Oh, and you have to promise me one thing."

Tess paused and narrowed her eyes. That sounded ominous. "What?"

"You need to tell me about this whole 'firebug' thing."
"Oh my God, shut up."

Chapter 20
A Chance at Redemption

Trish

"You know this is a bad idea," Trish said not long after Bianca got off of the phone. She leaned against the counter, shoulders rigid with nerves. And here she thought revealing herself just to Bianca and Carlos was bad. "Tess doesn't like me, and I don't know what I can actually offer to help them."

"You knew Saul was behind this," Bianca argued. She poured them another cup of coffee and added a little salted caramel Baileys to take some of the edge off.

"No, I *suspected* Saul or Joseph might know about what was happening," Trish corrected her. She picked up the mug and glanced at the balcony. Staying in a cloister-run apartment building set her teeth on edge. At least Haley hadn't killed her on the spot, and Henry, adorable kid that he was, had upright forgiven her for the part she'd played in almost kidnapping him. He'd even given her a hug, much to the chagrin of his mother and to Trish's shock.

Avians were too damn forgiving.
"You still might have information they need," Bianca pressed. "Look, it's the least you can do."

Trish pressed her lips tightly together at the accusatory tone. She sipped her coffee and looked around the apartment to give herself a distraction. Paintings littered the walls, most of them hand-made, she guessed. Some were of Kat and Bianca together; others showed a golden wolf with a caracara on the canine's back.

She glanced at Bianca and caught the avian staring at a photograph of herself and Kat longingly. Bianca trailed her fingers lightly over the silver frame, swallowing a lump in her throat.

Trish tightened her hand on her coffee mug. "We'll get them back. I don't know how, but the pack at least isn't going to leave them there."

"I know. I'm scared we won't get there soon enough." Bianca stared at the swirls of Baileys in her coffee. "I was supposed to help protect them," she said in a whisper. "Act as the look out. Instead, I watched them get taken. I should have done something more."

"You would have ended up captured or killed," Trish said. "And then you wouldn't be able to help rescue Kat."

Bianca sniffed and brushed a tear from her eyes. "You sound like we're going to go on this heroic journey to get her back."

"Well your friends did that for you. Why not for Kat?"

Bianca glanced at her and gave a derisive snort. "You guys were up against two Hunters and a senka. We'll be against a whole group of Hunters. That's…a lot more dangerous, and we don't even know if Kat's alive."

Trish scoffed as she crossed her arms, mindful of her drink. "You didn't know if Tess's dad or friend were still alive, and you still helped. Are you going to give up on her so easily?"

"Of course not!" Bianca snapped. "I would never give up on Kat. I just don't want to lose anyone else."

Trish grimaced, her shoulders tensing again. She probably meant Gladus. *Again.* One day maybe people wouldn't hate her for that. "Glad to know you're not going to let her go."

"Never."

Trish fell silent after that. While Bianca sat at the kitchen breakfast bar, Trish huddled on the couch, sipping her coffee and trying not to feel overwhelmed by the smell of avian and wolf. She missed her coven.

Despite being forced to spend all her time inside, she missed them and the smell. Most of all, she missed Saul, which drove the stake deeper into her heart. She *hated* that he was behind this. It would have been easier to accept the betrayal had it been Joseph. Hell, she understood Saul's anger and want for revenge. But it twisted her insides, knowing their relationship might have been a lie. Of all the vampires Trish looked up to, she looked up to him the most. He'd been there for her since the very beginning.

And he'd been there after Gavin had died like no one else had.

She fingered the leather coat and brought it to her nose, breathing it in lightly. His scent had started to fade, but a whiff of it remained like the memories of him. Would those vanish over time too, leaving her grasping uselessly at a smoky smile drifting to the edges of her mind?

Trish blinked back a tear and glanced at Bianca. "You know how you feel right now? Terrified for Kat? Missing her? Afraid for your friends? Not knowing what's going to happen to them?"

"Yeah?"

"I know that no one is probably ever going to forgive me for what happened, but, that's how I felt when the Hunters threatened me. They'd already killed someone I …loved in front of me. And I was scared of losing the others." Her hands tightened around the mug, threatening to shatter it. "If I didn't obey, the rest of my coven would die. With Gavin's death still so fresh, I couldn't imagine that happening to anyone else. So, I obeyed. I know I hurt other people in the process, but I didn't mean to. I'm not evil. I don't want to be."

Bianca didn't say anything. She held her coffee and stared at her photograph. Trish sighed and leaned back on the couch, figuring that was the end of it.

"I still don't agree with what you did," Bianca finally said. "But, I think I get it. And I'm sorry you had to go through it alone."

Trish looked at her and met the avian's eyes. She nodded slowly, her throat tightening with barely concealed emotions. "Thanks. I don't talk about Gavin much, but he was a good guy. I wish the Hunters had given him a chance or killed me instead of him. He might have actually made the right decisions."

She set her coffee on her lap and rubbed her face. Her fingers trailed over a spot on her throat where her original sire had viciously marked her. Gavin had been the one to free her of his control. He'd given her a second chance at this new life. Why couldn't she have returned the favor?

"Hey," Bianca called. "You want something a bit stronger?"

"God, yes," Trish said and headed for the kitchen.

They were on their first glass of wine when Bianca's head suddenly shot up. The avian sprang from her chair and went over to her balcony. Trish watched her and then almost jumped out of her seat when she heard the clang of a grappling hook catch the metal railing. A moment later, two heads poked over the side, and Tess and a dark-skinned man with curly hair climbed onto the balcony.

"You could have used the front door," Bianca hissed as she ushered them inside.

"We didn't want to create a scene," Tess said. "Or have our scents get tracked through the front."

Bianca nodded then froze. She spun around and grabbed Tess, yanking her back and lifted her hand. Talons grew on the tips of her fingers as she rounded on the man. "What did you do to her?" she snarled.

It took Trish a moment to scent the elderberry in the air. She looked over at Tess and narrowed her eyes. The woman was dressed in torn jeans, a black shirt, and tattered jacket. Her cheek looked swollen and covered in deep, angry red marks like claws. Her entire appearance looked askew, like someone had beaten her.

And yet, Tess grabbed Bianca's arm without an ounce of weakness. "Bianca, stop, he didn't do anything. Look, see?" She held out her hand and a ball of fire sprang to life. "It's a ruse. He sprayed some elderberry-scented perfume on me so I smell like I'm subdued. It's part of our plan."

"And the marks on your face?"

"Paytah."

Bianca paused, and Trish lifted her head, surprised. Wolf claw marks? Those looked deep and vicious. Tess was lucky he hadn't gone for her neck!

Bianca gave herself a shake and narrowed her eyes. "Plan? What's going on?"

Tess sighed and motioned to the breakfast bar. "Let's sit, and I'll explain. By the way, this is Arjun."

Trish shifted a little to make room as Bianca, Tess, and Arjun joined her. She eyed the man up and down, taking him in. He smelled spicy; she almost sneezed. His eyes were sharp and alert like a bird of prey. He'd dressed in black pants, shirt, and jacket, and boldly wore his guns on his hips. She suspected he had more on him tucked away in his coat. The grappling hook brought an amused smile to her lips. Just how many tricks did he have up his sleeve?

He sat close to Tess while Bianca joined Trish.

"Okay, so here's the deal," Tess started and launched into a long story about their plan to invade the Hunter's den. Trish remained quiet, glancing at the tracking device and listening as Arjun explained his history with the Hunters and the whole good Hunter versus bad Hunter. She didn't really buy it, but, there were "*good*" vampires and "*bad*" vampires, so she supposed it wasn't impossible.

She propped her chin on her hand and looked the pair over. They stuck close to one another, Tess resting her hand lightly on Arjun's arm when she added to his statement, or Arjun gazing at her as she explained their plan. Vampires were very attuned to sexual tension and attraction. She could have smelled it radiating off of them a mile away. Did they even realize how much they were projecting?

Bianca held up a hand. "So what part do we play in this?" she asked. "I mean, I can identify Kat."

"We don't need you risking yourself, too," Tess said. "You can be part of the rescue party. We're only going in for intel."

Trish narrowed her eyes. "What was the point of talking to us about it then?"

Tess glanced at her. "Well, first, we wanted to make sure we had people on our side who would be willing to rescue folks once we found them. And two, we wanted to see if there was any information you could give us about Saul that might help. Especially if he's there."

Trish shut her mouth and looked down at her red wine. Oh, she had a world of intel about Saul. How he never squandered a drop of blood. How he only wore suits because that was what Fraula found the sexiest on him. How he managed to keep the coven functioning even when Joseph or his mate were away. He was the backbone of the coven. Without him, there would be turmoil, if Joseph didn't pull them together. "He's smart," she finally said. "Cunning. You won't be able to slip under his nose if he catches sight or whiff of you."

Arjun shook his head. "No one saw me when the assassination attempt happened. I made sure to cover my face and fight from a distance so I wouldn't be spotted. I don't think he'd recognize me."

"He'll recognize Tess," Trish said.

"I'll be Arjun's captive," Tess said and glanced at him. "So it shouldn't matter."

Trish wrinkled her nose. "And if you try to walk out of there after you've seen him, he's not going to let that happen."

Tess snorted and waved her hand lightly, causing the fire to dance on her fingers. "I'd like to see him try to stop me."

Trish rolled her eyes. Like a flash, she moved from her chair, slipped around the bar, and came up behind Tess, one hand to her throat, the other twisting the magus' arm behind her back. Tess yelped in surprise, and Arjun drew his gun, pointing it at Trish's head. She felt the cool kiss of the barrel, igniting every nerve and urging her to take him as her victim instead. She swallowed and released Tess, hands going into the air.

"Just a demonstration," she remarked. "Saul is older and faster than I am. If he doesn't want you leaving, he'll make sure that you can't. Before you use your flame, he'll take your head off. Even if your friend tries to kill him," she added, eyeing Arjun.

Tess rubbed her wrist while Arjun kept the gun level to Trish's head. Slowly, he holstered it and touched Tess's arm. "Are you all right?"

She nodded and glanced sideways at Trish. "She has a point. So then, what do you suggest we do?"

Trish breathed out through her nose and bowed her head. It was smarter to do nothing, but Tess wouldn't take that for an answer. "If you were smart, you wouldn't go in at all. But, it's probably better to send in a small group to scope out the place so you know what you're up against than to send everyone in at once." She tucked her hands in her trench coat pockets. "Let me come with you."

"What?" all three said at once.

"If any Hunters give us trouble, I can charm them so they'll leave us alone. It'll make it easier for us to get through the compound. And if Saul sees us, I can take care of things with him. You can even offer to 'sell' me over to him as an act of goodwill. Basically, I'm your contingency plan if things go south."

Arjun lifted an eyebrow. "And why should we trust you?"

Trish threw her head back and barked out a laugh. "This coming from a Hunter? Wow. What choice do you really have?"

"But why?" Bianca asked. "Why put yourself in that situation?"

Trish half shrugged. "Let's say that it's my way to try to make things right. Besides, I'll be able to spot if any of my vampire brethren are there. Maybe they'll be alive, too."

Trish glanced at the trio and couldn't help but be amused by their little group. Avian, magus, Hunter, and vampire. What a mix. But also all part of being in the District, right?

Even if it did mean pitting her up against someone she cared about.

Bianca sighed. "I don't like it, but you're all right. We need someone in there to scout things out. I can be on standby, and I can get the information to the pack and my cloister, especially if something goes wrong."

Arjun pulled a device out of his jacket and handed it to her. "It's a com piece. I'll keep one on. I should be able to send detailed messages to you, unless we're too far underground. That'll let you know, too, if we get in trouble."

Bianca grimaced and slid the piece behind her ear. "There's still no word from Legion?"

Tess shook her head. "The last I heard from Paytah, Legion didn't want to be involved except for a consulting agent, so it's up to us." She looked at Arjun. "If Trish is coming with us, do you have some kind of mistletoe you can use on her that won't take away her charm abilities?"

Arjun nodded. "I have something I can use." He tapped the tracker. "But we should get going. Depending on what your friends are going through, this may not last long."

Tess slid off of the bar stool. She rubbed her arm and looked sideways at Bianca. "I'm sorry about Kat and for failing to protect you both. We'll get her back. I promise."

Bianca went to her in an instant and wrapped the magus in a tight hug. "You get yourself back home safely."

Trish moved to the side and shifted anxiously from foot to foot. She wanted to leave and stop listening to all the sappy goodbyes. If she died down there, no one would care. Well, except for maybe Saul. Unless he'd been playing her this whole time.

"Hey, Trish?"

Trish glanced over at Bianca. "Yeah?"

"Be careful, alright? You better come home, too."

Trish blinked at her and pressed her lips together. Instead of saying anything sentimental, she nodded once and headed towards the balcony. "Can we get this over with?"

Before Arjun or Tess could say anything or exchange more

sentiments with Bianca, Trish climbed onto the railing. She gazed down at the concrete below her and couldn't help but wonder if this was a suicide mission. At least, if she died, she'd be reunited with Gavin and could make amends with Gladus.

Maybe.

She leapt off the cold railing, listening to it ring softly behind her as she fell towards the ground. She landed lightly on her booted feet and looked up as Arjun stuck the grappling hook on the balcony. He wrapped his arm around Tess and leapt over the side, carrying her down like a fragile treasure.

Trish's belly burned with jealousy, but she smothered it quickly. Now wasn't the time for that.

"This way," Arjun said and guided them towards a car.

Tess walked at his side. They were halfway there when Trish heard a buzz from Tess's back pocket. The magus pulled out a cellphone and frowned.

"Who is it?" Arjun asked.

"Rozene." She gripped the phone, hesitated, then ended the call. "She'll have to wait," she said and turned the phone off.

Chapter 21
Training

Nick

Nick dropped to his knees, wheezing, from a crushing blow to his stomach. He leaned over in the sandy pit, fighting back the urge to throw up. Blood dripped down his nose and lips, tainting them red and leaving a metallic taste behind. It pattered into the sand, creating a morbid work of art. Every muscle in his body trembled with exhaustion and begged him to collapse and welcome the blissful world of darkness, but he knew that would make things worse for him when he woke up.

"Come on! Get back on your feet!" Hendrickson shouted.

Nick waited for the shock of the collar, but it didn't come. Likely the Hunter didn't want to knock him out completely or risk losing one of his "prized fighters." He spat blood onto the ground and slowly pushed himself back to his feet, his fists shaking.

Brighton staggered upright across from him, looking about as haggard as Nick felt. They hadn't been allowed to shift yet, except for claws since the Hunters wanted to see how strong they were in their human bodies. They could both take a punch, but Brighton was older and stronger than Nick.

Brighton put up his wrapped fists again and threw himself at Nick.

Nick dodged and nailed him in the stomach with his knee. He heard the air whoosh out of Brighton's lungs before Nick slammed his elbow into Brighton's back. The man stumbled and fell to his knees, gasping.

Nick made it another step before dropping again. They'd been training for hours. Was it customary to kill off their fighters before an actual battle? He *hated* fighting Brighton, but they both knew what would happen if they didn't obey. At least one of them would suffer, and then Augustine, Kat, or Yanlei would be tossed in instead.

He glanced over to the holding cell where the three women waited. Augustine paced, her eyes already taking on a wolfish glint. Kat huddled near the furthest corner, trying not to watch the bloodshed. And Yanlei, calm, poised Yanlei, sat on a bench, legs crossed, eyes shut to the torment going on around them.

Theirs wasn't the only training ring. Other Hunters pitted their warriors against each other to choose the best one for the main fight. He'd already spotted Slater dragging three men over to a cage. So far, one had been carried out with a broken neck. There was no sign of the other two.

Hendrickson kicked the cage wall. The violent move made him grimace and grasp his shoulder in pain, like he'd been injured. Gale wore a thick bandage over part of her face, and both were supporting cuts and bruises. Nick had to wonder if they'd actually gone after Paytah. It looked like the Hunters had lost either way, and that put a smile on his face.

"They lasted longer this time, but still not long enough," Hendrickson complained. "Slater has stronger wolves. These two need to build up their strength, or we're not going to last in the tournament."

"They won't get any stronger if you kill them," Gale reminded him curtly. "Let them rest and see what the women can do. So far, the new one has outlasted almost everyone."

Nick glanced at Augustine. She was spitting for a match; it was the only way she could keep her mind distracted from Ray.

Hendrickson stalked towards the holding cell. "We'll let the two little ones fight first and winner can take on the new one. Or maybe we should do two against one and give her a challenge."

"No," Gale said. "She can fight the winner, and then she can fight the winning male." She tapped the side of the cage closest to Nick. "Get up and go into the holding cell. Both of you."

Nick knew better than to argue. He rose slowly and glanced at Brighton. It took the man longer to get to his feet, but he managed, and they shuffled towards the cell like a pair of beaten soldiers. He passed Yanlei and brushed his hand along her back to offer some comfort then went to Kat.

She touched his bruised arm. "You look awful," she said softly, her voice quivering with nerves. Her eyes darted towards Hendrickson then back to Nick, searching his face for, what, he didn't know. Comfort? Protection?

Nick gave a lopsided smile. "I've had worse. Do your best in there, Kat."

Kat glanced at the ring and swallowed. "It…it makes me think of *him*."

Nick's gaze hardened, and he pulled her into a hug. "*He's* not here. And we won't be here much longer. We know our friends will come. Keep your chin up. Remember what Paytah, Rozene, and I taught you. You're stronger than you realize, Kat."

She hugged him back, though not too tightly, and nodded. He reluctantly released her and watched as she walked timidly into the pit.

Hendrickson smacked the bar closest to Yanlei. "Hey! Get in there."

Yanlei opened her eyes and slid off of the bench. She met Nick's gaze once, and he nodded his support, not that she needed it. She could stand on her own two feet, but it made him feel better to do something.

She slipped out after Kat, and the cage slammed shut.

Nick and Brighton dropped down onto the bench beside each other. Brighton held his side and took a shaky breath. "Using what I taught you against me. Classy," he murmured with a tired laugh.

"You're one of the reasons I'm still on my feet," Nick said. He tipped his head, wiping sweat out of his stinging eyes. "Sorry."

"Yeah, I'm sorry, too."

Augustine paced by them and growled under her breath. "I don't know why they won't let me fight. I'm tired of *waiting* and *watching*."

Nick didn't try to stop her from prowling around like a caged animal. "You'll get your chance. Try not to wear yourself out before that."

She snarled at him and resumed pacing.

Nick sighed. They were losing her. At first, she'd dealt with the pain of her mate's death with tears. But the longer they were held captive, the more she let anger consume her rather than grief. Nick understood. He'd done the same after his father died, and it had taken Paytah knocking him across the head a few times to realize it. Rozene taught him peace. Paytah taught him how to redistribute his anger and energy. And Brighton taught him some of the dirty moves. It all kept him alive.

But he didn't know for how much longer.

He leaned forward and clasped his hands as he watched Yanlei and Kat face off against each other. He hated it, watching them fight. He cared about them both, and there wasn't a damn thing he could do to help them except call out encouragement and make sure Kat obeyed.

Yanlei stopped at one end of the ring and stretched her arms over her head, her expression the perfect picture of calm. On the contrary, Kat huddled near the other end and paced, eyeing Yanlei nervously. Nick yearned to go in and shake Kat to remind her, again, of her self-worth, but she listened to Bianca more than him these days. Bianca could break her out of her fear.

"Well?" Hendrickson snapped. "Fight!"

"Do you want us as humans or wolves?" Yanlei asked.

Hendrickson jutted out his chin and then grunted. His eyes gleamed lasciviously, but before he could act on his primal desires, Gale interrupted him.

"Wolves. Bipedal form."

Hendrickson shot her a look, but Gale ignored him and leaned against the cage to watch. She slumped a little, her eyes closing briefly as if to fight off pain. She touched her bandaged cheek then took a breath and regained her composure. Nick took note of it.

Yanlei started the change instantly. Her body twisted and expanded, fur rushing over her in place of her skin and clothing. Her hands almost ballooned to twice the size with vicious claws on each digit. Nick heard her bones popping and reshifting, but their werewolf genes naturally helped with the pain. Still, the sound made him wince.

Kat's transformation looked slower and less graceful, which had nothing to do with her ability. Nick knew how beautiful she could look when shifting. But the fear distracted her from her true skills. Golden fur glistened on her skin in a tattoo pattern before breaking through flesh. She took on a larger form than Yanlei, towering about half-a-foot higher over the other wolf.

Nick swallowed and ran his hands along his face as she finished and crouched down, one front paw digging into the dirt. Brighton touched his shoulder. "They'll be alright. They're both strong."

"I know," Nick murmured. He watched Kat curl her tail between her legs, every aspect of her body language screaming fear rather than strength. "But Kat can be delicate, and Yanlei is more trained. I don't want either of them to get too hurt."

"If they don't go all in, you know those morons will shock them," Brighton said. "I think we should hope they make it a true fight."

Yanlei took the offense and rushed Kat. Sand flew up around her paws in puffy clouds. She spread her mighty digits and lashed out. Kat ducked beneath the attack and twisted out of the way, sending Yanlei staggering forward. Yanlei caught herself quickly, spun, and launched at Kat again. Kat dodged a second and third time, dancing away from Yanlei's violent blows.

Not once did Kat return a strike.

Nick groaned and glanced over at the Hunters. Gale's expression remained unreadable, but Hendrickson started to thump his boot impatiently on the ground. His battered face twisted into an ugly scowl.

"Come on," the Hunter growled. "One of you get a hit in!"

"Calm down. Maybe she's trying to wear the other werewolf down," Gale said.

"Or she's being a coward."

Kat flicked an ear towards them and then ducked another strike. She jumped away and backed up, putting space between herself and Yanlei. Yanlei rose slowly and huffed in frustration at Kat. Nick couldn't hear them, but he imagined Yanlei giving Kat a mental lashing. Kat shook her head and looked at the cell where Nick, Brighton, and Augustine were being held. The worry and fear glistened in her beautiful eyes.

Nick stood up, gasping in pain as his sore ribs protested. He gripped the cell bar, thankful it wasn't silver. "You can do this," he mouthed. "You're strong."

But Hendrickson had had enough.

Yanlei dropped with a roar of pain, clawing at the collar on her throat. Hendrickson held the controller up and glared over at Kat. "She's going to get hurt one way or another. You want me to be the one to lay her out?"

Kat snarled at him furiously and stalked towards the wall closest to the Hunter, but of course she couldn't get to him. Instead, she positioned herself between him and Yanlei's thrashing body. She snorted, her head rising above the Hunter.

Hendrickson grinned and took his thumb off the button. "Good. Get to it, bitch."

Yanlei struggled to move. She made it halfway up when Kat struck her across the face, knocking her onto her back. Yanlei snarled at her and fought to stand up again, but once more, Kat pounced, bringing her down to the ground, brutally.

"What is she doing?" Nick asked, his voice rising with concern.

"Trying to end the fight quickly," Brighton said. "She doesn't want to battle Yanlei, but she doesn't want that asshole to hurt her either. So, if she takes Yanlei down quickly, then neither one of them has to suffer."

"The Hunters won't like that," Nick hissed and looked over at their captors. "They like the fights to last and get bloody."

Brighton shrugged. "He pushed her, so she's going to act. I'm guessing Yanlei encouraged it, too."

Kat lashed out again, but this time, Yanlei smacked her wrist away and threw herself forward, crashing into Kat's gut. The blow drove Kat backwards. She dug her paws and claws into the sand and leaned forward, putting all her weight onto Yanlei to slow her down. Yanlei roared before striking out at two pressure points on Kat's leg and side.

Kat's leg dropped beneath her, and she fell to the dirt with a yelp. Yanlei followed her towards the ground and elbowed Kat first in the chest then grabbed her head and smashed it onto the ground. Nick grimaced in sympathy as the loud smack of skull against sand and concrete echoed in his ears. He hoped that would put Kat down, but to no avail. Kat jerked her head free and snapped her teeth down around Yanlei's arm.

Yanlei cried out in pain and struck Kat in the face several times with fist and claws. The fifth blow finally broke Kat away from Yanlei's arm, leaving deep gouges in the dhole's flesh. Blood soaked into the golden fur on half of Kat's face, giving her a sickening duology of beautiful werewolf and vicious beast. She spit blood out of her mouth and bunched one of her legs close before sending it like a battering ram into Yanlei's stomach. Yanlei flew back with a pained yelp. She went to all four paws and prowled around Kat, giving her a chance to recover and stand up. Yanlei started limping, her arm oozing blood into the sand.

Kat hobbled, likely waiting for the feeling to come back to her leg. She bared bloody teeth at Yanlei and went down to her paws as well. They paced around each other, snarling, posturing as only werewolves could. As Kat passed near him, Nick caught her eye.

His stomach dropped.

The worry in her eyes had vanished. Instead, he saw an angry, vicious creature ready to tear apart anyone who tried to touch her. It was easier to feel braver and safer in the werewolf body. But that didn't mean the mind stayed safe. She'd let the animal instincts take over to spare her the trauma of her emotions, and her memories of her years of abuse.

"Kat," Nick called to her.

She snarled at him in reply and launched herself at Yanlei.

Nick could only watch helplessly as his two friends ripped into each other with teeth and claws. Yanlei caught Kat on the scruff of the neck with her teeth and threw her into the bars. Kat recovered and pummeled Yanlei's side then face with sharp claws. They bit, scratched, snarled, and howled, driving each other across the fighting ring, trying to bring the other down.

Yanlei knocked Kat onto her stomach, but before the wolf could get onto her feet, Yanlei leapt on her back. She wrapped one of her muscular arms around Kat's throat and yanked, cutting off her air.

Kat froze. For a moment she didn't fight back. Every muscle in her body went rigid and her pupils narrowed to pinpricks. When she came back to her senses, she grappled at Yanlei's arm frantically rather than trying to buck her off. Whines and whimpers escaped her muzzle, her breath coming in ragged gasps. No one could ignore the pure panic which drove her to fight for her freedom.

Yanlei frowned and looked over at Nick, not quite understanding Kat's reaction.

Nick shook his head firmly, trying to tell her to let Kat go. Yanlei waited a moment longer then jerked her arms back and took a few steps away.

Kat crumbled into a broken ball on the ground and trembled, tail tucked between her legs. She couldn't stop whimpering in absolute terror.

Nick's heart broke for her. He knew some of the things Kat's old lover had done to her and what could trigger her. Unfortunately, Yanlei had hit one of those triggers.

"Get up!" Hendrickson shouted and smacked the bars.

Kat huddled into a smaller ball. After a moment, she started to shift back into her human form. Her frame shrunk, her fur slipped into her skin, and her clothing flowed back over her body. The moment she finished the transformation, her whimpers turned into shattered sobs.

Yanlei hunched down. She exchanged looks with Nick and took a step forward as if to comfort Kat, but Hendrickson acted first.

He grabbed his controller and pointed it at Yanlei. "Get back in the cell."

Yanlei didn't argue. The bars came up, and she slid inside, remaining in her bipedal form as he hadn't asked her to change back. It made the holding cell more cramped, but they adjusted. Nick wiggled past Brighton and touched Yanlei's arm comfortingly.

He swallowed, watching anxiously as Hendrickson advanced on Kat. *Let him take you out of the cell*, he thought silently. *Just obey*.

Hendrickson nudged Kat roughly with the tip of his boot. "Get up."

Kat hid her face more from him.

The Hunter rolled his eyes and reached down for her hair.

"Don't!" Nick shouted, but too late.

Hendrickson twisted the golden tresses around his hand and jerked.

Kat's response was instantaneous. She rounded on him with a scream of rage and struck him across the face with her wolf claws. "Get away from me! Don't touch me!"

Hendrickson dropped her and staggered against the wall, clapping a hand over his bloody face. "You bitch!" He fisted his hand around his brass knuckles and swung at her.

Kat wrapped her arms protectively over her head, letting her shoulder take brunt of the blow. Nick threw himself at the bars and tried to squeeze through.

"Leave her alone! Stop it!"

But Hendrickson ignored him and brought his fist down again, leaving a bruise across Kat's folded arms. As he reached for her hair a second time, Nick's cell suddenly exploded, sending broken bars flying. Unbeknownst to him, Augustine had shifted into her bipedal form. The wolf barreled through the flimsier section of the gate and rushed the Hunter. Hendrickson didn't even have a chance to get his hand on the controller before Augustine literally bodied him away from Kat and clawed him across the belly. Four bloody streaks appeared through his clothing, but they weren't enough to kill him.

Kat scrambled away from Hendrickson while he tried to recover. Augustine trotted after her and positioned herself protectively over Kat, her hulking frame dwarfing the younger wolf. "Augustine," Kat whimpered.

Augustine nuzzled her affectionately but bared her teeth at Hendrickson.

Madness filled the Hunter's eyes. He pulled a knife from his belt and ran after Kat, shouting obscenities. Augustine squared her body, acting as a barrier between him and Kat. It lasted all but five seconds before Hendrickson pulled out his controller and shocked Augustine. The werewolf howled in pain and wobbled, almost falling on Kat as she struggled to endure the pain.

Kat crawled out from beneath her to avoid being crushed, but that put her closer to Hendrickson. Hendrickson towered over Kat and Augustine, the blade held tightly in his right hand. He didn't try to grab her hair this time. Instead, he raised the knife to plunge it into her.

Suddenly, Gale appeared at his side and grabbed his wrist. "*Stop*," the woman said.

Hendrickson fought her while holding his bleeding gut with his other arm. "Let go! She deserves this! I'm not going to let some stupid wolf think she can get away with attacking me. I'll kill her before she kills me!"

"And killing her will mean one less person for the pit. We can throw her into a fight we know we won't win, and we won't lose anything worth our time and effort." Gale shifted in front of him and grabbed his chin, forcing him to meet her eyes. "*Think*. That big fight's coming up, Hendrickson. We need all the money we can get. She won't kill you. I won't let anyone take you from me, you know that. We made a promise."

Hendrickson panted, hand quaking. Blood ran down his

stomach, staining his shirt and pattering like rain on the floor. He slowly looked at Gale and clenched his teeth. "She deserves to be punished. All the monsters deserve it."

"They do. You did punish them. Let it be and go get your stomach tended. Make sure that they didn't get any of their venom on you." She touched his chest lightly. "Hendi, come on."

Hendrickson growled under his breath and jerked his arm free. He bowed his head to his sister before squeezing her shoulder lightly with his good hand. "I hate them," he said, almost too quiet for Nick to hear. He glared down at Kat and Augustine one more time and spit at the ground before stalking off.

An eerie silence fell over the fighting pit save for Kat's frightened pants. Gale stood in front of her and glanced over her shoulder at Augustine. The werewolf curled her lip over her teeth but didn't try to attack. They all knew what would happen if one of them killed a Hunter; enough people had died already. With a grunt, Augustine went to Kat and nuzzled her, trying to urge her back to her feet. But Kat didn't want to move. Augustine whined under her breath and looked at Nick imploringly.

Nick nodded. "Please, can I come get her?" he asked Gale.

Gale pressed her lips together and eyed Kat. After a few long moments, she curled her finger. "You, and only you."

Nick touched Yanlei's shoulder and pushed past Brighton. He slipped through the broken gate and limped to Kat's side. "Kat, it's Nick. I'm going to help you up, okay?" He knelt and moved his arm closer to her, letting her see his dark skin and smell his scent.

She sniffed and looked up at him. Suddenly, she sprang into his arms and pressed her head against his shoulder. Her entire body shook like a leaf. "I want to go home. I want Bianca."

"I know," he whispered and stroked her hair. "I know you do."

He stood up and carefully helped Kat despite his own wounds. She leaned heavily against him, turning her body away from Gale as much as possible. Augustine positioned herself protectively on Kat's other side, prowling close like a silent guardian. Nick glanced at Gale, and he saw a look in her eyes that surprised him.

Sympathy.

"That's enough for today," Gale said. "I'll return you to your cells first and then get the others. You," she motioned to Augustine. "Change back and stay with those two."

Augustine growled in protest, but Nick reached out to brush her fur. "Listen to her," he whispered.

Begrudgingly, Augustine pulled away from Kat and stalked towards Brighton.

Nick followed Gale with Kat still pressed up against him. He rubbed her arm, mindful of the new bruises, and kissed her hair. "You nailed him pretty good," he whispered. "He's going to feel that for a while."

"I thought he was going to kill me. I just wanted him to stop. If Augustine hadn't been there..."

"I know. He's an idiot to take you on. Can you imagine the look on Bianca's face when she finds out you fought a Hunter?"

Kat blinked back a few tears and looked up at him. "I didn't do it alone."

"You still defended yourself," he said. "I bet if he'd grabbed you again, you would have ripped his throat out. And he would have deserved it, too."

Gale cleared her throat ahead of them. "You know I can hear you, right?"

Nick didn't apologize. Why should he after what they'd done? He hugged Kat harder as they made their way towards their cells. In the back of his mind, he considered taking Gale out himself, but two things stopped him. One, and most importantly, there were so many Hunters around, he wouldn't get five steps before either getting shocked or stabbed to death. And two, he grudgingly had to thank her for what she'd done for Kat. True, she'd convinced Hendrickson to back off by treating Kat like some kind of commodity, but she was still alive. Bianca still had her mate.

Thank god for Augustine, too. He couldn't believe she'd managed to break through the gate to get to Kat and also had enough sense *not* to kill the Hunter. Maybe there was hope for her yet.

Gale brought them to his cell, but instead of separating them, she let them go inside together. Nick sat down with a grunt and helped Kat beside him. He held her close and watched the Hunter lock the cage then turn to leave. "Hey," he called. When she looked back, he nodded. "Thank you."

Gale's face remained emotionless. Without a word, she headed out of the cave, leaving him and Kat alone.

Nick leaned back wearily. "Damn, girl, you did more damage to them than I have. I'm jealous."

Kat snorted and hugged his arm. "I almost got myself and Augustine killed. What if they take it out on Yanlei?"

Nick grimaced. He didn't want to think of Yanlei getting hurt either. Deep down, he still felt love for Kat, but more like a brotherly love now that she'd found Bianca (or at least he tried to convince himself of that). The more he got to know Yanlei, the more he found himself drawn to her. Her calmness. Her brilliance. Her stubborn nature. She'd been with them since the beginning, and he couldn't imagine losing her any more than he could Kat.

Paytah teased him that he thought with his heart too much. Apparently his alpha was right.

Yanlei, now in human form, was brought to the cell next alongside Brighton. While Gale forced Brighton back into his cage, she put Yanlei in the one with Nick and Kat. It made their quarters cramped, but Nick didn't complain. He opened his arm for Yanlei, but she shook her head and touched his leg instead before turning her attention to Kat.

"I'm so sorry. If I had known what I did would frighten you, I never would have put you in that choke hold."

"It's not your fault," Kat said, still clinging to Nick for support. "I didn't realize I'd react like that." She looked at Yanlei and lowered her eyes in shame. "I'm sorry you were shocked. I didn't want to fight."

"I don't like it either," Yanlei said. "But it's the only way we can survive." She crossed her legs and sat beside them, her hand never once leaving Nick's leg. He put his hand over hers and squeezed it tenderly.

Augustine returned to them kicking and snarling. Gale had her chained up again, not able to trust the furious wolf, and used the pole lead to guide her back to the cell. She shoved Augustine inside and locked the door, barely avoiding a swipe from the angry woman. Augustine glared at her then settled near one side of the cell, hands trembling with too much energy.

Nick grimaced. The room vibrated with her nerves. "She needs to fight," he told Gale. "Or she's going to explode from all that pent up rage. I'll fight her."

"That's not your decision to make," Gale said and left the room.

Nick sighed and settled against Kat to comfort her and himself. He'd lost track of the days they'd been there, the amount of fights they'd been forced into. Brighton was going to have a permanent limp before the end of this, and Nick didn't think he was too far behind. He would have expected Paytah or the pack to move in sooner than this, and the more time that passed, the more he wondered if they'd ever be found.

Kat rubbed her bruised arm slowly. "What if they don't find us?"

"They will," Nick said with less conviction.

"But what if they don't?"

Nick opened and shut his mouth. What could he say? The collars would take them down if they fought back. Hunters guarded the exits and entrances. They were all exhausted. What chance did they stand?

"We'll find a way," Yanlei said. "Wolves have escaped the fighting pits before, and we'll do it again. We must bide our time. Learn. Conserve our strength. We can't give up hope."

Kat looked at her and offered a smile. "Thank you."

Nick squeezed Yanlei's hand and felt her return the warm gesture. Hope. He wasn't sure if he still held hope in his heart, but he stubbornly refused to die here, locked in a cell while his friends were trapped around him. The Hunters wanted him to give a good fight? Oh, he'd prove why you didn't mess with a wolf pack. And he'd see his friends freed.

Somehow.

***

Nick fell asleep hours later within the warm embrace of his pack. They were awoken at some point for food, which Nick couldn't ignore. He drank and ate, making sure both Yanlei and Kat had plenty first. A healing tonic must have been added because, as he devoured his meal, he felt his wounds start to mend and his energy return to him. For people who hated parahumans, they definitely enjoyed using their magical elixirs.

They settled in to rest again with nothing else to do. Nick was curled up contentedly with Yanlei and Kat beside him when lights suddenly blazed in their cave. He hissed in pain and put his arm over his eyes. He'd started to adjust to the darkness of the cells. The light shone even brighter than the ones in the rings.

He blinked a few times then grunted in surprise when he saw a dark man holding up a light to illuminate him. That was...no...it couldn't be.

"Saul?" Kat whispered.

Saul looked over at them without an ounce of care in his eyes. He glanced around the room then turned his head towards Gale and Hendrickson. "You'll be compensated if they are taken out of the ring too quickly. But I want them all in."

"Why are you so worried about *them*?" Gale asked.

"Because you two couldn't handle a simple job," Saul snarled. "You had one target, and you both fled before it was done. And now I've been recognized."

Gale stiffened. "We weren't the only ones who failed. You were tossed off the balcony because of that damn fire magus first. And I wasn't going to let my brother get killed. We lost enough following your orders." She gestured to her bandaged cheek then to Hendrickson who lightly touched his shoulder.

"I'm not just talking about that night. I mean the car crash, too." Saul advanced on Gale, staring down at her with furious eyes. "You assured me the werewolf wouldn't survive or at least there'd be permanent damage."

Hendrickson slid between them, despite being shorter than Saul. "Maybe next time you should finish your victims off yourself."

"Hendrickson," Gale hissed and grasped his arm as if ready to jerk him out of the way of an incoming attack.

Saul snorted down at them and glanced at the captive wolves. "It doesn't matter now. They might recognize me, but they have no way of finding out where we are. Still, I don't want them to have the opportunity of getting their wolves back." He shot Gale a look. "I've already paid you a hefty amount. This is my last order. Once the matches are done, take whoever is left and leave. You can find other wolf pits elsewhere."

Hendrickson scowled but neither looked interested in arguing with the vampire. Gale nodded and passed a pole over to Hendrickson. "I'll get the money."

"Gale," he said in warning, grabbing her wrist.

"I'll be fine," she replied and nodded to the cages. "Do what he says." With that, she left with Saul and the bright light.

Nick blinked a few times and looked at Hendrickson. The Hunter gripped the pole with such force, Nick expected it to snap in half. After a moment, the man stalked towards Nick's cage, and he tensed, waiting for a fight.

"A vampire?" Nick asked. "You hate parahumans so much, and yet you're working with a vampire?"

Hendrickson glowered. "He pays better than the matches do. And I hate vampires a lot less than werewolves."

Painful shocks hit Nick, knocking him to the floor. He thrashed, gasping for breath while Yanlei and Kat shouted his name. The door flung open, and Hendrickson thrust one pole in, grabbing Kat around the throat. She choked as he dragged her to her feet. He grabbed Yanlei by the arm and yanked her out before slamming the cage shut.

The pain subsided.

Nick rolled to his knees and scrambled to the front of the cage. He reached out for them, ignoring the silver that bit at his arm. "Yanlei! Kat!"

"No, no! Please let me go. Don't do this!" Kat cried.

Hendrickson jerked both women along, leaving Nick, Augustine, and Brighton to shout their outrage. Nick beat against the door so hard he felt his fingers start to burn and bleed. But there was nothing he could do. He slumped, helpless, as Hendrickson dragged both wolves away towards battle and possible death.

Chapter 22
The Hunters' Den

Tess

"Well, this is the place." Arjun lowered the tracking device and stared ahead at the gaping entrance of the subway.

Tess leaned forward to get a better look down the dark stairway that led under the city and frowned. There were no visible signs of Hunters or parahumans coming around here. A light brush of magic didn't tell her anything, but maybe they weren't close enough. The entrance looked like any other abandoned subway. She looked at the dot and shifted on her feet. "It's like we're right above her."

"Maybe we are," Trish said. She turned slowly in place, taking in the area. Arjun had fixed her up to look more like a battered, broken down captive. Her hair was about as messy and dirt-filled as Tess's, her clothing tattered and ripped in places. Trish had stopped them from tearing her jacket though, leaving it folded in Arjun's car instead. Cuffs bound her wrists in front of her, like Arjun had done to Tess. Neither liked being bound, but it would be more convincing this way. Unlike Tess, Trish had a "vampire muzzle" on, a sort of cage over her mouth that allowed her to speak and breathe but prevented her from using her fangs. "I can smell wolves and vampires. Mostly wolves, though." She glanced at Tess. "No magical signatures?"

Tess shook her head. "Not yet, but that doesn't mean there's not something there. We might have to get underground first."

Arjun pressed his lips together and stuck the tracker back into his pocket. "I don't like it. They could have left a Hunter mark behind to at least tell me where to go." He grabbed the chains attached to their cuffs and tugged lightly.

Tess walked behind him slowly, keeping her head down in case they were being watched. Trish still kept her distance, tugging now and again on the chains for show. No vampire in her right mind would allow herself to be dragged into a Hunter's den, even if it seemed like she was dosed with mistletoe.

They slipped into the dark entrance and down the dusty stairs slowly, carefully, Arjun always keeping in front to check for clues, and to protect them, Tess thought. She and Trish were more powerful than him, but if a Hunter came upon them, they'd be targeted first.

They reached chained gates, but Arjun used a few tools to get the locks undone. The doors opened with a rusty moan that made all three of them flinch. They slipped through and waited, but still no one appeared.

He shut the gate quietly behind them. Tess looked around, but there wasn't much to see. Arjun turned on a flashlight and shone it around, but when they reached the Washington-Madison mezzanine, they were greeted by the barren remnants of the station. Thick, dirty beams kept the street and buildings above from crashing down on them. Red paint peeled off of the railings, while a blue coating covered part of the wall. She could barely make out the word "Washington" in faded white paint. A couple remaining signs, once lit with directions, held no power and could only reflect Arjun's flashlight. Others had been ripped down, leaving exposed wires behind.

"*I don't like this,*" she said mentally to them. Trish could respond back, but Tess had to keep an Ether pathway open so that Arjun could "think" his thoughts to them. "*What if the tracer fell off here, but they were taken somewhere else? Wouldn't they have guards?*"

"*Not necessarily. They might have cameras or something up to keep an eye on the tunnel. Or there are secret entrances only Hunters would know about. Which could give us some trouble. But having guards constantly around while trains run through here would be suspicious.*"

"*Some trouble?*" Trish thought, her mind-voice rising with annoyance. "*Do you have a contingency plan for this, mighty*

Hunter? Or are we just going to hope we don't get shot?"

Arjun glanced back at her in frustration. *"I'm doing the best I can to help your people. Trust me a little on this."*

"Trust a Hunter, he says," Trish mocked.

Tess wrinkled her nose. *"Says the vampire who worked with Hunters."*

Trish grunted. *"Touché."*

Arjun guided them along without comment, taking the concrete path through the subway. When they got near the underground tunnel over the tracks, he pulled out the tracker before shoving it back into his pocket with a grunt. *"We're moving further away from it."*

Tess bit her lip. *"What do we do then? What if—"*

"We're not alone," Trish cut in. *"I smell a human."*

Tess looked at her and then over her shoulder. The tunnel was eerily quiet except for the occasional creak or the patter of rubble falling. Arjun shone the light behind them then turned and flashed it ahead.

A man stood in the glow of the light.

Tess jumped backwards with a start and Trish jerked against the chains, but Arjun held fast and yanked her close. He kept the flashlight trained on the tall Black man. For a moment, Tess panicked, thinking it was Saul, but as her vision cleared, she realized the man was actually bald and stood taller than vampire. He stared down his nose at Arjun and glanced briefly at the two chained women, but he didn't seem alarmed at their predicament.

"Who are you?" he asked in a deep bass.

Arjun bobbed his head. "Hunter Arjun. I heard rumors of a fighting pit around here. I'm hoping to either sell these two off or bet on them in a fight."

"Prove it."

Arjun blinked. "Excuse me?"

"Prove you're a Hunter."

Arjun lifted his chin. Tess expected him to shake their chains to show them off again, but instead, he reached for his clothing and shined the flashlight on his tattoo.

The man eyed it before his gaze swept over Tess and Trish again. "Kind?"

"Magus," he said, pulling down his shirt. "Vampire. Both dosed."

The other Hunter crossed his arms and squared his shoulders. "We don't typically take in magi. Too much trouble to keep them under control."

"I wasn't sure about your policies. The one in Wisconsin likes magi. I don't have to sell it here. But I don't want to leave it alone while I find a use for the vampire."

Trish jerked on the chains again, almost pulling Arjun off of his feet. He growled and yanked hard, causing her to fall to her knees at his side. In a swift move, he pressed a taser at the back of her neck. "Don't make this harder on yourself," he warned her. The taser buzzed an inch from her throat.

Trish froze in place.

The other Hunter chuckled. "You're young, aren't you?" he remarked. "Is this your first catch?"

"Um, second," Arjun said and put the taser away. "The first didn't quite make it all the way to the pit."

"Wisconsin?"

Arjun nodded.

The man sighed and motioned with his hand. "Well, follow me, *Hunter* Arjun before the next train comes through. My name is Slater. You've come at a good time. We're having a tournament, and the pit is alive with a spectacle of fights. Hopefully, your vampire can stand her ground against at least one opponent."

Arjun hurried after him, tugging on the chains until Trish and Tess fell into step behind him. Tess bumped her shoulder lightly into Trish and gave her a look, silently asking if she was alright. Trish offered a subtle nod in answer.

"Are you not in the tournament?" Arjun asked.

"My early brackets are already complete," Slater explained. "I have two moving on to the later rounds, but I have to wait for the other brackets to finish up. Some of the fights have been quite bloody. Fights to the death and the like." He glanced at Arjun. "I hope you have the stomach for that."

Arjun snorted. "If it means seeing the end to these monsters, of course. How did you know I was here?"

The man folded his arms behind him and raised his chin. "We have cameras to make sure we don't have parahumans trying to invade and save their companions. Have to be careful. Someone alerted me to your presence. As my fights are complete, I thought I'd see for myself what the trouble was." He turned towards a wall and reached out. Before he touched it, he looked back at Arjun. "Don't be alarmed," he said then stepped forward.

Slater vanished from sight.

Tess jolted. How was that possible? She reached out tentatively with her power and felt it bounce off a magical barrier. "*They're using magic! Who would help them?*" she asked Arjun.

Arjun didn't reply, which was probably for the best. She didn't need someone else noticing her active magic.

Tess followed him through the wall and was immediately bombarded by noise and stench. She stood on an upper steel platform that circled around the fighting pit. Stairs led down to the main floor, but from her vantage, she could see everything beneath harsh fluorescent lights. Cages and cells filled one corner of the room likely where parahumans were forced to fight. She watched as werewolves crashed into one another, clawing at each other's face. Parahumans, mostly young and fit, sat dejectedly inside of prisons as they waited to be dragged into the next fight.

The main attraction, though, was a giant fighting ring at the center of the room. Bleachers encompassed the field where Hunters sat, cheered, and booed the combatants. Two wolves in bipedal form raced around each other. A black wolf grabbed the grey around his waist and hurled him across the ring. The gray smashed into a wall and collapsed to the ground, blood staining his head while Hunters roared with excitement.

Tess looked away in disgust, her heart pounding in her chest. Was this what her father and Nick had been going through all this time? Had they been forced into the ring to fight to the death? Were they even alive?

Panic rose inside of her, clawing at her throat and stealing her breath. She stumbled back and hit the side of a wall near the hidden entrance. Arjun glanced at her, but he obviously couldn't comfort her in front of Slater.

Trish backed away from the stairs with a hiss and stopped next to Tess, blocking her view from the battle field. "*I know you're scared and angry, but you need to pull yourself together. Your pack needs you.*"

Tess sucked in a breath and glanced at Trish. The vampire was right, but the panic argued its point by tightening her chest and making her stomach twist until bile rose in her throat. Only Trish's presence in her mind kept her steady. She breathed slowly, as she'd been taught, and brought the anxiety down to a reasonable level, at least for the moment. *I'll be fine.*

"*Good.*" The vampire looked down at the battle while Arjun and Slater talked.

"How long have you been here?" Arjun asked.

"Oh, our operation has been running for years. We were in another section of Chicago before we were betrayed. They thought we'd fled, but we simply moved here. Such a shame. We had a bigger space back then."

Tess sucked in a breath. A bigger space than this? How many parahumans had died *there*?

Slater headed for the stairs, and Arjun quickly followed. "Are the parahumans just from Chicago or other places?"

"What was it like in the one in Wisconsin?" Slater asked, glancing back at Arjun.

"Mixed. There were two fighting rings I remember. One only had Wisconsin-based parahumans. Another was a trading ground. But neither one can compare to the size here."

Slater smiled. "The larger cities generally have the most space. The one in New York is the biggest, so if you're ever in that area and need to trade, go there."

Arjun nodded and grinned. "Good to know that we're putting these creatures out to pasture. We don't need any more of their kind running around, killing people, or spreading their disease."

Tess swallowed as she listened to his tone. She was glad to know he was on their side, because he definitely didn't sound like it. Even Trish gave her a nervous look. Tess shrugged and walked carefully after them.

"How did you come up with the hidden entrance?" Arjun asked curiously. "I'm surprised you'd be using magic if you can't keep magi-users under control."

A coy smile lit Slater's face. "Oh, I can't divulge all our secrets. Trust that we're safe."

They walked past the main pit and Tess looked inside at the combatants. Two wolves in biped form again. This really was a wolf pit, wasn't it?

Arjun and Slater paused as one of the wolves was thrown onto his back and the larger male pinned him with arms over his neck. "Are you familiar with the game?" Slater asked.

"It's different in every area. You said there's a tournament going on?"

"Yes. Generally Hunters bring in their prey, and they can fight for keeps. If my creature wins, then I keep the loser's. We can exchange money, too. We guess which one will come out on top. You can make some good money." He glanced at Trish and Tess, looking them up and down. "Well, if you had a male wolf you could. Vampires don't often last long down here, especially not women. You won't find many buyers for your magus."

Arjun shrugged. "I'll be moving on soon enough, so I can take her to another trading ground. Like I said, Wisconsin's more magic friendly."

Slater chuckled. "Maybe you aren't so inexperienced after all." He motioned for them to follow him.

Arjun tugged on the chains and the women moved along. Tess passed the cage as the fallen wolf was dragged out and the other crowned the winner. They didn't even bother to clean up the bloody ring. Instead, a Hunter shoved a bedraggled man out to fight, his pants tattered, his hair messy, his face bruis—

Tess tripped in shock. *Dad*!

Her father panted as he faced off against the other werewolf. He shook himself and started to transform into his bipedal form, rich fur rushing over his body. He barely changed before the winning wolf attacked. Her father snarled and ducked away before clawing the other one on the back. His reward came in the form of a chest full of claws, forcing a howl of pain from his lips.

Tess couldn't help herself. She yanked on the chains and tried to get closer, panic rising. Not her father. Not here! She'd hoped to find him caged, not forced to fight in the ring. She searched the cells and found Nick waiting in the wings, watching intently as her father battled the new wolf.

"*It's Nick! And my dad!*" Tess shouted mentally at Arjun and Trish.

Arjun grunted as she jerked the chains. He pulled her hard, causing her to stumble back towards him. Trish bumped into her and grabbed the back of her arm tightly.

"*Stop it! You're going to draw too much attention. And if they recognize you, we're screwed.*"

"*But my dad—*"

"*If he's survived this long, then he can survive a little longer,*" Arjun thought to them gently. "*Tess, I know this is hard, but this is why we're here. To find your family and friends. We find the rest, then we get out and get help."*

Tess fought back tears. Each blow to her father's body sent a shock down hers. She wanted to jump into the ring and burn the other wolf for his transgressions, but he was as much a captive as her dad, wasn't he? And what about Nick? He couldn't stand up to that sort of fight, could he?

She tore her eyes away from them to another, smaller ring where a familiar golden wolf fought against a smaller reddish-hued wolf. A sharp strike knocked the golden wolf backwards, and she skidded, trembling, across the ring.

Oh Kat, she thought to herself. She was grateful her packsister was still alive, but not like this. Bianca would murder them, or Tess, over what had been done to her. The urge to use her magic and break everyone free burned inside of her, but she also knew they wouldn't make it out of the fighting ring. And it wasn't like she had teleportation abilities. She wasn't talented enough for that.

"Just how big is this compound?" Arjun asked.

"There are many levels here. The amount of Hunters comes and goes daily. New missions. New places to go fight with their prizes." Slater glanced around. "We aren't at full capacity yet, though that's happened before. I expected the tournament to bring more out." He looked over at Arjun. "How long have you been in the Hunter business?"

"A few years, but I'm still getting my feet wet."

Slater smiled a little. "Interesting. Normally a new Hunter wouldn't be able to take down both a magus and a vampire, and with so little fighting, too. Despite some outbursts, you seem to have them cowed."

Tess glanced over at Slater and cursed inwardly. She and Trish were supposed to at least be acting like captives. Shouldn't the sight of this place be a big enough excuse to reason why they weren't battling Arjun?

Trish took point, though, and suddenly twisted the lead around her hand and snapped it towards Arjun's back. The metal hit his spine, and he hissed in pain before jerking the chain forward and knocking Trish to her knees. He shoved her face-first into the ground and planted his boot on the back of her neck. "I wish it was so easy," he commented. "I'm sure the look of the fighting ring has them scared, but this is what they're used to attempting. Idiots." He pushed Trish's face harder into the dirt. "Don't know what's good for them."

"That they don't," Slater said with a hint of amusement in his tone. "Well, then. What you haven't seen contains the holding cells, which I can show you after you sell your vampire."

"If I find a good enough buyer," Arjun said with a grin. He moved his foot, allowing Trish to struggle to her knees. She spit dirt out and coughed, fighting with the cage over her mouth. At least it had protected her nose from shattering. Arjun grabbed her wrists and yanked her back up to her feet before following Slater again. "Do you have buyers I could speak to?"

"A few. I—"

A fierce howl rang out followed by shouts and curses. Tess looked back towards the ring where Kat fought and saw the golden wolf start thrashing her opponent. A Hunter tried to come in after her, but she beat him back with claws and snaps of her powerful jaws. The other Hunters started crowding in, obscuring Tess's view. She heard more roars and shouts.

Suddenly, the loud snarl of a gun echoed through the room.

Tess froze. Her heart skipped a beat, and she tried to peer through the Hunters to see what had happened. *Don't be dead. Don't be dead*, she begged silently.

The bodies parted, but before she could see anything, Arjun pulled her away.

Slater snorted. "Some of the other younger Hunters are still having issues controlling their beasts. A handful of the wolves shouldn't have been entered into the match. Then again, maybe it's a way for them to get rid of useless merchandise."

Useless merchandise.

The words cut Tess like a knife to the heart. She spun towards Slater, her fear for her pack, and her hatred of the Hunters consuming her sense of reason. She didn't bother reaching for the fire inside of her. She launched herself at Slater, fist flying for his face.

Arjun wrapped his arm around her waist and jerked her back before she could hit the other Hunter. "*Stop it! Don't make me hurt you!*" he shouted mentally to her, their connection still open. He threw her back, sending her tumbling to the ground.

Tess hit the dirt and panted, her gaze burning with rage.

Slater looked down at her with cold, unfeeling eyes. He walked past Arjun and crouched next to her. His hand streaked out like a snake and caught her by her chin. "And this is why we don't keep magi here. Such emotional creatures. They try to pass off as human, but they'll stab you in the back just as quickly for being *normal*." He glanced at Arjun. "You should be rid of her before she does you in next."

"I'll take that into consideration," Arjun said. He pulled the chain, bringing Tess closer to him. She got up and took a step away from Slater, chills running down her spine. She didn't like Hunters in general, but something about him scared her more than any other one ever had.

She fell into step beside Trish while Arjun and Slater spoke amicably about the fighting ring. Tess listened as much as she could, but she couldn't stop looking around at all of the bedraggled parahumans.

"Are there other entrances to this pit?" Arjun asked.

Slater chuckled. "Well, we have several. The one you took is a main one, but there are more. Since you know where that one is, that's the only one you need to know about. No sense in revealing all of the locations."

"Of course. You want to keep your secrets safe," Arjun agreed.

Tess glanced sideways at him. He sounded so calm, so natural. How long had he been a Hunter? He said he went into pits like this and helped others, but had it always been that way? Or had he been like *these* Hunters at some point in his life?

Stop doubting him, she thought to herself. *You know he wants to help, and that's all that matters.*

They stopped near a hallway at the border of the fighting pit. "The holding cells are down here. I can show you around if you—"

"Slater!" someone called.

Tess glanced over her shoulder as a woman walked towards him, pulling along a limping bound man behind her.

Slater nodded. "Yes?"

"The next brackets are up. You're first."

Slater pressed his lips together. "I'll be there shortly. Thank you. Are Gale and Hendrickson finished?"

"They're cleaning up the last mess."

Slater nodded and tilted his head towards Arjun. "Wait here for a moment. I'll go speak to them and see if they can show you around while I'm occupied."

"Of course." Arjun replied.

Slater departed with the woman, though not before she looked back at Arjun and grinned, her eyes roving over him hungrily. Tess almost scowled at her but decided not to draw more attention to herself than she'd already done. She watched the Hunters for a moment as they headed towards the fighting ring where Kat had been battling. The field was clear of bodies, but blood flooded the ground in several patches. Her breath caught in her throat. She could only hope that Kat had survived.

She began to turn away when she noticed Slater walking towards another female Hunter. It only took Tess a moment to recognize her.

"Shit. Oh shit. He's talking to one of the Hunters that took Augustine and Kat. If she sees me, she's going to recognize me."

Arjun followed her gaze and swore quietly under his breath. *"Come on. We'll slip out of the main room for now. If she gives us trouble, we'll deal with her out of sight."*

Tess grimaced but didn't argue. She and Trish followed him into the hallway and moved past openings in the walls that led to caged rooms. Tess glanced at them as she passed, spotting parahumans chained or trapped behind silver bars. The smell of sickness and unbathed bodies hung heavily in the air, almost suffocating her.

They rounded another corner when Trish tugged on the chains. *"Wait, I smell something familiar. I think it's your pack, Tess."*

Tess skidded and looked over at the tunnel Trish stopped near. The trio exchanged glances before Arjun went towards the room. A few lanterns dimly lit the way. When Tess stepped inside, she wanted to vomit. The smell of blood overwhelmed her. Four cages filled the room, each holding chains and thin pads for the captives to rest on. She moved towards one of the open doors and looked inside, imagining her father bound like some animal.

Trish wrinkled her nose. *"I smell him."*

"Who?" Arjun asked.

"Saul. He's been here."

Tess looked over at her then back at the cages. If Saul had been in there, then he was likely walking free, a problem in and of itself.

"We shouldn't stay," Arjun whispered. "At least we know where they're being held."

He turned and headed towards the cave entrance.

Tess followed reluctantly and exchanged nervous glances with Trish. They neared the opening when a dark shadow fell across them. Tess tensed, expecting the female Hunter.

It was worse.

Saul.

Chapter 23
Betrayal

Saul's foreboding frame loomed in the entrance, blocking their escape. His eyes darted first to Arjun, then to Tess, and finally to Trish. A raised eyebrow was the only indication that he might have recognized her.

"What are you doing in here?" he asked in a cool, collected voice.

"*That's Saul,*" Tess quickly informed Arjun.

Arjun, to his credit, didn't look caught off guard. He remained calm as he yanked on her and Trish's chains, bringing them closer to him. He pulled out a gun and pointed it at Saul, his eyes narrowed. "I should be asking you the same thing *vampire*. What are you doing out of a cage?"

Tess almost snapped at him for being an idiot, but then remembered that he was supposed to be playing the part of a Hunter. They sometimes had ways of *knowing* what parahumans were. A sixth sense.

Saul sighed in boredom. "Put that away. I have more right to be here than you do." His eyes drifted to Trish. "Are you coming to sell your property? I'm working with Gale and Hendrickson Telmar. They'd be interested in having another vampire in their *employment.*"

Arjun snorted, the gun still raised. "And you have *permission* to purchase? They're fools for not keeping you collared."

Saul chuckled, the sound deep and threatening, though he made no move to attack Arjun. "You're just like the rest of them. And yes, I have permission. What do you want for her?"

"Depends on how much you're willing to spend. Make me an offer."

Tess noticed the way that Arjun had shifted to put himself boldly between her, Trish, and Saul. She glanced at the female vampire who stared at Saul with wide, shocked eyes. Trish tugged a little on her chains and tried to move closer to Saul, but Arjun held out his hand, blocking her.

"S-Saul? What are you doing here?"

"*Quiet*," Arjun growled aloud to her.

Saul held up his hand. "Let her speak. I know her." He smiled sadly. "I was afraid that you'd been caught up in the pit when you disappeared from home."

"You've been helping them all this time? How could you? After everything our coven has been through?" Her shoulders stiffened and she threw her arms down in frustration. "After everything the coven put *me* through because I joined Hunters?"

Arjun glanced between the two vampires and smirked. "You know her, hm? Well, don't think you can take her off my hands so cheaply."

Saul's tenderness vanished as he bared fangs at the Hunter. "Don't play me for a fool, *boy*. I know the costs of parahumans, and if you ask too high, you'll be laughed out of here. No one is going to want to spend their hard-earned money on a female vampire who can't fight, or a magus either," he added, glaring at Tess.

Tess clenched her hands into fists. "You're the reason my father and the others are held captive here, aren't you? We thought just the Hunters were behind this, but it was one of our own District members this whole time. You bastard. How could you betray us like this? And your own duke! Does Joseph even know you've been letting vampires get sold, too?"

She waited for his explosion or for him to slip up, but she should have known better. Saul played the game far better than she did.

He brushed dirt off of his jacket and lifted his chin. "Why should I follow a Violet Marshall who isn't held accountable for his crimes against me and for the murder of my mate? Why should I follow a duke who whimpers at the heels of the Marshall and doesn't defend his coven?"

He looked at Trish. Again, softness filled his eyes and he held out his hand towards her. "You know it to be true, Trish. You went missing, and he never once sent someone out to find you. Our own vampires have vanished, and he did nothing to help them, and I can assure you, I had no hand in their disappearance. He looks out for himself, alone. His hunger for power drives him, and he gets rid of the ones who want to challenge him, like his wife. Haven't you noticed that she's never around?"

Trish bowed her head and shuffled anxiously in the chains. "We're supposed to help each other. That's the point of being in a District. But when I helped the Hunters, everyone wanted me dead. And I was only trying to protect the coven."

"Exactly. You were trying to save us, but you were nearly killed for it. Joseph wanted you branded and banished, but I convinced him to let you stay so you could be safe. You belong with the people who care about you, like I do, Trish." He spread his arms. "Stay with me, rule the coven with me, and I'll protect you."

Trish lifted her eyes, her body quaking with nerves. "You mean it?"

Tess shot her a look. "*What are you doing? You can't be buying this.*"

But Trish didn't respond to her.

Arjun grunted and pulled Trish closer, wrapping a strong hand around her bicep. "How about you continue your heart-felt bullshit later and make me a deal."

Saul sighed and drew out a checkbook. "Very well, *Hunter*." He scrawled down a number and turned it around to Arjun.

Tess had never seen that much money before in her life. It was a small fortune, and would take care of a person's needs for years. She didn't miss the surprise in Trish's eyes either.

Arjun holstered his gun. "Generous. But still not enough."

Saul snorted. "Go and ask around. See if anyone else will purchase her for anything more. You'd best give her to me."

"I'll consider your proposal," Arjun said. "But for now, I bid you good day." He held fast to the chains and made to move around Saul to get them out of the room.

Saul didn't budge. He tore out the check and handed it to Arjun with more force. "Give me the girl."

Arjun glared back at the vampire. "No."

They were saved from their squabbling as someone else stepped into the cave.

Though Tess realized quickly that "saved" was the wrong word to use.

Gale marched up to Saul, a lilac fragrance following in her wake. A bandage covered the side of her face that Tess had burned. "Have you seen a new Hunter and his two slaves? Slater said— *you*." Gale took one look at Tess and pulled a gun from her belt. There was no warning, no pleading, no chance to bargain.

The Hunter met Tess's eyes and fired.

Tess heard the impact but never felt it.

Arjun moved in front of her, taking the bullet through his side. He fell to his knees, clutching the injury. The chains fell away from his hand, clattering to the floor, as crimson blood flowed between his quivering fingers.

Tess couldn't stop herself. She scrambled to Arjun's side and grabbed his arm so she could see his wound. "How bad is it?"

"Tess," he hissed in warning.

Saul grabbed Gale's wrist and jerked it back, spinning her towards him. "Are you mad, woman?"

"No, that little bitch has been the bane of my existence since we took on your stupid mission." She jerked free and pointed the gun again. "She survived the car crash when we took her father. She stalked us. She managed to escape us when we took the rest of her mutts. She burned my face and saved the alpha. I'm not letting her get away again." She kept the weapon trained and sneered at Tess and Arjun. "And it looks to me like she's playing us again. What Hunter would step in front of his slave?"

"She's *my* property," Arjun said between clenched teeth.

Gale leaned forward. "Give it up, boy. You're working with them, aren't you?"

Arjun bowed his head and gasped for breath. Tess tightened her hold on his arm fiercely. She couldn't let him die, not after he'd saved her. She placed her hand on his back and pushed magic into him to help mend the wound, or at least stop it from killing him. She tried to keep the power hidden from sight and subtle enough that Saul wouldn't notice it.

Saul stood up taller and looked at Trish. "Is this true? Is he working with you?"

Tess waited for the denial but none came.

Trish looked down at Arjun and Tess, Gale's gun still fixed on them both. Without a word, she reached up and undid the cage around her mouth. She dropped it on the floor then jerked the chains down on her right knee, snapping them. The tiny metal fragments tinkled as they hit the cold stone floor. Arjun had left a flaw in them, so if they had to escape, they could.

"Of course it's true," Trish said calmly and walked past Tess. Tess stared after her, eyes wide. "*Trish! What are you doing?*"

But the woman's mind remained closed to her.

"I brought them to you as a gift," Trish said and sidled up beside Saul, her hand brushing his arm affectionately. "They said they had a way to find this place, and I went along with them so I could find you. You're right. Joseph is terrible at leading the coven. He's not a duke, not like you. And he doesn't give a damn about me. No one in the District does." She laughed. "I even got that stupid bird to believe I turned over a new leaf. She should know better. Vampires stick together." She glanced cautiously at Gale, as if waiting for her to turn the gun on her next.

Saul held out his arm to block Gale and bring Trish to him. His eyes softened further and he hooked a finger beneath Trish's chin. "You came looking for me?"

"Yes, I suspected you were involved, but I couldn't figure out how to find you without the Hunters trying to kill or enslave me." She kicked dirt back at Tess and Arjun. "He's playing you. He never meant to sell us. He just wanted information." She rushed into his embrace and held him tightly. "I missed you, Saul."

Tess gripped Arjun's arm harder. "You conniving lying snake," she hissed at Trish. "I knew I never should have trusted you."

"And yet you did," Trish said. "You're an idiot." She leaned against Saul. "Did you mean it? That I could stay here with you and serve at your side?"

Saul smiled and looked imploringly at Gale.

Gale rolled her eyes. "*Fine,* but let's be rid of these two first." She leveled the gun at Tess's head.

"Can I do it?" Trish asked, holding out her hand towards the Huntress.

The question struck like an arrow to the heart. Tess had wanted to believe the woman was telling the truth. She'd wanted to believe that Trish had repented for the part she'd played in Gladus's death.

But the same monster stood before her that Tess had grown to loathe.

Gale wrinkled her nose.

"Let her do it," Saul said, his voice rising with pride. "Let her prove herself. If you want to kill the magus, at least let her put down the Hunter."

"Fine," the woman groused and shoved the gun into Trish's hand.

Trish grinned and ran her hand over the cool metal. She pointed it at Arjun and met Tess's eyes. "Sorry about this. No hard feelings."

Tess tightened her hold on Arjun, her magic burning within her, willing a shield to form that would be strong enough to ward off a bullet. "Go to hell."

Trish smiled.

Suddenly, the vampire spun, cracking the gun across Gale's jawline and sending her crumbling to the ground. Before Saul could move, Trish flew at him, fist in his stomach, one across his face, and the butt of the gun clacking off of his temple. He dropped like a sack of potatoes next to the Huntress. Trish stood over them, panting, the gun lying in two pieces on the floor.

Tess stared, mouth hanging open. "Did you—"

"I'm not a monster," Trish rasped. She looked back at them, angry tears in her eyes. "Did you really think I would sell you out so easily? I was trying to give you time to heal him before they noticed." She went to their side and quickly broke the chains off of Tess's wrists. "You need to get out of here before they wake up."

"What are you talking about?" Tess hissed. "You're coming with us. We're not leaving you here."

"He's losing a lot of blood," Trish said.

Arjun's face had taken on a ghostly pallor, his grip weakening by the minute. "I'll be fine," he said in a mumble.

Tess heard the lie in his shaky voice. She touched his cheek and steadied him. "Don't you die on me," she snapped. "That wasn't part of the plan." She shot a reproachful look at Trish. "And neither is staying behind. We can kill them and get out."

"And if their bodies are found? Slater's going to know we did it, and they'll kill your pack for this." Trish blew out a breath. She crouched down and draped her hands between her knees, head bowed. "I can manipulate Saul's memories, and the Hunter's. I can make them think you attacked us and escaped, and I'm still with them. That way…if things go south, you'll still have a contact. I can still *help*."

"Trish—"

"We knew there was a chance this would fall apart," Trish said, glancing sideways at them. "If I can get to Slater, I can change his memories too, but I can bet you he's on a dose of mistletoe so not even Saul can corrupt him. Get out of here, and tell the pack where we are before it's too late. With any luck, I'll get rescued with everyone else pretty soon."

Tess stared at the vampire and swallowed. A familiar panic swept through her, causing her to flash back to leaving Ray and the others behind, even though she'd had no choice at the time. She had a choice now, and yet… "Don't die," she whispered. "And I'm sorry for what I said."

Trish smiled sadly and shrugged. "Hey, it's not the first time someone thought I was a lying conniving snake." Her face turned somber. "Get out of here, Tess. Use your cloaking spell."

"I could bring you, too."

Trish shook her head. "I've made up my mind. Besides, healing him is draining your powers. You'll have to focus on hiding the two of you. I'll clean up any messes you leave behind."

Trish started to rise, but Tess reached out and squeezed her arm. "I won't forget this. We'll get you out of here." She hefted Arjun's arm over her shoulder and hoisted him to his feet. He struggled not to cry out in pain.

"You should leave me here," he whispered. "I'll slow you down."

"I'm not losing both of you," Tess said and wrapped magic around herself, hiding them both from sight. They shuffled to the door, Arjun growing heavier on her with each step. Just before they left, Tess glanced over her shoulder at Trish as the woman knelt beside Saul. "For what it's worth," Tess called, "Gladus was right to help you. She'd be proud."

She didn't wait for Trish to respond. Instead, she clutched Arjun harder and slipped out of the cave.

Blood pounded in her ears as she guided Arjun through the tunnel. Her magic flowed around her and in him, healing him, keeping them out of sight. Anyone sensitive to Ether would notice it (which was why she hadn't brought them in shielded in the first place), so she hoped and prayed that Saul was the only parahuman the Hunters had employed in the immediate vicinity. Guilt gnawed at her for leaving Trish behind, but the vampire was right. They'd need help if things went wrong.

The battles still waged in the main room. She held Arjun against her and watched a pair of werewolves being led towards a holding cell while Hunters made bets on a smaller ring. Somewhere in the mix, she knew Slater was commanding his own slaves to fight for blood.

"*This is stupid,*" Arjun whispered through their mental link. "*We're going to get caught. Your pack needs you more than they need me.*"

"*Hey,*" Tess said. "*You saved my life twice now. Time for me to return the favor for once.*"

"*You're not returning the favor if you get killed helping me.*"

Tess shushed him and waited for a pair of Hunters to pass before she moved with him across the room. The exit seemed an eternity away. Anything could go wrong, and while she might be able to stand up to some bullets, she couldn't fight off a barrage. She peered up at the stairwells, trying to remember which one they'd taken. There were several entry points which meant that while they had more ways to get in, it also made it harder to know the right way out.

As they neared a set of stairs, Arjun's legs gave out on him.

Tess caught him and dragged him over towards a dark corner where they couldn't be seen easily if her shield faltered. She leaned him against the wall and knelt beside him. As she rolled up his shirt, more blood gushed out. "*Damn. I thought I'd sealed it enough.*" She placed her hand over his hot, damp flesh and focused. "*My shield may flicker. Warn me if anyone is coming near us.*"

"*Tess,*" Arjun said softly. He lifted a shaky hand and brushed it along her cheek. "*Go, please. I don't want you to end up a captive or dead trying to save me.*"

"*Well you shouldn't have taken the bullet for me, idiot,*" Tess said, her voice laced with worry. "*Shut up, I need to concentrate.*"

"*Tess…*"

She ignored him and focused on the wound. Ether slipped inside of him like warm liquid and wrapped around the bullet lodged in his flesh. She wished it had gone out the other end and been a clean shot, but it would have hit her too. Removing it might cause more damage. Could she close the skin around it, trapping it in place until someone with more skill could help him? She didn't have much time to decide. So, she pushed the magic through his skin, closing the flesh and blocking the blood from spilling out of his body.

Arjun gasped in pain. She grasped his hand and squeezed it to comfort him, and he squeezed back, his hold tightening the longer she worked.

"*I'm sorry,*" she said. When she finished, she sat back on her heels and looked at him. The remaining color had drained from his face, and his eyes reflected like a glassy pool. His pale complexion and clammy cheeks made him a perfect candidate to greet death's door. Panic rose in her and she touched his cheek, ignoring the blood on her hand. "*Don't, please don't. I can't lose anyone else.*"

Arjun released a weak chuckle then winced. "*I'm just a Hunter.*"

"*You're more than that,*" Tess said, shaking her head. "*You put your life on the line for my pack, for my District. You saved my mother. You saved me. And even now, you're asking to be left behind so I don't get caught. I can't. I won't do that. Why…why did you have to be so stupid?*"

Arjun closed his eyes and smiled a little. "*I have my reasons.*"

Tess ran her thumb along his cheek. He opened his eyes and stared back at her, a little color returning to his flesh. "*Oh yeah? And what are those?*"

Arjun curled his finger, urging her to come forward. She leaned towards him, turning her head to hear him better, but Arjun caught her chin lightly in his hand. He pressed his cool lips to hers, their mouths locking.

The world didn't fall away and there was no sudden spark like she would have expected. But something else ignited inside of her, something that she could only describe as home. She kissed him back without reservation and held their entwined hands to her chest. Her heart pounded so loudly she swore someone would hear it.

Arjun broke the kiss first and leaned back with a satisfied sigh. "*I guess I'm not the only idiot,*" he whispered.

Tess blinked a few times. She met his eyes and shook her head. "*Guess not. But you're not allowed to call that a goodbye kiss. Let's get out of here.*"

Before he could protest, she helped him back up to his feet and half-guided, half-carried him over to the stairs. She grabbed the railing and pulled them up step by step, inch by inch. They reached the top platform, and Tess moved towards the hidden exit.

"Hey? What's all this?"

Tess looked back and spotted a Hunter standing at the bottom of the stairs. He pointed at the railing where she'd left bloody handprints behind.

She swore to herself and jerked Arjun out of the hidden pit. A chiming noise rang behind her which she hadn't heard when they entered. It set its own alarm bells off in her head. She moved faster, despite Arjun's pants and groans.

It was a good thing, too, because no sooner had they neared the gate to the stairs than she heard voices coming behind her. Hunters ran down the subway, calling to one another, shining lights in every dark crevice.

Tess swallowed and slid through the gate, shutting it softly behind her. She fairly dragged Arjun up several stairs before she pushed him against the wall, flattening her body over his as people raced past the gate. For the moment, they were trapped. If she tried to move him and made a sound, the Hunters would come tearing up the stairs after them.

So she held Arjun and watched his eyes flutter and felt his body grow colder. "*Don't let go,*" she said mentally to him. She filled his mind with magic, warming it, and did the same for his body, trying to keep him awake.

Time, too much time, passed before people started to walk slowly back into the tunnel.

"I didn't see anything," one said.

"It could have been left over from a fight. Maybe one of the losers was getting dragged outside and didn't want to go."

"But the chime?" another said.

"Malfunction?"

They muttered to each other as they disappeared into the darkness.

Tess watched them go then looked at Arjun.

His eyes had shut, his breath coming in slow, weak gusts.

Using her magic, she helped carry him up the rest of the stairs and over towards his hidden car. She settled him into the backseat and fiddled with his pants until she found his keys. She climbed into the front and backed up, keeping the lights off. The moon had dipped in the sky, the soft rays of sunlight starting to peek over the horizon.

Tess reached into the console and pulled out her phone, turning it on with a press of her thumb. In the faint glow of the screen, she saw she had two missed calls from Rozene. Ignoring the messages, she called the werewolf.

"Tess?"

"I'm heading to the hospital. Arjun's been shot. And I have news Paytah needs to hear about the Hunters and their pit."

Chapter 24
Invasion

Tess

Tess chewed on her thumbnail as she paced outside of Arjun's hospital room. He'd been brought back from surgery some time ago, but he still hadn't woken which wasn't entirely unusual. He'd been shot after all. She followed the rise and fall of his chest, his arms limp at his sides. He looked helpless, hardly the powerful Hunter who had taken a bullet for her or fought against other Hunters.

A hand settled on her back, causing her to jump.

"Just me," her mother said.

Tess blinked and fought back tears. "Mom," she whispered and pulled her into a tight hug. Her mother held her close with one arm then cupped her cheek.

She looked Tess over and her face turned blotchy with emotion as she reached for her battered face. "Oh, honey, your poor cheek."

"It'll heal," Tess said and caught her hand, but she didn't pull it away. She buried her head into her mother's shoulder. "You're okay," she said, reassuring herself. "I didn't…after Paytah…I'm sorry I didn't check on you. I was so scared you might be—"

"I'm fine," her mother replied. She did look healthy enough, despite her wounded arm being in a sling. It could have been so much worse, but she was alive and free, which was more than Tess could say about her father. "The doctors took good care of me. I need a little more time to heal and rest." Her mother rubbed Tess's back and shoulder and leaned her head against her arm. "You can go in there and sit with him, you know."

"I know. I don't want him to think I'm hovering."

Her mom gave her a look. "What are you doing right now?"

"…Hovering."

"Hmm." She closed her eyes. "I should be furious at you for going into the Hunter's den without telling me, or anyone for that matter. I couldn't handle losing both you and your father. Bad enough Paytah made the decision to banish you." Her hold on Tess's arm tightened. "Did you see him? Your father?"

Tess sucked in a breath sharply. "Mom, I don't really want to answer that question."

"Tess, *please*."

She'd tried to wipe the memories from her mind, but they were as clear as glass. She diverted her gaze. "I saw him fighting in a ring. He'd been injured, but he held his ground. Dad's always been a tough old wolf. If he's survived this long, I don't think he's going anywhere."

"And Nick? Kat? Augustine?"

Tess shut her eyes. "Nick and Augustine were in holding cells. Kat was fighting against someone else. I…I don't know who won. I heard a gunshot. I'm hoping it was just to break them up." She turned towards the hospital room window and rested her hands on the sill, teeth clenched. "I wanted to free them, or stop the people attacking them. But I couldn't. Not without drawing attention to myself."

"I'm glad you didn't," her mom replied. "I don't know if you would have come back."

Tess glanced sideways at her. "Paytah called Legion?"

"Yes, they're sending someone here to talk to you. If you have the exact location of where the captives are, they can send people in to help them."

Tess snorted. "So, when we tell them our people are missing, they do nothing. But if we feed them the rest of the information on a silver platter, *then* they'll act."

Her mom shrugged. "Be glad they're willing to come at all."

Glad. How could she feel glad about any of this? She'd left Trish behind. Her friends and father were still captives. Arjun was badly injured. And she still didn't know if Paytah could even bear to look at her. It was why she'd told everything to Rozene and the rest of the pack. They could tell Paytah. Maybe he'd believe *them*.

Arjun rolled his head and lifted his hand slowly. Tess stiffened until her mother touched her arm. "Go to him. He needs you, too."

"But, you—"

"I'm *fine*. He's the one who needs you now."

Tess glanced back at her mother and smiled sadly. She kissed her on the cheek. "I know you're pissed at the pack, but don't do something you'll regret like leave them. They're family, and sometimes family bickers."

"I know, firebug."

"Mom, don't…" she sighed. "Never mind. Call me firebug all you want." At least it would keep her father alive in their minds while they waited for him to come home.

After giving her mom a final hug, she opened the door and slipped inside. She'd drawn the shades to make it a little darker for him. Arjun rolled his head a few times and then blinked. His eyes settled on her after a moment. He forced a weak smile.

"Hey, troublemaker."

"Hey, yourself." Tess sat down in a chair next to his bed and took his hand. His fingers felt like ice against hers. "You gave me a scare. Doctors said the bullet almost tore apart your kidney, but they were able to save it. You're gonna be down for a while healing, though."

"I figured as much, if I pulled through at all." He turned his hand and laced his fingers between hers, sending a delighted chill up her spine. "I think I have you to thank for stabilizing me and keeping me alive long enough for them to treat me."

"I'm also the reason you got shot in the first place."

Arjun rolled his eyes. "Were you holding the gun? I don't think so. I just happened to be my heroic, charming, idiotic self and stopped that woman from hurting anyone else."

"You have the idiotic part right," Tess teased. She ran her thumb over his warming flesh and brought his hand to her lips to kiss it gently. "You scared me."

"I scared myself." Arjun watched her with tired eyes and tilted his head. "Now what? Did you get the information to your alpha?"

"The pack knows, and Legion is going to come in and help, finally. If everything goes right, maybe we'll have everybody back by tonight."

"You don't sound confident."

Tess bowed her head. She held onto him for support so the world didn't sweep out from beneath her feet again. "I've made a lot of dumb mistakes which have cost my friends' their lives or freedom. I'm afraid to hope and lose them all over again." She swallowed the lump rising in her throat. "I almost lost you."

"But you didn't. I'm right here, Tess."

Tess nodded and fought back the tears of relief, grief, and exhaustion threatening to pour down her cheeks and drown her. The weight of the world hung on her shoulders, making her slump forward. All these days of worrying and trying to find her family were taking their toll on her, and she didn't know how much more she could handle. Was it too much to want her pack to be safe? Or *the* pack she supposed.

Arjun squeezed her hand. "So tell me, when all this is done, when you're done playing the hero and have rescued everyone, what are you going to do?"

"I haven't given it much thought," Tess said. "I mean, I'm not part of the pack, and I'm kind of pissed with Vic that he didn't do anything to help us, so I don't really fit in with the magi either." She gave a nervous smile. "I was sort of hoping that maybe you could teach me how to be a Hunter."

Arjun shifted and sat up a tiny bit, though he couldn't get far. One thick eyebrow arched high. "Do you know what you're asking?"

"To learn the way of the people who have hunted mine for eons? Yeah. But I don't mean I want to be like *them*. I want to be like you. I want to use my magic and my talents to help free parahumans from these awful pits. There's only so much good I can do in Chicago."

Arjun bit his lip. "It's not an easy life, Tess. You have to give up a lot to do what I do, and you never know if you're going to walk away from a mission alive."

"I gathered as much. But when you're living with a wolfpack and have Hunters after you, there's no guarantee you're going to survive that either. Ask Ray. Oh wait, you can't, because he's dead." She fought back the pain in her chest, though tears threatened to flood her eyes. "I want to learn how to better defend myself and others so I don't always need someone to save me."

Arjun sighed and settled his head back on the bed. He looked up at the ceiling and drummed his thumb on her hand. "On one condition.”

"Yeah?"

"You're a magus because you're born with that extra chakra, the one that gives you magic. But there are witches out there, people who aren't born with power but can still use Ether." He glanced at her. "I want you to teach me how to use magic."

Tess sputtered. Now *that* she had not expected. "Do you even know what *you're* asking?" she said, echoing him.

"I wouldn't be asking if I didn't."

"And you do know witches and magi don't exactly get along."

"Yeah, because you guys can be kind of pompous arses about your abilities. But you're both magic users. So teach me. It'll give me an extra defense if my other techniques don't work. Plus, that healing magic is amazing."

Tess hesitated and shifted in her chair. "I'm not sure how good of a teacher I'll be. I had to learn a lot through trial and error, and I was born with magic."

"Same with me and being a Hunter. And I've never trained Hunters, so you'll be my first. We'll both be out of our element." He smiled. "What do you say?"

"You might never even learn how to use it."

"Won't know if I don't try."

Tess knew she should say no. Teaching magic wasn't her strength, but maybe it could be. Maybe they could be the first magic Hunters off on daring quests to save people in danger.

Heh, I can dream, right? she thought.

Before she could answer, the door slid open. A woman with blond hair tied back in a ponytail stepped in. Her body was swathed in black except for her badge which was in the shape of a silver ouroboros and a bright red L.

Legion.

"Jay?" Tess asked in surprise, recognizing the woman from a former encounter.

The Legion agent nodded and walked towards them with a tablet in hand. "I'm shocked you remember me. I was told you both had intel about a fighting pit?"

Tess exchanged looks with Arjun and nodded. While she might have been pissed at Legion for not stepping in sooner, at least she felt she could trust Jay. She pulled out the tracking device from her pocket and passed it over. "This is what we used to find them. He put a tracer on one of my kidnapped packmembers." She glanced at Arjun. "I took it out of your pocket before you went into surgery."

"Glad you did. Would hate to lose that."

Jay looked it over and made notes, her fingers swiping rapidly over her tablet screen. "Well, it looks like they're still in the same location you mentioned to your alpha. What else can you tell me?"

Tess and Arjun wasted no time launching into the story of going into the pit. While Arjun focused primarily on the layout and the amount of Hunters, Tess talked about the captives, the fighting, and the holding cell treatment. Between them both, they were able to paint a pretty clear but bleak picture of what they'd found. Tess's stomach flip-flopped all over again.

Jay lowered the tablet onto her lap. "You're lucky you made it out alive. I don't think I have to tell you how stupid it was to go in there without backup." She sighed and tugged her nose. "*But*, I also understand. I've been on a few suicidal missions of my own." She offered a comforting smile as she rose. "We'll be going in shortly."

Tess stood. "I'll come with. There's a secret entrance that I can show you."

"No need. We may be able to teleport into the pit itself."

Tess frowned and tried to get around the agent before she left. "Please, let me help. My father is in there."

"Even more reason for you to stay behind, Tess. It's personal for you. We'll go in and get them out and report back to you as soon as everyone is free."

Tess clenched her fists, fighting back panic as her father's bloody face and Trish's sacrifice flooded her mind. "There's a vampire amongst them who's acting like a Hunter when she's really not. I told her I would come for her."

"Trish, right? Oh, I remember her. She and I spent a few sessions talking about her involvement with the Hunters before. I'll be sure to get her out."

"You're not listening!" Tess shouted and struck the top of Arjun's hospital table with her fist. "I'm not staying behind. I have healing magic. I can help!"

Jay lowered the device and lifted an eyebrow at Tess. "And we have healing magi as well." Her voice softened. "Tess, I understand how you feel. I've been kept out of missions that have involved saving my family, and I hated it. But we can't let civilians go down there and risk their lives. It seems you were lucky once." She nodded to Arjun. "You might not have that luck again."

Tess's shoulders slumped. Again she couldn't help. Again people were putting themselves at risk, and she couldn't be there to save anyone. She slumped down in her chair and ran both hands roughly through her hair.

Jay tapped her fingers thoughtfully on the table. With a sigh, she pulled something out of her pocket. "Do you have a phone with you?" When Tess nodded, Jay held out her hand. "Let me see it."

Tess grabbed her phone and handed it over. Jay attached a small device to it and tapped a few numbers into the phone. When she passed it back, Tess saw a black screen with the word, "offline" on it. "What is it?"

"That's a connection to my personal camera feed when I go in on missions. You can watch from the hospital room when we go in to save your friends so you can at least see how the mission is going." She settled a warm hand on Tess's shoulder. "I know what it's like to wait on the sidelines. Sometimes, it helps to at least know what's happening. Once I turn my feed off, the device attached to your phone will fry, so don't think to use it for other Legion missions. And don't show that to anyone else. I don't need my superiors on my ass."

Tess held the phone tightly to her chest. "Thank you."

Jay nodded. "We'll be going in in a few hours. Make sure the phone stays charged. You both get some rest for now." With that, the Legion agent turned on her foot and strode out the door.

Tess quickly pulled the table over and propped the phone up on it so that she and Arjun could watch. "Do you really think she connected us to the feed?"

"I'd be surprised if she did," he said. "But thankful, too. All we can do now is wait."

***

Waiting ached worse than a body full of elderberry, but wait they did for the phone to turn anything but black. Tess watched with trepidation as the battery life slowly withered away. Arjun had fallen asleep sometime after the nurses came in to check his vitals. So far everything looked good; Arjun simply needed time to heal.

Tess chewed on her thumb again and glanced at him as he snoozed. He wouldn't miss her if she slipped out for a moment to find a charger. She squeezed his hand then slipped out of the room. She knew where Paytah was staying, so she avoided that room like the plague and headed for the waiting area instead.

To her surprise, most of her pack lingered there, even the kids, Heidi, Phoebe, and Eliza. Mikayla saw her first and flew out of her chair.

"Tess!" She scooped Tess into her arms like a ragdoll and held her close.

Tess hugged her back and almost cried when Jackson came over and offered her a warm embrace.

"Glad you're safe," he said. "We were worried."

"Thanks, I was, too."

She glanced around at the other wolves. Pedro and Quince looked away from her, but Becky offered a smile, as did Tamara. It hurt to take in how much smaller their pack looked without Ray, Augustine, Nick, Kat, and her dad.

"I'm sorry for all the trouble I caused," she said. "I never meant for anyone to get hurt. Especially not Ray."

Mikayla held her tighter. "We're just glad you're alive and not a captive with the rest of them."

Pedro hugged Eliza in his lap. "Though if you'd listened to Paytah, maybe Ray, Augustine, and Kat at the very least would still be with us."

Tess dropped her eyes in shame while Mikayla shot him a dirty look.

"Not cool, Pedro."

"No, I'll tell you what's not *cool*," Quince growled. "It's watching my dead packmate wheeled past me after he's been filled with bullets. It's having to bring Paytah and Rozene to him and watch them crumble once they see his mutilated body. It never had to happen, Tess. If only you'd listened to Paytah."

"*Enough*," Jackson rumbled deeply. "That's neither here nor there, Quince. Ray is gone, and we'll mourn him. We can free the rest of our pack because of Tess. We should be thankful for that."

Quince muttered something and leaned against his husband.

Mikayla snorted and patted Tess's back. "Ignore them," she whispered. "We know why you did it. Why don't you sit with us?"

Tess shook her head. "I can't. I'm trying to keep an eye on Arjun. I was actually wondering if someone had a phone charger."

Pedro barked out a laugh. "She's more concerned about her

Hunter then the rest of her pack. Why does this not surprise me?"

"Pedro!" Jackson snapped. "If you can't keep your mouth shut, then you and Quince can go to another room."

Neither spoke again, but their eyes burned into Tess, forcing her to shift closer to Mikayla and out of their heated glares.

Mikayla held up a finger and went to her purse. She searched around and held out a cord. "Should connect with your phone. How is Arjun doing?"

"Healing," Tess said. "The doctor says he should be fine." She wrapped the cord in her hand and swallowed. "I…should get back."

"I'll walk you," Mikayla said and draped her arm around Tess's shoulders. As they left the waiting area, Tess heard Pedro speak up again.

"She's a threat to the pack. Paytah was right to kick her out."

"Don't you listen to them," Mikayla whispered. "They're angry and need someone to take it out on. If Saul was here, they'd rip into him instead."

Tess chuckled bitterly. "I feel like I should be offended that I'm being compared to Saul."

Mikayla hugged her again. When they neared Arjun's room, the wolf stopped Tess and turned her around. Mikayla looked her up and down and touched her cheek, her fingers pressing shy of the claw wounds. "I was really scared I was going to lose another packsister. Please don't think the pack hates you. Quince and Pedro will get over it, and I know Paytah will, too. You're not alone, Tess. I'm still on your side. So's Carmen, Tamara, and Jackson."

Tess fought back tears as she smiled. "Thanks, Mikayla." She wrapped the woman in another hug. "That means a lot."

They stood together in a warm embrace, Tess feeling the pain in her stomach unravel a bit. At least one of the wolves didn't despise her.

"By the way," Mikayla whispered. "I saw your Hunter. Girl, he is *cuuuute*."

Tess laughed and pushed Mikayla back playfully. "Mine," she said.

Mikayla held up her hands. "Hey, I know not to get between a woman and her man. You go get him, Girl. Just make sure he treats you right, or I'll have something to say about it."

"I'll give him the warning," Tess winked. "But I think there's already a line."

They exchanged smiles before Tess looked down at the charger in her hand. "I should get back in there."

"Of course, go on. Let me know if you need anything."

Tess watched the wolf head off before she went back to the room. She opened the door. "Arjun, I found—"

"It's started," he interrupted her and turned the phone towards her.

A live feed appeared on her phone, showing the large tunnel they had gone through to find the pit. Tess scurried over and plugged the charger in then attached it to her phone. She pulled the chair around so she could get a better look.

"This is where she said it would be," Jay said and turned towards the hidden entrance.

"Guns at the ready," another said. "Magi, bullet shields."

Jay moved to the back of the group, a gun held tightly in her hands.

Tess pressed her hand over her mouth until Arjun took it and held it softly. She couldn't stop her fingers from shaking.

The Legion agents waited a moment then burst through the entrance, guns at the ready.

The feed went black, sending a chill of fear down Tess's back that Jay had lied and cut the camera all together. But she still heard noise. Startled voices. Groans and moans. Flashlights illuminated the backs of the Legion agents before spreading out into the pitch-black room.

"What the hell?" someone asked.

Jay pointed a flashlight down and lit up the twisted, mangled body of a werewolf in his bipedal form. "I got a body," she said.

"I got one here," another called.

Tess's heart skipped a beat as the icy claws of dread snapped her up in its clutches. She looked at Arjun. "What's happening? Where are the lights and the Hunters?"

His face paled as he stared at the phone. "No," he whispered.

"What? What is it?"

But the dying moans of parahumans gave his answer. Tess stared back at the phone in horror as the agents moved through the darkness, searching the grounds. They came across body after body, most dead, others writhing in agony as they bled from bullet or stab wounds. One wolf had nearly been decapitated.

Tess clapped a hand over her mouth.

"Can we get lights on in here?" someone asked.

Feet and machinery scuffled before the sound of a generator turned on. One by one, the lights illuminated the pit.

And the bodies covering it.

All the cages had been broken down, and the bleachers as well. The only sign that there had been anyone there were the skeletal stairs, the lights, the trash, and bodies left behind. Tess stared at them in shock, searching fearfully for sign of her father or anyone that she knew.

"Why would they kill them all?" she whispered.

"If the Hunters thought they were going to be caught, they would disband. Normally they would take all their captives with them. The only time I've seen this kind of carnage was if they wanted to leave a warning. These could merely be the people who died during the tournament."

But Tess heard the doubt in his voice. The Hunters were leaving a message behind.

Don't follow us.

"I got a live one over here!" someone shouted. Jay looked over as a few Legion members rushed to the survivor. She kept walking through the carnage and knelt down to check pulses here and there.

She turned towards the cell tunnels, and her camera showed a woman curled up on her side, long strands of golden hair chopped up around her.

Tess grabbed Arjun. "Kat? Oh God…oh God, no." Her throat tightened until she could only release a strangled whimper.

Jay walked towards the woman and crouched down. Blood covered Kat's back and side. Someone had hacked off almost all of her hair, and right in the center of it rested the tracking device that Arjun had planted in her tresses.

Jay reached for Kat's neck.

Tess jerked to her feet and moved away from the phone. She couldn't look. She couldn't hear those awful words.

"Tess," Arjun whispered.

"I got a live one!" Jay's voice cut through.

Tess turned sharply and looked back at the phone. Jay had rolled Kat on her back, her chest bloody and naked from claw marks that another wolf had given her. She panted for breath and blinked through the bright glare of light.

"Easy," Jay said softly. "We're going to get you help."

"They knew," Kat rasped, her eyes darting around wildly. "They knew help was coming. They killed so many." She started to sob, her entire body trembling with stress.

Jay pulled something off of her back and wrapped a thin cloth around Kat to try to keep her warm. "Shh, rest. Did you have friends here?"

Kat sobbed and nodded. "I don't know where they are. I don't know what happened. They're just gone!"

Tess dropped into the chair. Her father. Nick. Augustine. Gone. But gone how? Captives? Dead? She wanted to scream the questions at the phone, but she knew Kat wouldn't hear.

Two people rushed over, and a magus planted her hands on Kat's body and started to heal her. Kat fell unconscious within moments, her head lolling to the side as they stabilized her injuries.

Jay sighed deeply. "I'm sorry," she said to the camera.

Suddenly, the feed went dead.

"No!" Tess shouted. She tried to tap the phone, change the volume, do anything to get the feed back. But the little device plugged into the phone popped, sizzled, and fell onto the table. "No!" she shouted again and dropped the phone.

"Tess," Arjun said.

"This is all my fault," she sobbed. "I should have helped them when I had the chance. Now they're gone. And I don't even know if they're dead, or…or something worse has happened. I should have done something!"

"*Tess*," Arjun said with more force. "There's nothing you could have done. If you'd revealed your powers, they would have killed you. They figured it out somehow. Maybe Trish wasn't able to charm the Hunter or Saul. Maybe they found out some other way."

"You saw the tracking device," Tess said. "They knew Kat was the bait. The only way they could have found that out was if someone told them." But she couldn't imagine Trish betraying them. Not after getting them out. Maybe Saul had read her mind or forced her to tell the truth. If he could control Joseph, he could control Trish. "I never should have left her there."

Arjun stared at her then at the phone. Without a word, he pushed the table aside and slowly scooted over in his bed. "Come here, Tess."

She wanted to resist, but her heart shattered into pieces.

Everything *hurt*. Her failure hung heavily over her and the only person who seemed to give a damn that she'd at least tried to help was Arjun. She went to him and curled up in the bed beside him. He wrapped her up in his arms and held her as she wept into his chest.

Chapter 25
The Message

Paytah

Paytah steepled his fingers on the elegant rectangular table in the middle of Duke Joseph's dining room. A week had passed since the failed attempt to rescue his wolves from the pit. To say he was furious would be putting it lightly. He was still on the mend, but he had enough energy to come out and speak with the other leaders of the District, as well as his pack. The wolves waited outside of the room for him. Rozene rested beside him, while Joseph, Vic, Mia, Akeno, and Carlos sat at other sections of the table surrounding him.

Joseph's wife Selene, a dark-eyed Grecian beauty with curly brown hair, tan skin, and a fierce complexion, had returned from her travels and sat beside her husband. Since the discovery that Saul had charmed Joseph and corrupted his mind, Selene had taken over as Duchess of the coven. But she stubbornly refused to be at the meeting without her mate present.

"We still rule as a pair. Joseph is a victim as well," she'd told Paytah sharply over the phone. And so Paytah had agreed.

A dark, somber aura encompassed them, as was to be expected. They'd found remnants of Joseph's lost vampires left behind, though they'd been little more than flesh on brittle bones. Kat, despite the Hunters' best efforts, had survived and was currently being nursed back to health by Bianca and a mix of avians and wolves.

Much to their relief, Nick, Augustine, and Brighton hadn't been discovered amongst the dead.

But they hadn't been rescued either.

He glanced to his right where Rozene sat with stiff shoulders and worried eyes. The fate of their pack weighed as heavily on her, if not more so with her motherly disposition. Tess and Arjun sat further down the table, both who seemed to know more than any of them. As much as he'd tried to talk to Tess, she kept refusing his calls. Rozene had encouraged her to come to the meeting more out of obligation to their kidnapped wolves than out of loyalty to Paytah.

Paytah tried to ignore his bruised emotions.

"So," Mia said quietly. "On the plus side, the Hunters are gone, and no one else has vanished. But we have no idea where they've disappeared to, do we?"

Paytah shook his head. "No. The tracking device that the Hunter put on Kat was left behind. Trish, supposedly, went with them as a false ally, but we've received no word from her. So either she's turned tail yet again and joined them, or she's unable to reach out to us."

Tess spoke up, her voice firm. "It's more likely she can't reach out yet. She was adamant about wanting to help us."

Vic snorted. His mussed hair and dark eyes made him look about as haggard as Paytah felt. "She's served Hunters before."

"Yes," Selene agreed. "But she also helped save Arjun and Tess from the Hunters' grasps. Had they been caught, we wouldn't have known where the pit was to begin with."

Akeno drummed his fingers on his tablet. "This is true, but their going in must have tipped off the Hunters and sent them running. We have no idea where they are, and my locator spell isn't enough to find them." He looked over at Vic. "Do you have a magus who is stronger with such spells? Do you think one of them, or you, could track them?"

Vic raked his fingers through his hair. "They already tried, and none of them had any luck. Somehow, I think there's a magus helping to keep them cloaked."

"I think it's more than just a magus," Tess said. "I felt a very strong magical shield down there. It didn't *feel* quite like Ether."

Vic set his jaw grimly and pinched the bridge of his nose. "I know of a stronger locator magus, but she lives up in Wisconsin."

"Wisconsin…" Tess murmured and looked at Arjun. "You said a pit or two existed up there, too."

Arjun nodded. "Yes, but that doesn't mean that they'd go there next."

Mia leaned forward, her claws turning sharper with her growing Cheshire smile. "Where would they go then, dear *Hunter*?" she said in a mixture of a purr and a hiss. "If you know them so well, then *where* would they have taken the parahumans?"

"I can't know for certain." Arjun trailed his fingers along his mustache, thinking. "They could have found another spot in Illinois. They could have decided to join with another pit to increase their forces, defenses, and their chances." He waved a hand. "Either way, the message they left behind was clear enough. 'Don't follow.'"

Mia chuckled. She leaned back, draping her arm over her chair. "And since when have we ever listened to Hunters' threats?" She glanced at Paytah. "Your golden wolf. Has she said anything?"

"She said she'd been shot, stabbed, and left off to the side to die because of a fight she started in the ring. But she saw them break down the fighting rings and start killing parahumans. She said the cages crumbled in on themselves, like with magic, which is probably how they got everything cleaned up and moved so quickly. Someone commented, 'This is why we shouldn't let these things near *her*.' That's all she remembers though. Someone came and chopped her hair off to find the tracking device and then knocked her unconscious. That's all she remembers."

Carlos folded his arms and gripped his biceps tightly. "So we know about as much as we did before Legion went in to save them. They're taken, and we have no idea how to find them. Unless you think your magus friend can help, Vic."

Vic nodded. "She may be able to, or her wife can. I think that's where we should go next. We need to send a warning to the other Districts that the Hunters are on the move. If we create a network of communication—let each other know if parahumans go missing —we might be able to narrow down where they've gone." His gaze darted to Paytah. "Legion said that they would be available to contact for help, right?"

"Yes. But, Legion also told us to leave it alone, as they're now planning to handle it."

Carlos grunted and tilted his head back, his eyes rolling

towards the ceiling in annoyance. "Of course they are. What's the point of Legion if they aren't going to help until it's too late? All they do, it seems, is come in and clean up the mess."

Rozene sighed, reaching to taking one of Paytah's hands before his own claws could grow and pierce still-healing flesh. "They have their reasons, Carlos, you know that."

The room fell quiet again, the mood darkening. Paytah finally stood up, though he had to wrap his arm around his stomach as a streak of pain passed through it. He impulsively squeezed Rozene's hand by accident. As she went to help him, he gave a subtle shake of his head. He couldn't look weak in front of everyone, not now when they needed strength. She withdrew her hand, but not without giving his a loving and supportive squeeze.

"For now," Paytah began after catching his breath, "let's get the messages out to the other Districts in Illinois. You each contact fellow leaders, and I'll talk to the Violet Marshalls. Vic, reach out to your friend. The rest of you, take care of your people and watch over them. We don't need anyone else slipping away to help the Hunters, charmed or not."

Joseph bowed his head while Selene glowered at Paytah at the unintended jab.

The leaders rose and started to depart. Akeno walked over to Paytah and grasped his arm. "My heart grieves for your loss, my friend. If there's any way my grove can help, please tell me."

Paytah clapped his shoulder. "Thank you, Akeno. That means a lot."

The man bowed and departed, Mia on his heels.

Tess and Arjun quickly followed them out.

Paytah glanced at Rozene. "Ask Tess and Arjun to wait before they leave. I want to speak with them, but I need to talk to Joseph and Selene first."

Rozene nodded. "Be quick, my love. I'm not sure how long I can hold them."

Paytah kissed her cheek and went to the end of the table where Selene and Joseph sat together. He pulled back a chair and took a seat across from them, noting how Selene's back straightened. "It's good to have you back in town, Duchess Selene."

"Thank you. I only wish I'd been here sooner to help when Saul's betrayal came to light." She stroked Joseph's hair gently. "I'm working to mend things for my husband."

"I'm glad for it." Paytah cleared his throat. "I don't mean to be curt when I ask this, Joseph, but how is it that someone as powerful as you, a duke, was able to be charmed by another vampire?"

Joseph kept his eyes down and sighed. "I've been wondering the same thing. It's easier to charm someone if you play on emotions they already feel. And I can't deny that I felt a certain sense of jealousy when Gladus named you Violet Marshall. She groomed many of us, and I thought I had a chance. But, I was glad to remain a duke and not have all of the Purple Door District on my shoulders." He rolled his shoulders. "I was also still cross over what you did to Fraula, though I knew you had no choice. Saul must have gotten into my head and focused on those negative emotions. He is a strong charmer. Stronger than any other vampire I know. And I trusted him. Easier to charm someone who trusts you."

"He's been a loyal man," Selene said and ran her hand soothingly along Joseph's cheek. "Up until now. His mate's death changed him. He's old, Paytah. And he and Fraula had been together for decades."

"But to work with Hunters and put other vampires at risk, you don't think his situation is like Trish's do you?" Paytah asked.

"No," Joseph said with bite. "Trish, despite her ignorance, didn't cause any vampire deaths while she helped them. Gavin was an unfortunate loss. But that was no fault of hers. They've found at least four vampire bodies that belong to my coven. Trish would have protected them." He ground his teeth, his fingers digging into his palms. "No, Saul is working *with* them. He is no longer part of my coven. He will not come under my protection, and we will not house him if he tries to return. He's dead to us."

"And Trish?"

Selene smiled in such a way it made Paytah think of Mia. "If what Tess says is true, and Trish is trying to act as a contact to help us, then of course she'll be welcomed back to the coven with open arms and as a hero." She looked at Joseph and reached for his hand. "I think Saul had you send me on those trips so I'd be blind to his schemes. I spent very little time with you, him, and Trish. I would have noticed if something was wrong. I won't be away again. I can promise that."

Paytah bowed his head. "Thank you. We'll stay in touch." He rose and made to leave, but Selene touched his wrist lightly. "Yes?"

"Not to be presumptuous, but, it seems we've both had little lost lambs. We're working to get Trish back. Whatever things Tess has done, I'd strongly encourage you to bring her back into the fold. Despite her transgressions, she thought she did it for the good of the pack."

Paytah smiled. "I appreciate the advice. I'm going to speak with her now. I was blinded by pain and my own fear; she shouldn't have to pay the price of that."

"Good," Selene said and settled back beside her mate. "We'll be here if you need us."

Paytah nodded and walked quietly out of the room. Each step jarred his stomach and made his hip snarl in pain, forcing a painstakingly slow gait. Werewolf healing had saved his life and mended most of the wounds, but a few of those stabs had dug too deep. It would take longer than he was willing to admit to return to his full strength, and even longer before he could change comfortably.

He emerged from the dining hall and found Rozene waiting near a guest room. She gestured to him with quick jerks of her fingers. "They're inside," she whispered. "Tess looks ready to run, so be gentle."

He kissed her forehead. "Come in with me, then. She's always felt more kinship with you."

"Of course."

They stepped inside, and Paytah shut the door quietly behind him. Arjun sat in an ornate chair that might have very well been centuries old, knowing Selene's taste in antiques. Tess paced in a corner near the Hunter like a trapped mouse. No, a wolf. Arjun shot worried glances her way when he wasn't busy eyeing Paytah.

Paytah would never be able to understand how a man could call himself a Hunter and yet try to help parahumans. "Tess," he called.

Tess jumped and looked over at him. She strode to Arjun's side as if afraid Paytah might take his head off this time.

Paytah held up a hand. "You can relax. I don't have any misgivings with your friend. After what I've seen and heard, I am doing my best to believe that he means well."

Tess's posture remained stiff. She kept her hand on Arjun's shoulder and waited, her dark hair blowing softly in the breeze of an open window. The scars—the ones he'd marked her with—stood out against her pale skin. She looked so young, just a child in his eyes. "What did you want to talk about?" she asked cautiously.

Paytah shifted on his feet, taking pressure off of his wounds. "I know you were doing what you thought was best, and it was an unfortunate circumstance that those other Hunters attacked at the same time that you brought Arjun to me." He eyed the man. "I'm still not certain I can trust him completely, but he has my respect for what he tried to do to save the pack." He held out his hand to Tess. "Come home, Tess. The pack and I miss you."

Tess stared then looked at Rozene as if silently asking if this was a trap. Rozene offered a smile in return. "Tess, we want you back."

Tess turned toward Arjun. They were silent a moment, likely exchanging a private conversation. When Arjun sighed and gave a resigned nod, Tess stepped forward. She reached for Paytah's hand.

And gently pushed it back to him.

"Thank you for the invitation, really, but I don't belong with the pack. I never did. Mom has a better knack for it, but I'm too hot headed. Too…free spirited, I guess you can say." She lowered her arm. "Arjun is going to teach me how to become a Hunter like him, and I'm going to make a witch of him. I can't sit by while the others are still in trouble. So, I'm going to become stronger, and I'm going to do everything I can to bring them home." She swallowed.

"Whether I'm pack or not, you're still my family, and I care about all of you. I can't continue to be a liability to the pack. I'm a magus, not a wolf. And now I think I have a new calling." She looked back at Arjun. "I can do more good in this world than just staying in Chicago."

Paytah's stomach lurched like he'd been punched. He'd planned on her accepting with undying gratitude, and welcoming her with a warm embrace. Instead, she wanted to stay with this man. This…this *Hunter*?

"Paytah," Rozene said softly.

Paytah set his jaw and breathed in and out through his nose. He counted down, like he'd taught Nick, calming his temper. "Is that what you really want? Or has something else swayed you towards him?"

Tess rolled her eyes. "I'm not leaving the pack because of my feelings for a man," she said. "I'm doing it so I can make something better of myself. I've screwed up. A lot. Ray's—" Her voice caught and she rolled her neck, fighting to maintain her composure. "He's dead because of me, and I need to find a way to make it all right. So, thank you, Paytah, for welcoming me back, but I'm going to be staying with Arjun."

Paytah pressed his lips together.

That was it. No questions, no promises that she'd come back when everything was said and done. He wanted to be angry. He wanted to storm out of the room and denounce her again for being a fool. But deep down, he felt a swell of pride that his little pup had grown into a fine young woman. Brash. Bold. Stubborn. She was all these things, but she was also loyal, kind, and willing to admit her mistakes.

Most of the time.

Paytah breathed out then stepped forward. She tensed, but he wrapped his arms around her and pulled her into a hug. "When did you become so stubborn?"

She relaxed a little in his hold and chuckled. "You and my dad are pretty good examples. You can blame Augustine a bit, too, once I get her back."

Paytah smiled and hugged her tighter. "Be careful, pup. No matter where you go, you can still call the pack home. Your mom will need you, especially while your father is lost."

"I know," Tess said. She nuzzled her face against his chest like she used to do when she was young to drink in his scent. "I know," she whispered again. Her body shook suddenly, threatening to explode with emotion. "I'm so sorry for using my magic against you," she said in a strained voice. "I never meant…I…I'm sorry, Paytah."

"Oh, little one," Paytah whispered. He lifted her chin and brushed his thumb near the scars on her face. "We both let our anger take hold. I'm sorry, too."

Tess sighed in relief. "Thank you." She squeezed him again and pulled back slowly from the hug. "We're not going far, not yet. We'll train each other and keep searching for our friends. Don't think you can't call on me for help. Just promise me you won't try to take Arjun's head off again."

Paytah snorted. "I won't, not unless he hurts you." He stared at his little wolf then gently touched the scars on the side of Tess's cheek. To his surprise, she didn't flinch.

She held his hand over her marks.

They stood together for a moment, letting the familiar feeling of family return. Her body relaxed against him as the tension flowed out of her and the smile he loved so much blossomed on her lips. He lifted his eyes over her shoulder and narrowed them at Arjun.

"You take good care of her, boy. If I hear a peep that you've harmed her, we'll have words, you and I."

"I don't doubt that, sir," Arjun replied. "Call on me if you ever need me."

Paytah grunted but still offered a nod. He patted Tess's shoulder and smiled at her. "Don't be a stranger."

"I won't. Go get some rest, Paytah. I have a feeling we're all going to need it for what's to come." She squeezed his hand. "Will we have a funeral for Ray?"

"Not until we get Augustine back. Quince convinced Vic to cast a spell on Ray's body to keep it from…decomposing until we're ready for a funeral. For now, the pack will stay focused on getting our family home. We'll mourn later."

"When the time comes, and Ray's laid to rest, I'll be there to show respect to my packbrother." She stepped towards Arjun as he rose, her hand slipping out of Paytah's. She took Arjun's instead and lifted her chin. "We'll find them, Paytah. I don't care if I have to go through Hell and back, I will bring them home."

Chapter 26
Transit

Nick

It felt like a jackhammer was going off in Nick's head. Pain and blood pounded through his ears with each rumble of the truck. He wasn't sure if his ailments were due to the drug the Hunters had used to put him out, or the amount of wolfsbane they'd shoved into his system. His entire body buzzed like a colony of angry bees swarming his veins, and there wasn't a damn thing he could do about it.

He huddled on his side, wrists and ankles chained. He glanced to his right in a neighboring cage where both Brighton and Augustine were similarly tethered and kept unconscious. Augustine's body displayed a mosaic of wounds from fighting the Hunters. The moment they'd heard the Hunters had been discovered, the parahumans had fought to get free, but to no avail. Augustine had suffered brutal hits, but her tenacity and strength caught Gale's and Hendrickson's attention.

They wanted to keep her as a fighter.

So along with the bonds, she had a mask over her head, keeping her blind, deaf, and silent to the world. Brighton slumped next to her, his face bruised from the tournament fight. But he was alive.

Unlike Kat.

Tears pricked Nick's eyes, not for the first time, but he held back the broken sobs. He curled up on his side as best he could and scooted closer to Yanlei as she slept beside him.

He'd watched it happen, all of it. One moment Kat and Yanlei were in a fierce battle together, and the next, Kat had lost herself in her fear and nearly defeated Yanlei. Hendrickson took her down with one shot to the side to stop her. But that hadn't been enough for the bastard.

Once the order was made for them to clear out, he'd jerked Kat out of the cage and stabbed her.

"We have to leave a message for them," he'd sneered at Nick and dragged her limp body out of the room. Nick screamed in rage after him until his voice gave out.

Nick swore he'd make Hendrickson pay for her death, even if it sent Nick to his grave.

Kat, I'm so sorry. I promised to protect you, and I failed.

And that failure tore into him more than any amount of wolfsbane.

He still didn't understand what had prompted the move. The tournament had been going as well as could have been expected, at least for the Hunters. To end it all right in the middle of the match baffled him and made him wonder how close to rescue they'd been.

Yanlei shifted and turned her head to look at him. "Ow," she murmured.

"I know, me too." He rested his chin on her shoulder. "How are you feeling?"

"Sore. But I'm alive." She sighed and nuzzled him. "Nick, I'm so sorry about Kat. I tried to keep the fight going as long as possible to wear her out. I would have managed it, too, if the Hunter hadn't…I'm sorry."

"It's not your fault," Nick assured her, though his breath caught in his throat when he said it. "He did this. At least she won't be in pain anymore." Yet that brought him little comfort.

He stared at Brighton and Augustine. Others were in the truck with them, but he couldn't see them. They were all sectioned off, property belonging to different Hunters. Quiet sobs and whimpers from their captured companions filtered through the flimsy dividers. What sickened him the most was he thought he heard the wretched cries of a child. And if that was the case, these monsters deserved no mercy or redemption.

He buried his head into Yanlei's shoulder. "What happens now?"

"We get transported to another fighting ring. It'll take time for them to rebuild. We'll likely be forced to build the arenas for them. But it means it'll give us time to heal. There won't be as much fighting."

"Your granddad told you?"

"Yes. He learned it from another captive." Yanlei shifted. "I wish I had had more warning that we were leaving and parahumans were going to be left behind. I would have tried to do something."

"No," Nick shook his head. He nuzzled her as best he could with his nose. "Please, Yanlei, don't do anything stupid. I can't lose you, too."

She turned her head, her short hair falling along her cheek. "If there's a chance to help everyone escape, I'm going to take it, Nick. You'd do the same, wouldn't you?"

He didn't reply, but that was answer enough. Of course he'd give anything to free his family. But if someone had to die, he'd rather it be him, not Yanlei, not Augustine, not Brighton.

And definitely not Kat.

He fought back tears, not wanting to cry again, but he knew it would happen anyway. Kat was one of his best friends. And it broke him to think what Bianca would go through once they found her dead. So he sobbed and showed no shame as Yanlei turned and snuggled up against him to comfort him. He pressed his head against hers and shook, his cheeks and neck burning red both from the poison in his system and his grief. "I miss her already."

"I know. Remember that feeling, so if you ever question whether these Hunters are here to help us or not, you'll know your answer."

Nick nodded subtly and breathed in her scent, taking in every comfort she had to offer. At least Yanlei was alive and he hadn't failed her, too.

The truck lurched suddenly and sent them skidding in the cage. Nick grimaced and lifted his head, blinking through the tears. Now what?

A few minutes later, he heard the back door open and someone step inside. Heeled boots clicked quietly on the metal ground until the flap separating them from the rest of the truck moved back.

Nick gaped, the hair on the back of his neck standing on end. "Trish?" he asked quietly.

She looked down at him, a light in her hand illuminating her bright red hair. She was dressed in black pants and a leather trench coat which went up to her throat and down to her knees with a red belt tied at the center.

The thing he noticed most, though, was she didn't wear any cuffs.

"I thought you were back here," she said casually and stepped into the area, letting the cloth divider swing shut behind her. She cracked open a bottle of water and stuck it through the bars. "Open up."

Nick was too dumbfounded to do anything else. He drank the water slowly then watched as Trish gave some to Yanlei next. He brushed his mouth on his shoulder and frowned. His eyes darted, searching for some sign of a Hunter lingering close by. "What are you doing here?"

"What does it look like? Making sure that you stay healthy and are strong enough to put together your new home."

"You've joined them? You're working with Saul?" Nick's eyes burned with hatred and he curled his lip in contempt. "That's just like you, isn't it? A Hunter wants your help, and you go running."

Trish shrugged and stood up before crossing over to Brighton and Augustine. "I like to choose the winning side. Tess never figured that out. She thought I was helping her and her friend escape when they were looking for you. I only needed them to prove my loyalty to Saul so he'd welcome me back with open arms. I'm where I belong."

Nick narrowed his eyes. Tess? Tess was here? And who was her friend? He eyed Trish, not quite understanding what she meant. Either way, it looked like what he expected; she'd betrayed them again.

Yanlei squeezed his hand before he could snarl anything else, and he looked down at her. A faint smile touched her lips as she leaned in to whisper into his ear. "Listen."

"It's a shame, really," Trish went on and poured a little water on Brighton to wake him up. "Legion came so close to rescuing you. I guess your golden friend will have to give them the Hunter's message. Kat, was it?"

Nick jerked and looked at her in surprise. Kat? Kat was alive? "They shot her."

"You can get shot, and stabbed, and still survive," Trish said in a bored tone. "She'll just have to live another day and deal with the guilt of failing her friends."

"You're a bitch," Nick hissed, but it was more to keep up the act than to insult her. "I can't believe you'd turn your back on all of us again. What do you get out of it?"

"The winning side," Trish said, spreading her arms. "I'm tired of being a loser. Tired of being the one in chains. So, I'll do what I need to do to stay on top. And I'll get rid of *anyone* who gets in my way." She looked at him and raised her eyebrows. Neither Brighton nor Augustine woke, so she grabbed a tin from a container near the wall, slipped it between the bars, and filled it with water. "Rest. We have a long way to go before we get to our new home."

She passed Nick's cage, but a moment before leaving, he felt her mind brush his with a feathery touch. *"This is the only time I'm going to risk talking to you. Keep them strong and alive, Nick. I'll get you out somehow."*

"Screw you," Nick said aloud with a growl.

Trish chuckled and left, the dividing wall swinging shut behind her. He listened to the cold, calculating click of her boots as she passed the other cages, likely offering them water and "comforting" words as well. He kept silent until he heard the door to the truck slam shut and the engine rumble to life again.

"She's helping us," he whispered in disbelief to Yanlei.

"I thought as much. Don't tell your friends. The more people who know, the harder it will be to hide the truth." She smiled at him. "She's alive."

Tears pricked his eyes again and he gave a choked laugh. "She's alive. If one good thing comes out of this, it's that Kat's okay and back home with Bianca. That's enough to keep me going."

Yanlei nodded and settled down beside him again. "She said we have a long way to go. I wonder if we're going out of the state."

"I don't know," Nick said and curled around her to keep her warm. "But wherever they take us, I know Paytah and Tess won't be far behind."

About the Author
Erin Casey

Erin Casey graduated from Cornell College in 2009 with degrees in English and Secondary Education.

She attended the Denver Publishing Institute in 2009 and has been a recruiter ever since. She is the Communications and Student Relationships Manager at The Iowa Writers' House and the Director of The Writers' Rooms, a non-profit corporation that focuses on creating a free, safe environment for writers no matter their experience, gender, background, and income. Just like in her book, community is very important to her.

An advocate for mental health, Erin's written and published several articles on the Mighty, specifically about anxiety and depression.

She's also a devoted bird mom.

When not volunteering and working, she's querying her LGBT

YA Fantasy dragon book, writing short stories and blogs, and trying not to doze off to the glow of the computer screen while her bird sleeps on her.

Learn more about The Writers' Rooms:
www.thewritersrooms.org
Learn more about The Iowa Writers' House:
www.iowawritershouse.com

Follow Erin

Website
www.erincasey.org
Amazon
amazon.com/author/erincaseyauthor
Goodreads
goodreads.com/erincaseyauthor
Instagram
@erincaseyauthor
Facebook
@erincaseyauthor
Twitter
@erincasey09
Wordpress
erincaseyauthor.wordpress.com
Patreon
patreon.com/erincasey
AllAuthor
Allauthor.com/author/erincasey
BookBub
Bookbub.com/profile/erin-casey

www.ingramcontent.com/pod-product-compliance
Lightning Source LLC
Chambersburg PA
CBHW021132110726